A Novel ASHES OF REMEMBRANCE

A Novel ASHES OF REMEMBRANCE

BOOK THREE OF
THE GALWAY CHRONICLES

BODIE & BROCK
THOENE

THOMAS NELSON PUBLISHERS®
Nashville

Published in association with the literary agency of Alive Communications, 7680 Goddard St., Suite #200, Colorado Springs, CO 80920.

Published in Nashville, Tennessee, by Thomas Nelson, Inc.

Library of Congress Cataloging-in-Publication Data

Thoene, Bodie, 1951–
    Ashes of remembrance : a novel / Bodie & Brock Thoene.
        p.   cm. — (Galway chronicles)
    ISBN 0-7852-6620-8 (pb)
    ISBN 0-7852-8069-3 (hc)
    ISBN 0-7852-6865-0 (ie)
    I. Thoene, Brock, 1952– . II. Title. III. Series: Thoene,
Bodie, 1951–   Galway chronicles.
PS3570.H46A94   1999
813'.54—dc21
                                                                98-44605
                                                                CIP

Printed in the United States of America

02 03 04 05 PHX 8 7 6 5

Welcome to our world—
Ian Stone McCraw
—you are loved.

Other books by Bodie and Brock Thoene

The Galway Chronicles Series
Only the River Runs Free (Book One)
Of Men and of Angels (Book Two)
All Rivers to the Sea (Book Four)

Winds of Promise
To Gather the Wind
Winds of the Cumberland
The Legend of Storey County
The Hope Valley War
Shiloh Autumn
The Twilight of Courage
The Zion Covenant Series
The Zion Chronicles Series
The Shiloh Legacy Series
The Saga of the Sierras
The Zion Legacy Series

Prologue

Bind him to a pillar and leave him there til noon!
Bandage both his eyes and dress him like a fool!
Get a rope of cruel hemp and have him tightly bound!
Spit on him and rail on him with every mocking sound!
Beat him and flog him—Mary's only son.
Cut down a tree from the garden—the very tallest one!
—From "The Blessed Virgin's Keep," ancient Celtic poem

Beginning with the ravaging of Drogheda and continuing through the devastation of Wexford, the flood tide of souls pouring westward for safety never slowed that bloodstained autumn. August 1649 had seen the landing in Ireland of the English Puritan warlord, Oliver Cromwell. Fresh from his final victory over the Stuart king, Charles, and the king's execution, Cromwell was determined to reduce Ireland to submission as well.

To that end he brought a picked force of seventeen thousand of his Ironsides: fierce, hymn-singing soldier-fanatics. They had spent the better part of a decade roaming England during that country's civil war, stabling their horses in cathedrals, breaking out centuries-old stained glass with the bones of saints, and destroying or at least desecrating all things that smelled even faintly of popery.

Cromwell knew hounds weaned on steaming blood would not be satisfied with less when they grew older. Decimating Ireland would not only eliminate a stronghold of the hated Old Religion, it would spare England herself additional rampages.

Richard Burke, Lord Burke of Connaught, was seeing to his property over the border in County Roscommon when not only the refugees, but the war itself, swirled in upon him. "They are comin'!" shouted a wild-eyed youth from Longford, spurring his horse into the village square. "I saw them with my own eyes! A column of horsemen! Dragoons there were and cavalry. They'll be here in less than an hour."

Instantly, panic reigned in the streets. Men and women cried out in terror. Everyone had heard the horror stories: out of three thousand Irish soldiers at the garrison of Drogheda only thirty escaped alive. That much was the fortunes of war; what followed was not. For three days Drogheda was abandoned to the appetites of the Puritan warriors. Thousands of men, women, and children were slaughtered, many of them in the crypt of St. Peter's Church where they had fled for refuge. As Cromwell said to friends, "I thought it not sensible to restrain the soldiers from their right of pillage or from doing execution on the enemy."

Now the Ironsides were coming west to continue the butchery. "We must throw up barricades," urged Lord Burke. Despite his sixty-seven years, Burke was a doughty fighter, unafraid of combat with sword or pike, musket or cannon.

"There's no time," his friend Nicholas Lingard said. "And no chance of holdin' out either. We can only fly."

But it was already too late even for flight. Cromwell's column of cavalry and mounted infantry split into two. One charged straight into the village, the troopers slashing without discrimination at any who stood in their way. The other regiment circled the town, cutting off retreat. Soon those who had sought to escape farther west doubled back from the fresh assault, compounding the frenzy in the streets and rendering futile even isolated attempts at defense.

A mounted trooper, seeing Burke's unsheathed sword, attempted to ride him down. The master of Connaught stood his ground until the last second, then swung his blade at the horse. The animal reared and plunged, dumping his rider. Burke cut off the man's head with a single stroke.

Despite his successes, Lord Burke was pushed backward yard by yard. He yielded ground slowly, taking a greater toll of the enemy than he gave of himself. Even so, the grip of his sword was slick with the mingled blood of Burke and Puritan.

At the crossroads of the village was a stone cross, the site of public gatherings and celebrations. Clustered about its base in an agony of terror were three hundred women and children. Burke and those Irish fighters who remained alive were forced into a smaller and smaller circle until just a handful of armed priests and a dozen exhausted and wounded fighters protected the civilians.

"Throw down your weapons!" shouted Cromwell's general, Broghill.

"Not until we have your assurance that the women and children will be spared," Burke roared back with defiance.

"Then I swear you will all die together!" Impatient at the delay, Broghill ordered his men to charge. Two priests were trampled under hooves, and six armed men went down in the first rush. A Puritan dragoon snatched up an Irish child and used her as a shield to protect himself from injury. The girl, dead in minutes, was cast aside in favor of another living buffer.

Attacked from both sides, Burke blocked one thrust with his sword before the blade snapped, leaving only a foot of steel past the hilt. Just as a blow was aimed at a mother who cradled her infant son, Burke thrust out the broken weapon, managing to catch the descending stroke on the guard and turn it aside.

Another trooper drew rein and hacked at Burke's head. The Irish lord threw the useless hilt at the soldier's face. The blow was already descending when the dragoon jerked aside, the flat of his blade connecting with Burke's skull. As Lord Burke went down on the steps of the cross, the slain mother and child fell across him.

When Richard Burke awoke his head felt as if the trooper's blow had split his skull in two. It was pitch black, and even when Burke opened his eyes, he could see nothing. Had he been blinded, or was he dead?

"Where am I?" he muttered, wondering if he had been buried alive.

"This is the crypt of Holy Cross Church," said a voice nearby. "Rest easy. You are safe for now."

"Who are you?"

"My name is Father David of Ballygar," the man replied. "I was brought with nineteen of my brother priests, all of us herded from surroundin' villages by Cromwell's men."

"How long have I been here?"

"It is still the night of the massacre," the priest said.

"Do you know how many died?"

Father David's voice quivered when he answered. "May as well ask how many lived! You alone were spared. We were paraded in chains past the heap of bodies. Broghill has vowed to leave them there unburied as a lesson against resistance."

Richard Burke wept. "Why spare me?" he said at last. "To hang me later?"

Father David said gently, "No, we are to hang. Your chain of office identified you as a nobleman, and so you were dragged from beneath the corpses. It is said you will be sent as a slave to Barbados. A livin' slave is a more terrifyin' example to other Irish lords than merely one more execution."

Overhead a booming voice filled the church and filtered downward into the crypt. "English soldiers," it proclaimed, "you know me. I have fought beside you against the forces of Belial, against the idolatrous Canaanites. Now hear what I, Hugh Peters, say as your pastor: do not think because you have done good service this day that your work is finished. No! Not while the contagion of popery remains in this land. You must act as Joshua did after Jericho. 'Kill all that were of that city,' he said, 'young men and old, children and maidens.' Cease not from your holy war while one child of Belial remains alive."

Father David remarked, "Be grateful you were unconscious. Preachin' like that has been going on for hours. It is to inflame the English to further atrocities tomorrow. After the spectacle of course."

"What?"

"Outside of town there is a great oak, a venerable tree that would probably provide every room in every hall of your estate with furniture."

"I know it," Burke said.

"Yes, well, after tomorrow the whole country will know of it. The twenty of us priests are to be hanged together from its branches."

Richard Burke was silent for a long while and then he asked, "How old are you, Father?"

"Six and thirty years," was the reply. "But I have seen horror enough for a thousand."

"Even so, you are young and strong by the sound of your voice. Your height?"

"About the same as your own. Why do you ask?"

Burke smiled in the darkness. "Would you like to poke your finger in Cromwell's eye?" he asked. "I am an old man. The heat of the Indies will finish me in a month. But you, Father! You could do a work among the prisoners. You could carry the hope of God to the slaves, if you are willin'."

"How can this be, seein' as I am to hang?"

"Trade places with me. My chain of office, you said. No one knows me. Let us exchange clothin'. One will hang and one be enslaved, and the Ironsides will be satisfied."

"You would do this?" Father David said with amazement.

"I ask you to do me this service," Burke asserted firmly. "It will bless me to be of some use even in my death. It must be for this cause I was spared at the foot of the cross."

"It will bless you and your heirs from now till the end of the age if my prayers count for anythin',", the priest said. "If you are certain it is what you wish."

"I am set upon the course," Burke confirmed. "My son, who is my heir, is well able to run my estate, and he has a brace of sons to aid him. Only, if you can, I beg you: let them know my fate."

Chained hand and foot and wearing Richard Burke's clothing, Father David was brought to witness the execution of the spawn of the devil; the hanging of the popish priests.

Twenty men were forced to kneel in a circle around the giant oak. One of them attempted to speak the Our Father, but was rudely whipped across the mouth. "You are only kneeling for your execution," said the soldier who had struck the blow. "God does not hear prayers from such as you."

The priests were asked if any wanted to beg for mercy; none did. They were asked if they wished to save their souls by converting before their hanging; none would.

Each man had a loop of rope cinched around his neck, and then gangs of Ironsides hoisted the struggling, kicking forms into the tree branches. "This is how all traitors and idol-worshipers shall be treated," Pastor Peters exclaimed.

"God keep you, Richard Burke," Father David whispered. "May you and your children's children be blessed."

Then, as he was led away, the priest looked at the great oak, so terribly ornamented. "And may this tree stand as a memorial against brutality," he said. "A curse on whoever shall cut it down."

PART I

Oh the days of the Kerry dancing,
Oh the ring of the piper's tune,
Oh for one of those hours of gladness,
Gone, alas! like our youth too soon!

—Old Kerry song

1

It was meant, of course, to be an evening enjoyed only by the men of Castletown and Ballynockanor. But there was no keeping Mad Molly Fahey out. Squire Joseph was, after all, her little darlin'. She had nursed him as a babe, sorrowed for him as an orphan, mourned him in his absence, and rejoiced at his return to take his position as lord of the Burke lands. And since he had no blood kin to properly see him through his last night of bachelorhood, she would not be denied. Besides, she declared, had she not promised she would dance in honor of his wedding?

Joe Watty, proprietor of Watty's Tavern in Castletown, called the raucous gathering of fifty men and Mad Molly "The Bachelor's Wake." The party was held in honor of Joseph Connor, Lord Burke of Connaught, who was to be married to the widow Kate Donovan Garrity the following afternoon at the church of St. John the Evangelist in the village of Ballynockanor.

The Bachelor's Wake had been under way for six long hours,

occupied by a multitude of toasts. Reasons to imbibe were running low when Patrick O'Brien, the blind piper, raised his glass (or the glass of whoever was near) in remembrance of those who could not join the group. "Well now, Squire Joseph, a pity it is that Tom Donovan, your future father-in-law, could not be with us to see his daughter, the Widow Kate, wed to yourself, dead that he is."

"Aye." Mike O'Rourke, the fiddler, clucked his tongue. "Dead he is. And Aidan Clooney as well. It would be a fine thing to see Tom Donovan dance to the tune of Aidan Clooney's flute at Kate's weddin'!"

"A miracle it would be, nothin' less!" cried Adam Kane, steward of the Burke estates. He groped for his glass, which was in the fist of the blind piper. But Kane was so far gone that he took hold of Father O'Bannon's pint of temperance lemonade instead. "Here's to Tom Donovan! True patriot! Son of Ireland! Shot full of holes by the British sentries in defense of . . . what was it, Molly?"

Molly cocked an eye heavenward. "Beer! No blood in Tom's veins, only ale. He could have killed the English with his breath if only he'd got near enough."

"Never mind. He's dead."

Molly continued, "A blast of his nostrils could've lit a torch. A certain weapon against the English, it was! O'Connell might have used him to burn the British ships at Clontarf. Only Tom was dead by then."

"Where was I?" Adam Kane slurred.

Father O'Bannon, eyeing the temperance punch in Kane's fist, reckoned the steward would not notice what he was drinking at this point.

With a toothless grin, Mad Molly began to sing and dance. The blind piper joined in. O'Rourke added his fiddle.

I'd like to give a lake of beer to God.
I'd love the heavenly host
To be tipplin' there
For all eternity.
I'd make heaven a cheerful place.

I'd sit with the men, the women of God
There by the lake of beer.
We'd be drinkin' good health forever
And every drop would be a prayer.

After much applause, the bridegroom raised his punch and solemnly proclaimed, "I give you my father-in-law, Tom Donovan, and Aidan Clooney, who will not play at my weddin'! To heaven and their health, gentlemen!"

The cry was raised, "To heaven and their health!"

Voices and laughter from Watty's Tavern drifted up on the chill night air to the hills. A full moon shone high above Connaught, illuminating the ruins of the great Burke manor house in shades of grey and black, like a charcoal drawing. Broken chimneys pointed skyward. Scorched stone walls and burned timbers were all that remained of generations of Burke glory. In the servants' quarters in the stables, a few lights still burned in the windows as women waited for their men to return.

On the hill above the river fifteen mounted British troopers and one English landlord listened to the music.

"It's after curfew," said the captain, pulling the collar of his great-coat more tightly around his neck. "We could arrest the whole lot of them when they come out."

Colonel Mahon, a retiree from the British army who had been awarded Crownlands to the east of the Burke estate, coughed into his hand. "Arrest them all for breaking curfew? The rabble is inconsequential, Captain. It's Joseph Burke we're after." He snapped his fingers, calling his wolfhound, Flint, to the side of his mount. Mahon's sharp face pivoted to survey the wreck of Burke Hall. "When I set torch to that place, I thought it would be the end of him. They believe he is invincible, you know. Stood by Daniel O'Connell for Repeal. Paid back taxes with his last penny, thus depriving me of purchasing his lands by default. And he lowered the rents of his tenant farmers. Joseph Connor Burke is the center of Irish political hope here in the West. He thinks he has escaped the fate of O'Connell and the other rebels in Dublin who are arrested and charged. He walks freely about. But without the squire every peasant in West Ireland will cower and cringe and crawl docilely back into his hovel. Tomorrow Lord Burke marries. That is the moment for arrest."

The captain shifted uneasily in his saddle. "Tonight would be easy enough to take him. Then it's over and done with."

"After the wedding," Mahon replied.

"But after . . ."

Colonel Mahon raised a patient finger to redirect the conversation. "How is it you never married, Captain?"

"I've been more than once on the verge of it, sir. But my duties dictated sensibility. And you?"

"In my days as an officer, it was much the same. I was susceptible. Not that I cared for your blushing sixteen-year-old beauty fresh from the governess. My tastes ran more to the charms of experienced women with a little breadth to them."

The captain nodded. "An honest widow then."

"I confess a widow always was my weakness. I liked the notion of a woman who was quite over the awkward girlish years and knew enough to understand what she wanted and where she would go."

"My very thoughts on the matter," agreed the captain.

"And there is the matter of fortune. A widow has a decided advantage over spinsters if a man chooses carefully. An English woman of any breeding will not marry a man who lives in Ireland."

The captain nodded, then added, "I was nearly taken in by a girl here that her brother-in-law swore had an income of eight hundred a year. I could have retired. It came out that she had the eight hundred, but for one year only. I was nearly challenged to a duel over the word of the brother-in-law. Bad luck here in Galway."

At this, Mahon smiled thinly. "There's an ancient formula for calculating the fortune of an Irish woman. Take half the figure, divide by three, and what remains may be half the amount proposed." He snapped his fingers.

"Not in the North," disagreed the captain. "In the North they are well off. A race of clever, thrifty, Scotch, linen weaving, Presbyterian, yard factoring, long nosed . . ."

"So they are," assented Mahon. "Though I've never fancied a woman from the north of Ireland. But a wealthy Irish widow here in the West . . ."

"I know of none, sadly."

"I know of one soon-to-be widow after her husband is tried for treason in the court of Justice Lewis and hung in Galway City."

"Can you predict such a verdict?"

"Lewis is the judge of Kilkenny fame. And a correctly picked jury in Galway City will have no fondness for the Burke family."

"But after the wedding?"

"Arrest the man before the ceremony and his fortune passes to his infant son. Better to leave a widow behind with considerable property in her name."

The captain laughed loudly, making his horse stamp and snort uneasily. "Intend to marry, do you?"

Mahon was unruffled by the question. "Never. And not to a bog Irish woman like Kate Donovan at any rate. No, Captain, I intend to persuade the widow to sell her property to a gentleman who can manage it properly. That is myself."

"Persuade." The captain considered the word.

Mahon replied, "As all the Queen's men are bound to persuade the Irish that what is best for England is best for them."

Morning flowed down from the Galway hills like water washing the green valley in brightness. Clean and cold, the clarity of the air added crispness to the village of Ballynockanor.

Lining the rutted road were two dozen glistening white cottages, defined by light and shadow. A patchwork of verdant fields was bounded by rock walls that wandered up and down the swales, dividing the domain of one poor tenant farmer from another. Since the thin soil of western Ireland sprouted up a new crop of rocks each spring, the fences separating pasture from potato patch were broad and strong.

From the ancient stone cross of St. Brigit, high above the valley floor, Kate Donovan Garrity watched the stirrings of the village of her birth. Thin wisps of peat smoke drifted up from chimneys as the bells of the chapel of St. John the Evangelist tolled the morning mass of this first day of Advent, 1843.

While every farmer and his family scurried to finish chores before the service, Mad Molly Fahey capered up the lane toward the church-yard. Carrying two brimming buckets of fresh milk, Kate's twelve-year-old brother, Martin, emerged from the dairy barn while seven-year-old Mary Elizabeth fed the chickens. It all seemed so ordinary, as it had always been in Ballynockanor and always would be.

It was Kate's wedding day. Today, after a long year of troubles and doubts, she would finally marry the squire of these townlands, Joseph Connor Burke.

From this place of her pilgrimage, Kate imagined what her father, Tom, would say if he were alive. "Sure, and it's about time you came to your senses, girl! Joseph is a good man. Landlord he may be, but he's poor now as the rest of us. His great manor house burned down. Taxes have taken everything. He's sacrificed his own safety and lost a king's ransom for love of Ireland, as his father did before him. Kate, you're no daughter of Tom Donovan if you show no mercy to such a patriot. Take pity, girl, and wed him for what he's done for his country! And your martyred sister's babe . . . wee Tomeen . . . needs you to mother him as well."

As for Kate's mother? She simply would have asked, "But do you love him, Kate? Love him enough to stand by him no matter what may come?"

At the image of her mother's kind face, Kate smiled and glanced up at St. Brigit's cross. The tolling bells of St. John's echoed against the hills and fell away. Kate repeated the question, "Do I love Joseph Connor Burke, poor man that he is?" A lark sang from the brush. Soft wind swept over the nodding grass and touched her face. "Aye, Mother. That I do. I do love him. More than my own life."

The bell of St. John the Evangelist was pealing wildly, as well it might since the pullrope was firmly in possession of Martin, Mary Elizabeth, and Mad Molly Fahey. The two children and the one of childlike heart were gleefully churning the rebounding chime like a carnival ride at the grand Cong horse fair.

Mad Molly's daughter, harried and fearful of Father O'Bannon's disapproval, laid her hand on her mother's shoulder to draw her away from the game, but the good priest himself insisted the pastime continue. "'Tis little enough happiness abroad in *this* world to draw her back from her own on such a cheerful occasion," he said. "Let her alone."

The ecstatic reverberations brought smiles to the faces of the villagers of Ballynockanor. After all, many causes for celebration were wrapped up in this wedding day: one of their own, Kate Donovan, whom many of them had known since she was a wee lass no bigger than *that*, was marrying with Joseph Connor Burke. And even more significant: no further threat of Burke townlands reverting to the Crown or being taken over by the likes of Colonel Mahon.

"No cottages bein' tossed," remarked O'Rourke as he rosined up his bow. "No more American wakes."

"No Tom Donovan alive to see this day, and no manor house for the squire to carry his lady home to," observed Paddy O'Flaherty, owner of O'Flaherty's Pub in Ballynockanor, injecting a note of Irish melancholy into the proceedings.

"No," agreed the fiddler, "but the prospect of a host of wee Burkes to carry on for both himself, the Burke that was Joseph's father, *and* Tom Donovan." With that, O'Rourke struck up a jig on his fiddle.

Just that quickly there was dancing in the lane beside the church, and laughing and singing. O'Brien's pipes dueled with O'Rourke's fiddle, and the two of them contested for possession of "Whiskey Before Breakfast" until everyone's sides ached from the merrymaking and the cheering.

Kate Donovan twirled in the arms of her husband, then was swept away from him by Adam Kane, who was in turn captured by the maid Fern. Joseph escorted the cook, Margaret, while Kate found herself confronted by the twinkling eyes of Father O'Bannon. "Will ye play the fiddle for us today, little Katie Don . . . , I mean, Lady Burke? It was part of a covenant, I believe."

Molly Fahey spun past with Mary Elizabeth. "A promise, 'twas, 'tis true, Father. Just as I am dancin' at the weddin'." Beneath her coarse, woolen skirt flashed a red petticoat, a gift from Joseph Connor Burke.

From within a thickly padded fold of cloth Martin withdrew the precious fiddle and offered it to his sister. "Play for us, sister," he asked. "Da would like it."

From the top of the hill beyond Blood Field and in sight of the chapel of St. John, Colonel Mahon listened to the clanging of the bell and the first springing strides of the fiddle. Standing erect in his stirrups and stretching gratefully, he turned to the captain of the troop of English soldiers and remarked, "There's your signal, Captain. Now's your time." The wolfhound, Flint, shivered with excitement beside the horse.

"Men," advised the captain, "down there is Joseph bloody Burke. It was at his home that we were overtaken by Ribbonmen and shamed. Some of those same Ribbonmen may be at the dance right now. It is certain that those people hold rebel sentiments, and Lord Burke is responsible for much of the upheaval and unrest in this part of the country. That is to say, I know you'll do your duty." Belatedly he added, "Remember, this is an arrest of one man, not an attack. We'll have no bloodshed unless there is resistance."

Exchanging a significant glance, two of the troopers undid the frogs that secured their sabers.

"Good hunting," Mahon said, touching his cap in salute. "Not you, Flint. Stay!"

"Right," agreed the captain. "Let's go to a wedding."

Joseph looked about him with pleasure and gave a sigh of contentment. He caught Kate's eye as she stood tuning the fiddle, winked to encourage her, and received a dazzling smile in return. She was so beautiful. His heart felt like it would swell to bursting inside his chest. Joseph's one fear was that he would awaken to find himself alone in his bed and this moment only a dream. Involuntarily he closed his eyes as if to check the reality, then snapped them open again. To be able to look at her and not to do so was too absurd. For the rest of his life, Joseph vowed, she would be the last of his sight at night and the first of a morning. And in between the two as well, he reminded himself.

Kate tried a few runs up and down the scales, then pronounced herself ready and nodded to O'Brien and O'Rourke.

> *I will ever be your love,*
>   the fiddles and pipes sang.
> *From Spring till Spring the same.*
> *My heart, my life, my song, my all,*
> *Is yours alone to claim.*

The achingly haunting melody lingered on the air and swirled in Joseph's ears moments after other wedding guests heard the sound of hoofbeats approaching on the road. The troop of horsemen swept into view, divided into two columns, and surrounded the crowd. Sensing danger, Miss Susan, the wet nurse, grabbed the toddling Tomeen and retreated to the safety of the chapel steps.

Each man of Ballynockanor urged another to restrain himself. "What is the meanin' of this?" spoke up Father O'Bannon. "As you can plainly see, this is a weddin', and no concern of yours." O'Bannon grasped Kate's arm and held it firmly.

The captain chose to ignore the priest's protest. He nudged his horse forward through the crowd, forcing Martin to draw the blind piper, O'Brien, out of the way. The officer reined up with the head of the horse practically touching Joseph's chest. "Joseph Connor

Burke, I arrest you in the Queen's name," he recited solemnly. "Come along without trouble, and none of the others will be inconvenienced."

Mad Molly scrabbled in the dirt and threw a handful of dust in the air. "Sassenachs!" she screeched. "Foreigners. Be off with ye!"

"Restrain the woman," the captain demanded.

"Will you restrain her like you did me da?" Martin Donovan demanded. "Shoot her down?" An angry current of agreement greeted these words.

"Martin!" Joseph said with alarm. "You must not endanger the women and children." It was the right approach to take. Proud at being included with the adult males, Martin subsided. The point was well taken by the others too.

"I'll go with you, Captain," said Joseph.

"It is good you are sensible," the officer said. "You will mount the spare horse."

After Joseph had done as ordered, the captain directed the squire's hands be bound. "It is not necessary," Joseph commented. "I have promised to go with you."

Kate could restrain herself no longer as she saw her husband of one hour trussed up and about to be led away. Pulling free of O'Bannon, she thrust the fiddle at the priest, ran to the side of the mounted officer, and grabbed his stirrup. "But where are you takin' him? What is the charge?" she groaned. "Why are you doin' this?"

"Move out of the way," the captain commanded. "The prisoner will be held in Galway City. He is charged with treason. Move out!"

"Treason!" Kate and others gasped. "But that means hangin'! Joseph! Joseph!"

Kate was still clinging to the captain, trotting alongside to keep up. As he flicked his reins down on the neck of his horse, he also drew back his booted foot and kicked her on the right cheek. Kate spun away, stumbling and falling to the ground.

The troopers burst through the crowd, scattering them in all directions, then the soldiers cantered away toward the south. Mad Molly tossed handful after handful of dust after them, crying, "Sassenachs! They've stolen the Burke. Over the sea they'll take him. Ah, wee Connor, don't go! Don't go!"

They left Kate alone in her bed. Without a tear she wished them good-night. Miss Susan's voice drifted through the door. "They tore my man away from me just so. I weren't half so brave as Miss Kate be."

Words about courage made tears brim in her eyes at last. It was not bravery that kept her from sobbing, but fury and a determination never to let the English overlords see her weep. But she was alone now, alone on the night she had dreamed would mean the end of loneliness. Her gaze lingered a moment on the white satin of her wedding dress flung over the chair in the corner. She snuffed the candle out and lay back heavily on the crisp linen pillowcase. A single tear escaped. She brushed it away angrily with the back of her hand. "They will not break me," she whispered through clenched teeth. "They will not break me down, Joseph!"

Her right cheek was swollen and throbbed from the boot of the trooper. But she welcomed the physical pain as some slight distraction from grief.

The scent of fresh-cut pine boughs filled the room. Martin had cut the limbs that morning. Later, as Kate ironed Martin's shirt in the kitchen, she had listened to conspiratorial giggles as Mary Elizabeth joined him to decorate the bridal chamber.

Martin had laughed, then said, "Well, I've stolen the branches from his Lordship's own trees, but since Joseph is His Lordship and the bridegroom too I'll not be transported for the crime."

Woven branches above the window and door and at the head and foot of the bed masked the aroma of smoke from a hundred years of peat fires. The room smelled like a forest glade, clean and unbounded by the four walls of the tiny cottage. Now the darkness mocked their gift.

It was true that a child even younger than Martin could be transported for stealing pine boughs from a landlord's forest. Taking a loaf of bread from a baker's cart in Dublin was crime enough to be shackled and shipped seven months to the penal colonies of New South Wales as punishment. What then would be the penalty for

Joseph's crime? The accusation of treason against Queen Victoria and England had been proclaimed at his arrest. How many Irishmen had been hanged for an offense a thousand times less grave than that? The threats of the soldiers rang clear in her mind. Would she be Joseph's widow before she ever lay in his arms or felt his soul and body melt into hers?

"Joseph." She sighed. "Oh, Joseph, darlin', what will become of us?"

Overwhelmed by exhaustion and dread, Kate turned her face into the pillow and wept silently.

When Joseph laid a hand on the slime-covered stone wall, his palm came away coated in oily green scum. The only light source in the ten-foot-square room was a small window set high in the wall opposite the stairs. Too far above the floor to reach even by jumping, the opening was nevertheless further obstructed with rusting iron bars.

A bed of sorts, formed by a ledge of rock only some six inches higher than the floor, jutted out of the far wall. The meager layer of straw with which it was strewn had perhaps once been yellow but now was grey and sodden. Joseph dubiously inspected the furnishings his cell provided—the single threadbare coverlet, wooden bucket of water, and empty rusty pail representing the toilet facility.

There seemed to be less ooze on the treads halfway up the flight of steps, so Joseph sat there to ponder. That he had been arrested openly meant his enemies were confident of their evidence, manufactured though it had to be. That the seizure happened on his wedding day was not coincidence either; the British authorities wanted to make an example of him.

And what about Kate? How was she coping with this additional terror? Kate had already lost mother, first husband, and infant brother to a fire that left her scarred for life; not Joseph's arrest as well? Following only a year after the death of her sister Brigit, ten months after her brother Kevin's banishment to America, and six months later than her father's slaying by British soldiers, could she possibly have any strength remaining to face another loss? With his cleaner hand, Joseph gingerly touched the scissor nicks marking his closely hacked hair.

From the top of the gloomy passage came the jangle of keys, the rattle of a chain, and the creaking complaint of the bolt being drawn. Joseph stood and backed downward as the newcomer advanced until his features were revealed. Short and stocky, bald and stubble-faced were all things Joseph noted, but the most distinguishing mark was the scar: a welt of puckered skin ran from his forehead to right cheekbone. The sunken flap of eyelid announced the loss of the eye to the same stroke. "Stand by yer bed, croppie!" the jailer ordered, thumping a wooden truncheon against his palm. His manner suggested he would enjoy serving out correction if Joseph chose to disobey.

"I am Joseph Connor, Lord Burke," Joseph said calmly, "and I demand . . ."

"Shut yer gob 'fore I shut it with this," the guard menaced, waving his club. "You don't demand nothin', croppie. You are *Prisoner* Burke and nought more. In here I, Mister Gann, am your lord and master . . . executioner and undertaker too, come to that . . . so mind yer manners and don't speak 'less I ask summat, see?"

Joseph nodded, and a lopsided smirk turned the already misshapen countenance into a gargoyle's leer.

"Quick learner, eh? Right then, here's the drill. Bucket and pail at top o'steps at daybreak or no change till next day. Midday meal must be et in ten minutes, or you miss a day. Clear?"

Joseph nodded again.

"Don't guess you'll be here long enough to starve, croppie," Gann observed. "Treason means hangin'."

"Treason?" Joseph snorted. "I've done nothin' wrong."

"That's what all you croppies say," Gann retorted. "Well, chew on this, Prisoner Burke: if the Great Liberator . . ." The guard broke wind loudly as he uttered Daniel O'Connell's nickname. "If the leader of you bog-trottin' rebels is facin' the noose, why do you think *you'll* escape? Crush all such rats and burn out their nests, I say."

Tasting bile, Joseph bitterly wanted to retort that such had already been done, but he kept still.

"Do you see this?" Gann asked, turning his cheek more toward the light so that the scar glistened. "Scullabogue, croppie, in '98." Joseph could not repress the tremor that ran through his frame. "You know of it then?" Gann continued.

Indeed Joseph did know the atrocity of Scullabogue. Rebels, fleeing their defeat at New Ross in the Rebellion of 1798, worked up a frenzy against innocent Protestant loyalists. Men, women, and children were herded into a barn and burned alive. Others were stabbed to death outside.

"Two hundred of my kinfolk and neighbors burnt to death by rebels," Gann said. "And when I, only eleven years old, tried to stop it, a big lout stuck me with his pike and laughed as he slung me around." Gann's narrative stopped, then he shook his head. "No matter," he concluded at last. "In less than a month, I seen that same rebel hanged, then burnt in a barrel of tar . . . good job I still had one eye, eh croppie? And this eye will always be watchin' you."

The square patch of dim twilight hanging on the wall of Joseph's cell faded to inky black. The slowly rolling waves at the harbor mouth beyond the confines of his prison made the bell of an entrance buoy toll mournfully, like the solemn call to a requiem mass.

Joseph sat motionless on the stones, staring at the window till the last gleam disappeared. Body and soul were both cloaked in darkness.

Joseph wrapped the lone blanket, its repugnant condition disguised by the night, around his shoulders. He thought how he would get word to Daniel O'Connell, who could surely arrange Joseph's release, then regretfully reminded himself that O'Connell was also in fear of his life. The Liberator had a battle of his own to fight.

The squire of Burke Hall vowed to enlist the assistance of his other friends in the Repeal movement, even while wondering if they were incarcerated or in hiding. As for other influential landlords who could sway the British authorities—they were probably celebrating his downfall, since they regarded Joseph as a turncoat to their class.

The people of Ballynockanor might wish they could rally to his defense, but Joseph knew that they were powerless. Tenant farmers, even those as fairly treated as the ones on Burke land, could barely feed their families and survive from one Gale Day to the next. It was neither wise, nor possible, for them to interfere on Joseph's behalf.

Who was left? Father O'Bannon, certainly. The aging priest of St. John the Evangelist would spare no effort to secure Joseph's freedom; he was probably working even now to get word to someone in Dublin about Joseph's arrest. Then what?

Only Kate remained to be considered. Following a circular pattern of tortured thinking, Joseph's reflections returned to her yet again. Kate would move heaven and earth to get him released, would contact every possible assistant, bombard every official, no matter how remotely connected, with pleas and demands.

Joseph could see her now: her face flushed with indignation and resolute pride, her chin raised in defiance at injustice, her brown eyes flashing. How he loved the waves of her chestnut hair, the way he could fold her in his arms and she fit so perfectly against his chest. The warm, earthy aroma of vanilla came from her neck as he buried his face in its nape.

Putting out his hand in the darkness, Joseph encountered not the soft warmth of which he had been dreaming, but the dripping wall of his prison chamber. If he were not locked in this hole, this dungeon, he would be in the Donovan cottage with Kate at this very moment, in her arms . . .

It was the same tormenting image from which Joseph's thoughts had retreated during the previous cycle . . . and the time before that . . . and the instance before that. The images were too painful to be borne.

He would bribe the jailer to send word to Derrynane, he mused. Daniel O'Connell's home was at Derrynane, just down the coast from Galway City. Perhaps a fishing boat could carry a message to O'Connell's retainers. But no, all Daniel's family and associates were helping prepare for the trial in Dublin . . .

2

The first Castletown market day since the arrest was bitter cold and grey. Wrapped and mufflered, wind-stung farmers and their ruddy-faced wives tended stalls as the townfolk hurried to make their purchases and retreat to the warmth of their hearths. Few took time to share the usual gossip. Some hurriedly commented on the fact that the new Lady Burke had set up a booth among her husband's tenants to sell Donovan cheese, butter, milk, and cream as she always had in the days before her marriage when she was plain Kate. There was, however, a sense of deference displayed toward Kate that made her uneasy. Was it just the cold that made longtime friends lower their eyes when speaking to her, then hurry away as though she were changed?

With Squire Joseph in a Galway City dungeon, most thought Kate was prudent to stay on at the dairy and continue with her life as if there had never been a wedding. After all, was it not likely that she would be a widow before she had a chance to be Squire Joseph's wife? And was the marriage valid anyway, considering that there had not been a wedding night to follow the ceremony? None dared ask Father O'Bannon the church position on such a delicate matter, but such questions were discussed quietly over a pipe and a pint at Joe Watty's.

One new item of information was circulated among the farmers and the townfolk: the Lady Burke stated flatly she would not move onto the grounds of the estate. She said the Donovan dairy was her place until her husband came back and took her to his own home. Along with Martin, Mary Elizabeth, and Miss Susan, Kate intended to continue milking cows and mucking stalls. She would not know how to do otherwise. She would raise Squire Joseph's baby boy, Tomeen, as if the child were not heir to the Burke lands. The infant was half Donovan after all.

"He'll be a better man for it," O'Rourke said to Adam Kane.

"'Tisn't proper," disagreed Kane. "Kate's rightful place is behind the gates of the manor, not in a dairy barn. I've been to Galway to see Squire Joseph about this and other matters. They'll not let me speak to him, but I think I know his mind on the matter." His quick eye fixed on the figure of Colonel Mahon moving through a pen of ewes. Mahon's dog, Flint, sat watchfully outside the sheepfold, eyeing the woolly creatures with undisguised interest.

Tall boots gleaming, Mahon tapped the bleating sheep out of his way with a silver-headed stick. "There's a wolf among the sheep of the townlands," Kane continued, indicating the colonel. "That one there'd have his fangs in the deed to the Burke lands, and I'd feel easier if the Lady Burke would give up her dairy herd and move onto the estate."

But years of facing tragedy had given Kate the strength and control to stand in a harsh wind with her head erect. She did not display her emotions, and none spoke openly to her about the fact that her new husband would likely be hung.

"Kate Donovan bears the strength of St. Brigit's cross on her face," commented the Widow Clooney to Margaret, the cook of the Burke household. "Storms may blow, but she is ever rooted where she was planted. Sure, and I think she'd crumble to dust if she moved away."

Margaret sighed as she picked through a heap of beets. "Still, Kate's always been good company when she's stopped in the kitchen to bring the butter and the milk. I was lookin' forward to havin' her to cook for. And that sweet baby boy playin' by the hearth. Nothin's gone as it should. Nay. And not likely to either."

"If they hang Squire Burke she's better off where she is," Widow Clooney said knowingly. "Familiar surroundin's are a comfort. At least she's got the warmth of the moilies t' lean on while she's milkin'."

"Aye. If he's t' be hanged, then what'll become of us who serve him?" As she said this, Margaret dropped a cabbage into her basket. Both women stared down at it as if they pictured a severed head landing below an executioner's ax.

Widow Clooney raised her eyes as Colonel Mahon climbed out of the sheepfold. "That one'd snap up the estate quick as a wink. Any of us who ever paid a penny to help Repeal would be tossed, and our farms turned to grazin' lands. My dear Aidan, God rest his soul, never did trust the English colonel."

"Look at him there," Margaret whispered in astonishment, leaning closer. "He's walkin' straight toward herself! Lord a'mercy, Widow Clooney! The colonel is speakin' to her!"

"A bold one he is," agreed the widow.

All heads in the market pivoted to watch as Colonel Mahon approached Kate, tipped his hat, grinned pleasantly, and offered what appeared to be words of consolation and encouragement to her. She thanked him with evident coolness, then turned to assist Mrs. Watty in the weighing of a pound of butter. Colonel Mahon watched her a moment as if he had something more to say, but she did not look at him again until he selected a wheel of cheese. She told him the price. He paid her without bargaining and, after lingering more, snapped his fingers for the hound and walked away.

Without missing a beat, Widow Clooney remarked, "She's one of us."

"That she is," concurred Margaret.

"If Squire Joseph is hanged, and we're all tossed, that is when we'll see Kate Donovan close her dairy and follow us to the ships."

Martin's changing tenor cracked with resentment as he stared hard at Mahon's retreating back. "And what did the English landlord want of you?"

"Cheese," Kate replied without emotion.

"More likely he's after some bit of information about Joseph."

"Well, all he's taken away is a very fine wheel of cheddar, Martin."

"He's a spy, you know. Working for Dublin Castle, they say. Don't speak with him again, Kate. He's got his eye on Joseph's land."

She might have smiled if her heart had not been so heavy. Martin was the man of the house until Joseph was released, and he took his charge seriously. "He may put his eye anywhere he pleases, Martin, but it does not mean he'll get any other part of himself on it."

"The Ribbonmen know how to deal with the likes of himself."

Kate whirled in anger at mention of the Ribbonmen. Pulling him behind the cart, she rebuked him in a harsh hiss. "Sha, Martin! Would you be speakin' of the criminals who oppose the things Joseph is in prison for? O'Connell says violence will bring nothin' upon us but more violence."

"I could wish a night visit and a hangin' for Mahon."

"Then keep your wishes to yourself! Speak aloud of such matters in the marketplace and when Mahon is hanged some dark night by the Ribbonmen the authorities will be comin' after yourself! Would you be hanged for speakin' your mind? Or deported like your brother, Kevin? Keep a sensible tongue in your head, Martin. We've lost enough Donovans to foolishness!"

Wrenching himself free, Martin glared at her. "Seems you should be preachin' from the rooftops about what these English landlords are doin' and not just to Donovans, but to your husband and every honest Irishman. Are you scared of them?"

"Aye," she said fiercely. "Every breath I take I remember Joseph is locked away in their prison. Scared? I scarcely sleep at night for fear I might say or do somethin' to give them evidence against

Joseph for the charge of treason. I lock my fury away and smile at every villain who passes by and inclines his head to hear my words."

Martin gulped and backed up a step. "Of course . . . I mean . . ."

"It's talk of hangin' the likes of Mahon that could get Joseph convicted. Peace is what Joseph preached at O'Connell's side. It's peace for Ireland he'd die for . . . so he may be called to do so too. But he'd not kill for any cause. And I'll not give his enemies anything more than my smile and . . . a bit of cheddar to chew on. Have you spoken like this to anyone else, Martin?" Bitter tears stung her eyes.

Martin, pale and ashamed of his carelessness, looked away from her. "Aye."

She drew herself upright. "You mustn't. You'll help the hangman put a noose around Joseph's neck." She put a hand on his shoulder. "Do you understand what I'm sayin', Martin? Mahon may be a spy. May well be. Probably is. No doubt reports every word we say to Dublin Castle and the authorities. But there are more spies than himself right here in Castletown. Even in Ballynockanor there are some who would tell what they know and make up more besides if they could gain from it. Hold your tongue, lad."

"Aye." He was beaten and knew it. "That I will, Kate."

"Tip your hat when that devil walks past, lest he notices you and turns on you and me and Joseph. Do you understand, Martin? If Joseph goes down, then every tenant farmer on his lands will fall with him."

He nodded. Kate saw the remembrance of a dozen separate foolish conversations, today alone, pass through Martin's mind. He had been dangerously open about his feelings and wishes. She chided herself for not warning him sooner. Among friends it was completely understood why Martin Donovan would want all Englishmen—soldiers and landlords—to die a horrible death. But to speak it!

"I'll be more careful, Kate."

"Give them nothin'. Perhaps then Joseph will come home to us soon."

An iron panel in the cell door slid back with a clang loud enough to jolt Joseph out of his stupor. "Where are the buckets, croppie?" Gann's voice demanded. "Hurry up!" he ordered, banging on the panel with his club.

When both containers had been passed through the hatch, Joseph asked, "When do I see the magistrate? You can't just keep me locked up without a hearin'."

The only reply was the slamming shut of the grate.

For three days running Joseph asked the question; for three days there was no response. Slop jar and water bucket were exchanged just after dawn each morning. Half a loaf of coarse, grit-filled bread and a quart of watery soup were shoved through at noon. These were the only signals that anyone even knew of Joseph's presence in the dungeon.

By the morning of the fourth day, his beard was ratty, his clothing foul, and his eyes red from worry and lack of sleep. He bent mechanically to retrieve the fresh water from beside the grate when he realized that the panel had not been closed. A pair of boots could be seen in the passage on the other side. "Visitor comin'," Gann announced gruffly. "Stand off under the window and don't move till the door shuts again."

Grabbing up the container of water, Joseph stumbled down the flight of steps as he leaped to comply. His mind was spinning with the thoughts of who it could be. Father O'Bannon? Daniel O'Connell? Did he dare hope that it could be Kate? He plucked nervously at his wrinkled and slime-smeared shirt, and hurriedly splashed water on his face and the worst of the muck on his trousers.

The hinges of the door shrieked, and it was pushed narrowly open. There was a long pause during which Joseph's pulse raced, and then into the cell stepped a diminutive young man wearing spectacles and carrying a satchel. He was completely unknown to Joseph. The newcomer advanced three steps down the stairs. When the entry banged shut behind him, the little man jumped and spun about as if anxious to flee back the way he had come.

"Who are you?"

Adjusting his glasses, the slight figure offered in a deferential voice, "Sweeney. Jasper Sweeney."

"Do I know you, Mister Sweeney?"

"Dear me, no," Sweeney said. "No, no, no." His monosyllabic comments were offered in a tone of pious horror, as if to assert any prior connection between himself and Joseph was completely unthinkable. "I am your defense counsel."

"My lawyer?" Joseph responded in puzzlement. "Who sent you?"

"Well, my, you see, that is, it's complicated. There was a request made for you to be represented by Daniel O'Connell."

"Good," Joseph said with a sigh of relief.

"But, no," Sweeney corrected. "That would be quite impossible. Mister O'Connell stands accused of treason himself. He could not possibly defend you."

"But he sent you in his place?"

Sweeney managed to look even more shocked. "I have absolutely no connection with political demagoguery and seditious conspiracy. No, no, no. I am a completely loyal subject of Her Majesty the Queen."

Exasperated and losing patience, Joseph took a step toward the short man wearing the high starched collar and perfectly creased brown suit. "Then who sent you?" Joseph shouted.

"Take one more step, and I shall call the guard," Sweeney warned. He clutched his briefcase to his chest in preparation for flight.

"Wait," Joseph offered in a quieter tone over raised hands. "I am anxious for news about my family and about what is happenin' here. Can you tell me anythin'?"

"That's better," Sweeney said, but he made no move to get closer to Joseph. "Since your associates stand accused of treason the same as you, yourself, the magistrate has appointed me to see to your defense."

"Who is the magistrate?" There were many local judges Joseph knew. Few of them were well-disposed toward the Repeal movement, but many were fair-minded men before whom Joseph had the chance of an impartial hearing.

"The magistrate was specially appointed for this case," Sweeney said. "His name is Lewis. He's not from this part of the country at all, not at all. He's from County Kilkenny."

Joseph's heart skipped a beat, and he swallowed with difficulty. "Lord Lewis of Callan?"

"The same."

There was no way the news could have been worse. Magistrate Lewis had begun his career in jurisprudence at the time of the Rising of '98, when he had been known as "the hangman of Kilkenny." He had received the brutal nickname after supervising the building of a scaffold on which thirty rebels could be hanged at a single time. It was widely known that Lewis had remarked to a visiting British army officer, "I hate dribble-drabble work. Hanging by ones and twos is so inefficient." Lewis's delight in increased productivity had led him to hang several hundred men.

"And you are to defend me before Judge Lewis," Joseph repeated. "How many capital cases have you handled before?"

Sweeney removed his glasses and polished them with a clean handkerchief before replying. "I've never actually appeared in a courtroom before," he admitted. Then, swooping into his satchel, he produced a leather-bound volume of *Blackstone's Commentaries*. "But I've been studying very carefully . . . very carefully indeed."

3

It was mid-morning. Martin and Mary Elizabeth were away at the Burke estate school. Miss Susan had gone to town to see about a length of corduroy for Martin's new trousers. Kate and Tomeen were in the garden when Adam Kane rode to the gate.

His look was sober in spite of the glorious warmth of the day.

"Well, it's the rent collector?" Kate jibed. "Hello, Adam. I paid my taxes and my rent."

He tipped his cloth hat and approached the vine-covered fence, snatching off the cap before entering the garden. "G'day, Your Ladyship."

"It's always Kate to you, Adam."

"Beggin' your pardon, Your Ladyship . . . Kate. We all, that is, us on the estate, figured you'd be movin' into Castletown."

"When Joseph is released."

"It's likely to be some time before that."

"I can wait. I don't fancy livin' in the shadow of the ruins alone."

"But you wouldn't be alone. There's all of us. Fern, Margaret, Molly. The house staff needs someone to fix and carry for. And Squire Joseph had a fine place furnished for you. Before the weddin', that is. It's not a bit gloomy."

"I've been fixin' and carryin' for myself and my own too long to be waited on, Adam. And I'm less lonely here, dreamin' among my own things."

But Adam Kane continued to encourage Kate to pack up her belongings, bring the children, and move onto the grounds of the estate. "You're the Lady Burke now," he said, standing at the end of a furrow as Kate dug turnips for supper. Tomeen ran his stubby fingers through the earth and drooled happily as he gazed at the steward.

Kane continued his argument. "And wee Tomeen is the new Viscount Burke. Fern and Margaret were sayin' it ain't fittin' for him to grow up like a common tenant farmer's child."

Kate broke the clods away from the bulb. "But he is just that. The child and grandchild of a tenant farmer, Adam. For that is what I am and so was his natural mother, my sister. And our father and his father before him."

The steward's brow wrinkled. "But milkin' cows and muckin' stalls and makin' milk deliveries, Kate . . . the wife of Squire Burke?"

"And if I don't do it, who will?"

"I could find a hundred."

Kate shook the turnip at him in gentle reprimand. "Ah, but none would love it as much as myself, Adam. How else would I learn the news from every household in the parish?" She chuckled. Her lightness seemed to trouble him more deeply.

"Squire Joseph took the furniture we rescued from the fire, see. And Dick Dooley's put walls and doors in the old barn until it's hard to see it wasn't always a house."

"The barn is it?" Kate laughed. "Why should I leave when I've got a house, a real house, right here at the Donovan dairy?"

"It would be simpler, Kate . . . ma'am, for Martin and Mary Elizabeth to go to school if you lived inside the gates of Burke manor. They could walk across the green, and there they'd be."

"They ride with me to Castletown on the milk run every mornin'. I wouldn't give it up for the whole world."

Kane hung his head in somber thought. "But there's the nights, Kate."

"Aye," she said, acknowledging in her thoughts that the nights without Joseph were indeed long. Would they be easier in a new place unfamiliar to her? "I know the mornin' always comes here. I can point to the crag on yonder hill and tell you just where the sun will rise."

Shuffling his boot in uncharacteristic uneasiness, he replied, "Times have changed, Kate. A woman alone . . ."

"I'm not alone."

"A woman and children alone, then. Let me speak, woman."

"Woman, is it. What happened to Lady Burke?"

"I need a word with practical Kate. Kate Donovan, daughter of a plain Irish farmer, if you don't mind."

"Well, then."

He jerked his chin down in satisfaction. Plain, practical Kate would listen to his warning. "There's been talk."

"As there always is."

"It isn't safe for you and Miss Susan and the children here any-more."

"You're making too much—"

"Squire Joseph, Daniel O'Connell . . . well, Kate, politics in Ireland is a nasty business. Like it or not, you're the wife of a man who has become a target for the opposition. Two of the lads at Watty's heard a big, wild-eyed chap in the market square at Cong. He was talkin' against the Repealers, the wives and children of his enemies. The family of your husband, you might say." He coughed into his hand and did not look her in the eye. "Threats, Kate. Almost biblical it was. Dashin' babes against the stones and such to rid the land."

Instinctively Kate picked up the baby. Holding him on her hip and brushing back his red curls, her mind flitted to old tales of mas-sacre and destruction. "Anything directly about Ballynockanor?"

"No. But Cong's not more than a mornin's walk from here, Kate. Listen to reason. We can't keep watch over you or this wee one from all the way over in Castletown. There's plenty who'd benefit from Squire Joseph bein' dead. After the squire comes you and that baby you're holdin'. And for the time bein' the squire is better protected behind the prison walls than you and Tomeen, Miss Susan, and Mary Elizabeth and Martin. Don't think they would hold back from killin' the witnesses as well. Now look here. There you stand with a child in your arms. What would stop a man of wicked intent from killin' you both and ridin' away? Come back with me, Kate."

"I'll think on it," she promised. She did not reveal that his words made her tremble inside. "I'll speak with Father O'Bannon on the matter. For now Joseph's fate alone is concern enough."

They'll bring Joseph into the courtroom through that door, daughter," Father O'Bannon said to Kate when they gathered for Joseph's first hearing.

She was grateful to have some place in the packed chamber to focus her attention. Her stomach churned as it had when she had been caught in a storm on Lough Corrib in a coracle. There were rough waters ahead, she knew, before she and Joseph came again to safe harbor, if ever they did. She had not even been permitted to see her husband before the arraignment.

"Pray silence in the court!" intoned the bailiff in a manner that brooked no debate. "Special court of assizes, County of Galway, Province of Connaught, assembled in the year of our Lord, eighteen hundred forty-three, is now in session. His Honor, Justice Lord Lewis presiding!"

An oak doorway to the right of the high seat of justice opened to admit the robed and bewigged figure of Magistrate Lewis, the hangman of Kilkenny. "God save the Queen and this honorable court!" bellowed the bailiff.

At the tables occupied by the crown prosecutor, the court clerks, and the counsel for the defense, there was a hearty response to this acclamation. Particularly enthusiastic in his acknowledgment was

Squire Mahon, seated just behind the prosecution and wearing a look of smug satisfaction.

But the responding invocation probably never reached God's ears, for it rose no farther than the level of the gallery at the rear of the court, packed with two hundred spectators. Their groaning, growling, and muttering muted and then overpowered the call for solidarity and respect. The bailiff cast a hurried glance to see that the armed pairs of red-uniformed guards were in place beside every entry before scuttling to his place in a corner.

Peering over his reading glasses at the crowd of onlookers, Judge Lewis's rat-like features became even more pointed. "I will tolerate no disturbance of any kind in my court," he warned. "One outburst, no matter how light, and I will arrest the perpetrator and clear the court. Let the prisoner be brought in."

At the other end of the bench another doorway opened to admit Joseph. Despite the judge's admonition, there were several in the throng who could not refrain from gasping. Was this Squire Burke, so recently part of the life of Castletown and Ballynockanor? At Father O'Bannon's stern look, Kate clasped her hand over her mouth and forced herself to keep still.

His leg irons clanking as he shuffled forward, Joseph was also manacled to Officer Gann. He had dropped at least a stone of weight, and his eyes looked sunken and unnaturally bright. His head had been recently shorn for his court appearance, and in place of his familiar, collar-length blond hair was a short bristle bearing the marks of many gouges.

"Ooh, sister," Mary Elizabeth moaned, tugging on Kate's sleeve. The vision of Joseph caused Kate real physical pain.

Martin, on the other side of Mary Elizabeth, jerked his elbow into her to urge her silence. Though his twelve-year-old face was a mask of fury, there was no way Martin was going to be ordered out of the court! The anger on his countenance was mirrored on the features of Adam Kane and Joe Watty, on O'Rourke and the usually timid Fern. Even the kindly visage of Father O'Bannon looked to have been cut from stone.

"Read the bill of specifics," directed the judge.

Below the bench a clerk stood and announced, "Joseph, Lord Burke of Connaught, is charged with high treason against Her Majesty, Queen Victoria, in that he did conspire to overthrow Her Majesty's government, did knowingly aid and abet others to do the same, and did keep an unlawful school for the purpose of indoctrinating others in the same principles of treason and sedition."

"Prisoner at the bar," said Judge Lewis with a thinly disguised sneer, "how do you plead?"

"Not guilty, mi'lord," said Joseph firmly.

"The plea is duly noted. The prisoner is remanded to his present place of incarceration, there to await trial."

For the first time Joseph's meek and furtive-looking defense counsel appeared to have something to say. "If it please the court," Jasper Sweeney said with an apologetic wave, "Lord Burke, though not appearing in the same court, is codefendant with the honorable Daniel O'Connell and others. Those others are also awaiting trial, but have been released on their on recognizance. I pray the court grant similar clemency to my client."

"Denied," grunted Justice Lewis. "This is my court, not one in Dublin. Treason, conspiracy, and sedition are heinous crimes that lead to open rebellion and armed insurrection. There will be no ill-advised clemency, particularly for an educated member of a privileged class who cannot even claim to have been led astray by others. Take him away!"

In the fleeting instant before his exit, Joseph turned his face upward to search the gallery. As his eyes locked on Kate, he managed a slight smile, a nod, and a wink to tell her he was bearing up and so must she. His strength passed to her in that instant. She inclined her head and mouthed the words *I love you,* just as he passed from her sight.

The strong west wind blew a flock of seagulls inland. Calling frantically, they circled over the hulk of the ruined manor house. Mad Molly, hearing their cries, emerged from the kitchen as Martin and Mary Elizabeth passed on their way to the school.

Mary Elizabeth nudged her brother, who sighed in resignation and greeted the old woman as she fell in step behind them.

"G'day to ye, children."

"Hullo, Molly," Mary Elizabeth replied glumly. The girl had scarcely smiled since the wedding day had been ruined and the bridegroom hauled away.

"Would ye care for supper?" Mad Molly blinked her eyes rapidly and screwed up her face as some strange thought leaped into her addled brain and out again.

Mary Elizabeth frowned. "We et porridge."

"He's flown away." Mad Molly looked toward the birds. "Altogether lost he is. Poor, poor Connor. Poor Joseph Connor Burke. Flown away."

Her incantations, which usually meant something, worried Mary Elizabeth. Porridge or not, school notwithstanding, the child was inclined to skip arithmetic and stay awhile to hear what Mad Molly Fahey had to say.

"We're late for class, Molly." Martin pulled Mary Elizabeth along at a quicker pace.

"Aye." Molly danced sideways along the road. "Sums, is it?"

"Arithmetic," Martin said.

"Sums and sums. Large sums and simple sums. There's nothin' more that devil loves than his sums. May one. May two. May three. That's why he's thrown poor Joseph in the dungeon." After inspecting each of three fingers as if she suspected them of treachery, Molly continued, "Kate must know the sum of it, or two and two shall never be four."

"We'll tell her you said so, Molly," Martin assured her.

"Do that." She cocked her eye at the birds. "The wind'll carry him far, I fear. Poor Joseph. Far from where he wants to be."

Mary Elizabeth pulled free of Martin's insistent grasp. "Let go a'me, Martin! She's at it again! Talkin' in riddles, she is, and about Joseph too. It means somethin'!"

"Mary Elizabeth!" he scolded. "School!"

"Aye," Mad Molly cackled. She had them now. "School, is it. They'll use that against him sure. Ah, the seabirds. What're they doin' so far from home?" She waved her spindly arms in the air and called to the wayward fowls, "Be off with ye! Back to port! We'll not have ye here screamin' so's a body can't hear the lark!" Then, suddenly calm again, she winked at Mary Elizabeth. "Have ye heard from your poor brother Kevin, banished to America?"

"A message or two," Martin answered for his sister, who was speechless in her effort to decipher Molly's ranting.

"A message or two. Aye! There's the cause of the mishap, Martin. A day late. Every message they send a day late. And poor Joseph can't know the news." Lifting her sharp chin skyward, she shouted at the flock, "The wind'll carry him where he doesn't want to go, y'see! Get back home, y'fool! The shores of Ireland! Get home! That way!" She chucked a stone in their direction. It missed. Shaking her head sadly, she turned abruptly and wandered back toward the kitchen. "Two and two is never four in the devil's sums, see? And every message a day late."

The assistant to the Lord Chancellor of Ireland, one Burtenshaw Suggins by name, belched loudly into his fist. From the pocket of his brocade waistcoat he removed an enamel snuff bottle, painted with a miniature scene of a stag hunt. Suggins snorted a quantity of finely powdered tobacco into each nostril, then exploded with a thundering sneeze. Blinking his watering, piggish eyes, he peered around the first-floor drawing room of his town home on Dublin's North Great George Street. "Bless me!" he said with satisfaction. "Delightful. Care for a pinch?"

This offer was made by vaguely waving the snuff bottle between the other two occupants of the room. Edward Lucas, under-secretary to the Lord Lieutenant of Ireland, declined with thanks. Colonel Mahon merely scowled. The cause of Mahon's annoyance was not so much his disapproval of an unfashionable habit as it was the delay in getting to the substance of the meeting. "And what is Your Lordship's response to my proposal?" he demanded again.

"I say that the Repeal movement is dead, at least for this year,"

Suggins boasted. "We will keep O'Connell fearful for his life until the trial and therefore harmless—convict him and lock him up for some length of time, but not enough to give him a halo, you understand. Meanwhile, we will work undercover with his more radical associates, planting the notion that O'Connell has sold out the side to save himself and thus divide the cause of Repeal irreparably."

"Exactly what I explained to Colonel Mahon," Lucas interjected. "Joseph Burke is no longer of any consequence whatsoever."

"He is to me," growled Mahon. "And he was to you when you wanted him dead."

"I can't imagine what you are referring to," said Suggins coldly, wiping his cheeks and nose with a silk handkerchief. "In any case, it no longer signifies. Now is not the time to create any martyrs to a cause already on its deathbed."

"But I have Burke locked up and charged with treason with Justice Lewis to try the case!"

Lucas and Suggins exchanged a wary glance, and Suggins motioned for Lucas to summarize. "Precisely why we insisted on seeing you," the slim man said. "O'Connell will be tried and convicted, but not for treason."

"What!" Mahon demanded, bolting upright in his chair as he saw his scheme collapsing around him.

"As I say, not for treason," Lucas continued smoothly, "but for the lesser charge of conspiracy to disrupt the peace. The maximum term is ten years."

"This has been decided in the highest offices," Suggins rumbled. "Politically this *is* the course we will follow. Do not presume to overreach yourself, Colonel Mahon."

Mahon's mind was racing. No charge of treason meant no death sentence. And now that he had revealed his scheme to Suggins, there was not even a way to help Joseph to an untimely "natural" death. "Can you do this much," he pleaded. "Keep the information about the reduced charge secret as long as possible?"

"That is already the strategy," Lucas conceded. "It serves our purposes to cause Daniel O'Connell as many sleepless nights as possible and thus break him down."

"When will the accusation of conspiracy be made?"

"Not until just before the trial, now set for the first week in January," Lucas concluded.

"Good," Mahon uttered thoughtfully. "Very good. There is time. Gentlemen," he said, standing, "I thank you, but I must leave at once and hurry back to Galway." With that brief salutation he departed.

"Keep an eye on that one," Suggins ordered Lucas after the colonel had left the house, yelling vehemently for his coachman to hurry. "Perhaps another glass of this excellent port?"

4

Something was wrong. Martin knew it from the distant barking of a dog, the bawling of the cattle, and the frantic clanking of the cowbell before he and Mary Elizabeth ever reached the pasture.

"Sounds like dyin'!" Mary Elizabeth ran ahead to clamber over the stone wall.

Martin's twisted right foot slowed him down. He called to his sister as her dark curls bobbed up and then out of sight. "What is it?"

"Martin! Oh, Martin! Martin!" she shrieked above the bellowing and then, after a silence, "Get out! Leave her alone! Get on with you!"

Martin cursed his crippled limb and struggled up the rocky slope, coming at last to the enclosure. Climbing over the fence he saw Mary Elizabeth, disheveled, holding a stone and weeping among eleven milking cows. In the center, bloody, torn, and struggling to stand on a horribly broken foreleg, was Daisy, the lead animal of the herd. Panting and wild-eyed, the beast lay on her side, raised her head, tried to brace her weight beneath the jagged bones, and collapsed instantly in agony.

"It was a dog!" Mary Elizabeth sobbed. "I saw it there." She pointed to the far wall. "A wolfhound it was, tearin' her to pieces."

Martin put an arm around Mary Elizabeth, gave her a squeeze, then knelt beside the bovine. Placing a hand on its neck he held the terrified creature down and tried to calm her with soothing words. There would be no saving her. "It's ripped her belly out," Martin said, wincing. A glance at the rest of the herd showed that three others also suffered wounds in flank and abdomen. "Wolfhound."

"Aye. Great hairy devil with bloody fangs. I threw a stone and hit it. It ran away. But we're too late. Ah, Martin. Poor, poor Daisy girl."

Martin exhaled slowly, trying to think what to do. "Who would have such a dog in the parish?"

A gruff English voice answered from the far side of the fence. "I do." It was Colonel Mahon. He stepped from his hunter and hopped easily over the stones, then strode toward the suffering animal.

The gore-covered hound followed at his heels.

Terrified, the milch cows bawled and ran to the end of the pen in panic.

"You!" Martin's fists were clenched as he rose to his feet. "Get it away from my cows!"

Mary Elizabeth shrieked and hurled the rock at the dog, which dodged and returned patiently to its master's side.

"Look what it's done! Get it out!" Martin grasped a jagged hunk of granite and threatened the squire with it.

In reply Mahon halted, pulled his pistol, called the dog to sit, put the muzzle between its eyes, and fired.

The report of the weapon resounded in the hills as the body of the dog collapsed, jerked, and then was still. Mahon, his boots and riding breeches stained with blood, stepped over the body of the beast and strode toward Martin and the dying moilie.

He reloaded his weapon, glanced at Martin's crippled limb, then ordered Mary Elizabeth, "Go fetch your sister and that servant woman. Tell them what's happened. Bring the wagon for the carcass. There's no use letting this meat go to waste." With that he fired a second ball into the cow's brain.

Mary Elizabeth cried hysterically and rushed to Daisy's side. "No! No! No! No!"

Mahon, a hint of disgust on his hard features, took the girl by the arm. "Get on with you! Do as I say!" In one deft movement Mahon flicked open a clasp knife and slit the throat of the cow to drain the blood. Martin sat pale and shaken on the ground. "You, boy. Get up. We'll skin her out here. There's hide and tallow and meat to salvage."

The exhausted hysteria of Mary Elizabeth twisted the tale of horror into an incomprehensible jumble. Kate held the sobbing child just long enough to get the drift of her meaning. Someone with a pistol shot Daisy. Something terrible with dripping fangs attacked. The dairy herd panicked and injured. Bring the wagon. Go now.

"Mary Elizabeth! Where is Martin?" Kate held the child's shoulders. "Listen to me. Is Martin hurt?"

Mary Elizabeth managed to shake her head before she collapsed.

A glance of comprehension passed between Kate and Miss Susan. "We should fetch Mister Adam Kane," the wet nurse said.

"No time. And I'll not risk takin' Mary Elizabeth or Tomeen out on a night like this."

"Y'all ought not go alone if them Ribbonmen is maimin' cattle," Miss Susan warned ominously. "We got's us no Tinker man to skeer 'em away like the other time, God rest his soul."

"I must." Kate grabbed her cloak and the lantern off the hook. "Mary Elizabeth, I'll be back. Do you hear me, child?" She lit the wick and cast a rapid glance around the cottage to see if there was anything else she might need. Hooking her arm through her sewing basket, she stashed a bottle of whiskey in her pocket. There might be an injury that needed stitching and cleaning on the spot. A handful of tallow candles completed the supplies. It would be nearly dark before Kate reached the far field. "See to her, Susan. Stay with the baby. Bar the door till I come back."

The wind was up, stinging Kate's cheeks and whipping her hair. Lowering its head into the teeth of the gale, the donkey plodded too slowly up the incline. Kate leaped from the seat and, clutching the reins, led the animal through the twilight.

The gloom was thick before she arrived at the field. All was silent except for the howling of the wind. Holding the lantern aloft she called, "Martin! Martin Donovan! Where are you, boy?"

Martin stepped from the shadows into the reach of her light. Ghost-like, he did not speak for a time. "Daisy's dead. Me and the squire cleaned the carcass. There'll be beef to hang and can."

Behind him Colonel Mahon said flatly, "Lady Burke. Entirely my fault. I've killed the brute. He'll not be hamstringing cattle again."

Kate, speechless, progressed into the scent of the slaughter. The dog's carcass told the whole story: Irish wolfhounds, bred for bringing down the deer and elk on the grounds of the vast hunting estates of the gentry, were born to maim and kill. The animal had merely followed its instincts.

Daisy's head stared at Kate from beside the hide. "She was my best milker."

Martin replied, "We may lose Sal, Goodlady, and Sunshine too."

"The hound did the devil's bidding." Mahon was dark with the stains of his gruesome work. "My sincerest regrets, Lady Burke."

Kate tossed her head in bitter reply. Regret would not restore Daisy or repair the damage to the herd. Kate moved among the other moilies, studying gashes and puncture marks in the soft hides. "Poor darlin'," she murmured. "Poor, poor darlin'." It would take a barrel of whiskey to cleanse the injuries and strong stanchions to hold the animals motionless for the work. "Let's get them home to the barn."

Grudgingly Martin added, "The squire's helped me."

Kate agreed, but could not trust herself to speak civilly to the man.

Colonel Mahon turned his back on her and set to his task. "You'll need a man to help tend the wounds, Lady Burke. But you're likely to lose those two." He jerked his thumb in a matter-of-fact gesture toward two moilies lying nose to nose in misery. "Now lend a hand, boy." He and Martin hefted a hindquarter of the beef onto the wagon. "It's good that it's cold. Keep the meat right enough until you've got the chance to can it. You'll want the guts for sausage."

It took fifteen minutes to load the wagon. Then, as Martin picked up Daisy's bell and managed to urge the two injured cows back upright, Mahon bade them good-evening and rode away as though he had simply passed them by on the highway.

It was just after midnight when two riders approached outside the barn where Kate, Miss Susan, and Martin doctored the cows.

Torn udders, gashed necks, slit flanks, and exposed intestines told the tale for Sunshine and Goodlady. They, like Daisy, would have to be killed to end their suffering and save the meat.

Kate barely looked up from stitching Princess when two men entered the warmth of the barn and announced themselves.

"Pardon, Lady Burke, ma'am. We are Dan and Andrew Glen, ma'am. Dairymen we are, sent from His Honor, the Squire Colonel Mahon, to lend a hand."

They were twins, identical from their coarse red beards, rose cheeks, bright blue eyes, thick necks, and stout bodies. They differed only in the color of their kerchiefs—one red, one blue.

Miss Susan eyed the two suspiciously. "Which is who?"

Martin reared up in fury. "We'll take nothin' from the devil."

"Peace, Martin. They know dairyin'. That makes them our kin," Kate noted. Then, to the brothers, "You're welcome."

"Lad, would you see to our horses?" asked Blue. "We've rode them hard to get here."

"See to your own," Martin spat.

Kate rose from the milking stool and glared authoritatively at Martin until he blushed and looked away. Throwing down his whiskey-soaked towel, he strode resentfully from the barn.

With a jerk of her head, she returned to her work. Dan and Andrew moved from animal to animal examining the damage.

By morning light Sunshine and Goodlady were butchered and dressed. The wounds of the others were stitched and cleaned. The dairymen assessed the damage with the same sad eye as Kate. Three milkers dead. Four in the herd damaged badly enough that they would surely go dry. Seven out of a dozen fine moilies had been rendered useless by one errant hound.

Blood Field!" Mad Molly flapped her arms as though she would fly from the circle of schoolchildren. "'Tis a cursed place, it is. Blood Field!" She fixed her eye on Mary Elizabeth, who shrank back from her. "Ancient slaughter! Treachery! Ah! Turn loose the wolves among the lambs. Happened there before, ye know. Ask wee Connor who fled from the dogs that terrible night. His own dogs too, they were, eh, Martin? Tell us more!"

Martin, angry that Molly had turned her ranting toward the slaughter of the Donovan cattle, replied, "Leave it be, old woman."

She seemed surprised at his rebuke. "Old woman, is it now? Sure, and I'm not as old as some."

"And who then?" Martin urged her thoughts along a different path from that which led to carnage.

"Well, I'm not as old as . . . St. Patrick."

"He's long dead."

She held up a bony finger in correction. "Nay! Alive with all the saints, praisin' God in heaven, he is."

"You're older than any in Ballynockanor." He was pleased with the new subject of verbal combat. She had forgotten Blood Field.

"Nay! Not as old as Jehovah who walks the Seven Bens daily. Why, I'm a spring chicken. A hatchlin'. A heifer!" Her eyes rolled in memory. The addled brain clicked from heifer to cattle and back to the carnage of Blood Field. "Aye. A heifer. As I was sayin', Martin . . ."

"You're old as . . ." The game was over and he had lost.

"A fine dog it was too. Licked the boots of the squire. Then!

Mother's milk spilled upon Blood Field! It's the why and the why and the why of it that escapes me."

Colonel Mahon did not dismount from the sorrel hunter as he spoke to Father O'Bannon. The priest mentally noted that this was the first time he had ever seen the English squire without the wolfhound at his side.

"Good day, Squire, Colonel Mahon," said Father O'Bannon.

"Good day, Your Honor."

So far Mahon seemed pleasant enough for the devil incarnate.

"You're far from home, then, Squire." Father O'Bannon said this to send the message that Mahon was on Burke land and that it would never be home to the likes of himself.

"I've come on an errand of penance." Mahon reached into his pocket and tossed down a fist-sized leather pouch that had the distinct clank of coins when it landed in the priest's hand. "This is for Lady Burke. I did not think it proper to present it to her myself. Twice the worth of the cows. Will you see she gets it with my heartfelt remorse?"

Father O'Bannon hefted the pouch and closed one eye in thought. *Penance, did the man say? Heartfelt, was it? Remorse, is it?* In spite of the good priest's doubts, here was a purse of hard, cold cash to back up the villain's claim that he had some wee-tiny-pea-of-a-heart thumping away in that hollow-shell-of-a-landlord's-breast of his.

"Well now," replied the priest, hefting the coins. "Aye. I'll give her your gold, Squire. But this'll not replace her sweet companions. Kate, the Lady Burke, set a high store of affection on those little creatures. Friends they were to her. Daisy. Sunshine and Goodlady." He did not mention that Kate had brought them each in turn for the blessing on St. Francis's feast day. "Many's the time I heard her singin' to them as I passed the Donovan barn."

At the coolly relayed information that even the colonel's gold might be scorned, a hint of sorrow passed briefly over his features.

"I regret . . ." He stopped, and with a slight inclination of the head, said, "Good day." Then he rode on.

Twenty-one gold sovereigns were stacked in seven piles on the table between Kate and Father O'Bannon.

"Three sovereigns for each killed or injured cow," commented the priest. "Give the devil his due. Colonel Mahon pays his debts."

"Three times more than the value." Kate sighed. "But still not touchin' the worth of my little friends. I'll miss them, Father. They were good company and always gave their milk without complainin'."

"Aye. Strange isn't it, daughter? All things livin' on earth know how to be what God made them to be . . . except for mankind." He tapped his finger on a stack of coins. "Ah, well, then. There's more money here than the House of Burke has seen since payin' back taxes with the de Burgo treasure."

"And more than the House of Burke is likely to see again for many a year. There's another notice of more Crownland taxes owed since Joseph's arrest. Adam Kane brought me the bills as though I'd know what to do."

"Ye'll need to be thinkin' of yourself as Lady Burke now, Kate. Joseph needs someone on the outside tendin' to business."

"It never ends, and I'm not the one to know such business. I'm still the daughter of a dairyman. A common tenant like the tenants I'm now responsible for. If it hadn't been for the murder of my herd and now the Squire Mahon payin' damages, I hadn't cash to pay the servants, let alone the Crown assessment."

"God provided for ye as He promised He would, girl. Now Adam Kane says you're travelin' again to Galway City to see if ye can visit Joseph before the arraignment?"

"That I will. But they've turned me away at the prison twice before."

The aged priest gave a wink. "Colonel Mahon's left ye the key, daughter." He held a newly minted coin to the light. "Young Queen Victoria. Sure, a noble sovereign she's made of herself. Her golden cheek pressed against a greasy palm'll bring the most unpleasant prison guard to attention. I ask ye, who would argue with the sovereign herself when she says, 'Open in the name of the Queen'?"

It was the darkest midnight in December when the Burke coach arrived at the inn in Galway City. Adam Kane was at the reins, and Kate, Miss Susan, and the baby within.

The steward hammered at the door of the half-timbered and galleried building. It took a full five minutes before the knock was answered by a sleep-dulled man wearing a red flannel nightshirt and carrying a candle.

Kane instructed, "A room for the Lady Burke, her servant woman, a child, and myself."

At the mention of the Burke name, the innkeeper's eyes widened. "The traitor's wife, is it? No room for the likes of a Burke. Fools we will shelter, but never felons, sir, lest we be caught in the web of their conspiracy."

The door slammed shut.

It was two hours before Adam Kane finally procured a room for the little entourage. He did not mention the family name again in Galway City.

The Spanish Arch, located beside the old quays where the river Corrib opened into Galway Bay, had been built in 1584 to protect the harbor of Galway City, which was then outside the city walls. Here the Spanish merchantmen unloaded their ships. Here too unruly sailors were imprisoned, and mutineers kept in shackles until they were led down the Long Walk to be hung from the yardarms of a vessel.

Joseph Burke was a mutineer to the ship of state. For this reason he was placed in the deepest cell of the Spanish Arch to await his trial. Through the jailor, Gann, lay the only approach to Joseph.

Beyond the Spanish Arch, on the west bank of the river, was the
Claddagh. From medieval times this flat, stony shore had been home
to a fiercely independent, Gaelic-speaking fishing community. They
scorned the English minions who kept watch on the city walls. It
was there Kate and her group found shelter for the night.

She awakened at first light to the soft sound of Gaelic voices at early
mass: "Is robhrea an stor ata ag Rina Gloire duinn in aisce . . ."

> *Wonderful is the treasure that the King of Glory has in
>   store for us.*
> *His own blood and flesh as a sustenance against sins.*
> *Do not put your hope in gold or in power for they are
>   a lie.*
> *Like a mist, compared with the glory of the heavens.*

The words somehow calmed her. She had slept little through the
night as she considered facing Joseph's jailor and presenting him
with the gold coin in hopes of seeing her husband. How would the
man she'd heard about, the evil-tempered Gann, respond to the
bribe?

While Miss Susan fed Tomeen, Adam Kane found a waterman to
row Kate to the landing on the opposite side of the river.

Against the objections of Kane, she went alone up the Long Walk
to the prison. She carried a wicker hamper of fresh clothes, baked
meat pies, and loaves of bread for Joseph. She prayed as she walked,
fingering a dozen shillings and the one gold sovereign she had
reserved for Gann. The innkeeper in the Claddagh had told Kate
that this one-eyed demon was a brute too evil to live outside the
sulfurous vapors of hell. The dungeons of Spanish Arch, a near copy
of Satan's dwelling, were thus suited to the likes of Gann.

Kate's heart pounded as she passed under the thick, stone arch-
way and approached a youthful, redcoated British sentry on duty at
the entry of the prison.

She wrapped her shawl around her chin and tucked her head
slightly to hide the scars of her burn. Smiling, she addressed the man
as though she had met him before.

"Good mornin' to you, sir. Have you been on duty the whole long night?"

"Aye, ma'am." His weary eyes betrayed exhaustion. "A cold one it was too."

"Well you're nearly off watch, then," she said pleasantly. "A hot cuppa will set you right."

"That it will, ma'am."

"I wish I had it to offer you. But I've come on another errand."

"What can I do for you, ma'am?"

"I've come to have a word with the jailor Gann about a prisoner. I've brought a few things."

Surmising she was the wife or sister of someone in the dungeon, his eyes betrayed an instant coolness. His tone became gruff. "I'll fetch Gann."

He left Kate waiting outside the door, returning a few moments later with word that Gann did not care to be seen, no matter what the errand.

Kate pressed a shilling into his palm. "Try again for me, will you?"

He slipped the coin into his tunic pocket, bobbed his head rigidly, and once again retreated behind the thick, plank portal.

Minutes passed before he emerged. "Sorry, ma'am. He says he'll have none of you."

Kate's brow furrowed. Another shilling in the hand of this lowly soldier would not change anything. She remembered the instruction of Father O'Bannon. Clearing her throat, she said, "Tell Mister Gann that the sovereign herself would like a word."

The blank expression of the youth filled with comprehension. "The sovereign," he repeated and retired inside for the third try.

There was a longer pause, giving Kate hope that Gann himself would come for the bribe and escort her to Joseph's cell.

Instead, the crestfallen soldier came out. "He says . . . ma'am . . . I cannot tell you exactly what he says to your offer. But he'll have none of it or yourself. He's steadfast to his duty, he says, and will arrest any who try to corrupt him." The young man returned the shilling to her. "You'd best be off, and that quickly. He's a coarse man, and women who are committed to this prison are ill-treated.

Do you understand me, ma'am? Very ill-treated, indeed. I have a sister myself back home. You're a pretty one, and he may take a fancy and arrest you for his own purposes."

The threat made her shudder. She nodded, certain the soldier was speaking straight with her.

"Can you get these provisions to prisoner Joseph Burke?" She set the basket at his feet.

"Gann'll have it for himself." The sentry nudged the container away with the toe of his boot. Lowering his voice to an urgent hiss, he added, "Please, ma'am. Take it and be gone. There's a window in the wall. He watches from it sometimes. Hurry on."

Kate swallowed hard, aware of the nearness and threat of evil. "Aye." Taking up the hamper, she hurried away from the shadow of the Spanish Arch and the watchful gaze of Jailor Gann.

The beef from the Donovan cows was divided and distributed among the families of the parish of St. John's for the holiday. On the morning of Christmas Eve, Kate, Miss Susan, and the children returned from church to find dairymen Dan and Andrew Glen standing in front of the closed door of the barn.

"Good mornin' to ye, Lady Burke," said Red.

Blue added, "Looks like we'll have sunshine on the Nativity."

In spite of the brightness of the morning it was bitterly cold. Kate, friendly but reserved, asked the two in for a cup of tea beside the hearth. The rest of the herd were recovering right enough, though the tragedy had slowed milk production to a quarter of what it had been.

Blue touched the brim of his cap in thanks. "Ah well, ma'am, we can't stop for tea. The squire, Colonel Mahon, sent us to ye on a Christmas errand, and we've stayed too long already."

With those words the brothers stepped back and flung the barn doors wide. In the shadowed interior a half-dozen unfamiliar heifers milled about.

"These are brought for you, ma'am. Six of the finest Springer heifers in four counties. Me and Andrew have been on a treasure hunt, ye might say, at the squire's biddin'. Find her the best there are, said he. Each of 'em due to calve within the month, and ye'll have the dairy back on its feet in no time. So, you see, six heifers, six calves. What was a most turrible tragedy becomes a blessin' to yourself and to the folk of your parish as well. With his compliments, ma'am."

The brothers grinned and blushed identically at her gasp of pleasure. Tears came to her eyes as she entered the barn and moved from one young cow to the next, stroking velvet muzzles and rubbing silken necks. The squire had more than made up for her loss. "His Honor, the squire, has done overwhelmin' right to the House of Donovan and Burke. Tell him he is forgiven, indeed."

"They're well-mannered too," remarked Blue proudly. "We made certain they'll stand patient and easy as you milk them."

"Not a heathen among the lot. Fine, sweet-tempered Christians they are, every one," added Red. "A woman alone without a husband . . ." He scratched his beard and shuffled uneasily. "These are cows fit for a gentle lady, ma'am."

Red pointed to the bulging bellies of the animals. They seemed as wide as they were tall. "The squire, knowin' how Springer heifers may sometimes be trouble with their first calvin', says you're not to worry. If you lose one he'll buy another for you. Me and me brother are to be sent here to lend a hand come calvin' time." He reached into the pocket of his coat and produced an envelope with Colonel Mahon's seal. "Here's the bills of sale for each and a letter from the squire that he says you may read at your own pace. No answer required. He wishes you and your tenants well and says he hopes to be on more cordial terms in the future."

"All this and not even a cup of tea to warm yourselves?" Kate asked.

"Nay, Lady Burke. The squire is a hard master, and we're above an hour late in this task as it is. There'll be the devil to pay if we don't hurry back."

Kate read Colonel Mahon's letter aloud to Martin. The message was brief and to the point:

> *Lady Burke,*
> *It is my hope that replacing your dead and injured cows with new stock may lift your spirits and restore me to your favor.*

Martin harrumphed, "There's nothin' to restore! His devilship never was in your favor."

Kate read on.

> *I am in your debt. If there is anything further I might do to assist you or yours, please do not hesitate to send word, and I will do all within my power for your benefit.*
> *I am your faithful servant,*
>
> *Colonel Mahon, esq.*

Martin scoffed. "Anything further to assist? He's not assisted any a'tall. Only repaid what he owed and made right what he made wrong. And it's still not enough."

Kate tossed the sheet onto the table. "That's somethin' anyway. Rare for any of his upbringin' to think of rightin' a wrong."

"Don't defend him, sister. It's men of his kind put Joseph in chains. It's Mahon himself who knows every crooked judge and politician in Ireland. He's a regular visitor at Dublin Castle. No doubt knows more about Joseph's case than we'll ever know."

Kate's head snapped up. Her eyes became bright with some unspoken thought. "Aye, Martin. You're right, God be praised!"

"Right about what? God be praised for what?" he asked suspiciously.

"Dublin Castle. Mahon. Knowin' more about Joseph's case than we. He's put himself in my debt. You heard the letter. He can get me into the Spanish Arch if any can!"

5

The tall, cadaverous steward of the Mahon estates towered over Father O'Bannon in the foyer of the great hall of Mahon Park.

Although the role of emissary had at first made the elderly priest uncomfortable, Kate's desperation and his own thoughts of Joseph's well-being urged him on.

"I've come on behalf of the Lady Burke," Father O'Bannon explained to the caretaker. "Colonel Mahon sent word that if the lady had a need, he'll do what he can to aid her."

The hawk-nosed administrator peered down at the cleric as though he were a mere sparrow come into the nest of the raptor at peril of his own life. "The squire, my employer, Colonel Mahon, has instructed me that no papist scum is ever to set foot in his house. If ever there were a papist, you are he."

O'Bannon was not intimidated by the steward's reluctance to fetch his master.

"Young man," said the priest, although the agent looked over fifty, "if ye do not do as I bid ye and fetch your master, there'll be hell to pay, I warrant. The squire, Colonel Mahon, has sent word to Her Ladyship that he is most eager to be of assistance. Now she's sent me, I've come this whole long way, and ye'll be makin' me welcome and fetch the squire, or he'll have a word to say to ye when he gets word ye've treated the Ladyship's emissary in such a shabby manner."

"Arrogant rodent." The steward's eyes narrowed angrily at the challenge.

"And after ye fetch your master, I could do with a hot cuppa tea."

"You'll have nothing more from me but my boot."

"Aye. Your boots, a yard of your worthless hide, and your badge of office if ye insult and refuse my errand further."

"We'll see about that!" The steward pulled his height erect and reached for Father O'Bannon's neck. Just then the whistle of a riding crop whipped past the priest's left ear and landed soundly against the steward's shoulder. With a startled yelp, the man fell back.

At the sight of his attacker he became as docile as a well-trained dog. "Ahhh. Squire, sir. Colonel Mahon, sir. I was about to dispose of this Catholic heretic, sir. He claims . . ."

Mahon's eyes blazed with fury against his employee. "Get out, Riggs! You're aware of what has passed between me and Her Ladyship. Well aware, sir! And now you mistreat her representative in such a manner? Pack your kit, and be off my lands before morning!"

Father O'Bannon smiled as he smoothed his cassock and cocked an eye at the discharged steward. He gave a knowing shrug as the man hurried past him in confusion and terror.

Mahon extended his hand to O'Bannon. "Apologies, sir."

"Sure, and don't turn the fellow out. A loyal creature it is that doubtless does the biddin' of its master. No doubt my errand is confusion itself to the man."

Mahon, unsmiling, nodded once and rang the bell to call a second servant as he led Father O'Bannon to the massive library.

"You have come from the Lady Burke."

"That I have."

"I have pledged to help her as I can."

"She holds ye to your word, sir."

"How may I be of service?"

"That is for herself to explain to ye, Squire."

"She'll meet me face-to-face then?"

"Aye. She'd like a meetin'."

"Only name the place."

If Colonel Mahon felt uneasy about Kate's selection of a meeting place, he did not show it.

Kate was beside Father O'Bannon in the front pew of St. John's while the English landlord sat in a ladder-backed chair across from them and in the shadow of the crucifix.

The choice of the church for this discussion was made by Father O'Bannon.

The cleric's reasons were clear: "It's hard for any man, be he Protestant or Catholic, landlord or tenant, to deceive another in the presence of the crucified Christ. Only a man with a heart of stone and no regard a'tall for the only true judge can tell a lie with the Lord before his eyes. If it works as we're hopin', then the murder of your milk cows will turn out to be the greatest blessin'! But if this fellow's got ill motives for offerin' peace and aid to the wife of his political opponent, we'll see it in his eyes; we'll plainly see fear of divine judgment on his face."

Kate studied the smooth, handsome features of the colonel. His expression seemed untroubled, even relieved as Father O'Bannon opened the parley by warning each participant that Christ was witness to the proceedings.

Mahon cleared his throat. "I thank Your Ladyship for the opportunity to make amends."

"Your help is kindly accepted," Kate replied.

Mahon's eyes flitted to Kate's burned hand. The sight of it made him falter an instant. Then, "What with the bad news from Dublin about O'Connell, I was hoping Your Ladyship would contact me."

Kate and Father O'Bannon exchanged looks. "What news?"

"You haven't heard then?" His brow furrowed.

"There's been no news a'tall," Father O'Bannon interjected.

"Well, then, here it is. There's no sign the prosecutors will lessen their charges. It's treason for O'Connell and the penalty of death they're after. Dublin Castle has treated O'Connell with more leniency than your husband has met with here in Galway. Judge Lewis is notorious. It's a certainty, Lady Burke, that he will extend the maximum penalty to Lord Burke."

A dull ache squeezed Kate's chest. She bit her lower lip. "They'll not let me in the prison to see my husband. I've tried. I hoped you could help in the matter since you are . . . well . . . your politics are well known and agreeable to the authorities, sir."

"The very point, Lady Burke," Mahon responded, struck by some idea. "I believe I can help save your husband from the gallows."

"Speak on, man," the priest urged.

"He has pleaded not guilty to all charges, thus opening himself up to trial, conviction, and execution. And he will surely be convicted and hung if he persists in this course."

"What choice is there?" Kate asked.

"An admission of guilt to a lesser charge, Lady Burke. The charge of conspiracy holds a maximum penalty of only ten years."

"Transportation to New South Wales," Father O'Bannon murmured flatly.

"He'll be alive," Mahon shot back. "There is always a chance of appeal or pardon or parole . . . hope."

"If he's alive," Kate replied softly as the sense of his argument came clear.

"I'll intervene with Judge Lewis if Lord Burke will agree to it." Mahon's offer was reasonable. "You'll need to speak to your husband."

Father O'Bannon remarked, "You'll need to arrange that as well, Squire. There's a devil named Gann who stands guard at Spanish Arch. A heart made of stone. Hot sulfur runs in his veins."

"I'll see to him," Mahon promised.

Now a doubt entered Kate's thoughts. She glanced at the figure of Christ on the cross and then at Mahon's eyes. "Why would you do Lord Burke such a kindness?"

Mahon smiled. "For the return of your good opinion of me, ma'am, after the carnage my animal wreaked upon your livestock and livelihood."

"But you have more than made up for it."

"Does that mean I am forgiven?"

Again Kate looked at the cross and then at patient Father O'Bannon. The priest's look urged her on. "Aye. That is my Christian duty, sir."

"Then say I do this for friendship, Kate, Lady Burke."

This last explanation troubled Kate in the long days and nights that followed.

6

Defense Counsel Jasper Sweeney pivoted slowly in place as he examined the drab but dry offices of the prison warden. "Now this is better," he observed. "Quite a change from that dripping dungeon." Sweeney shuddered as if *he* had been the one imprisoned below ground for weeks.

"A significant change *and* an interestin' one," Joseph noted. "What do you suppose it means?"

"Oh, I thought it was already clear," Sweeney said with astonishment. "I had it from the Crown Prosecutor himself. Giving you a respite from your cell is a token of good faith; a gesture to support the sincerity of the bargain you are being offered."

Joseph maintained an attentive silence.

"The *quid pro quo* is," continued Sweeney, "if you will plead guilty to lesser charges and save everyone the bitterness of a trial, then your life will be spared."

Joseph snorted and turned away from the nattily dressed Sweeney to stare morosely at a carved stone crest of the family Lynch imbedded in the ancient wall that formed part of the newer barracks.

"I understand completely," Sweeney said sympathetically, even as he moved away from Joseph's ripe aroma and nearer an open window. "You are thinking, 'Why should I trust the Crown Prosecutor?'"

Laughing aloud, Joseph corrected, "You will have to pardon me, Mister Sweeney, but I was also thinkin' what reason I have to trust you."

Sweeney looked dismayed. "But I am your . . ."

"Spare me your protestations of devotion," Joseph said in a tired voice. "What are the details of the message you have for me from the Crown?"

"The offer is based on political considerations," Sweeney said in a tone rich with injured feelings. "If you are hanged, as you surely will be if you are convicted of treason, as you surely will be . . ."

This is the attitude of my defense counsel, Joseph thought with bitter sarcasm, but he refrained from snorting again so as not to interrupt Sweeney's speech.

"Hanging you would create a potentially explosive situation that is in no one's best interest."

"Not even mine," Joseph offered gently.

Sweeney looked to see if he was being mocked before continuing. "Therefore, the authorities are prepared to offer you a bargain. Plead guilty, and your sentence will be transportation."

There it was, out in the open at last. Acknowledge himself to be guilty of conspiracy and, in place of the hangman's noose, Joseph would be shipped to New South Wales to a place of living death, away from his home and loved ones, away from any protection he could offer to the families of the Burke townlands. "And if I refuse?"

"Unthinkable," Sweeney squeaked as though a shrinking loop of hemp encircled his own delicate throat.

"I will have to correspond with Daniel O'Connell," Joseph mused aloud. "Such a deal would not be offered me if it were not also going to be presented to him. I cannot act without consulting him."

Defense Counsel Sweeney plucked at his collar. "There is no time,"

he said. "The Crown Prosecutor has made it clear that your deci-
sion must be rendered at once—by tomorrow in fact. You know the
attitude of Magistrate Lewis. The judge is only barely susceptible to
political pressure. If he thinks you are balking at all, he will force
the trial to go to its disastrous conclusion. Your life hangs by a thin
thread that even one day's delay may sever."

Joseph stood and escorted Sweeney to the corridor door outside
where Jailor Gunn stood guard. "Good night, Mister Sweeney," he
said. As Sweeney began to argue further, he added, "Come for my
answer tomorrow." Then as a memory struck him, he grasped
Sweeney's elbow and gestured toward the arms of the clan Lynch.
"I need time to wrestle with my thoughts," he said. "Things are not
always what they seem. Security may not exist in what appears to be
true. Take the original ramparts of this fortress, built in the 1500s
by the Lynches."

"And so?" Sweeney said with confusion.

"My family and the Lynch tribe were mortal enemies," Joseph
concluded. "One of my forebears was murdered by the original
builder of this fortification. Good night again, Mister Sweeney."

"By the way," added Sweeney in his turn, "as an additional token
of good faith, the warden is permitting your wife to come and visit
you here for eight hours tonight."

Far from having the last word, Joseph found himself speechless
and unable to grasp how Jasper Sweeney could possibly have offered
that earthshaking piece of news as an afterthought.

The sleeping quarters of the warden was neither house, nor cottage, but a private room built into the wall of the courtyard of the
prison barracks. Stark and cell-like, the space measured twelve feet
square of stone blocks. A cast iron kettle hung from a crane above
a peat fire burning low on the hearth. The cubicle was furnished
with a narrow rope bed, one chair, and a rough wood table topped
by a half-burned tallow candle, a tin bowl, and two tin cups. Next
to the peat bricks were a full bucket of water and a dipper. A window

containing four panes of glass and framed by red calico curtains provided the only light and color.

"Lord Burke'll be along to the bridal chamber shortly," mocked the guard. "Wait here." He slammed the thick plank door behind Kate.

As grim as the place was, Kate was grateful for it.

Her heart pounded with anticipation as she placed her basket of provisions on the table, stirred the fire, and set the kettle to boil. For the first time since before the wedding she was promised they would be alone together; have some word together without the prying ears of a prison guard outside the door. It had been nearly three weeks since she had briefly spoken to him through the bars of the visitation cell as Gann leered at her and jangled the keys in his meaty fist. Tonight she would convince Joseph to take the only course that would save him from the gallows. Her argument had been perfectly rehearsed, but words left her now as she thought of finally feeling his arms around her.

Then she heard the clank of chains and the rough voice of Gann outside. "Well, Yer Lordship," Gann said, laughing, "y'think the bride'll have the likes of you?" The door crashed back as Kate rose from the hearth. Silhouetted in the doorway stood a figure Kate hardly recognized. Clothed in a filthy striped uniform, Joseph stood with the awkward stance of a man in leg irons. He had dropped another stone of weight. The ragged hair was matted, and the beard on his hollowed cheeks revealed weeks of growth. Hands were clasped before him, wrists manacled. He raised his haunted eyes to meet Kate's. He remained silent, as if speaking her name in front of Gann would be somehow profane.

Reading this determination in his expression, she held herself from reaching out to him or uttering even one word of grief or joy in the presence of Joseph's chief tormentor.

"Here's a happy reunion. Not even hullo, Yer Lordship! See how she's missed you!" Gann snorted and shoved him roughly, sending him sprawling at her feet.

Kate did not move from her place. "Take off his chains," she demanded. "It was part of the bargain."

At the word *bargain,* Joseph looked up sharply.

"Remove His Lordship's leg irons? What? Before the hangin'? What do you take me for?"

"It was promised . . ."

Gann spat on the threshold. "They'll come off with me own hand when his body is lowered from the gallows. Think about that over a cuppa tay, Your Ladyship!" He kicked Joseph's chains. With a satisfied guffaw, he left them alone, slamming the door and locking it behind him.

For a long moment Kate hesitated, thinking that Gann would return to mock them. Then Joseph struggled to rise. She rushed to kneel beside him.

Joseph whispered hoarsely, "Kate, no . . . don't touch me, darlin'. I'm—"

She stroked his head. She was crying in spite of her vow to be strong. "Ah, Joseph! Joseph! It doesn't matter."

"Please. They've given me no water to wash."

Saying his name again and again, she gathered his head into her arms and cradled him like a child who had fallen and needed comfort.

Minutes passed. She could not tell how long she held him.

"Kate." He sighed. "Ah, Kate. What bargain? What promise did they give?"

She stiffened as he pulled away. Behind her the water in the kettle hissed to a boil. Wiping her tears, she drew herself erect. "A little soap and water'll put you right again." Her voice quavered as she fumbled in the basket. "I brought a fine big bar of soap."

"Aye. Soap is most welcome in such a place." His tone was weary; filled with infinite sadness.

"So I was told. And a puddin' I brought. A leg of mutton. Soda bread. A jug of milk. Butter and potatoes."

"A feast."

She could not reply as she poured steaming water into the tin bowl, refilled the kettle, and set it over the fire again. He knew some bargain had been made, some promise given. Clutching soap, towel, and basin, she knelt beside him. She felt his searching stare on her face. She could not look him in the eye as she struggled to remove the ragged shirt from around the manacles. It could not be done.

"They promised," she muttered, tearing the seam of the shirt.

"What did they promise you, Kate?" He grasped her wrist, forcing her to look at him. "Sweeney's already told me what they want from me."

The knowing in his gaze searched her soul. Her bravado left her. "O'Connell is likely to be hanged for treason. But you . . . if you'll plead guilty . . ."

"I'm guilty of nothin', Kate. Nor is Daniel. If we're hanged, it'll rally all of Ireland."

"Ireland, is it! What about me? What about Tomeen? How will I go on if you're dead?" She pulled away from him, sitting back on her heels.

"It won't come to that. They're not so stupid that they'd give millions of Irish a new crop of martyrs to rally 'round."

"Will they not?" Kate was suddenly furious at his patient acceptance of his predicament. "Maybe not in Dublin, but this is Galway. They say Justice Lewis carves notches in the doorpost of his chambers for every rebel Irishman he's hanged, and he's set his sights on you, Your Lordship! I have it on the surest authority."

"Who told you?"

"Mahon."

Mahon's name settled heavily on Joseph. If anyone knew the intent of Judge Lewis, Mahon would. "Mahon would like to see me hanged."

"That he would. The Burke estate would most certainly fall into his hand if you were dead."

"And when I am halfway around the world in a penal colony?"

"Ten years. They told me only ten years. And you will be alive. I can manage. You'll be alive."

He raised his hands to touch her cheek. "You're a young woman, Kate. Ten years . . ."

"Is not forever!" She broke. "I'll wait for you. Do you not know I've waited my life for you, Joseph Connor, and the waitin' is not half the pain of livin' without hope of ever holdin' you in my arms again?"

He fell into a pained brooding at her pleading. She dipped the towel into the basin and washed his face as he wiped her tears.

"Let me," she said, kissing him on the mouth. "Please, please, let me . . ."

He nodded once in reply. The tender glance of his desire sent warmth through her like sap rising from the earth to nourish a tree.

Suddenly the tears came to her again as he surrendered himself to her will. Closing his eyelids and leaning his head back against the wall, he appeared to doze as she stripped his prison rags and poured soothing water over his body one dipperful at a time. Her fingers trembled with longing as the soap lathered on his skin, then flowed away in this baptism of love.

"Stand up now," she instructed him in a matter-of-fact tone as she set a fresh kettle to warm. "I'll scrub your back."

His eyes snapped open. He stood effortlessly as if he were not wearing chains. "And may I not return the favor, Kate Donovan, my Lady Burke of Connaught?" He smiled down at her.

She lowered her chin, suddenly shy, as she fumbled with the buttons of her blouse. Her voice cracked with emotion. "Aye, Joseph. I was hopin' you would ask."

His gaze hardened with desire as the fabric fell away. It seemed to her he did not see the scars where flames had marred her beauty. Her shyness melted in the heat of his passion for her.

"Kiss me then, my Kate." He pulled her against him. "A kiss to fill my dreams awhile."

7

It was beside the lone oak sheltering the mortal remains of the murdered Tom Donovan and the three victims of the smallpox epidemic that Father O'Bannon arrived at a hurriedly convened meeting with Adam Kane.

"Thank you for comin' to meet with me on so short a notice, Father," Kane acknowledged.

The aging priest, still puffing from his speedy hike across the downs that separated Ballynockanor from Burke Park, leaned against the trunk of the oak to catch his breath and nodded. "Your message conveyed the urgency," he said, wheezing, "but did not explain the need for such a clandestine meetin' place. Could you not just as easily come to the chapel?"

"Indeed I could not, Father," Kane said, examining the landscape in all directions and even inspecting the winter-shorn limbs of the oak for lurking listeners. "Lately every pint I raise in Watty's Tavern and every tune I whistle skirtin' the churchyard," Kane continued, casting an uneasy eye at the four still-mounded graves, "every time I spit gets more than passin' interest from strangers."

O'Bannon nodded gravely. "You are not the only one," he admitted. "I have, myself, noted those at mass who hang on my every word, and I do not credit my old age with a sudden wellspring of eloquence."

"Just since the squire's arrest," Kane added. "Crown agents, belike?"

O'Bannon shrugged. "Aye, or in the employ of Colonel Mahon, scoundrel that he is. The difference is small potatoes. Undoubtedly they are listenin' for more treasonous sentiments to lay against Lord Burke's account."

Kane frowned at this. "Beggin' your pardon, Father, but eavesdroppin' on such as we for what weak beer of sedition we might be brewin' seems like a waste of manpower—seein' as how they can manufacture evidence at will. Could they not be wantin' . . ."

"What, my son?"

Kane idly picked a flake of bark from the oak's girth, then thumped his solid right fist into the tree. "There is somethin' you have not yet heard, Father. Squire Joseph is offered a bargain: plead guilty and escape hangin'." O'Bannon's bushy eyebrows knit together in surprise. "We are so isolated here from the doin's in Dublin," Kane resumed, "though the Liberator likewise faces the scaffold. Might we not be well advised to consult with O'Connell?"

"Treachery," O'Bannon muttered. "Men like Magistrate Lewis and Colonel Mahon do not offer deals unless they stand to gain by them. Yes! Can you leave tomorrow?"

"At first light."

"Come by the chapel on your way. I'll write a word to Daniel's private secretary, Mister Daunt. You may trust him, but no other. See what you can uncover and do it quickly!"

They had been behind him ever since Dublin; of that Adam Kane was certain. Even though he had met with Secretary Daunt in the Merrion Square fastness that was Daniel O'Connell's own town house, left by its sidedoor under cover of night, and ridden out far north of the city before turning west, somehow they were on to him.

It did not matter to Kane who they were; their identity was of as little consequence as the color of the chestnut horse surging and straining beneath him. All that mattered was the speediest return to Galway City with the news. God grant Kane would arrive before Joseph went to sentencing!

He had gained ground on his pursuers when by the blessing he had arrived at a coaching inn with only a single remount for hire. Whether those following remained on their same jaded mounts or were forced into a delay while seeking others, the result was the same: Kane had added at least a precious hour to his lead.

But as darkness swallowed him on the road beyond Athlone, the steward missed the turning for the Aughrim that led onward toward Galway City. Even though he quickly found it again, pounding hooves were coming along the track back of him. He doubted that there could be more than one occasion for foolhardy travel on such a blustery night. No, the enemies of Repeal were on his trail again and coming up fast.

Splashing into the ford of the river, Kane urged his mount onward against the shock of the icy water and the force of the current. The noise he made alerted his pursuers to his proximity, and he heard a muffled cry of excitement. Off to the north, the moon illuminated the decaying remains of a hilltop castle, and the bone-chilling wind fluttered banners of mist from the ghost-warded battlements. The night felt of unseen eyes, spectators of ancient battles being replayed over and over.

On the far side of the watery boundary that marked Kane's return to the Province of Connaught, the bank sloped gently upward over the inch, a clear patch of boggy grass free of tall brush and exposed to moonlight. The chestnut's forelegs caught at the mud bank and his hindquarters gathered under him. With a spring the horse pulled free of the stream, for a moment silhouetted and static against the inch. In that instant Kane saw the trees ahead of him illuminated as by a flash of lightning, though there was no storm. His mount tossed its head awkwardly and stumbled. Then came the report of the musket, booming across the water. A second blast followed the first, but neither horse nor rider was hit by the subsequent shot.

For two more strides it seemed the horse was not seriously wounded. Then, his neck curving downward and his body following, the chestnut crumpled, thrashing, flinging Kane off forward. The steward tumbled in a ball, protecting his head from the flailing hooves of the dying animal.

Kane crouched against the muddy pasture. The nearest sheltering trees were a hundred yards away. The pursuit—there were two riders approaching—was in midstream already. Even though there had been no chance for his foes to reload, if he tried to make a dash for it, they would run him down. No doubt soon after there would be another musket ball ready to be fired.

The weaponless steward fully expected to be shot dead at once. There had been no call for surrender, no threat of arrest. Capture would certainly end in death and an unmarked grave.

Resolving not to sell his life cheaply, Kane's hands scrambled over the earth for a stone, a tree limb, anything with which to fight back. His fingers encountered a stout rod, buried in the matted roots of turf. Working feverishly, Kane pulled it free. It was a pike staff, ten feet long. The rusting blade was still in place, bequeathed to Adam Kane by some Irish soldier of the war against King William.

Kneeling as the pikemen of 1690 had been instructed, the steward awaited the onslaught. He placed himself so that the two riders would have to diverge around the body of his slain mount. That would give him a momentary freedom to deal with them one at a time.

When they came crashing up out of the river, one was more eager and in advance of the other. Standing in his stirrups, the one in front caught sight of Kane and gave a hallo as if he were on a foxhunt. He spurred his horse directly toward the steward, expecting to ride over the top of the man.

Holding his breath and his nerves until the charge was only a dozen paces away, Kane erupted upward with a shout of defiance and a thrust of the pike that passed between the ears of the mount. The tip of the pike entered the man's open mouth, piercing the back of his throat even as Kane danced aside from the rush. The attacker was knocked backward off his horse and the pike wrenched from Kane's hands.

"Roger!" called the horseman who was later arriving. "What's happened?"

As the second rider circled the scene, Kane used the body of the dead chestnut horse as a springboard. Running up its back he flung himself toward the remaining pursuer. The third mount shied from the vaulting form, but Kane caught a loop of reins and his weight pulled both horse and rider down.

The steward was up quicker than the other. He had his hands clenched around his attacker's neck before noticing the man was unconscious. Kane stood and caught the trailing leather ribbons of the shuddering horse. Mounting quickly, he looked down at the bodies of his enemies. "King James may have lost Ireland right here a century and a half ago," he muttered, "but I have paid back a wee part of his defeat this night." Breathing a silent prayer of thanks to God and the long-departed Irish pikeman, he spurred off again toward Galway City.

Justice Lewis swept imperiously into the Galway City courtroom. After his demand for quiet had been moderately fulfilled, he ordered the prisoner brought in. The entire audience of court and gallery caught its collective breath and leaned forward as one creature to see Joseph's arrival.

No longer chained to his jailor, Squire Burke was also much cleaner than at his last public appearance. He was wearing the grey trousers and yellow jacket of a convicted criminal, but he entered the hall with his head up. Gann hovered nearby, a dragoon pistol thrust conspicuously into his waistband.

There was a delay during which Defense Counsel Sweeney and the Crown Prosecutor conferred with Lewis. No one could hear what the conversation involved, though there were many whispered inquiries of "What are they about, then?" from the assembled citizens of the Burke townlands. Martin shushed Mary Elizabeth, who begged Father O'Bannon to tell her what was happening. The good father, in turn, was anxiously concerned about something outside the stone walls, but he was the only spectator whose attention was focused elsewhere.

Kate did no craning of her neck, nor did her eyes inspect the meeting at the bar. Her gaze was fixed on Joseph, though he had not yet elevated his face toward hers. She had vowed that she would not miss his briefest glance, nor omit the slightest opportunity to pour her love and concern into Joseph's soul.

From the square outside the courthouse came the clatter of hooves on cobblestones. Muffled shouts and angry voices echoed upward through the lancet windows, but only Father O'Bannon noticed. He clutched his fist to his chest and tried to push aside those who crowded in against him, but without success.

The two barristers returned to their respective places and the murmuring stilled. Lewis cleared his throat, liberally distributing a scowl to the whole assembly. "I have been informed that the prisoner wishes to change his plea and that the Crown is prepared to urge clemency in exchange." Lewis formally inquired of both sides if this was indeed correct, then said, "Joseph Connor Burke, you stand accused of treason. If you enter a plea of guilty to conspiracy you will forfeit your right to trial by jury. The penalty you deserve is death, but the Crown is willing to show mercy and commute your sentence to transportation. Do you agree that such is your wish?"

Only then did Joseph seek Kate's strength with his eyes. She dipped her chin minutely. *Go on*, her motion said. *You will live, and we will be reunited.*

"It is," Joseph agreed.

"Then, Joseph Connor Burke, hear the sentence of this honorable court: You are to be taken from your present place of detention and confined as Her Majesty's government deems fit, there to await transportation to the penal colony of New South Wales . . ."

The clamor in the lobby outside the court grew in volume and intensity. The sentries posted beside the doors looked nervously around, and the captain of the guard drew his sword halfway free of its scabbard.

"For the term of your natural life."

The room turned to bedlam in an instant. *Your natural life . . . natural life . . . natural life* bounded to the ceiling, dropped to the tiled floor, was flung upward by a hundred throats until the glass in the windows rattled. It was a life sentence; it was exile; it was banishment forever.

What? What? What did he say, Kate?" Martin grasped Kate's sleeve. When she did not answer, he turned in desperation to Father O'Bannon. The old man's knees were buckling, and he staggered. "Transportation for the term of his natural life? What's it mean, Father?" Martin queried.

The priest slumped in stunned silence as the realization sank in. "It was only to be ten years," he said. "Kate, daughter! They said the maximum was only ten years."

Kate was reeling. Voices took on a dreamlike quality. Could this be happening? One quick look at Mahon told her that the sentence had been known ahead of time. But why? Why had he gone to the trouble to warn her? The outcry in the courtroom provoked an instantaneous and violent response from the magistrate who banged his gavel and called for order.

Ashen, rigid, and unmoving, Kate took her cue from Joseph. From the dock he glanced upward, catching her gaze, and in his look commanded her to dignity and self-control in the midst of chaos. *Do not let them see you break,* his eyes warned her.

Mary Elizabeth, shaken by the tumult around her, clung to Kate and began to cry. "Is it terrible then, Kate? Why is everyone shoutin' so?"

Martin leaped to his feet and sprang up to stand beside the tenants of the Burke townlands as they shook their fists and jeered down the judge.

The priest reached for the boy, calling him back, but Martin evaded his grasp and clambered into the center of farmers. Below the balcony a belligerent pro-English faction formed, led by Colonel Mahon.

Ten times the bailiff cried, "In the name of the Queen," but not even the authority of Queen Victoria could halt what was sure to be a bloody confrontation. The noise was deafening, shutting out any one voice. The expression of Judge Lewis was black and threatening as he stood behind the bench, gave a command to the bailiff, and faced what had become a mob.

"There'll be a slaughter," said the priest to Kate as he levered his creaking body upright and pleaded with his parishioners for calm. They did not seem to hear the old man.

Within seconds a dozen rifle-bearing, redcoated soldiers swept up the stairs and lined the back of the gallery. "The first man who advances against us is a dead man!" a grim-faced sergeant warned.

Weapons ready, soldiers stood beside Mahon's men, likewise aiming upward at Joseph's supporters.

O'Bannon cried, "Men of Castletown! Of Ballynockanor! Sit down now! All of ye! What use is dyin' today for a case that will surely be changed in appeal?"

Mahon cupped his hands around his mouth and jeered at the priest. "The sentence stands with the guilty plea! No appeal! No appeal!"

The clamor began again. Kate's arms encircled Mary Elizabeth protectively.

Emotions stretched to breaking. Then Joseph's voice rose above the din.

"Men of Ireland!" he cried out to the mob, but his gaze was locked on Kate's ashen face. She nodded encouragement. The crowd fell silent. "Above all, the call of Repeal is a call to unite, Protestant and Catholic, for peace and justice in Ireland!"

A hum of remembrance vibrated in the courtroom.

Joseph had them. "How many of us stood shoulder to shoulder with Daniel O'Connell at the monster meetings of Galway City and Mallow and Tara? We heard his proclamation that liberty would come through peace or not at all! How many of us turned back from Clontarf and the mouth of British cannon for the sake of sparin' the movement the loss of even one drop of Irish blood?" He paused. "Rejoice! My blood is not spilled for my country today. Do not offer your lives on the altar of violence! Praise God! I am alive to carry on. Distance from these shores will not turn my heart from you! With life I have the power to pray, and hope, and dream, that in my natural lifetime we will be free!" A cheer reverberated, bringing tears of pride to Kate's eyes. "And I pray God for the unity of all men of Eire and that Repeal will soon be a reality. Then, still strong and young, I will return to a homeland of freedom and peace!"

As the disturbance finally subsided, Adam Kane's voice could be heard ringing out in the antechamber of the law court. "Squire! Don't plead guilty!" the steward bellowed. "O'Connell is not charged with treason, only conspiracy. Squire, d'ya hear me? Five years at most. Don't do it!" Kane, pushing two young soldiers ahead of him as if they were made of straw, burst into the courtroom.

Magistrate Lewis, his sharp features converging into dagger points of fury, shrieked anew his demands for order and silence. "Guards! Remove that man!" roared Lewis, overtopping the volume of Kane's impassioned cry.

"There'll be no hangin', Squire! Don't do it!"

Violence, so lately restrained, threatened to burst its bonds. The confused jabbering of the crowd mixed "No hangin'," with "five years" and "his natural life!"

Lewis's order changed to, "Guards! Silence that man! At once, do you hear?"

The two troopers already had grasped Kane's elbows. As they absorbed the frenzy of the judge's command, they bore the steward roughly to the ground, pummeling him into stillness.

Jailor Gann cocked the hammer of the firearm and presented the muzzle against the side of Joseph's head. Without words, but with no less certainty, he ordered Joseph down to the floor.

"This is riot!" Lewis screamed. "I will give the order to shoot! Do you hear? The soldiers will fire!"

Now it was Kate's voice that rang out above the crowd. "Stop! Stop now! Don't give them excuse to kill him! Please!"

A fearful hush fell at once.

"The plea is entered and sentence recorded. No change is possible," Lewis intoned. "Gann, remove the prisoner. Guards, clear the court. A six o'clock curfew is imposed. Anyone found abroad more than two hours from now will be arrested and charged with insurrection!"

8

The jailor, Gann, looked out of place as he stood on the floral tapestry carpet in the study of Colonel Mahon's Galway City town house—like a toad sitting on a fine china dinner plate.

"He bears up well, Your Honor." Gann wiped his nose on his sleeve and shifted uneasily from one foot to the other. "Cheerful he is, in spite of the verdict. Certain he'll not be in prison long."

Mahon tapped his fingertips together and considered the situation. It was possible, even likely, that O'Connell would get off with a light sentence. Therefore any legal judgments rendered against his subordinates, Joseph Burke in particular, would be reconsidered.

"Cheerful, is it?" Mahon remarked.

"His wife and that papist devil, Father O'Bannon, have stayed behind in hopes to see him."

"No visits are to be allowed from his family, Gann. The woman. Understood?"

"Aye, Your Honor."

"That'll sap the cheer from him." He half smiled. "No news. No letters."

"And the priest?"

"Your prisoner will be needing spiritual comfort."

Gann nodded. "When I'm finished with him. That's a fact."

"Last rites. Yes. Let the priest visit with word that he is to be moved in the morning."

"Well done, Your Honor. We'll see how cheerful he is after that."

"I'm counting on the fact, Mister Gann, that Lord Burke will not manage the sea voyage well. If good news should come to Kate, the Lady Burke in Ballynockanor, as to his release, it will come too late. I predict that under your watchful eye he will not survive. All within the bounds of punishments allowed by the law." He tossed a gold sovereign to the jailor.

Gann's features spread into a hideous grin. "I thank ye, Your Honor, sir. Just the thing to help me get a start in New South Wales. And sure, as to Burke, ye don't need to doubt I'll do me duty."

The jingle of keys and the harsh clank of the bolt announced that Gann was not yet finished with Joseph.

His voice resounded in the corridor outside the cell. "If it was up to me, you'd be off to New South Wales with Burke."

Who was he talking to? Joseph stood as the door swung open. Father O'Bannon stood framed in the passageway with the grimly creased visage of Gann scowling behind him.

"God bless all in this house." O'Bannon crossed himself and entered the cell.

Gann spat on the hem of the priest's cassock. "Here's your papist warlock come to send you off to hell with a pocketful of spells, Yer Lordship."

Neither Joseph nor the aged priest responded or spoke to one another until the cell was locked behind them, and they heard the retreat of Gann's heavy boots.

Then Father O'Bannon gave Joseph a quick embrace and a pat on the head as though he were a small boy. "Are you well, Joseph?"

Joseph's questions came in a rush. "Is Kate holdin' up?"

"You'd be proud of her."

Joseph nodded in relief and sat wearily on the edge of his bunk. "Will they let me see her, Father? Before I'm sent off?"

"This province is a world apart from Dublin. Men like Justice Lewis and your jailor do as they like here, for there be none in the wide world who care if there is justice or mercy in Galway. However, a few coins in the right palm may do it."

"I want to tell her not to be afraid for me."

The priest smiled and delved into his deep pocket to produce a letter. "She wanted to say the same to you, I'm thinkin'."

Joseph held the envelope to his lips and breathed in her sweet fragrance. "Kate," he whispered.

"Read it later, boy. Her words are only for yourself to savor. They've given me a few minutes. We'll have no more time together after this. Certain I am that there'll be a priest or two on board whatever ship they send ye on. Or at least an honest Irish Protestant parson condemned for marchin' with the United Irishmen. But I've been hearin' your confession from the time ye were a wee boy and, old man that I am, Christ may call me to His presence before ye're back home."

"Word among the prisoners is there'll be no priest or Protestant preacher allowed to minister. Prison ships are English soil. Neither Catholic, nor Presbyterian, nor any worship but the Church of England'll be allowed. There's a floggin' for any who violate the edict."

Father O'Bannon nodded. He knew the rules prohibiting freedom of worship among the prisoners as well. "In the meanness of their own souls they made God small enough to be useful."

Joseph bowed his head and murmured, "Aye. But Christ's love is large enough to go into the pit of hell with me and yet still stay behind to comfort my own dear Kate as well. I believe. Christ help my unbelief."

O'Bannon smiled. "Ye would've made a fine priest, Joseph lad.

And for a time the Lord has called ye to suffer with the sufferin' and minister to those who have less faith than ye."

"Pray for me, Father. It is said that one of my ancestors was by Cromwell sent as a slave to Bermuda, but his fate was never really known. 'Tis certain he never came home. I'll need more strength to take with me than I have at this moment. When I think of years away from Kate and the baby . . . They are my homeland. I find no words deep enough to pray for myself or them."

"He'll pour out strength when ye need it most. That's the meanin' of grace." The old man let his hand rest on Joseph's head in blessing. "At the moment of His greatest sufferin' Jesus prayed for us who would suffer in this life. When ye can't find words to pray on your own, then pray the prayer He taught us. The Our Father begins with praise, follows with daily needs, confesses sin. It commands us to forgive our enemies so that we'll be forgiven. Reminds us that to God alone is power, glory, and honor forever. Neither monarch nor jailor can control your soul. If ye live, you are Christ's. If you die, ye are Christ's. So hold your life loosely, dear Joseph; place it in God's lovin' hands. When all other thoughts desert ye, pray the prayer Christ prayed. Meditate on its meanin', and ye will bear your cross without complaint as a Christian called to rejoice in sufferin' and help your weaker brothers."

Joseph sank to his knees in the cell and made his last confession to the priest of Ballynockanor. He received the holy bread of Christ that had been shared at mass by the congregation of the parish that week. It would have to last him a long time.

Then Father O'Bannon reached again into his pocket and produced a small lead cylinder shaped like a fishing sinker and tied to a leather string. The old man slipped it around Joseph's neck. "Who can say how long it'll be before ye share the Eucharist among us again? I've made an ark for ye to carry with ye, then. And in it is the holy bread last broken and shared by those who love ye in Ballynockanor. When the hours seem unbearable, touch this, and remember love is tangible. Christ has died, Christ is risen, Christ will come again."

Joseph clasped his fingers tightly around the tiny casket. Emotion closed his throat until he could not speak. The sound of Gann's hobnails echoed in the hallway without. The priest and the prisoner embraced one last time.

Kate waited in the cubicle that passed for the office of Spanish Arch prison. Warden Gann escorted Father O'Bannon to Joseph's cell. Kate hoped she too would be allowed to see him.

"Last rites. Is that what ye papists calls it?"

Kate appraised Gann with an aloof glance. Gann was as twisted inside as he was on the exterior. Perhaps she could find room to pity such a pathetic soul. He was doing a job he loved, she reasoned— like a gargoyle glowering down from the gates to keep love from entering.

When she did not reply, he prodded, "Not speakin' to the likes of me, is that it?"

"You're at least an honest villain."

"Not like the Colonel Mahon, eh? He sent you to do his biddin', knowin' that Burke's guilty plea would carry him off to New South Wales forever. Well, well, ye've no friends in high places to help ye today." Gann held the ring of keys up before Kate and then, with a satisfied smirk, pocketed them. "No visitation of women in my keepin' for a prisoner condemned to transportation."

Kate held herself proudly and met his cruel amusement with an outward dignity that surprised and irritated him. Though her emotions were at the breaking point, she reminded herself that here was a man who would scorn any show of anguish. To lose control would mean that Gann gained power over her and ultimately over Joseph.

"What?" Gann exclaimed. "No tears, Lady Burke?"

"I reserve my tears for moments of joy. On the day O'Connell is liberated, then Joseph's sentence will be dismissed."

"If the fool lives so long in hell, then maybe you'll see him again. But he'll be less a man after the stroke of my lash."

"No lash'll ever touch his soul, sir. And that's where the true man resides."

"So you may think, madame, but I say the man'll rot in chains in the belly of Her Majesty's foulest prison hulk. Like Jonah." The lips curled back in a grin, revealing his rotted teeth.

"God was with Jonah even in the belly of the whale."

"God, is it? I see your thoughts! Aye! Ye say to yourself that at least in such a place Joseph Burke'll be away from Jailor Gann! Now here's news! I'm to sail to New South Wales with him. I'm promoted to a post among the convicts there. For the term of his natural life, says the judge. It may well be a short term." He chortled and leaned back in his chair, putting his boots on the desk.

Struggling to keep her voice even, Kate replied, "I know where Joseph'll be when God releases him from life. Every man's term on earth is too short. And where will you be goin' when your term here is up?"

Her words did not intimidate him. "Hell, I hope. Satan needs a reliable prison warden there. Aye. One who wields the cat-o'-nine-tails so well he can lay open a backbone with one stroke. Ever seen a convict whipped to death, have ye? Great crack it is. We wager on how long a croppie can stay alive with his flesh in ribbons oozin' down his back."

Kate felt the bile of fear and fury rising in her throat. When she gulped air, he knew he had her.

"Will you allow me a last visit?"

He continued unabated. "Throw the body over the side, and the sharks come swarmin' for a nice meal."

"A final word with him?"

"I was aboard a prison ship once. A dozen croppies died of dysentery. Wasn't much left to feed the sharks after that. But still they tore away arms and legs like dogs fightin' over scraps. Last rites is what your priest is givin' him, sure."

Kate gathered her shawl close about her. "The room is foul with the smell of somethin' not quite human."

"At your service, madame." He mocked her, proud of his cruelty.

"I'll wait for Father O'Bannon on the quay."

Gann guffawed at her retreating back. He had won a small victory, but she had not been broken.

If she had stayed longer, Kate knew she would have been sick. The sea air revived her, but she could not hold back the tears any longer. Turning her face toward the rough stone of the wall, she whispered her farewell to Joseph and hoped somehow he heard her.

The tawny red sails of Galway hookers scudded across the bay. Father O'Bannon said little to Kate as the two shared a seat on the Galway mailcoach bound for home. Kate was grateful for the quiet. She could not have spoken without crumbling inside. Fifty years of hearing the hearts of his parishioners pour out had given the good priest a sense of when to wait and when to listen. He sensed Kate's need to compose her thoughts.

When at last the horses strained up the grade leading north from the city, Kate drew a deep breath and asked, "Was he well?"

"He's plannin' on bein' home by next Christmas."

"It seems a very long time, Father."

"He's more worried about what ye'll face while he's away."

"I'll be waitin'."

"More'll be required of ye than waitin' patiently, daughter. Mahon has his eye on the Burke lands. That's the only explanation for his treachery. What has been done legally to Joseph will take a while to be untangled. But untangled it will be. And in the meantime ye must hold fast to the land and the people, Kate. Joseph trusts ye to fight the good fight in his absence."

"That I will, Father. But I scarcely know where to begin. He's married a simple girl from Ballynockanor. Other than the business of dairyin', I know nothin' of overseein' property."

O'Bannon nodded. "Mahon is countin' on that. A simple girl, daughter of a Connaught tenant farmer. Aye. He's countin' Burke acres and figurin' what grazin' land he'll have once he tosses Ballynockanor and drives us to the sea."

The elderly cleric was challenging her to rise up and fight the dragon. "Mahon." She repeated the name flatly. "Ah, Father. I'm sick with missin' Joseph. I'd give the last stone in Connaught to free him. There's the truth of it."

"He'll not have that truth from the woman he loves, Kate. Strength is why he loves ye. Ye've got a will strong as granite. Ye'll have to live for him awhile now when he's away. Every hour ye'll need to ask yourself, *What would Joseph do? What would he say?*" They rode along, silent for a few moments. At last Father O'Bannon tapped his temple. "Think of it, Kate. Ye'll have to fight smart against an opponent so clever. Mahon will take all ye have and all ye are unless ye learn to fight like Joseph Burke would fight."

∾ 9 ∾

The wagon that carried the convicts to the detention cells at Cork was innocent of any springs, any shelter against the rain, and any seats, except for the driver and the guard. Two dozen prisoners were crammed into the bed in a space that would have been crowded by half that many head of sheep.

Convicts were shackled together by the ankle, the right leg of one to the left of the man next to him, and so on around the circle. Pen Brophy, a coarse Limericker being transported for assaulting a constable, laughed and said if they were dropped in the ocean that way they could all drown together. Their corpses would make a pretty daisy chain.

The prisoner bound to Joseph Burke's right leg, Laurence O'Halloran, was a slip of a boy only sixteen years of age and so slight that he looked no more than thirteen. The lad, already shivering from the February damp and the wind, shuddered even harder at this image. He had been convicted of stealing a candle and a half pound of butter; his sentence was seven years.

"Squall ahead!" called the prisoner to Joseph's left. By this warning he meant he had spotted yet another pothole in the road ahead. First the left front wheel and then the rear in turn dropped with successive crashes. The abrupt impacts made the leg chains hammer unwary knees and caused the shackles to dig deeper gouges into already scored flesh. "Sorry, mates," Patrick Frayne apologized. "I din't see that'un soon enough." Joseph judged from Frayne's speech that he was a sometime sailor. He had heard that Frayne was being transported for fourteen years, but beyond that did not know the man's story.

Of the two dozen men in the prison transport, eight were under twenty years of age. Ten were to serve terms of seven years and six others fourteen; Joseph and seven more were being sent away "for the term of their natural lives." All seven of the other permanent exiles were either murderers, arsonists, or violent repeat offenders.

"How much longer will it t-t-take?" O'Halloran stuttered to Joseph.

"Not long now," Joseph said kindly. "We passed Blarney castle an hour since. It can't be much farther."

"I never been so far afore," O'Halloran explained. "I never been past Tipperary."

Joseph knew the boy's home was in Cashel; Tipperary was no more than fifteen miles distant. He reflected somberly how the notion of being carried halfway around the world must be inconceivable to such a one. Indeed it was to Joseph himself.

"Keep quiet, croppies," said the sentry riding beside the driver. "Be a shame to arrive at your new accommodations with your face all bloody, now wouldn't it?" Jailor Gann slapped his favorite cudgel against his leg and laughed.

The stone-walled prison dormitories at Cork held bunks for two hundred fifty convicts. The arrival of the wagon carrying Joseph Burke pushed the total incarcerated there to over four hundred.

Gann prodded, bullied, threatened, and made liberal use of his truncheon in unloading his charges into the dusty prison yard. "Get on w'ye, croppies," he snarled, poking O'Halloran in the ribs with his club. "Move sharp and line up straight."

For the edification of the new arrivals, a disciplinary matter was scheduled for their observation. Just after the two dozen men formed themselves into two rows facing the barracks, a prisoner was dragged out in front of them and manacled to a triangular frame with his hands at the apex and his feet spread apart and tied to the lower corners. His shirt ripped from his back, the shaved head of the convict hung down as he heard himself pronounced guilty of having stolen a loaf of bread. The sentence was two hundred lashes.

At a nod from Major James Boyd, governor of the prison, a burly guard stepped forward, shaking out the tangles from a nine-ribbon leather whip. The cat whistled through the air and snapped against flesh. Blood flowed at the first blow. At the sixth the convict screamed. By the twentieth the skin of the prisoner's back could no longer be seen. By the fiftieth the man sagged from the bindings, mercifully unconscious as the flogging continued for another one hundred fifty blows.

Laurence O'Halloran, his young face the grey-green of seawater on a darkly clouded day, continued to retch while tears of fear ran down his face.

"You new men will observe that we do not tolerate any failure of discipline here," Boyd lectured. "Mister Gann," he continued, "you will escort your prisoners into their quarters. But first, which of you is Joseph Burke?"

When Joseph did not speak up soon enough to suit Gann, the guard clubbed Joseph in the back of the legs, knocking him to his knees. "This is he, Yer Honor. Shall I teach him better manners?"

"That is not necessary, Mister Gann. Remove the others while I speak with Burke."

When the two men were alone, Boyd said, "That was uncalled for. I did not mean for Gann to treat you harshly. I will warn him not to abuse you."

"Compared to what we witnessed here," Joseph observed, gesturing toward the dangling body of the still-unconscious and un-attended recipient of the flogging, "why should I think him harsh?"

"What I mean is," Boyd explained, "you are not a common criminal—no counterfeiter or rapist or drunken brawler. There is no reason you should have to suffer indignity while here."

"Meanin'?"

"Your stay can be quite comfortable. Private room. Better food. Privileges. You are Lord Burke, after all. The only difficulty is our limited budget." Boyd cleared his throat meaningfully.

"Save your breath, Major," Joseph suggested. "Titled I may be, but I have no money with which to bribe, nor inclination."

Boyd continued to smile, but his eyes took on a harder edge. "You may change your mind," he said. "If you want to see me, send word by Mister Gann."

Summoned from the barracks, Gann accompanied Joseph to his detention. "Be warned, croppie," Gann said, "there's those who would be glad to see you dead and those who think you worth more livin'. I've been well paid to keep a close watch on you, clear to Australia. Watch what you say to the governor about me. If you think two hundred lashes rough, you have no notion how miserable I can make your life."

Once in the dormitory, Joseph found the available space already taken. Patrick Frayne moved aside to offer Joseph a tiny scrap of floor beside him and O'Halloran.

A heavy hand thumped Joseph in the back. Joseph turned, expecting to see Gann again, but instead found Pen Brophy staring at him. "We don't like them as has private meetin's with the gov'nor," he said coldly. "There's worse things than floggin', and the worst we saves for informers. You mind what I say, Lord Mighty Burke. You are a marked man."

Martin and Mary Elizabeth were asleep. The wedding clock ticked above the mantel. Miss Susan's dark skin glowed mahogany in the firelight as she nursed Tomeen. The child's flame-red hair and porcelain complexion contrasted against the breast of the wet nurse. A beautiful picture it made, Kate thought.

"I envy you," Kate said, glancing up at the woman and child.

Miss Susan chuckled. "Why you say such a thing, Miss Kate, when you gots this pretty baby boy to raise?"

"Like a wee calf, he is, turnin' his face to your breast, drawin' life from your milk. It's true. I envy you."

"All my babies was took from me. Some was sold away by the man. Some in heaven. Nursin' this chile is a comfort to me. Rests my heart to have Tomeen at my breast. But he ain't mine. He already call you Mama."

"He thinks you're the sun and the moon."

Miss Susan brushed back his curls. "He be weaned mos' anytime now. Adam Kane tell me there's a baby to be born to a sickly woman in Cong. Reckon I'll be goin' on over there when word come."

"I was hopin' you'd stay. You're fine company," Kate said, then faltered. How could she tell Miss Susan how much she dreaded being alone? "And I could use the help."

"Martin help you like a man with the dairy. Mary Elizabeth fusses with Tomeen like she were born to be a mama herself one day. Y'all don't need me. I cain't stay if a new baby need my milk and Tom be weaned from needin' mother's milk. This boy's drinkin' straight out the cow's tit. I seen you squirt him and the kittens whilst you was milkin' this mornin'." She shook her head. "He open his mouth and laugh and laugh. Lick his lips and cry for more. Truth to tell, only reason I keep nursin' him is so's I don't go dry."

"I'll miss you."

"Yes'm. And I'll miss y'all. Now that's the truth." The two women sat in silence for a few minutes. Then Miss Susan said, "There was times after they took my man away I thought I like to die." She studied Kate with knowing brown eyes. "But you won't die."

Kate nodded slowly, not daring to look up from the darning. "I know."

"Back home they set fire to the canefield before they cut the cane. Burn away the leaves and rubbish so's they can press the cane to make sugar."

"Aye," Kate replied curiously. Where was this leading?

"Life ain't nuthin' but a canefield. Sorrows burn away the trash.

A person finds out what matters and what don't. What's left is the sweetness. Pressed out, boiled down, and purest crystal. One day, Miss Kate, you tastes the sugar and don't remember the ashes no more."

K ate felt the presence of the watchers before she saw them. For two days before Miss Susan left to nurse the newborn baby in Cong, Kate told herself that the vague uneasiness was nothing more than getting used to the idea of living alone again. But the wet nurse had left this morning, and Kate had not recovered from her sense that something was not right.

It was Mary Elizabeth who first identified the feeling as something tangible. It was a quiet supper. Martin was speaking of Adam Kane's insistence that they move into the grounds of Burke Hall and live behind the locked gate where he could keep an eye on them.

"Move the cows from grazin' here in Ballynockanor, says he. I told him he's not a dairyman or else he'd know how upsettin' it is to the sweet things to be moved away from home and hearth." Martin passed the potatoes. "There is somethin' lonely, though, about Susan bein' gone." He chucked Tom under his chin. "Miss her, do you, Tomeen? Well, you'll have to be a big boy now. Her teat won't stretch all the way from Cong, now will it?"

Kate cuffed the boy lightly. "Sha! Enough of that. You talk like a stablehand. What'll you be sayin' next?"

"You'll be surprised, what I'll be sayin' now." Martin laughed and so did the baby. It was a fine camaraderie Martin had with small Tom. They were more like brothers than uncle and nephew. "Lord," Martin added, "he does look like Brigit when he laughs, don't he, Kate?"

Kate spooned another mouthful of soup into Tom and agreed wistfully, "Aye. A beautiful child, he is. And sometimes I feel as if Brigit's smilin' down on us from heaven."

Mary Elizabeth brightened. "There are three pilgrims on the hill. Up at St. Brigit's cross they are, lookin' down on us."

A chill coursed through Kate. "What do you mean?"

"They must have a powerful load of sin to do penance for, because I've seen 'em three days, every day now. How long does it take to say ten Our Father's and get down the hill anyway? But there they are."

"Why didn't you say somethin'?" Martin glanced nervously out the window at the night sky.

The girl shrugged. "What difference does it make?"

Kate left the table and slid the bar across the door. "Do you know them?"

"They're too far off, sister." Mary Elizabeth caught the chill of fear in the room. "Bar the shutters on the windows as well, will you?"

Kate was already at it, leaving only one set of shutters unsealed. There were torches alight at the top of the hill. She counted eleven lights burning in an irregular circle. "How many days since you saw them first?"

"Two days ago first and then this mornin'. They came after Miss Susan was called away to Cong," Mary Elizabeth replied. "They were still up there when I locked the barn. One had a . . ." She pantomimed a spyglass held to her eye. "One of those things he had, lookin' right down at you, Kate, as you were takin' down the washin'. Tomeen was in the laundry basket, and the man looked at him a long time."

Martin and Kate locked eyes in understanding as the torches fanned out and began to move down toward the valley floor.

"Unionists, you think? The Mayo Ribbonmen burned out a Protestant family last week. There's been talk of retaliation."

Martin said, "Sure. The wife of Joseph Burke. Who better? Too late for us to make it into Castletown."

"Put the candles out!" Kate whispered as the bobbing torches snaked in single file down the path from the hill. "Martin! Mary Elizabeth. Get your cloaks and hats."

There was no time to think of gathering anything personal. Her fiddle remained on the mantel. Martin grabbed up Da's blackthorn walking stick as a weapon. Kate wrapped Tomeen in her mother's wedding quilt. If the visitors were set on burning the place, only that among the precious keepsakes could be saved. Throwing on her cloak, Kate urged the children out the smallest window in the kitchen. The rectangular frame was too tiny to permit a man to climb in. With the door barred and every window but that one shuttered, Kate hoped the loyalists would believe Kate and the children were still inside. It would buy the foursome time to escape while the nightriders were taunting and threatening an empty house.

"To the river, Martin!" Kate held the baby close against her. Mary Elizabeth clutched her hand. Martin wordlessly led the way, his mind certain of every stone and rut even in the pitch-black of the night. Behind them and above them the points of fire grew together in a clump of approaching light. Kate looked back briefly. The upper bodies of their pursuers were a vivid, monochrome glow of orange. They seemed legless, demonic, gliding as they descended the trail.

"Hurry, sister Kate," Martin hissed. "Hurry! Their light will touch us!"

With a sudden horror it came to Kate. "They'll kill the herd!" Hadn't the Ribbonmen slaughtered Protestant cattle in Mayo? "Martin! Take the baby! Run to Burke Park! Don't look back!" She passed Tom into the boy's arms and, dimly aware that Mary Elizabeth was weeping softly, she shook her sister's fingers free from her cloak.

"Don't go back, Kate," Mary Elizabeth begged.

Kate stooped, kissed her, and said in a barely audible voice, "Go on with you, Mary Elizabeth. You and Martin take care of Tomeen. My fine new heifers! These men'll kill my moilies, sure, though they're neither Catholic cows nor Protestant. For the sport of it they'll kill 'em, and I can't have it. Get on to Burke Park. Tell Adam Kane where I am. Go!"

The footsteps of the retreating children diminished, then vanished beneath the footfalls of the nightriders' boots. The light of their torches was still one hundred yards away from the cottage. There was time, Kate told herself, although blood was roaring in her ears, and her heart was racing.

She crouched low and moved along the outer perimeter of the

stone wall of the calf pen. Inching her way to the barn, she formed her plan: while the nightriders occupied themselves with the house, she would enter through the back portal of the barn, unlatch the gate of every stall, and drive the cows out and down the hill to the road. They would scatter along the riverbank and cover her own tracks if any man should take it in his head to follow. Perhaps some of the herd would be hunted and killed, but, just as surely, some would survive.

She slid over the wall and into the muck of the pen. Instinctively she dabbed mud on her face to dim the reflection of the approaching fire. Rising up to watch, Kate saw the circle of tormentors cross the lane and step onto Donovan land.

Now light and footsteps became voices circling the Donovan homestead.

"Kate Donovan! Lady Burke!"

The sound of her name startled her. She scrambled across the pen, slipped under the rail of the gate, and hugged the back wall of the barn as she inched toward the door.

"Kate Donovan! Friends of your rebel husband have burned the house and barns of Mike Wiley in County Mayo!" There was a murmur of rage among the mob. "We've come to repay the deed."

So they meant to burn the barn as well! Kate slid the long bar from its rings across the passage. The hinges creaked.

"We're not for butcherin' women and children as your papist monsters do to Protestant families."

She slipped into the building. A glimmer of light shone through the thatch. The words of the day's reading raced through her thoughts unbidden: *Rachel weeping for her children and she would not be comforted, because they were no more.*

"Come out then, and you'll not be harmed!"

They meant to torch the house. The image of flaming thatch made her panic.

"Your husband's comrades killed Protestant livestock. We'll have an eye for an eye."

She whispered, "Oh God! Oh, Jesus! Lord, help." The cows stirred, uneasy at the commotion outside the barn.

What was the praise sung in mass that morning?

We were rescued like a bird from the fowlers' snare.
Broken was the snare, and we were freed.

"Free them, Kate," she said, urging her trembling fingers and forcing her legs into action. Gathering her wits, she hurried from stall to stall, unlatching bolts and swinging open the barricades. The cows bawled protests as she swatted each on the rump and pushed them from lethargy to near panic.

"Come out of the house, Kate Donovan," bellowed the leader of the terrorists. "Unlatch your door, or we'll send you to hell in flames for the Catholic heretics you are!"

"Aye!" cried another. "And the children too! Bring them out into the yard, or we'll not spare any of you the flames!"

A cheer—no, a unified, bloodcurdling shriek of assent rose up from the men.

As Kate unhooked the final gate and drove that last heifer into the corridor among the others, a bright arc illuminated the sky.

The first torch flew up above the house and spiraled downward, landing on the thatched roof.

Don't look, Mary Elizabeth!" Martin grasped his sister's arm and propelled her along the riverbank. The sky was a brilliant glow behind them, making willowy shadows run before them on the path.

"They've set fire to the house!" Mary Elizabeth cried. "Martin! The roof of the barn's burnin'!"

Martin could not help but turn to see. In the instant of that glance he stumbled and fell, spinning to the side to shield Tomeen from the blow. The baby began to wail, sending a surge of desperation through Martin. What if the riders heard them?

"Quiet now." He tried to soothe Tomeen, but the infant would not be silenced. His cries reflected every emotion Martin felt as his eyes locked on the tongues of flame consuming thatch and beams and licking the night sky!

"Kate's there with the cows," screamed Mary Elizabeth. "She was goin' back to save 'em! Goin' back!"

Memory of another inferno paralyzed Martin. He grimaced as he remembered the fire that had consumed the leg of his trousers and the flesh of his leg, leaving him crippled forever. Sean, Kate's first husband, had died. Mother had died with the baby in her arms. Kate had been burned. On that terrible night there had been neighbors to help. Where was the help tonight?

Martin heard a voice say, "We have to hide! They'll know we're not in there! Kate'll make it. She has to! They'll come lookin' for us!" It was his own voice, detached and certain of the danger to come.

He spotted the heap of boulders that tumbled half in water and half on the shore. There was a cleft, a sort of cave where Martin had taken shelter in thunderstorms in times past. It was his own secret place.

"Kate!" Mary Elizabeth shrilled in near hysteria. "Oh, Kate! She's in the barn, Martin!"

Martin smacked her across the cheek. "Stop it! They'll hear us! Find us! They'll hurt Tomeen! Come on then." He pulled her toward the jumble of stones, then shoved her in ahead of him. "Take the baby," he ordered, climbing in after.

Only moments passed before Little Tom fell into an exhausted sleep across Martin's chest. In a stupor of terror, Mary Elizabeth shivered against Martin's arm. Finally as the reflected light dimmed, she too, slept. Then Martin nodded off as well.

Martin awakened to the sound of a solitary cowbell ringing in syncopated time with the gurgle of the river. He opened his eyes and squinted up at the light of morning.

With a rush the events of the night came to his mind. The night-riders. The fire. Kate going back to save the herd.

Kate. Where was Kate?

Above the sound of the cowbell was a croaking, discordant hum.

Mary Elizabeth raised her head. "Mad Molly's got loose again."

As if on cue the old woman exclaimed, "A troop of horse at the mouth of the pass! A wild fight! A ding-dong fray of footsoldiers!"

"Where's Kate?" Mary Elizabeth was ashen. Dark circles were beneath her eyes.

Tomeen slept on.

"I don't know." Martin's arm was asleep. His legs were stiff. "We've got to go."

"Are the bad men gone?"

"Molly's wanderin' about. They must be gone."

In that instant the wild face of the crone beamed in at them. "There they are, Molly! Look! Their cottage ashes, but they're in a house of stone. Never mind! Never mind! Hooray!"

"Mary Elizabeth, stay here with Tomeen. I've got to see about Kate." Martin struggled to stand.

Molly chortled. "Kate's a wonder! Aye! A wonder, Kate is! We've found every cow but one. And then there's the children. Where's the children, Kate wonders. Well, here they are now! And there's the last cow too."

Martin squeezed into the open. "Where's Kate, Molly?"

"Lookin' for the three of ye. Never mind the cows. Near out of her mind, she is. But Molly found ye!" She winked and pinched his sallow cheek. Then she gave a loud *halloo* into the air. Another wink. "Smile, Martin. We'll be neighbors, lad. Ye'll be movin' home to Burke Park now as Adam Kane said ye ought to. Donovan cottage is naught but a heap of rubble. Politics is all about burnin' down houses, ain't it?"

From within the boulders Mary Elizabeth called, "Can I come out, Martin?"

Martin sighed. Burke Park. Life behind locked gates. Mad Molly as a neighbor. "You say Kate's all right then?"

"Aye. Mad as a hornet. I'd not say too much to her lest she bite your head off."

"Can we come out now, Martin?"

Molly leaped agilely onto a stone. She thumped her chest and began to recite the ballad "Wild Irish":

He does not set his heart upon a feather bed!
He would prefer to lie upon the rushes!
A wild fight . . .

Molly scratched her head as the words left her memory. "Well, somethin' like it, anyway. He's comin'! He's comin' home, Martin!"

"Joseph?"

"Nay. The Tinker's on his way."

"He's dead."

"Joseph?"

"No. The Tinker."

"He's comin'. The message ye see. It's a day late. And off sails Joseph. But not the Tinker and the gospels. Four of 'em. Or the four horsemen? Fishermen? Fighters? Aye, that's it! Fight a ding-dong fray they will with mayhem. Mayhem. What's his name? Mayhem?" She brushed the thought away like a fly. "And we'll be neighbors one and all. The potatoes may run short. Who'd think it could happen? But we'll be neighbors just the same."

Martin exhaled loudly in exasperation. Over Molly's shoulder he spotted Kate, blackened face, muddy clothes, marching toward him like she was going to war.

"Martin!" Kate called joyfully as she broke into a run. "Oh, Martin!"

Colonel Mahon was raging as he stormed round and round the pair of thugs seated in his office. The two men looked as shame-faced as schoolboys caught in a classroom transgression.

"How utterly incompetent! You managed to locate neither the woman nor the tiny infant? How grossly inept!"

"Yes sir, Your Honor," Kirby O'Meara said. "We—"

"Silence!"

Kirby obediently clamped his mouth closed. He tried to look earnest; but the touch of canine-like sincerity was somewhat spoiled by his crooked jaw and flattened cauliflower ears.

"Did you light a single torch and run away like any hooligan setting fire to a neighbor's haystack? How can you come back here and tell me that you don't know what happened to any of them? Let me tell you: the whole family, now more on their guard than ever, has moved behind the walls of Burke Park!"

"Yes sir, Your Honor, Squire," Kirby apologized, "we know that now, and we're awful sorry. But you see, fact is, they was already bolted when we surrounded the cottage. Otherwise, we'd a seen them go."

"Meaning your clumsy surveillance had already warned them to flee."

Kirby looked anxiously around at the portraits hanging on the walls of the office as if they would coach him in what to say next. "I, that is . . . maybe it depends on what Your Honor means by surveyin'." Mutely he appealed to Scully Deane for assistance.

"What me mate is tryin' to say, Squire," explained Scully, "is that the cottage were barred from inside and the windows likewise, except one small one too little to use as a bolthole. We thought they was just keepin' close, till that thatch blazed up. Nobody coulda kept mum through that."

Mahon actually let Scully finish his account uninterrupted. This was not because of any particular respect he paid the brigand with the leprous patches of baldness separating tufts of wiry black hair. Mahon's silence had more to do with Scully's eyes. The hooligan's left eye turned toward the ceiling while his right glared straight ahead. Deciding which eye to address kept Mahon unusually sedate.

Noting that the colonel appeared calmer, Kirby ventured to say, "And then them cows started bustin' out of the dairy, and we knew village folk would be comin', so we departed."

"That explains it," Mahon mused. "They had some notice of the attack and were already hiding in the barn. The woman and the baby. Blast! All right, here's what we'll do next."

10

The employment of rotting carcasses of ships waterlogged and far past their seaworthiness, barely floating wrecks called *hulks*, had been banned from use as British prison facilities since the late 1830s. Disease and rats had thrived individually and together, but not prisoners, and so after fifty years of service to British penal institutions, hulks were altogether withdrawn from service—everywhere except at Cork. Last on the list to transfer excess convicts to the new Richmond Prison in Dublin, the jails in Cork and nearby Cove still assigned their surplus human baggage to Her Majesty's prison ship *Tartar*, permanently moored in Cove Harbor.

Each afternoon the two hundred forty-six prisoners crammed into *Tartar's* foul air below were allowed one hour to walk about in the sunshine and breeze. This privilege was believed important to the health of the convicts. Widespread use of the lash notwithstanding, Warden Quintle truly cared about the medical condition of his prisoners, at least until he was relieved of them by the transport captain.

This was because the transport captains were paid by the head for each criminal they carried, and Quintle received his bit of corrupt compensation for each living soul conveyed. If they died on the day after sailing, it was no longer any concern of his.

Consequently, the convicts were marched around the deck—one half hour clockwise, followed by thirty minutes the opposite way. Each man was required to keep his right hand on the shoulder of the prisoner walking in front of him. Faltering was not permitted, and the ever-present Jailor Gann encouraged the pace with applications of his truncheon.

"Move along, croppie!" he prodded. "How you gonna outrun them tigers if you don't exercise?"

Gann delighted in terrorizing the more dull or gullible prisoners by filling their heads with wholly fictional dangers awaiting them in New South Wales. Most of the prisoners, including Joseph, trudged in silence.

O'Halloran, plodding along behind Joseph, was one of the more susceptible. "Gann says them tigers springs from trees and b-b-bites your head off at one whack," he whispered.

"Don't fash yourself, Laurence," Joseph muttered back. "There aren't any tigers, and even if there were, Gann's smell would keep them away."

The afternoon delivery of fresh meat and drink arrived—for the guards of course. The prisoners lived on oat gruel and salt beef so ancient it had been condemned for army use years before. This afternoon the bum boat also brought a Dublin paper of only three days earlier. Gann swooped down on the printed page, snickered, and rushed across the deck to walk beside Joseph, thrusting the headlines under the prisoner's nose. "See what it says there, croppie?" he demanded. "Right there plain as day? It says Daniel O'Connell is convicted of conspiracy. Guilty as sin, that's what! Guess that puts paid to any notion of an appeal, eh, croppie?"

Joseph, who had stopped walking when Gann shoved the paper in his face, was hurriedly trying to scan the text of the story. Daniel was convicted, he read. Sentence was not yet imposed. Six others also found guilty.

Whack! Gann's club descended on the point of his shoulder, numbing Joseph's right arm. "Who told you to quit movin?" Gann inquired. "You're holdin' up the parade." *Whack!* the bat fell again. "Get your hand up and move on, there."

The weary circle shuffled forward again. Joseph had to use his left hand to support his deadened right. Gann called after Joseph's back, "Here's one for you, croppie: maybe O'Connell will be shipped down here to join you. Neither one of you will get an appeal. Wouldn't that be a fine Repeal party, then? Repeal has no appeal, eh, croppie! Ha!" Then Gann called, laughing, to another guard, "George, here's a hot one. Listen to this . . ."

On the afternoon when the convict ship *Hive* sailed into Cove Harbor, the prisoners were again at their daily exercise. That the three-masted transport stood in for the mooring between the prison hulk and the shore gave away her purpose even before her name was known. Among the prisoners and the guards who were to be leaving Ireland there was intense interest in the vessel destined to be their quarters for six months. Since all alike were thinking that the *Hive* would carry them eighteen thousand miles away from home, the normal prohibition against talking was relaxed.

"She has an evil look," Patrick Frayne muttered. "Slovenly and ill-handled."

Pen Brophy spat over the rail with an oath. "There's that for your 'evil look,'" he said. "Anything to get off this hulk, I say, and good riddance to this land of misery."

Joseph Burke, together with Brophy, Frayne, Laurence O'Halloran, and the unavoidable Jailor Gann, were to join close to three hundred others on the *Hive*. More transportees would follow on later sailings.

The following day the transfer of prisoners began. Two hundred seventy-five men and twenty-five women were being forcibly removed from the land of their birth. Some, like Brophy, were eager to go; many, like O'Halloran, were terrified; the rest stoically accepted their fate.

Though the mail packet *Mercury*, a sidewheel steamer, bustled in and out of Cove Harbor every day, the *Hive* hailed from the ages when wind power alone ruled the seas. She was three decks deep, one of them below the waterline. Tiers of slatted frames were provided to stack humans three high. Before the abolition of slavery in Britain and its possessions, the *Hive* had been a *blackbirder*, a slave ship. Hearing this, Frayne made the sign against the evil eye. "I told you she was an ill-omened vessel," he said as the convicts were marched below.

"She is what we make of her, and that's a fact. Don't you agree, friend Holt?" commented a ruddy-complected, cheerful prisoner to his thin, pale-visaged comrade.

The man identified as Holt signaled his acceptance of this proposition. The two men were of much the same small stature and age. The rounder, jollier one was Father Walter Talbot. His lean companion was Presbyterian pastor Henry Holt. Talbot was being transported for refusing to divulge evidence heard in the confessional. Holt was being transported for defending his friend Talbot. Both saw their removal to Botany Bay as the calling of God.

"We are not in a position to cry the *Hive* either ill or evil," Talbot said. "Things are just what they are. It is the use that men put them to that determines their moral value."

"But has not the life of this boat been one atrocity after another?" Joseph asked.

"Aye," Holt said in a Scots-Irish burr. "So it is up to us to give it a different future."

"It is too grim for us to change," commented Frayne.

"It is of no importance a'tall," Brophy said, shrugging.

Joseph said nothing, but only fingered the teardrop-shaped casket hanging around his neck.

The ashes were only barely warm in the remains of the Donovan cottage and dairy, but the tempers of the townsfolk were blazing. "Who would do such a thing!" Paddy O'Flaherty said, scowling.

"If I so much as catch sight of the evil, blackhearted rapparees who done this I will tear them to pieces!"

Mike O'Rourke, looking half dressed in the absence of his fiddle, was quieter of expression but no less incensed. "Tom Donovan, and his father and grandfather before him, were stout, true-hearted Christians, and his children the same. It's a black day for Ireland. Those lousy, Protestant Orangemen! May they rot in . . ."

Father O'Bannon, sifting through the rubble in pursuit of a single unbroken dinner plate, seized on the comment. "Don't even say such a thing!" he admonished. "Whoever did this are no true Christians, whatever label they may be hidin' behind!"

Kate helped Mary Elizabeth lift a heap of ashes that had been the thatch over the girls' bedroom. With a cry of discovery, Mary Elizabeth pounced on a hand mirror. The glass was cracked and the silver frame bent. "This was your grandmother's," Kate said in a weary voice. "I know you don't remember her, Mary Elizabeth, but once she went all the way to Belfast to visit a cousin, and she brought this lookin' glass back from that trip. She held it wasn't the thing that was important, it was the memory. 'Things are just place-holders for memories,' she used to tell me." Kate stared over the debris and turned slowly in place. "Remember my words, sister. You may have to speak them to me."

Margaret, who was packing the meager quantity of rescued furnishings for the trip to Burke Park, was so angry and talking so sharply that Fern jumped every time the cook spoke. "'Twas them Mayo Protestant boys did this," Margaret raged. "Cowardly wretches! Come here and attack our folk, then hightail it back across the border. Fine, brave lads they are, huh!" Fern dodged aside as Margaret brought a broom smacking down on a rock as though squashing the skull of a Protestant nightrider. Fern nodded, wishing she were as daft as Molly Fahey. Then the timid housemaid could, like Mad Molly, be skipping stones down at the river, and no one would pay her any mind.

Martin and Old Flynn, the Burkes' stablemaster, were sorting through the remains of the dairy. The boy found the blade of a turf spade with the handle burned completely away. He studied the iron implement, then flung it from him with a savagery that astonished the man. "It wants but a new handle to be mended," Flynn observed.

"'Tis not the shovel," snarled Martin back. "It's the whole world that needs mendin'! A decent man like Joseph is shipped away in chains while wickedness burns down homes by night and walks free by day. If I could only catch them!"

"They're over the border and back in their holes by now," Flynn observed.

"Not the biggest rat of all," Martin countered, "and his hole is just there." Even to Flynn's rheumy eyes, Martin's infuriated gesture pointed unmistakably toward the property of Colonel Mahon.

When the extent of Mahon's treachery against Joseph became clear to Kate and the people of the parish, there was talk of retribution among the folk at Watty's Tavern and in the market square. For fear of some outbreak of violence, the British had strengthened the garrison in Ireland with a force of men far greater than their army in India.

Mary Elizabeth came home with the details.

"They say someone ought to drop Mahon down a well. But that'd stink up the well, so they won't do that. But someone ought to do somethin', they're sayin'. And if Kevin were back here from America, he'd do it, sure."

"Kevin's not here," Martin said, poking at the turf fire with an iron poker. "But I am." He held up the tool and studied the sharp point.

Kate looked away out the window to where Old Flynn was leading Joseph's hunter across the stableyard. She felt the weight of some guilt. It was she who had convinced Joseph to plead guilty to the lesser charge. Now Martin was sitting there, considering doing murder to Mahon.

"Don't dwell on it, Martin," Kate warned.

"How do you know what I'm thinkin'?"

"Because I've thought of it myself."

"And why shouldn't I?"

"They'll hang you."

"I'll get away. Like Kevin. I'll find Kevin in America and have a life without a thought of this place."

"And what of those you'll be leavin'?"

"You'll come too. I'll catch him when it's dark . . ." He raised the poker as if to strike.

"Then there's the matter of murder."

"An eye for an eye is what they say. Murder? Look what the man did to us. Mahon set his dog upon the herd. I do not doubt that's just what he did; then he played the role of the so-sorry fellow. Killed the dog, though the creature had only done its master's biddin'. Paid you in gold and then sent the heifers just so you'd believe he meant no harm and carry the word to Joseph yourself." Martin slammed the rod against the stones of the hearth, sending a shower of sparks into the air. "Aye. You believed him too. Played into his hands. Now Joseph is banished."

Kate sank tiredly onto the stool beside the fire. She gazed at the glowing embers for a long time. Martin was entirely right. She had trusted that Mahon had some spark of goodness or repentance in him.

"Sure, I've thought it through myself. His kindness was meant to rule me. To deceive me. He did it well."

"You're an innocent," Martin said, scowling.

"You mean a fool."

"Sometimes it's the same thing."

"Well, you're right, and I take the blame for it."

"Blame is it! Blame for your good heart? Because you'd never do such a thing to anyone, you can't think anyone could do such a thing to you! You've got no more sense about wickedness than Tomeen!" With the heel of his boot he ground out a burning coal that had tumbled onto the wood plank floor. "You're not to blame, sister, but you've been deceived! There are people in this world who know how to use fair deeds and soft words to work their own evil! Such men should be stamped out like embers that roll outside the hearth and would burn the whole house down! Warmth and light they may give outside the bounds of what is right. But kill the deceitful warmth!

Destroy the wicked light, before it's too late! They're a danger to us all!"

"Or find some way to move it back where it belongs."

"You may think I'm just a boy, but didn't I learn from Brigit? Didn't I? Wake up! Father O'Bannon says sweet words from the mouth of a godless man are a certain destruction! Didn't Mahon pay? Wasn't he sorry for the cattle? Didn't he offer friendship? Aye. And look. You trusted him, and now the devil is at the gates, Kate! He has many arms, many faces in this world, and more names than I can count. One of them is Mahon! He needs to die."

His words shamed Kate. "'Tis true, Martin, about me bein' too willin' to trust that there was some good in him. Father O'Bannon warned me long ago that Jesus knew what was in men's hearts and so never trusted them. But He pitied even evil men, Martin. Gave Himself for every man. So pity the soul of the man who's deceived us and wronged us. One day Mahon'll face the judge, and there'll be no mercy without repentance. Leave him to God, Martin. If you kill him with your own hand, then it's yourself who'll be condemned in heaven and on earth, and true evil will have won *your* soul. Give hatred no corner in your heart, or it'll grow and grow and finally take over. Didn't I learn that from Brigit? Didn't I? So now I'm on to another lesson. The hardest one yet. How to be wise without bein' bitter. How to forgive without bein' a fool. I'm still at sea with this one, Martin. But I'll not sit quietly while you contemplate smashin' Mahon's brains out with my fire iron."

He was not willing to listen to her. His face became a sullen mask, and he refused to speak another word that night.

∞ 11 ∞

Fourteen fervent horsemen spurred their mounts in an eager dash to be the first with the news. Between Westland Row rail station and the gates of Richmond Prison, there were three collisions, a wagonload of beer was upset, and an aging veteran of Waterloo fired off his musket in the mistaken belief that the French had landed and were invading Dublin.

Hurtling from his horse and attacking the steps to the prison governor's house with the same pell-mell enthusiasm as he had ridden, Adam Kane almost garroted himself on the drooping lanyard of a flag being lowered at sunset.

When he recovered from his spill, he found that he was not the first to bring the word: Daniel O'Connell's conviction of conspiracy had been overturned on appeal. O'Connell and the other traversers were free men once more.

Screened away from the Liberator by O'Connell's supporters and well-wishers, it was some time before Kane could break into the inner circle with his specific request. Once there, however, O'Connell understood the urgency.

"And so, Your Honor," Kane said, "if Squire Joseph is to be spared a sea voyage to Australia, something must be done at once."

"Must and shall be done," O'Connell agreed. "As a gesture of good faith; a semiofficial apology, if you will, I have already extracted from Dublin Castle a pardon for forty-two other prisoners. The name of Joseph Connor Burke is first on the list."

"Thanks be to God," Kane murmured. "Now if Your Honor would excuse me, I have some furious ridin' yet ahead this night."

"Not a'tall," the Liberator corrected. "For I have an even better idea."

The square-rigged sloop *Flying Cloud* was specially chartered by Adam Kane through the offices of Daniel O'Connell. The owner of the shipping concern, though English by birth and Protestant by conscience, was also a passionately reform-minded Whig. As such, after examining O'Connell's note, he urged the Burke steward into a coach and ordered the driver to take them to the Pigeon House packet station near Poolbeg Anchorage before Kane had even finished explaining.

The lamp burned late in Colonel Mahon's study.

Again and again he read the letter from Justice Lewis and the roster naming the men pardoned with Daniel O'Connell. Mahon was undisturbed that Joseph Burke was on the list. What would the pardon mean if Burke was dead? Gann would take care of that detail.

But there was another matter that Judge Lewis now drew to Mahon's attention. Joseph's original guilty plea to the charge of conspiracy had opened the door for Mahon to press the Crown for legal confiscation of the Burke lands. With Justice Lewis as magistrate it would have been a small matter for Kate Donovan Burke and the child, Tom Burke, to be forced to forfeit everything to the Crown—rights, titles, and property. But now! The exoneration of Joseph Burke meant that his estate was no longer threatened by legal action. The twenty thousand acres of Burke Park could not now be legally confiscated and sold for pennies as Mahon had planned.

Even with Joseph Burke dead, his son Tom would inherit the title of *Lord Burke* and the lands that went with it. Kate would be named guardian until the boy came of age.

But what if the child should meet with some tragic accident?

After the death of the baby, Kate Donovan, Lady Burke of Connaught, would be next in line for the inheritance.

Colonel Mahon counted Joseph a dead man the moment he sailed on the *Hive* with Gann. But there were still two people who blocked the path to Mahon's goal.

It was the last of Ireland.

There were no longer any possible delays. The wind that had blown steadily into the teeth of Cove's harbor mouth had backed overnight and now filled the eager sails of luggers and fishing boats and tugged at the rigging of the *Hive*. Late-arriving officials had at last appeared, including Andrew Parker, a new assistant governor for a prison station of Van Diemen's Land. Frequently promised and equally often unfilled orders for supplies were at last complete. These accessories to the cargo of human misery ranged from barrels of ship's biscuit to clandestinely stashed crates of contraband wine. It had all been stowed by convict labor, shrinking still further the available space for prisoners.

And as the last night passed and the grey fleece of dawn gave way to the yellow satin of morning, so too dwindled Joseph's last hopes of pardon, reprieve, appeal, and deliverance. Daniel O'Connell was incarcerated in Richmond Prison, Repeal was dead, and Joseph was bound away from home, hearth, and, worst of all, from Kate.

What was she doing this day? Was she even now thinking of him as he was of her? How much time would pass before he saw her, kissed her, held her again? He whispered a renewal of his vow to come back to her and prayed her and all his family into God's keeping.

Convict ships had no reason to carry a full complement of crew. Beyond topmen for reefing and setting the sails, prisoners could haul as well as trained hands and could be flogged as needed. So it happened that Joseph was on deck with a gang of men pressed into service at the capstan as the *Hive* got under way and thus had a view of the shore.

"Haul away!" roared the mate of the watch, and the capstan began to revolve, the cable winding around the barrel with the dull clicking of the pawl, accompanied by the trudge of feet.

It was not expected that prisoners would sing out as they worked, but to Joseph's surprise a clear tenor voice drifted up from someone imprisoned below.

> *Green were the fields where my forefathers dwelt, Oh!*

And a few hands at the capstan bars uttered the refrain:

> *Erin ma vourneen! Slan leat go brah!*

And when the soloist sang,

> *Though our farm it was small, yet comforts we felt, Oh!*

An even greater number joined in the Gaelic for:

> *Ireland my darlin', forever adieu!*

Pen Brophy, despite his tough talk, had tears coursing down his grizzled cheeks. When the next verse came round, he was bellowing in a discordant baritone,

> *Forced from my home, from where I was born, Oh!*
> *To range the wide world, poor, helpless, forlorn, Oh!*
> *I look back with regret and my heartstrings are torn, Oh!*

Thereafter the entire ship's company joined in with,

Erin ma vourneen! Erin go bragh!

The anchor broke free of the seabed and, as the foretopsail fluttered in the breeze and then was sheeted home, the *Hive* gathered herself like a beast stirring from a long sleep.

"Cat the hook!" roared the mate, and the anchor was secured.

"You men get below!" ordered Gann roughly, prodding them along. "Mustn't work you too hard, eh croppies? Have a fresh batch along now to do the haulin'. Get below!"

Ordinarily being spared further labor would have been a welcome novelty, but this time the crew dismissed milled about and lingered at the sight of the green hills already dropping astern. "Get below!" Gann bellowed, lashing out at Patrick Frayne with his club. The men reluctantly disappeared beneath the ship's deck.

One of the hindmost in line, and thus the last to leave the free air, Joseph watched as the course of the *Hive* carried it across the bow of an incoming ship. It was too far off to make out details, but it was plain that the ship tacking toward harbor was in a terrific hurry. Her masts were crowded with all possible sail, and the sloop's canvas was taut. The new arrival threw out a foaming bow wave in her haste to reach port, and she looked to Joseph like a whole flock of white birds being driven before a storm.

How different the two attitudes: the reluctant departure, and the eager homecoming!

The cloud of sails on the advancing ship was for an instant backdropped by the brick buildings of Cork. The red and white spire of St. Ann's Church formed an exclamation point at the end of the farewell view.

"I love you, Kate," Joseph murmured.

It was the last of Ireland.

Adam Kane was pacing the deck of the *Flying Cloud* as dawn rose over the south coast of Ireland. By his calculation he had already walked twice the distance from Dublin to Cork while the boat was sailing. Not a patient man at the best of times, Kane felt frustrated that he could not spur a ship as he could a horse, nor could he call up a more favorable wind as he would call for a fresh mount. He understood that O'Connell's notion was sound: *Flying Cloud* could make the journey in under twenty-four hours. The best a rider could manage was two days, even if he made every relay without difficulty, provided he stayed awake and did not break his neck.

Besides, Kane told himself yet again, what was the likelihood that the transport ship would leave just as freedom was arriving for Squire Burke? Either it was still in harbor, or this mad dash was already in vain. The irony of anything else would be unbearable.

Still, Kane could not keep from pacing and pacing, squinting at the set of the sails, which he understood not at all, and whistling incessantly. He had been told by the ship's master that sailors always whistled for a fair wind.

The stratagem seemed to have worked. Just as full light showed the entrance to Cove Harbor, the *Flying Cloud* was spanking along. The ship's rush into the swells on its starboard quarter reminded Kane of a well-bred horse on a right lead. For the first time in twenty-four hours, the steward was satisfied with his progress.

"That's Cork off to port," the *Cloud*'s master pointed out. "And Cove lies dead ahead."

Another ship was getting under way, setting out from the land. Kane watched the bulky form of a brig slowly gain momentum, and the two ships swung past each other. The Burke steward did not give the outgoing vessel a second thought. His attention was entirely focused on carrying the official pardon to the governor of the prison. Kane could just imagine the surprise and delight on Joseph Burke's face at the news.

PART II

Wilt thou steer my frail black bark
O'er the dark broad ocean's foam?
Wilt Thou come, Lord, to my boat
Where afloat, my will would roam?
Thine the mighty, Thine the small,
Thine to make men fall like rain.
God, wilt Thou grant aid to me
As I come o'er the heaving main?

—"Crossing the Bar," a nineteenth-century poem
by Cormac MacCuilleanain

12

The first day out from Cove Harbor was appalling for most of the souls aboard the *Hive*. This situation occurred not just because of the realization that they were leaving their homeland behind. Mostly, they were miserable because they were seasick.

Aside from a few sailors among the convicts, like Patrick Frayne, or those of more travel experience, like Joseph, the rest of the passengers had never been on the ocean before. (Some, like Laurence O'Halloran, had never even *seen* the ocean.)

There had not been a problem while the *Hive* remained at her sheltered mooring. In fact, no one felt anything amiss until the brig cleared the headland, and the Atlantic rollers started playing with the ship. The less hardy souls headed for the slop tub at once. Others held out until the aroma of boiling salt meat reached them; then they also literally added to the difficulty with the already fetid bilges.

Nor was the predicament with mal de mer limited to the convicts.

Andrew Parker, the new assistant governor of the Van Diemen's Land prison station, was severely queasy. So nauseated was the man that after fifteen minutes of dry heaves he determined that something was terribly wrong and that Captain Clarke, a retired officer of the Royal Navy, must turn back and put him ashore at once!

To this end, Parker crawled from his bunk to the passageway and up the companionway leading to the poop deck. Nearing the top of the ladder, Parker was struck with the thought that it was undignified for a government official to be seen on hands and knees, so he levered himself upright just as the *Hive* broached the crest of a wave and slammed down into the following trough.

Parker went down the ladder much more precipitately than he went up, managing to bounce heavily on the deck and dislocate his hip.

There was instant pandemonium.

Parker's wife screamed, "He's killed! He's killed!" leading Captain Clarke to believe that an outbreak of violence among the prisoners had begun.

When the true nature of the problem was discovered, Clarke called for the ship's surgeon. Unfortunately, Surgeon White's personally preferred remedy for seasickness was imbibing a large quantity of gin, a physic by whose power he was already suspended in uselessness.

Turning back to port to explain a damaged assistant governor was more than Captain Clarke thought wise, so he scoured the ship for stand-in surgeons. "Do any of you men have any medical training?" he inquired among the mostly moaning prisoners. Baleful looks made up the replies, except for Father Talbot and Joseph. Both men asked if they could be of any assistance and willingly accompanied the captain to Parker's cabin.

The government official was howling and panting by turns, his right leg seemingly separated from his body and lying at an impossible angle.

After examining the misplaced joint, Talbot observed in an aside to Joseph, "Straightforward dislocation. Nothin' broken, praise be. Ever set one of these before?"

"Not on a man," Joseph commented. "Had to fix somethin' similar on a dog once."

Parker howled louder than ever and thrashed on his bunk while his wife wrung her hands.

"Send for a block and tackle," Talbot directed the captain. "Actually, make it three. And two of your strongest men."

Following Talbot's instruction, the corridor outside Parker's berth was soon a complex tangle of rigging that ended with a knot around the official's ankle. "You men hold him down," the priest commanded, "whilst Squire Burke and I perform the delicate realignment."

On a count of three, Joseph and the priest strained on the line that ran through three pulleys and terminated at Parker's leg. The eyes of the assistant governor bulged even more than his injury as what appeared to be some modern version of the rack was set in motion.

For a moment nothing happened, and then with a snap so audible that not only Parker but also his wife fainted, the displaced joint was reduced.

Father Talbot whistled happily as he took apart the apparatus.

"Most impressive," offered the captain with his thanks. "Will he be all right now?"

"Oh, he'll do well enough, with the blessin'," Talbot observed.

"I am in your debt," Captain Clarke said.

On the way back to the prisoners' quarters Joseph inquired, "And just what was that snarl of cat's cradle and fishin' line all about? I never saw the like. Could not we have accomplished the same result with less fuss?"

Winking, Talbot said, "Very likely, but it would not have been 'most impressive.' And likely you heard the captain: he's now in our debt."

Pardoned!" Kate breathed the word and groped for a chair as Kane presented the document bearing the official government seal.

"Aye. O'Connell handed me Joseph's amnesty with his own hand. I rode that very hour to catch a sloop to Cove." His expression told her it had not gone well.

"Where've they sent him, Adam?"

"As I was sayin', a coastin' ship she was. The *Flyin' Cloud*. We made good time to Cove, with me thinkin' every minute how glad you'd be when I brought Squire Joseph home. And what a celebration there'd be when he'd rested and recovered a bit."

"Adam!" Kate rose to her feet. "Tell me why he's not come with you!"

The steward hung his head. "So . . . we cut a fine swath. The seas were calm all the way from Dublin round to Cove Harbor. The wind was fair, and I thought we'd surely be there with days to spare." Unable to meet her gaze he looked helplessly out the window.

She finished for him. "But the prison ship had sailed."

"Aye. That she had. I didn't know until I took the pardon to the warden. 'Here it is,' says I. 'From the hand of the Liberator himself. Set Joseph Connor, Lord Burke, free, if you please, and I'll be takin' him home to Galway.' But they'd sailed away. I ran back to the docks, but the *Flyin' Cloud* had left for home. There were no other ships of a size to catch the *Hive*. That's the name of the prison ship he's on. I begged the captain of a boat, promised him a reward if he'd take me after them. Nearly had him convinced, but the tide was wrong, and then the winds came up fierce and hard as they do. He'd not take me out in it. So I've come home to tell you your husband's a free man, though he be still in chains."

"You've got the news of where the *Hive* will call?"

"Aye." He pulled out a rumpled itinerary from the pocket of his waistcoat. "The Canaries first."

Kate snatched the paper from him and studied the list of ports and the estimated day of arrival in New South Wales several months from now. "Are any ships sailing that could catch her?"

"In three days a merchant vessel sails from Galway City. The *Blossom*, she's called. Bound for the Cape of Good Hope, I hear. The harbormaster says she'll call at the Canaries, same as *Hive*. There's nowhere else they can provision."

"Then you're going." Kate pulled up a plank in the floor and disgorged the leather pouch still containing ten gold sovereigns.

"Not I, ma'am. But I'll send word to O'Connell that we've got to intercept the prison ship."

"There's no time for you to ride back to Dublin."

Kane rubbed his hand wearily over the stubble on his cheek. "Kate, girl."

"It's Lady Burke to you if you think you'll change my mind!"

"All right, then. Lady Burke. Listen to reason."

She shook her head in refusal. "I've listened to reason when what I most wanted in the world was to trade this place for Joseph's freedom. Do you know the sort of monster who has charge over his life? There's not a day to wait. Not an hour, Adam. You'll never dissuade me from this. Take half the Burke fortune." She separated the coins into two stacks. "This is all we have left. Take these, kiss Fern good bye, and go!"

"But Kate!"

"The sooner you bring Joseph back to me, the sooner you'll be back to Fern. In the meantime, we'll muddle through without you."

"I'll not leave you to manage the estate on your own," Adam Kane reiterated as he paced about the kitchen. Kate calmly watched him from the table.

"There's no man I trust but yourself," she said. "If you're thinkin' of continuin' to work for the House of Burke, then you'll pack your sea chest and be off."

"And what of Mahon?"

"What of him? We've won. Joseph is pardoned. When you fetch him back, what will Mahon be able to do?"

"He lusts after this valley. Grazin' land he's after. Ballynockanor is built upon the best in Connaught."

"He'll have to find it elsewhere. Joseph is pardoned. You'll sail to Botany Bay if you can't intercept his ship. Present the papers to the governor, and Joseph comes home." She paused and considered that the simplicity of her words did not reflect the months that would pass before she saw him again. "Then all will be well with us."

"It's not Squire Joseph's return I'm thinkin' of. It's the weary weeks between now and when I find him and get him home. Mahon intends to bring you down—and everyone in the townlands. How will a woman manage alone?"

Kate's eyebrow rose imperiously at the jibe. "I'll not be patronized. That's the new motto I intend to carve upon the Burke crest." She said it again, emphasizing each word. "*I will not be patronized!* I'm a Donovan and a Burke and a Christian before I am a woman."

He half smiled. "That you are, ma'am. But you'll not be fightin' any duels while I'm away now, will you?"

"If I may choose the weapons."

"And with what do you intend to fight Mahon and Dublin Castle, if I may be askin'?"

"My wits, sir."

He bowed to her. "Sharp enough sword to do damage. Well, then, God help them all. A formidable weapon indeed."

When Kane reached Galway City, the weather was oppressively cold. A strong northwester was blowing, keeping the more timid ships snug in the harbor. But there was one ship in Galway Bay that was headed immediately to the Canary Islands and then to Cape Town. The harbormaster directed Adam Kane to the merchant vessel *Blossom*.

Her captain, one Costello by name, was acquainted with Daniel O'Connell and had heard of Joseph Burke. He had read the Repeal paper, *The Nation*, and recollected seeing the name of Lord Burke among the gentlemen pardoned with O'Connell.

"Bound and in chains, you say?" Costello queried. "Carried off on board the *Hive*? A plague pot, a blackbirder, that one. Ran the slave trade from the Gold Coast to the Bahamas for too long." He shook his head. "I always wondered why God in His mercy didn't send her to the bottom, for if ever there was a sample of hell on earth, that is the *Hive*."

Kane figured correctly that Costello was the right captain for such a task. He had an inherent hatred of tyranny. "That's why I'm my own man. Captain of my own ship. I'll not be bullied, threatened, or told where I may sail or when I must arrive."

Kane explained to him the urgency of catching the blackbirder before she sailed from the Canaries. "There's trouble brewin' in the west. Lady Burke is driven off her farm by nightriders who threat- ened her and her family with death unless they give over their author- ity to a loyalist named Mahon. She's shut behind the high walls of the estate, but there's none but servants on hand to keep her safe if Mahon's men return. I'll only need to sail with you as far as the Canaries, free Squire Joseph, and then catch the fastest ship home."

"The weather's bad." Captain Costello studied the sky. "I'd thought to lay up awhile until it cleared. Can your stomach bear sailin' on rough seas?"

Kane was uncertain of the answer, but replied that he could man- age as well as any man.

Costello thumped him on the shoulder. "Then we'll sail on. Tomorrow mornin'. If *Hive* is fightin' this storm, it'll slow her down. We'll catch her all right."

13

The women convicts were assigned to cook for the ship. This meant preparing a gruel of oatmeal for breakfast and boiling either potatoes or stringy salt beef for supper. The wretched fare was a source of much grumbling among the convicts.

Each day Gann also picked out certain of the less dangerous criminals to act as kitchen helpers. Among these were Laurence O'Halloran, Joseph, and both of the clergymen.

On a certain evening O'Halloran had already carried three buckets of swill to be dumped over the side when he made the error of taking the fourth pail to the windward rail. A few paces away stood Jailor Gann, in conversation with another sentry.

As Laurence upended the bucket, a gust of breeze spattered the back of Gann's neck, and the warden exploded. Jerking the whip from his belt, he proceeded to lash the boy across the face. "You stupid ape!" Gann berated. "Are you too daft to go to the lee side? You soiled my uniform, you ignorant clot!" Each syllable of this tirade was punctuated by another slash of the cat. The youth was babbling, "I'm s-s-sorry," but Gann paid no heed to the apology and continued raking the whip backward and forward over the boy's head.

When O'Halloran threw up his hands to protect his already bloody cheeks, he spilled the remainder of the bucket of garbage onto the deck.

"Now look!" Gann screamed. "Foul pig of a papist bastard! Clean that up!"

As he spoke those words, Gann reversed the cat in his grip and swung the steel-knobbed handle toward the boy's skull.

At that moment Joseph and Father Talbot intervened. The two men had just emerged from the aft part of the ship where they had been checking on Parker's hip when they saw what was happening. Joseph threw himself across the deck and seized Gann's hand upraised to strike. When Gann drew back his other fist to clout Joseph, Talbot grabbed it, and the two convicts pinioned the guard between them while O'Halloran cowered on the deck.

"Get your hands off me," Gann threatened. "I'll have every scrap of hide flogged off your carcasses! I'll have you hanged! Help me!" Gann called to the other watchman. "Shoot them!" Instead of getting involved, the second guard ran for assistance.

"Calm yourself," Talbot urged, his short, stout arms wrestling with Gann's wiry limb. "You might have killed the boy if you struck him so. We have prevented a tragedy, I'm thinkin'."

Frothing at the mouth, Gann babbled of dire retribution, but his rage was so intense that he was incoherent when Captain Clarke arrived, demanding an explanation. He ordered the two convicts to release Gann, then sent Gann forward and O'Halloran below while he got Talbot's full account.

"I have seen Gann's temper in action before this," the officer admitted. "And I do not doubt that he may have killed the boy. But convicts may never touch guards, no matter what the provocation. Both of you will be flogged."

Father Talbot shrugged as the men went below. "Put no trust in the faith of princes," he quoted. "So we see just how much it is worth to hold the captain's debt."

The prescribed punishments for shipboard infractions were known to the prisoners; they heard them read aloud by Captain Clarke at least once each week: stealing, first offense, six dozen lashes; second offense, twelve dozen; striking another prisoner, two dozen lashes; striking a guard, death by hanging.

The sails were backed, and the *Hive* hove to. A row of sentries armed with muskets lined the quarterdeck and another file watched from the forecastle. The prisoners were crammed into the waist of the ship to witness punishment.

Joseph and Father Talbot were already on the quarterdeck, well away from any attempted rescue or riot by their fellows. Captain Clarke addressed the company. "These prisoners are guilty of laying hands on a guard. There is no defense possible, and such conduct will not be tolerated."

At the starboard end of the row of guards, Gann smirked broadly.

"But since they did not actually strike the officer," Clarke continued, "I am reducing their sentence from hanging to flogging."

Gann still smirked, apparently picturing the torn flesh and dripping wounds of his special victims. Many such casualties died as a result of their correction anyway.

"And because of a special request for clemency by Mister Parker," the captain went on, "I am further reducing their sentence to two dozen lashes."

Starting violently, Gann stepped forward, only to be imperiously waved back into line by the captain. "Finally," Clarke concluded, "since the two of them are guilty of only one offense between them, the sentence is to be shared as twelve lashes each. Prepare the prisoners to receive punishment."

Talbot's shirt was ripped from his back, and his arms trussed up over his head to the shrouds supporting the port side of the mizzenmast. A short time later Joseph was similarly bound on the starboard side. "By the slow count," Clarke ordered, "One!"

The lash in the hand of the first mate shrilled through the air to land across Talbot's freckled shoulders. The priest grunted with the impact, but made no other sound.

"Two!"

The cat swung by Jailor Gann against Joseph's back cut especially deep; Gann had knotted bits of stiffer horsehide into the leather thongs.

"Three!"

When the sentence was completed, Talbot's back was dripping lines of blood that ran down onto the deck. Joseph's was a solid mass of red.

As Gann cut Joseph down, he hissed into the prisoner's ear, "Don't think this squares the account. Not by a long chalk, croppie!"

Later, as Pastor Holt rubbed sweet oil over both his friend's and Joseph's wounds, Pen Brophy stopped beside them. Ducking his head and pulling his forelock, he said, "I was wrong about you, Squire. You are a right 'un after all."

Blossom rode high on the waves of the Atlantic. Up a wall of water she climbed and down into the depths of the trough beyond.

Kane's stomach, which he had imagined was made of iron, was merely feathers and fluff weighted with watery putty. He was sick into his fine new hat once, and after that secured a slop bucket from the cook. But after the hat was filled, there was nothing left in his belly to toss in the other receptacle.

He came near to cursing his luck, but cursing anything, he knew from Molly, would change it from bad to worse. Still, the constant droning that filled his head had to be the product of an imagination so diseased no turn of fortune could worsen it.

Three days out the weather cleared. Captain Costello poked his head into the cabin, which was the size of a closet, and said cheerfully, "The Americans have a sayin' about raisin' Kane. I thought we'd need some sort of resurrection for yourself if the storm stayed upon us. But I see you're less green today. Would you care for supper? Three quarters of an hour."

And so Kane rose reluctantly from his wallow. He washed himself with lye soap and salt water followed by fresh, and shaved with difficulty, nicking his cheek with a straight razor twice. When he was done, he felt altogether scraped, stung, and hollow. He was grateful he had not run off to sea as he had threatened his father he might in his youth.

So to dinner.

Captain Costello ran a contented ship, as he was a pleasant man. The table was a rectangle capable of seating six men elbow to elbow. Every space was filled with other passengers as well as the captain and the first mate, Mister Doheny. Second mate on the *Blossom* was a Scotsman named MacDougall, and he played the pipes. A lowborn fellow, Kane surmised. While the beef was served, the Scot filled the paunch of the pipes with air. Grimacing and pop-eyed at the effort, he puffed his cheeks out and played for the diners—a horrid, rasping noise to Kane's ringing ears and aching head.

Costello leaned on his elbow and remarked, "Different from the pipes of our Irish pipers, eh?"

Kane could only nod. He did not know if the buzzing of the Scot's instrument was a sack of hornets or music. He had heard sweeter baying from a sad beagle locked in her kennel.

The piper tucked his chin and blinked his bulging eyes as the closing notes of "Scotland the Brave" reverberated in the close cabin.

Kane looked at the faces of each of the diners. Speaking pleasantly. Shoveling knifefuls of beef and peas and potatoes into their mouths. Was Kane the only one who could see that this was a Chinaman's torture device? Lock a man in a crowded room, put everything in motion beneath him and around him, serve him peas and salted beef, then set loose a hive of insects to buzz in his ears!

"Are you unwell, sir?" asked Costello.

"What was that?" Kane could barely hear the question.

"Are you unwell, sir?"

"Aye." Kane gulped, gasped, and looked desperately for some suitable container in which to spew. A bucket? None to be found. Struggling to free himself from the chair that held him down, he reached up, grasped the piper by the pipe, yanked the chanter from the man's teeth, and clung to it like a lifeline.

"Let me out!" Kane cried.

Too late. Clutching the deflating instrument to his face, he lost beef, peas, and potatoes into the folds of the tartan bag.

There was no music in the captain's cabin at mealtimes after that. Kane had made his first enemy on board. From then on, the Scots piper glared at him when he came on deck and swore that Kane had done what he did on purpose.

Two months had passed after their eight hours together before Kate knew she carried Joseph's gift in her body. A miracle, it was. Her miracle and Joseph's too. She told no one even when she was certain. Lying on her bed at night she strummed her stomach with her fingers and knew that within her an unchained part of Joseph had escaped the prison walls. Joseph's love, tangible, alive, and growing in her womb, remained behind to comfort her through every ordinary hour of the day and the longest nights. This secret dulled the razor edge of loneliness.

Often Kate dreamed of Joseph walking ahead of her on the narrow path to St. Brigit's cross. The nightsongs of birds serenaded as they passed. She sensed the nearness of those she loved who had gone before. Near the crest of the hill Joseph turned to her with unchanging eyes and said, "We're more together than you know, Kate." After that he faded away and the silence came. She opened her eyes and touched the empty pillow beside her. If it had not been for the child, Kate would have awakened to reality and been consumed by grief. But was this miracle not some proof that God was watching, loving, preparing a future for them both?

In the morning sighing winds swept leaves along the sodden paths that crossed the grounds of the Burke estate. Like the charred skeleton of the manor house, the gardens had taken on a ghostly appearance. Memories of troubled times, of sorrow and loss, weighed on Kate in that place. She accepted now that it was safe, sensible, and even correct for her to live behind the high walls of the Park. Beyond the safety of the compound English soldiers patrolled the highway, and there were always strangers lurking just within view.

She was a prisoner in the home Joseph had prepared for her. It had been converted from a huge stone-walled stable with ancient oakhammer-beam ceilings. Legend was that this place had once been the great hall of the castle built by the first Irish de Burgo. When fashion dictated that the noble family required a larger, updated residence in the years of the Stuart kings, the hall had become a stable. Oak timbers above the second floor still were adorned with roof bosses decorated with the faces of the men who constructed the hall. The wood was preserved from insects and dry rot by years of horse urine in the atmosphere. Slate floors were uninjured by centuries of horse dung, iron shod hooves, and carriage wheels. Haylofts became bedchambers. Downstairs where the stalls had been the walls were stripped, cleaned, and bleached. New partitions of oaklinenfold paneling, rescued from a ruined monastery in Donegal, were erected to form a sitting room, music room, dining room, library, and kitchen. It was a fine, big house again, filled with the things that had been saved from the burning of the manor. It retained the air of a pared-down castle, Kate thought: dark oak and heavy furnishings; portraits of Joseph's ancestors, swords, and shields on the walls. The first de Burgo would have been comfortable here.

She was acutely aware that, for love of her, Joseph had labored with the carpenters and masons who had created this grand house from its humble foundation. She had often seen him scribbling plans and figures on a scrap of paper as he sat beneath the oak tree at the lake. He had forbidden her to set foot in it until the proper moment. By this he meant the hour he brought her home as his wife.

Without him to share his gift with her, every room seemed melancholy.

But there was the one true gift he had given her; the joy of it grew quietly within her. Sure, for the sake of the unborn child, for Tomeen, for Mary Elizabeth and Martin, she would take no more chances of facing another night raid alone. But she missed the warmth of her home. Again and again she found herself walking out of the house and back to familiar places on the grounds. Unbidden, she returned to each spot she had ever seen Joseph. Beneath cold, grey skies, she retraced her steps to the lake where he had last stood beside her as a free man. She half believed she would find him waiting for her.

And where have you been, Kate? Ah well, the sound of his voice was clear in her memory. It had not altered or faded with time.

"I've been lookin' everywhere for you, Joseph," she said aloud. "Where are you, then?" She had no more tears to offer the loneliness. Instead, she let the memory of his teasing laughter make her smile again.

There was a rule made by the prisoners themselves that after dark they could not speak of women: not wives nor mothers; sweethearts nor any other female. The agony of memory was enough to drive even the strong to madness.

Tonight the lantern was extinguished; the hatch slammed down, capturing them in the tangible blackness and stench. An audible moan of misery rose from the bilges through the hold. Disembodied walls were countered with curses and sobs from those who saw visions of home and loved ones about them in the night.

Joseph closed his eyes and thought of Kate, her arms around him, her sweet breath on the nape of his neck. The press of loneliness was so crushing that he fought to keep from groaning.

Laurence O'Halloran began to weep. Pen Brophy threatened to kill him if he did not shut up. From beside O'Halloran, Father Talbot whispered the Our Father.

"Say it with me, Laurence," said the priest.

The boy, struggling for control, joined in the prayer. Joseph, clutching the lead pendant, followed, then Reverend Holt and the dozen others packed above and below them.

There was comfort for most in the prayer. A few like Brophy, declared he would strangle in their sleep those who prayed aloud to a God who had abandoned them.

"What if we have died already?" O'Halloran's voice quavered. "What if this ship carries us to hell? I try to think of home, but it's a dream, Father. Not real. Ireland. The dream. But this—'tis the nightmare I never wake from."

"Ireland's still there, boy," Joseph said. "It'll be there when we get back. And we must hold to it so we will live and thrive and one day return."

"Aye," added the priest. "Preserve our thoughts, O Lord. Think on whatever is pure and lovely. As sure as heaven, our homeland waits for us."

To sing would summon Gann. But a snatch of verse came clearly to Joseph. He spoke the words quietly:

Cenn Escrach of the orchards,
a dwellin' of the meadow bees.
There is a shinin' thicket in its midst,
a spring and a drinkin' cup.

The vision floated in the darkness above him. It made him smile. Reverend Holt spoke quietly in a singsong tone,

The dim night is silent,
and its darkness covers all of Galway.
The sun sleeps in the bed of the sea,
and the moon silvers the waters.

"Ahhhhh," sighed Father Talbot, seeing it quite clearly. "There it is." There was a broad grin in his voice.

Now there was silence as each man searched his memory for images and phrases to paint home. Pen Brophy, impatient with the lag, snapped, "Get on with it, then."

Patrick Frayne chuckled and whispered, "Aye, here's one:

The calm green lakes are sleepin' in the mountain shadow,
and on the water's canvas bright sunshine paints the picture
of the day.

"What about you, Laurence?" Joseph queried.

The youth breathed deeply as though inhaling familiar scents.

They grow, the quiet throng, fair gems of the realm of sun and wind.

The boy faltered, unable to finish.
The priest picked up the stanza where Laurence left it.

The hanging bells of the high crags, flowers of the rocks like cups of honey.

They lay there, unmoving, in the oppression of the evil *Hive*. But heaven and home came to comfort them: sweet brooks, green hills, and the scent of flowers and the call of blackbirds.

14

Even when the convicts and the motion of the ship were reconciled to each other, life aboard the prison transport was cramped and almost unbearable. Despite the overcrowding, apart from some few cases of dysentery, no illness had broken out, and two healthy babies had been born to women prisoners; an occurrence considered lucky by the superstition-prone Patrick Frayne.

After the punishment inflicted on Joseph and Father Talbot, there had been no further incidents. Captain Clarke kept a close eye on Jailor Gann, who stayed more indifferent than before.

The forecastle was reserved for the ship's crew and prison guards and her poop deck for still more guards, the ship's officers, and the voluntary passengers. The waist of the transport belonged to the involuntary passengers, the convicts, at least during their afternoon exercise period. The company of prisoners was divided into three groups of about a hundred, each hundred being permitted two hours on deck each day.

Since reaching the latitude of Portugal, the sun made it entirely
too warm to do anything except laze about, but everyone aboard
wanted the chance to escape the stench and the squeeze below.

Joseph sat alone at the foot of the mainmast, his wounds painful
but bearable. He was alternately thinking of Kate and overhearing
snatches of conversations. Near the larboard rail, Pen Brophy was
bragging to the impressionable O'Halloran about his exploits.
"Throttled the constable, I did, leastwise, one of 'em. If I'd had me
a mate to back the play, I could have gone clean, but me partner cut
an' run on me, see?"

Strolling in circles around the "cattle pen," as the convicts' yard
was called, Father Talbot and Pastor Holt talked theology. On their
third pass, Joseph overheard Brophy explain to O'Halloran, "Now,
the way you run a coney-catchin' is like this: You get a gal to work
with and you have her come on to a swell, and then when she gets
him up to her room, you busts in as the aggrieved husband, see?
And does he pay up, then? Course, you'll need to grow some hair
on yer face before that'll play!"

While Brophy was still chortling, Talbot snagged O'Halloran by
the arm. "Laurence, did you forget that you have school this day?
Come along now."

Brophy scowled but refrained from openly criticizing the priest.
After the incident with O'Halloran, both Talbot and Joseph were
highly regarded by the other prisoners. And since Surgeon White
had not been out of his berth since the day of sailing, he was rightly
deemed to be an incompetent drunk whose clutches must be avoided
at all costs. Father Talbot had offered his services as a substitute and
was therefore also admired by the captain and the others, except for
Gann.

Talbot and his friend Holt gave instruction to any who cared to
listen in such diverse subjects as grammar and geology, history and
histrionics. It passed the time, and the education was of genuine
interest to those who believed they would one day complete their
sentences and return to Ireland.

The current subject was geography.

"I overheard the sailin' master say," recounted Talbot to O'Halloran and the circle of students, "that we should make port in the Canaries in two more days. The Canary Islands—"

"Not named for the birds," Pastor Holt interrupted. "From the Latin, *Canis*, meaning 'dog.' Early explorers wrote that they found many dogs there—hence the name." Holt was overly proud of his training in the classics. "Actually, the ancient Romans called them *Fortunatae Insulae*, thinking the islands were the home of the departed happy spirits. *Fortunatae* . . ."

"As I was sayin'," Talbot continued smoothly, changing position slightly to ease the stiffness in his back, "these Canaries, or dog islands, or isles of the blest, what have you, are volcanic by origin. In fact, by this time tomorrow, we should see the mountain known as *Pico de Teide*. It sticks up twelve thousand feet and is still smokin' from its subterranean fires. The Canary Islands are not far from the African coast."

Talbot was here interrupted by Patrick Frayne, whom Joseph had not even known was listening. "Pardon, Father, but just how far from Africa would they be?"

Talbot stuck out his lower lip in thought, then consulted with Holt. "I don't know exactly," he admitted. "Not over a hundred miles, I shouldn't think. I can ask the master for a more precise figger."

"Not a'tall, not a'tall," said Frayne hastily. "Don't be botherin' the important man with such idle chatter. Go on with your lesson."

The summit of the volcano Pico de Teide on Tenerife in the Canary Islands was wreathed in clouds and smoke. Though Joseph assured Laurence O'Halloran fully half of the mountain remained unseen, the boy from the plains of Tipperary was too awed to be convinced. "Sure an' you're foolin' with me," he accused. "Why, it's already the greatest mountain in the world. How can there be more, unless it reaches to heaven its own self?"

For a lad raised where the Rock of Cashel stood only a hundred paces higher than the potato fields and the hills ringing his hometown were less than two thousand feet elevation, the concept of something so enormous gave rise to biblical speculations.

Despite being repeatedly told the peak's name, O'Halloran insisted that it was Ararat, because, as he said, "Since it is plainly the tallest peak in the world, Noah's ark must have run aground upon it."

The *Hive* did not run aground, but it did sail into a sheltered anchorage before the town of Santa Cruz de Tenerife, in the afternoon shadow cast by the volcano. As soon as the transport ship hove into sight, a dozen rowboats, sharp at both prow and stern, pushed off from shore. They were laden with bananas, onions, grapes, and wine.

For two days the convicts worked from dawn till dusk, loading refilled barrels of fresh water, stowing sacks of potatoes, and refilling bins of provisions with the fresh stores from the islands. This labor was not objected to, since the prospect of better and more varied fare cheered up the entire convict population.

Even though it was officially forbidden, impromptu private commerce also existed between shore and ship. The male prisoners worked in leg irons so as to prevent them from jumping ship and swimming ashore, but not even the most watchful of guards could stop every trading venture.

"Here, mate," Patrick Frayne called to an islander with a boatload of tobacco. "Give you sixpence for a parcel o'that." A nearby guard saw but chose to ignore the exchange. As the dory boat rose and fell alongside, Frayne passed over the money and exchanged a few words with the boatman. It seemed to Joseph that Frayne had spoken to the same vendor the day before, but he gave it no special importance. Anyway, Father Walter Talbot was lecturing loudly nearby. Coiling down a length of rope, the good father was again offering instruction, this time in history.

"This very spot," he said, waving his arm over the cove, "this seemin'ly peaceful, idyllic place, was the site of a turrible battle. Before the turn of the century it was. Himself, that was later Admiral Nelson of Trafalgar fame, was wounded so as to lose his right arm attackin' this place."

Laurence O'Halloran crossed himself at the image, but Pen Brophy cursed and said, "Blasted English navy! Bad cess to 'em all. A pity the great Nelson did not lose his head entire and the French win at Trafalgar. Things would be different in Ireland now, I can tell you."

"Now, now," admonished Talbot, waving a cautionary finger, "if you took the time to know your country's history as you should, you'd know that many a son of Erin fought with Nelson that day. The French of the Revolution were godless heathen."

Joseph reflected that both men had made good points. It was one of Catholic Ireland's many pieces of ill fortune to long for help from a France that officially rejected God altogether, and always promised more aid than it ever delivered.

Brophy was not disposed to continue the argument. With a downward slash of his hand, he stalked away to engage Patrick Frayne and the Canary Island boatman in close conversation. Perhaps it was an escape attempt in the planning, since both convicts looked around furtively and jumped back to work quickly when the guard reappeared.

Pastor Henry Holt, too frail to shift heavy crates, was employed as a clerk, accounting for incoming foodstuffs. He recorded the arrival of several barrels labeled MEAL, and officiously attempted to check the quality by prying off the lid of the last.

Patrick Frayne suddenly jumped up from his place and shouted as he pointed to another boatman. "See here, Reverend. I cannot make out exactly what it is this fellow is sellin'. Tell me, is it a good thing or no?"

"And what is it?" Holt inquired.

"Pepper, *señor*," was the reply. "Colorado. *Muy bueno y muy caliente.*"

"Pepper, eh? Just the thing to give some flavor to the stew," Holt vowed. "Sell me a pouch of that."

A few coins and a small sack of red pepper changed owners. "I'd be careful of that if I were you, Pastor," Joseph warned. "It may be warmer than you are expectin'."

Unwilling to appear ignorant about his purchase, Holt opened the bag and sprinkled some into his hand. He eyed the shilling-sized heap for a moment, then lowered his nose and sniffed it.

For an instant the onlookers studied him expectantly. Then Holt gasped, "Water! I'm poisoned! Frayne, you poisoned me!" Choking and wheezing, his eyes streaming tears, Holt looked as if he might dive into the ocean in search of relief before spying a newly loaded cask of drinking water and plunging in his head. When he came up, bubbling and spouting, he gurgled to his friend the priest, "Help me, Walter! I'm killed!"

"See, Laurence," Father Talbot said, laughing, "the Protestant, good man that he is, is in fear of dyin' and is callin' on me for last rites. Look how eager he is for the baptism!"

In the uproar of teasing that followed, no one noticed that Frayne and Brophy had hurriedly rolled the meal barrels away. Shortly after the *Hive* made ready to sail.

The Canary Islands. The port of Santa Cruz de Tenerife. Adam Kane stood at the bow of the *Blossom* and breathed in the dusty scents of sagebrush and dry land. Gulls circled above the billowing sails and called joyfully as though they recognized the ship's white canvas as some giant seabird come back to nest.

Kane shared their sense of delight. Most certainly, he reasoned, the *Hive* would be here among the host of merchant ships at port. A forest of masts stretched across the harbor. Provisioning boats scudded to and fro across the clear warm waters. Along the shoreline the red clay roof tiles and whitewashed buildings glistened, giving the false impression that Santa Cruz was clean and tidy.

This image and the belief that, within a few hours, Squire Joseph would be free, made Kane grin broadly.

Beside him Captain Costello remarked, "That there's English House." He pointed to a large stone building just up from the quay. "We'll be another hour gettin' you to the docks."

"So long?"

"You'll not be jumpin' ship on me?" He slapped Kane on the

back. "Relax. There's a prison hulk on the far side of the harbor. I spotted her as we came about."

"How can you tell?"

"Hard to miss. When you haul barrels of wine and wheels of cheese, or ladies' silks and satins, why nothin' will do but a ship that's clean and in fine trim. No tattered canvas. Teak for the decking. Seaworthy and altogether cock-a-hoop." With a wave of pride he added, "Like the *Blossom*. But for haulin' human freight? Nothin' but the worst vessel will do. Filthy and listin'. Sails ancient and scruffy as a dead man's shroud. I've seen the *Hive* at anchor in Cove. The worst of the lot. Unless I'm mistaken, that harlot of the sea is layin' off between two sleek American ladies of the line owned by the Coffin family. Never liked the name. Steer clear of those ships if I can."

"Can't we anchor closer? Row directly to her?"

"It's a regular day at the races out here. Twenty ships at anchor between us and them. The wind's wrong for it, Mister Kane. The *Hive*'ll keep a while. And you'll need to make a social call to the governor."

These last minutes before securing Joseph's release were the worst for Steward Kane.

The bumboats of three separate warehouses were racing to reach the *Blossom* in hopes of securing the business of Captain Costello. In contrast, the ship's launch bearing Kane was irritatingly slow and clumsy in its progress through the docks.

Kane reasoned he could have swum the distance faster. At one point, as the hot Tenerife sun beat down on his Irish woolen suit, he was almost tempted to strip and swim for shore. But it would not be good form to appear before the representative of Her Majesty's government naked, dripping, and insisting on a pardon for one of the prisoners being held in the port.

Kane leaped from the launch just as it was hauling up at a stone quay. With barely a glance back he entered the labyrinth of the teeming port. Far from clean, it was the epitome of all things vile in a seaport. The heat amplified the stench on the garbage-strewn cobbles of the lanes. Sewage ran down open gutters. Prostitutes of every size and variety and in various states of undress called out to Kane as he passed the doors of their dark cribs. Tucking his chin and keeping his eyes fixed on the ground, he climbed the steep incline to the house of the British official.

A single porter sat on a bench beneath a shade tree outside the gates.

Kane stood stupidly staring through the bars for a long moment until at last the man spoke.

"English?"

"Irish."

"All the same." The doorkeeper rubbed his nose with the back of his hand.

Kane might have blasted the fellow for such an insult, but he was in too much of a hurry. "I have arrived on the *Blossom* on urgent government business. I need an audience with your master."

"English. All the same. Speak the same."

"Will you unlock the gate, sir, and let me pass?"

"All in a hurry."

"Sure. That much is true, sir. I've come a long way, and a man's life may be at stake."

"Hullo. How-do-you-do." The sentry grinned, expecting appreciation for his mastery of the English language.

"Not well, thank you. I've been too long on the sea. My legs are doubtful beneath me. The world is rockin', and I'm about to lose my temper, which is an Irish temper."

"*Si*. Good ev-en-ing. All the same. I speak it good. I comprehend . . ."

Patience gone, Adam Kane grabbed the thin fabric of the blue cotton tunic and lifted the guard up until his toes barely touched the ground. Nose to nose he growled, "Then comprehend this. I am an Irishman, sir. You will let me pass, sir, or I'll impale your worthless, lazy, ignorant hide upon the spikes of this gate!"

Leaving the guard to return to his bench after unlocking the gate, Adam Kane ran up the steps, through the arch, and into the courtyard of the house of Her Majesty's agent in Tenerife.

At his recognition of Adam Kane's Irish accent, Lord Hampshire, the representative of Queen Victoria to the Canary Islands, ordered the butler to keep the steward waiting outside the dining room until luncheon was finished.

Kane paced the length of the anteroom and back again. He had a clear view of the official and his guests in the sunlit open-air dining room. Their leisurely conversation was enough to make Kane more than half mad. But Captain Costello had warned him that Hampshire was not fond of the Irish and would be quite pleased if he had some reason to arrest Kane and transport him to hell where, as Hampshire said, all the Irish should be bound.

The citizens of Tenerife called Lord Hampshire *El Boracho Gordo*, meaning, "the fat drunk."

Kane needed no interpretation when he eyed the dining room of the corpulent, balding, red-nosed official. Surrounded by a half-dozen captains from various ships, El Boracho was animatedly retelling the story of Admiral Nelson, who was killed at the naval battle of Trafalgar and whose body was stuffed into a barrel of brandy to preserve it during the long sail home.

At this point in the tale the government official looked almost wistful and remarked with an indistinct slur, "A fine send-off. One I should not regret for myself should I perish on this volcanic lump. Send me home like they did Nelson, and I shall die a happy man."

"You'd be dead, and so how could you notice, Your Honor?" remarked one grey-bearded naval officer.

"Aye," joked another. "Consul Hampshire'd never fit into a barrel of brandy."

El Boracho patted his ample girth. "The Admiral was short of stature as I am. But alas! He died young and did not have opportunity to enjoy life to the fullest."

The stink of liquor oozed from Hampshire's pores. Kane could smell his breath at a distance. It occurred to Kane that the gentleman was a candidate for spontaneous combustion. One dared not light a pipe in front of him for fear he'd go up in smoke. He was sipping a tumbler of whiskey as the entrée of veal and a mountain of potatoes was placed before him. Snuffling like a hog, he examined the dish and then attacked it, shoveling food past his thick lips like he was half starved. At one point he closed one bloodshot eye and paused long enough to contemplate the looming presence of Kane.

"Who is that?" he queried the serving man.

"As I said, Your Honor, he's that chap from Dublin."

"Irish, is he?"

"Aye, sir."

"That explains it." With a disgusted harrumph, El Boracho resumed eating and drinking.

The meal lasted another thirty minutes. Perspiration soaked through Kane's coat. He felt sick to his stomach. When at last Lord Hampshire wiped his mouth, belched loudly, and proclaimed himself in need of a siesta, Kane had suffered enough. Waving the sealed document containing the full pardon for Joseph Connor, Lord Burke, Kane charged past the trio of servants.

"Nay, sir!" Kane cried before the startled gathering. "You'll not sleep until I am on my way to release my master from the convict ship known as the *Hive*! Here is his pardon, sir! Common decency demands that you hear me before you sleep one minute!"

Hampshire seemed confused. "Who is this fellow?" he demanded of the servant.

"From Dublin, m'lord."

"Ah. Irish." He leaned on his elbow and spoke in a conspiratorial tone to a well-fitted-out American officer on his right. "That explains it. Ill-mannered louts. Had a shipload of them in port last week." He scratched his chin in thought. "The *Hive*."

Kane shot forward, slapping the papers before Lord Hampshire. "Aye. The *Hive*."

El Boracho was amused. "One of those Irish chaps, is he? You say your master's on the *Hive*?"

"The very ship. And here's his pardon to take him off and carry him home."

"So sorry," said Hampshire. "*Hive* sailed almost a week ago. Stinking plague pot! If ever you catch up with her, and your master, you'd best have a full barrel of brandy on hand to pack him in."

The *Hive* was six days out of the harbor of Santa Cruz and bound for Cape Town. Provisioning for *Blossom* would take a full three days. This put *Blossom* nine days behind the progress of the *Hive*.

Captain Costello figured that with a fair wind there was a chance that the merchant ship would sail into Cape Town before the prison hulk lumbered out of that port on its way toward Australian waters.

This was, Kane mused to Costello, the only time he had ever heard of a blossom pursuing a hive of hornets.

The first evening back on board the vessel, Kane gazed pensively at the lights of Santa Cruz and considered the consequence if *Hive* were not overtaken at Cape Town. The journey he had hoped would take only a few weeks had the prospect of lengthening into months or more.

Clumsily he took up his pen and scratched out a letter to Kate and another to his beloved Fern. His thoughts turned again to home and Galway. Impatience settled on top of the dull ache of homesickness and the subtle nagging of some undefined fear.

The taverns along the docks of Santa Cruz de Tenerife were packed with sailors. It was not difficult to find one among them who could carry Adam Kane's letter back to Kate.

Kane rapped on a table and shouted over the din, "Any man here bound for Ireland? Galway City to be precise."

A dozen answered the call for Ireland; some sailors were bound for Belfast and others returning to Dublin. Only one among them, Lieutenant Charlie Nesbitt, leaped to his feet and cried, "Galway City, is it? My home, sir! That it is!" He was the first officer on a British naval frigate bound for London where he intended to resign his commission and return to his family in Galway.

Nesbitt was a Protestant and had served in the British navy for thirty years. But he was first and foremost an Irishman. He seemed eager to help and grateful to be asked to carry a letter back to his homeland.

"Sure, and it gives a man a sense of purpose. When the Queen's officers ask me to stay a few more years as their guest, I'll look 'em in the eye and proclaim, 'Not I, sir, I've got a message to carry back to Galway City, and I cannot be delayed.'"

Kane clapped him on the back and ordered another round of drinks. "'Tis chivalrous of you, sir. The lady is waitin' the return of her husband, and I'll not have her pine another hour longer than she must."

Nesbitt leaned close to Kane and remarked, "I saw *Hive* as we were sailin' in. A more sorry-lookin' tub is not afloat. Plaguey, filthy-lookin' hulk. Sink in the first high sea. But as she's bound for New South Wales, I'll tell you somethin' to cheer you. 'Tis a fair and beautiful land. Skies more blue you'll never see and waters clear enough a man can count shells on the bottom. Sharks though. Not fit for swimmin' unless a man holds his life of no account. But that's of no importance. 'Tisn't home, but a man could call it paradise if he had nothin' to draw him back. All the talk of cannibals and head-hunters is overrated. Disease takes more than the dart of a savage ever did. The mosquitoes are so large I've seen them swarm a horse and drive it mad until it ran headlong over a cliff. But all that's of no account. I'll cheer her ladyship with good news, for I've seen the place with my own eyes and found it pleasant. Many's the convict who stays after his sentence is over. Pillars of the community they become. A thief always makes a fine businessman, I say."

There was the tone of an easy and honest nature in what Nesbitt said, so Kane spent the evening plucking information from him. Six or seven months en route. As much again to return home. And how long between? It depended on which vessel was sailing, the season of the year, and when a man could book passage.

Kane figured Fern could be married and have a family before he saw her again. The thought was not comforting.

∽ 15 ∽

Only ten days out of Tenerife the *Hive* picked up the north-east trades. The transport soon coasted smoothly past the Cape Verde Islands, when the relative calm of the vessel's passengers disappeared. One morning, just at daybreak, armed guards appeared below. Grim-faced and threatening, they ordered each gang of one hundred on deck and chained them together. Those remaining below were shack-led into their bunks, treatment that had not been used before. Instead of exercise that day, each group was given a turn sitting in the ship's waist in the tropical heat. The warmth of the sun at twenty degrees north latitude was such that tar dripped from the rigging and pitch bubbled from the seams, but the prisoners were not allowed to seek shade nor to have any water.

The rumor went round that weapons had been smuggled aboard in the Canaries. This was an offense punishable by four hundred lashes, enough to kill a man. Over the years during which the trans-port penalty had been operating, several convict ships had been seized by prisoners and several more attempts had been made. As a consequence, not only would the possessor of any weapon be punished, so would the members of his berth, since it was concluded that men sleeping five across in a six-foot-wide space could scarcely keep secrets from each other.

Jailor Gann took especial relish in tearing through the meager personal belongings of the prisoners. He dumped Joseph's satchel out on the deck, emptied Patrick Frayne's duffel bag on top of it, and tossed Father Talbot's books into the heap. When he had made similar jumbles of all the convicts' possessions without result, he started in on the provisions stored in the hold.

Gann reported back to Captain Clarke that he had located no weapons, but he had discovered one unusual item: there were empty barrels stacked where only full casks should have been. Bungs had been started, and this would have accounted for the loss if the contents had been liquid and it had leaked into the bilges. Surprisingly, the containers indicated that the cargo should have been grain, which could not easily have disappeared.

About this same time, the *Hive* was overwhelmed with a plague of rats. The transport had been fumigated before the convicts were embarked, and since that time it had never been tied up to a wharf where the rodents would have had easy access. Rats were an inescapable presence on sailing ships, but in large numbers they represented a severe health problem since they not only spoiled victuals, they also carried disease.

The blast of the coachman's horn sounded from the Galway mailcoach three times at the gate of Burke Park.

Mad Molly, plucking imaginary green beans from the empty trellis behind the kitchen, perked her ears and said to Mary Elizabeth, "The Tinker's come home, darlin'."

Mary Elizabeth and Martin exchanged looks. The Tinker had died the night the manor house burned. "Whatever you say, Molly," Mary Elizabeth replied in a singsong voice.

"Aye." Molly cupped her hand around her ear as the trumpet rang out again. "'Tis the Tinker, sure. Bringin' news of Joseph, my wee Connor Burke, he is."

"Molly." Martin's changing voice cracked with impatience. "The Tinker's been dead these many months. He can't come home."

The old woman lifted her skirts and danced a reel of joy. "He missed the weddin', sure, Martin, but he's been sailin' the seven seas. The messenger, buzzin' among the bees awhile. Sailin' from here to there. Can't kill the messenger. Kate'll need him handy until Joseph comes home."

Once again the trumpet called impatiently for someone to come unlock the gate. "Where's Old Flynn?" Martin said, scowling.

"Fishin'," Molly proclaimed. "Caught a seamonster for his supper. You'll have to let the Tinker in, Martin darlin'."

Resentfully Martin snatched the gatekey from the rack inside the kitchen door and trudged down the long lane to where the coach waited. Mary Elizabeth and Molly scampered after with Molly reciting a verse from "Wild Irish":

A troop of horse at the mouth of the pass, a wild fight, a ding-dong fray of footsoldiers, these are some of the delights of Donnchadh's son—and seeking contest with foreigners!

Martin could see a tall man, dark and strong beneath his greatcoat, standing patiently outside the bars. Mary Elizabeth chimed, "Well, he does look like the Tinker, Martin."

Martin retorted, "Shall I call you Mad Mary Elizabeth then? The Tinker's dead, and that fellow looks nothin' like himself." Martin said this, but indeed, there was some resemblance. It made him shiver.

Molly sang,

He does not set his heart upon a feather bed, he would prefer to lie upon the rushes; to the good son of Donnchadh a house of rough wattles is more lovely than the battlements of a castle.

"Molly!" Martin snapped. "Will you hold your tongue awhile?"

Molly obliged, catching her tongue between thumb and forefinger for the rest of the stroll.

The stranger at the gate was wearing the heavy oilskin coat of a sailor. On his head was a well-used seaman's cap. His beard was thick and black with streaks of grey. The eyes were deep brown, the nose hooked, skin swarthy, betraying some ancestry of the Spanish who wrecked their Armada upon the shores of Ireland in the days of Queen Elizabeth.

"I've come to see Lady Burke," he called pleasantly in the accent of a Galway man. There was nothing mysterious about his voice.

"Who are you?" Martin queried.

Molly let go of her tongue and whispered, "The Tinker."

The stranger replied, "Name is Nesbitt, lad. I've come from far to bring news to the lady of the house. I've come with a message about Lord Burke."

Molly began to giggle. "There," she said smugly. "Not always mad, is she?"

Tomeen played with a ladle and a tin pot beneath Kate's desk. Even over the banging Kate could hear the clamor outside.

Mary Elizabeth in high-pitched excitement: "Kate! Sister! A letter! A letter!"

Fern's gleeful, squeaking voice: "Has it come then? Some word from my darlin' Adam?"

Martin's reprimand: "Hands off, woman. This is meant for Kate! The stranger has come the whole long way to see Kate!"

Margaret, breathless: "Would the gentleman like a cuppa after such a long, cold journey? Perhaps a slice of bread and butter? A potato?"

Old Flynn's demand: "How'd he get past the gate then? Master Kane said let no one past who was unknown. Cut our throats in our sleep, he will."

Then Mad Molly's song:

A thousand praises to the Light of lights!
He's sent the messenger to cheer our nights!
The Tinker's knives shall fight Burke's fights!
A thousand praises to the Light of lights!

And finally Molly's demand: "Go fetch the toothless priest! What's his name, Mary Elizabeth? O'Bannon. This matter'll take prayin' over."

Kate had barely risen from her chair and scooped up Tomeen when the door banged open and the crowd, surrounding a large-boned, rough-looking man, tried to squeeze en masse through the portal.

The grim visage of the newcomer alarmed Kate. He turned his face to one side and cocked an eye at her as though he were peering through a spyglass.

He scooped off his cap and bowed, piling up the crowd behind him. "You must be Kate, the Lady Burke."

"That I am, sir. And whom do I have the honor . . ." She was miffed. No one had bothered to knock or announce this ragged fellow. For all she knew he could be an assassin on Mahon's errand.

"He's brought a letter, sister," explained Mary Elizabeth.

"From Adam." Martin waved the envelope in the air like a prize.

"From Adam," Fern joined in, restraining herself from grabbing it.

"He's the Tinker," Molly said, screwing up her face.

Now the big man smiled. "My name is Charlie Nesbitt, ma'am. As for you all, I'd think I'd landed in Bedlam Lunatic Asylum except that I shared a pint with Adam Kane in Tenerife. He warned me about the household and what I'd find. Who I'd meet." With a certain finger he pointed at each member of the committee and named them accurately. With an air of accomplishment, he remarked, "Now there's your proof I've been on friendly terms with your unlucky steward, Adam Kane, in the Canary Islands. He sends his love to Fern." At this the housemaid blushed and twittered. "He told me about your circumstance, Lady Burke, ma'am, and seein' as my own family is scattered and gone from Galway City, upon my return I've come there to offer my assistance, to stand in for your steward for a while until he gets home, you might say. Employment. I'm a steady hand at the helm. When you read the letter I've brung, you'll see plainly you need me too."

"Charlie Nesbitt." Kate repeated the name of the messenger as she retrieved the letter from Martin. From the tone of Nesbitt's words, the letter could not contain pleasant information. Silence fell over the group as she opened it and began to read to herself first and then aloud:

> *Dear Lady Burke and all,*
>
> *I am at sea as to how I might tell you what has come upon me. Being a man of few words except when I have need of many, I will get to the very point of it and tell you the bad news, for it is impossible to give you good news.*
>
> *The ship I have sailed upon is called* Blossom. *She has arrived in Tenerife too late to catch the prison transport holding Squire Joseph called the* Hive. *Hive sailed a week away from Tenerife before we dropped anchor.*

A united groan rose up from the audience. Kate continued, struggling to hold back tears of disappointment.

> *So you see why I am writing. I will continue my journey in search of the* Hive. *Our captain says every ship, including the one we pursue, will stop and provision at Cape Town on the Cape of Good Hope. Hope is what I have therefore, that I shall find Squire Joseph alive and well within the bowels of that dank and filthy hulk and shall bring him home again to his place in Connaught. Hopefully alive.*

There was more, because Adam Kane was truly not a man of few words, but they came to the same conclusion. Joseph was still a prisoner.

Kate scanned the rest of the scrawl, coming to a second note to

Fern. "This is for your eyes alone, Fern." Kate passed the love letter to the palpitating servant girl.

Fern studied the writing in a half-dozen different positions and then said, "I'd read it if I could read, but I never learnt how."

Mad Molly clucked her tongue. "Mary Elizabeth will read it to ye in the kitchen. Come along. Come along. Come along."

Everyone but Kate, Martin, and Nesbitt departed solemnly to hear Mary Elizabeth's recitation of the love note.

Charlie Nesbitt stood at ease in military fashion before Kate and Tomeen. Martin eyed him suspiciously.

Kate spoke first. "Obviously Adam told you a bit about us."

"That he did, ma'am."

"Did he tell you we're long on hope and short on cash?"

"Somethin' like that, ma'am."

"Then you know I've little to pay you."

"Aye. He's paid me already." Nesbitt held up a shining gold sovereign. "Said I should work on your behalf till he comes home with Squire Joseph."

"And you consented? Without meeting us first?"

Nesbitt raised a brow and shrugged. "Sounded like an interestin' mix, ma'am. Molly and the rest."

Martin glared at him. "That could be the coin of Judas. How do we know it was Adam sent you? He doesn't say a thing about yourself in his letter. Mahon could've paid you off. You could've stole Adam's letter. You could be sent from Dublin Castle to spy on us. And sayin' our names? A parlor trick. Everyone in Galway knows Mad Molly. She's the most famous loon in Connaught. And as for Fern, it's no secret that she's bespoke to Adam. And then there's myself and Mary Elizabeth. Margaret. Old Flynn. Mahon knows us all." He clenched his fists. "How can we trust anyone now?"

Nesbitt rubbed his forehead in concern at the boy's challenge. "There's been talk you've had a run in with nightriders."

"That we have." Kate ignored Martin's objections.

"I don't hold with terrorizin' women and children."

Martin interrupted. "Are you Catholic—or one of them?"

"I'm Irish, lad. As Irish as Wolfe Tone," Nesbitt snapped, referring to the Protestant Irish leader of the Rebellion of '98. "You can see by my complexion I'm no Ulster Plantation Scotsman." The matter was settled in his mind and suddenly in Kate's, as well. Nesbitt turned a brooding eye on Martin. "I'd like to serve your sister, and I'll do it with or without your approval. But you've got fire enough in your belly that I'd like you as an ally." To Kate he added, "I'll bring a few stout lads along with me, ma'am."

"But I can't pay . . ."

"Claddagh boys. Big lads. Brothers. A quartet of them. Built like oaks. Fishermen they were. Out of work. Love a ding-dong fray, they do. And hungry enough that two meals a day and a corner in the stable will be pay enough. They've taken the temperance pledge of Father Mathew. Liquor does not touch their lips. Single men whose mother is long dead. No one to worry about them. If there's to be a fight with Mahon, we'll need men without farms to lose or wives and children to care for."

Each morning Kate rose before dawn to milk the cows as she had done at home. She congratulated herself that the sickness that came upon many women when they were with child had not come upon her. It was, she mused, as if a lifetime of conditioning herself to a full day's labor before the sun came up had caused her body not to acknowledge morning.

It was a half-hour before daylight. The breath of the cows rose up in a vapor, making a haze in the stone dairy barn. Kate and Martin moved from cow to cow, filling buckets silently and methodically.

Three times Kate emptied the bucket into the tin receptacle and all was well. Then, as she stooped to lift the fourth, a wave of nausea swept over her. The rocks in the walls seemed to move. She clutched the handle of the bucket and leaned against the warm brown hide of the moilie.

She felt a hand on her shoulder. The voice of Nesbitt surprised her.

"How far along are you, ma'am?" he asked gently. "Three months?"

"Past three . . ." So he knew.

"It comes on some women sooner and some later. Well, then. Fern and Margaret can manage until the Claddagh boys arrive."

"What . . ." She spoke haltingly. "You're up early."

"I've been standin' watch. Those scruffy-lookin' chaps by the gate, you know. If they decide to come over . . ." He left the thought unfinished, but Kate was comforted. His hand briefly touched her arm. "Not fittin' for you to be tendin' all this, ma'am. The boys will learn dairyin' fine when Martin shows them. Never worry. Milk cows love the sound of the Gaelic tongue, I'm told. And add a ration of cheese and butter for their bread, and one Claddagh man will work like ten."

The very presence of Nesbitt on the grounds of Burke Park caused uneasiness among the trio of Mahon's thugs who watched outside the gates.

As an administrator, Nesbitt was an able man. He organized the servants and workers in their daily affairs like the crew of a ship. Within a week even the stubborn Old Flynn was calling him "Sir," and telling him that yes, indeed, he would welcome the help of the Claddagh boys in the stable. Fern and Margaret, who tended the dairy herd each night and morning, grumbled to Martin that there was much more to cheese and butter than they cared to know and said how glad they would be when Nesbitt hired on those Claddagh boys to do the work.

At last the day came for the scheduled arrival of the foursome. Martin and Mary Elizabeth had, at Kate's direction, packed a supply of cheese and butter for Father O'Bannon, as was the weekly custom. The two children were in the kitchen with Fern, Margaret, and Molly.

"It's too long to walk," Mary Elizabeth complained.

Martin knew the truth. His sister did not want to miss the arrival of the strangers. "It's no farther to walk from here back to Ballynockanor than it was to walk from Ballynockanor to here."

Mary Elizabeth considered this. "But what if they come on the Galway mailcoach?"

"They'll sail." Molly looked out the window toward the sky. She chuckled.

"They won't sail here from there," Fern chided.

"They're sailors, ain't they now?" the old hag intoned.

"Fisherfolk." Margaret sniffed authoritatively. "Folk from Claddagh speak only the Gaelic. Hate the English. If you ask me, when Mister Nesbitt said they was Claddagh boys I felt much better about himself."

"Aye." Molly winked at Mary Elizabeth. "Seen a man from Claddagh gut an English sergeant like guttin' a mackerel outside a pub in Galway City when I went t'visit me dear, Annie Rose Field." She capered a bit at that. "They hanged him too."

"The dead Englishman?" Mary Elizabeth tried to imagine such a thing.

Mad Molly snorted. "Nay, child! They buried the Englishman. They hanged the Claddagh man. Then they buried him, too, so's it came out even." She began to hum. "They boxed up the Englishman like a tin of biscuits and shipped him home. The Claddagh man had a proper wake at least. His sister sang the saddest keen. Made even Annie Rose shed a bucket of tears." And now she began to sing off-key,

> *Is arriu!*
> *Agus a leanbh*
> *Cad a dheanfaidh me?*
> *Oh child of mine,*
> *And what shall I do?*
> *You've been gone such a long time*
> *'Sariu!*

"Take your keenin' out of my kitchen, Molly," Margaret snapped. "'Tis bad luck to keen when no one's dead and loved ones are away. Adam and the squire too. You'll call ill luck upon them."

Fern, thinking of Adam Kane, daubed her eyes with her apron. "Life ain't the same without Adam," she whimpered.

Molly scoffed. "Adam Kane? A fine, lusty lad. Healthy as a horse.

Why worry? Why worry? He's likely met some pretty wee thing in Shalamazamba and settled down. But he ain't dead. Not that one."

This pulled Fern from her maudlin thoughts with a jerk. She glared at Molly. "You may look mad as a hatter, but underneath you've got the tongue of . . . of an adder." She stomped out of the kitchen as Molly's cackle pursued her.

"Mad as a hatter! Tongue of an adder! Nay! No snakes allowed in Ireland! Ask Saint Patrick!"

With Molly thus preoccupied, Martin shouldered the pack and shoved Mary Elizabeth out the door, lest the old woman take it in her head to stroll along the entire four-mile distance to Father O'Bannon and St. John's.

16

Martin and Mary Elizabeth first saw the four brothers of Claddagh approaching from a distance on the road to St. John's.

"It's themselves," Mary Elizabeth said. "As Nesbitt told us."

At the sight of them Martin felt something akin to fear. Yet it was not fear, he reasoned. No. It was standing in an open field when the winds spring up and thunderheads roil above the Bens. It was hearing the thunder boom a mile behind him when he was almost home and safe. These men of Claddagh had that look about them: lightning, thunder, wind, and rain.

They were almost the same height—a half foot taller than Joseph, Martin figured. This put them nearly six feet, six inches tall, and as thick as the wrestler from Tuam named Tim Muldoon who could pin any man alive. They were hatless, and as Nesbitt had told Kate, their coloring named them. One called *Rusty* had a scorching red beard and hair. The next was as dark as a Spaniard. His name was *Moor*. The third was fair and sunburned. Blond hair was long and tied back at the neck. This was the one called *Sonny-boy*. Martin wondered if the spelling could be s-u-n-n-y? The last of the quartet was an ugly man. His hair and beard were a mousy brown. His brow was low and heavy, the under-jaw extended to give him an almost ape-like appearance. He was called *Simeon*.

They were dressed in the oiled coats of fishermen with red flannel shirts and knee-length corduroy breeches. In spite of the chill they wore no woolen stockings. Feet were shod with the thin leather shoes called *pampooties*. The look of poverty was in their clothing, but not their demeanor. Nor did they look ill-fed.

Mary Elizabeth spoke what Martin was thinking. "It'll take a lot of potatoes to feed men so big as them."

"That it will," Martin agreed, moving onto the side of the road as they strode past. Like a team of draft horses wearing blinders, they pressed on and seemed not to notice the children.

Martin chewed his lip and stared after them.

"Should we speak to them?" Mary Elizabeth asked.

"They speak only the Gaelic, Nesbitt says."

When they were twenty yards on, the hulk called Simeon swiveled his misshapen head to glower back at Martin and Mary Elizabeth.

Mary Elizabeth gave a tentative wave. The giant's face erupted into a broad grin. He waved back, gave a delighted hop, then turned eyes front and marched on without missing a step.

The provisions laid in at Tenerife disappeared much more quickly than expected. Captain Clarke's steward accused the cook of pilfering from the fruit and giving it to the sailors and guards. The cook, in turn, retorted that the steward could not be trusted with a brass farthing, since the chickens the steward had purchased laid no eggs.

The store of *soft tack*, as bakery bread was called at sea, also vanished faster than planned. Many loaves were spoiled with gnawed places and polluted with rat droppings. Once again accusations flew back and forth, but no word of this conflict went immediately to the captain. Since his table always received the best of whatever remained in the stores, only the convicts immediately suffered.

The loss of foodstuffs was more repugnant because everyone had seen so much provender brought aboard. Shortly after leaving the Canaries, the prisoners were again eating hard tack, salt beef, and oat porridge. The grumbling about the food, largely quelled by the stop at Tenerife, returned much louder and more insistent than before.

Gann flogged two of the more vocal complainers for insubordination. He commented that prisoners were lucky to be fed at all and had no rights of protest.

The harsh discipline forced the angry feelings to simmer more softly, but did nothing to correct the problem.

Even when a woman convict opened a cask in preparation for boiling the morning gruel and found a whole nest of rats inside and the meal contaminated, Gann sharply ordered the clamor to cease. Father Talbot petitioned that the spoilage be shown to the captain, but this was refused.

"You can eat what's provided, or you can go hungry," Gann said. "It's a matter of indifference to me. But you will not open another keg till that one is used up, and you will not bother the captain with such drivel, or I'll have you whipped again, and this time you won't get off so easy."

It was in the middle of an otherwise peaceful night that Laurence O'Halloran woke up with a piercing pain in his right ear. Since after the convicts were bedded down each night the lights belowdecks were extinguished, the boy brushed at his head without seeing what caused the sudden stab. His hand encountered a lumpy, furry body with a long scaly tail. Far from being frightened away, the rodent bit down hard on O'Halloran's finger, making the boy shout louder.

Pen Brophy, who was sleeping next to Laurence, awoke raging at the world every morning anyway. He was even more hostile when roused at night, and his temper shot to new heights when he jerked upright, bashing his head into the bunk above. Brophy laid about him with his fists, pummeling Joseph and Patrick Frayne in his rage before seizing the rat.

Brophy launched the rat at the far bulkhead with such force that the impact broke the creature's neck. This would have been the end of the incident, were it not for the fact that Brophy swung his feet down to the deck and in so doing stepped on two more rodents.

The resulting uproar brought Gann, in his nightshirt and every bit as infuriated as Brophy, to the scene. The jailor had a lantern and three more armed guards backing him when he demanded the cause of the disturbance.

"Look here," Brophy said, shaking the limp body of the first creature at Gann's face. "Three pound if it's an ounce. It's bad enough they eats our vittles, but now they're gnawin' on us!"

"It's true," Joseph confirmed, turning O'Halloran's right cheek toward the lantern. "Look there." A trickle of blood oozed from an obvious bite mark on the boy's earlobe.

"We won't stand for it, see?" Brophy insisted. "Will we, mates?"

"No, by thunder," Frayne said, and a growl of agreement swept the compartment.

Gann seized a musket bearing a bayonet from a guard and stuck the point of the blade under Brophy's chin. "You will, by thunder, stand it," he corrected. "This is mutiny, Brophy. You'll have six dozen of the best tomorrow. And that goes for anyone else who wants to make trouble." Then, to the guards, he ordered, "This entire berth is to be locked down right now."

The hostile muttering increased, and the sentries looked anxious. The situation might have reached a flash point if there had not come a loud, female shriek from the stern cabin overhead where assistant governor Parker and his wife were lodged. The screech began at a certain note and climbed the scale in both pitch and volume, repeating this process over and over.

"Keep 'em covered," Gann said hastily, running off to investigate.

The remaining guards backed away to the ends of the compartment. Any shift of position or urge to scratch brought the instant swing of a gun muzzle.

In a few minutes Gann was back. He never explained anything to a convict and hated to ever justify his actions, but this time he was forced to. "Captain says no lockdown," he said gruffly. "Lantern to be left in the corridor and two guards to keep watch. Seems a rat got into Parker's bunk with 'em."

Contrary to Gann's threats, there was no flogging the following day. As each hundred came on deck for exercise, Captain Clarke addressed them.

"It has come to my attention that the *Hive* is infested."

There was some snickering at this phraseology, but Clarke was speaking with so much evident compassion that the ridicule was quickly stifled.

"Ordinarily I would not undertake to deal with this predicament before reaching port, but any further spoilage of foodstuffs would be unpleasant, and the increase of the pests represents a severe health hazard."

There was a hum of agreement at this frank assessment and even some "good-manning" by the convicts.

"Accordingly, here is what I propose," the captain continued. "We have aboard a quantity of sulfur. When lighted, the fumes will drive the rats out of the holds and berths and cabins. They can then be exterminated."

Widespread expressions of approval swept through the crowd.

"The drawback is that no one can remain below without risk of being stifled. Accordingly, all three hundred prisoners will be brought on deck at once while the operation is carried out. It will be cramped, but we will make the best of it."

Actual applause broke out, and Father Talbot raised his voice. "You can be sure we will cooperate fully," he said. "We thank you for acting so vigorously."

Still more cheering greeted these words. Joseph noticed that Patrick Frayne, Pen Brophy, and several of their closest associates were grinning even wider than the others.

With the arrival of Nesbitt and the Claddagh brothers, the omnipresent thugs in Castletown vanished.

A week passed, and Flynn had not seen Mahon's men lingering outside the gates or talking on the road to the British troopers who patrolled the highway three times a day.

The early morning was bright and cloudless. A hint of warmth was on the breeze. Kate bathed and dressed Tomeen in the kitchen, then announced she was going to confession and mass.

"Aye," remarked Fern dreamily. "My soul could use a good purge. Is Father O'Bannon comin' today, then?"

"I'm goin', I said," Kate explained.

"You don't mean goin'. Goin' to St. John's?" Margaret said, scrubbing harder on a skillet.

"Father O'Bannon has been bringin' mass to me twice a week. His bones are groanin' like rusty hinges. I'll not have him hobblin' all the long way from there to here this week."

Fern and Margaret exchanged dubious looks. Fern gathered up an armload of linens and slipped out. Kate heard her squeaking with an audible urgency and then the deeper voice of Nesbitt in response. "I'll dissuade her, my dear."

Kate tugged Tomeen's shirt over his head and buttoned the tiny pearl buttons as Nesbitt entered the kitchen.

"Don't say it," Kate warned.

"But ma'am, it's four long miles to Ballynockanor."

"This child'll not know what the inside of a church looks like if I don't take him. I've not had him with me to a proper mass since the house was burned. Little ones learn early, and I'll not have him a heathen before he's two."

"But ma'am, ye know it's not wise."

Kate kissed Little Tom on the head. "We're goin' to pray for Da."

"Ma . . ." Tomeen drooled.

"There, you see? Tom's all for it. The cold weather cripples Father O'Bannon so's he can barely kneel. It takes him the whole day to walk so far."

"I can't permit it."

"Since you and the brothers came, there's been no one about the place who isn't meant to be here. Even the Castletown men are terrified of offendin' one of them."

"The Claddagh boys are off cultivatin' that fallow field two miles east over the hill. I've got a meetin' with the smith at half-eleven to replace the hub on the carriage wheel. And another right after with Squireen Wilson about those ewes."

"I'm walkin'," Kate declared. "To church. Before my legs forget how."

Supported by a sling devised from her shawl, Kate carried Tom on her hip as she traipsed easily up the long slope toward St. Brigit's cross. It was the long way home from church by anyone's estimation, but Kate was in no rush to get back.

Noon mass had been joyful. The familiar smell of the musty old building and the echo of Father O'Bannon's prayers had been perfect. Kate felt the ease of her soul's homecoming.

Father O'Bannon had chided her for walking out unescorted, but only a touch. Truth to tell, he was grateful to be spared the long trek and overjoyed to see the baby so fit and pleasant.

"He's an easy child," Kate told him.

"So were ye, little Katie Donovan. Aye. Sweet-tempered like yourself, and he's lookin' more like ye every day."

His comment pleased Kate. She wanted to say, "Yes, Father, he is my own dear boy." But she held her peace and smiled.

Now wind ruffled the child's red curls. He raised his face and squinted happily at the blue sky. They had been inside too long! When they had last ventured out onto the grounds, the skies had been grey and forbidding, the weather too cold for a baby.

"It's spring, Tomeen," Kate explained. "We can't expect it to be like this every day for a while, but there's a promise in it."

The baby listened to her chatter contentedly. It felt right to have Tomeen there against her, to see him grinning up at her in adoration. He was her heart, her joy, the thing that made this separation from Joseph bearable. Kate spoke to him of birds that would soon fly home from the south and flowers that would bloom on the hillsides. And she spoke of Joseph's homecoming too. "You must remember your da, Tomeen. He loves you so, darlin'. He'll be back soon, and then there'll be no coldness in the clouds and the rain'll fall soft and warm against our faces."

At the summit, where the stone cross stood as sentinel over the green valley of Ballynockanor, Kate paused awhile. She spread her shawl and sat with Tom on the new grass. She unpacked a lunch of bread, butter, cold stirabout for Tom, and a jug of milk, which they shared.

He fell asleep with his head in her lap as she sat to overlook the dairy that had once been everything to her. The lime-washed walls of which she had once been so proud were scorched and blackened. The barn was a ruin. As if the earth knew the place to be no more fit for humans, the creeping vines were already claiming the walls.

But the valley! Green jewels beneath opaline clouds. The winding river reflected the brilliant azure of the skies. How unlike most other villages in Ireland this was! Joseph's father had a heart for his tenant farmers, just as Joseph had a heart for the people now. Clean, well-built stone cottages, tidy farms, and soundly mended fences were a sharp contrast to the stark poverty and drab mud huts of Mahon's tenants.

"God bless you, Tomeen. These people of Ballynockanor are your own folk. Your grandfather, who you're named after, lived there where that heap of stones is. And his grandfather and his before him. You'll grow to care for them as Joseph does." The thought came suddenly to her that perhaps Joseph would never be back. She closed her eyes and willed the fear to leave her, but it did not. What if it were true? How would she manage? What if she were left to raise Tom alone; how would she train him to become the kind of man a village like Ballynockanor must have to stay alive?

The nagging dread of that possibility robbed her of the sense of freedom she had felt only moments before. She was no longer Kate, the dairyman's daughter who lived peaceably in the cottage along the road through Ballynockanor. She had new responsibilities: facing an adversary who would tear down everything she loved and destroy the lives of those she loved. Mahon viewed this valley with a different eye. He looked at it with a scheme to destroy every house and break the fences of the pastures and fields. Cattle took precedence over people. Kate knew she would have to fight him while Joseph was away. And if Joseph was away forever? The worry came full circle.

With a heavy sigh she gathered up the bits of bread and spread them on the base of the cross for the birds.

Across a canyon and up another slope from St. Brigit's cross was a fairy rath. The hillside around the place was barren and grey, the circle of gnarled tree branches still so enmeshed in winter's desolate sterility that it seemed determined to hold back the coming of spring.

From the raised rampart of earth that marked the remnant of a Bronze Age settlement, Kirby and Scully examined Kate's picnic with Tomeen.

"Ain't that grand, Scully?" Kirby asked, mocking. "Ain't it just? We won't tell Squire, the colonel, just how easy this was, now will we?"

"Indeed we will not," Scully agreed. "He like to flayed us with his tongue last job. It'll take a heap of praises to grow my hide back, and I don't aim to mess it up."

"Come on, then," Kirby urged. "Daylight it may be, but there ain't nobody else in sight. Now's the time to settle accounts."

Regretfully Kate packed up the remains of lunch and prepared to go home. She longed to stay, but it would not do to worry Nesbitt or the others; it would be that much harder to get away the next time she needed solitude. Kate retied the shawl across her chest and shook the milk jug thoughtfully. There was just a swallow remaining, but Tomeen would likely want a drink when he woke from his nap. The curly-haired child was stretching even now.

"Ain't that a peaceful sight then?" said a voice behind her.

Kate spun round on her knees to see one of Mahon's thugs, the one with the mashed ears, approaching from one side of the stone cross. "Keep back, you," Kate said, hastily grabbing up the child and trying to keep hold of the milk jug also.

"That don't sound friendly, does it?" Kirby asked as a second hooligan emerged from the shadow on the opposite side of the monument. "Must be your ugly face, Scully," he added. "You're scarin' the missus. Course, she has no room to be castin' stones, now does she? Tell me, missy, did you get them burns when your last cottage burnt, or was it some other time?"

The two separated to encircle her. She turned to flee, but they were quicker and cut her off. From within the shawl sling Tomeen wailed his displeasure at the rude awakening. Kate backed away again until stopped by the stone marker. She brandished the milk jug. "Keep away," she repeated. Tomeen cried still louder.

"Taw, Scully. You hear that brat wailin'? Whose kid do y'think it is, then? Young Marlowe's? The traitor Burke's? If the truth were known, that red hair oughta be rainbow-colored for all the fatherin' that bastard had."

Kate smashed the container against the cross, leaving the neck as a handle for the jagged ceramic dagger in her hand. A stain of white milk spattered over the cross and dribbled downward.

"Feisty," observed Scully. "You can come easy or not," he suggested, "but come with us you will. Safer for you and the child to not force us to be rough."

Kate's voice was shaking as she vowed, "You shall not have this baby . . . now or ever."

"And who's to stop us?" Kirby questioned.

Kate raised her eyes toward the edge of the drop-off where the hill fell away toward Ballynockanor.

"That's a good trick, that is," Kirby snickered. "Makin' us think there's summat behind us."

The bass rumble of a clearing throat stopped Kirby's laughter.

Without looking at the source, he yelled to Scully, "Mind the woman!" and flung himself at the intruder.

The Claddagh lad known as Simeon sidestepped the rush like a bullfighter and chopped downward with his right hand as Kirby passed. The blow made Kirby stumble and then sprawl, plowing up grass with his nose. He rose at once, shouting for Scully to "Get the woman!"

Scully's single step forward changed to a leap back as Kate slashed the air with the spiked shard, narrowly missing Scully's face.

Kirby rushed Simeon again. Arms wide, he tackled the Claddagh man around the middle. To his surprise, Simeon gave ground easily, making Kirby overbalance. Simeon sank downward on his haunches and in the same motion lifted Kirby by the hips.

The next sensation Kirby experienced was of the top of his head being rammed into the earth. Simeon let go in gentlemanly fashion and stepped away.

When Kirby got up the third time he said, "What are you waitin' for, Scully? Give us a hand, then!"

The two thugs approached Simeon, one from each side, but their hearts were not in the struggle. When Scully arrived a fraction of a second before his mate, the Claddagh man grabbed him by his shirt-front and spun him violently into Kirby's stumbling charge. The pair of hooligans went down together.

When Simeon stepped toward them with his fists clenched and his face distorted with anger, he looked like a bear on the verge of breaking out of a cage. Kirby and Scully cast one more look at Kate, safely out of the way on the steps of St. Brigit's monument, and then fled down the hill.

"How did you find me?" Kate puffed, shushing the unhappy Tomeen and willing her pounding heart to do the same. She repeated the question in Irish.

In the Gaelic Simeon answered, "We drew straws. I have been following you all day."

17

Colonel Mahon was not known in Westport. Located where the river Carrowbeg flowed into Clew Bay, Westport was a day's ride across County Mayo for the Galway squire.

Still, he felt very comfortable there. The area owed its English settlement to King Henry the Eighth as he gifted it to a loyal follower named Browne. Two hundred years later a branch of this rootstock, still named Browne, founded the town of Westport. By the time of Mahon's visit, another century later, Westport was a tidy, landlord-friendly community where Mahon could be among his own kind.

Mahon would have been welcomed at Westport House, the limestone and marble seat of the present Lord Browne, Earl of Altamont, but that was not where he chose to go. Instead Mahon's path took him toward the estuary of the river, to a small cove containing a single rundown pub named *Molloy's.*

The inlet, not marked on any map, could well have been designated *Smuggler's Cove.* Within the dim smoky recesses of Molloy's, web-like schemes were spun for the duty-free importation of such contraband as French wines and other, less benign substances. Despite the fact that Mahon and all the English landlords swore their allegiance to the laws of the Crown, it also served both their appetites and purposes to bend those laws on occasion.

Molloy's represented the crossroads of international commerce of a sort. There Italian traders acquired Irish linen to exchange for South African ivory that had been purchased for Spanish gold in Morocco. It was very complex.

Mahon's commerce was much more straightforward. He was looking to hire some men to do a job, men who would ask no questions, leave no answers, and happily exit the country shortly after the duty was performed.

Molloy, the proprietor of the pub, a man who knew no color except gold and recognized no religion except greed, led Mahon to a corner table and left him with a pair of swarthy men of dark hair and furtive eyes.

"You are—" Mahon began.

"Please, *señor*," the taller of the two interrupted. "Without offense we prefer using only Christian names." Spreading his hands in a flowing gesture of Latin graciousness, he added, "If you know more, it is something that can be demanded of you later, yes?"

"Then how shall I refer to you?" Mahon asked.

"You may call me Iago," replied the original speaker, briefly flourishing a wicked-looking knife. "Him you may call Sebastian." The partner indicated formed his hands into a tight grip and compressed them like a very small collar.

Mahon nodded. Reaching under his riding cloak, he retrieved a leather pouch that made a satisfying *thud* when he tossed it on the table. Iago hefted it, peeked in, and observed, "Are you not afraid, *señor*, to bring so much gold into such a . . . disreputable place?"

"My own servants are outside," Mahon retorted. "Besides, we are both businessmen. That purse is just the earnest money if you accept my offer. But if you cross me, you will never see the rest."

Grins spread widely on both smugglers' faces. "Then this amount is . . . ?"

"One third of the proposal," Mahon explained. "The rest after the job is done."

"Tell us about this job," Iago said. "We grow interested."

"There is a woman," Mahon said.

"Ah, there is always a woman," Sebastian remarked, nodding sagely.

"This is a . . . a most inconvenient woman." Mahon leaned across the table and spoke still lower. He pushed over a scrap of paper. "All the details are there. Her name is Kate, Lady Burke. Her home is near Castletown in Galway. She and a small child—his name is Tom—they must both . . ."

"It is enough, *señor*," agreed Iago. "When?"

"As soon as possible."

"And the rest of the money?"

"To be left here with Molloy for collection after I send him word that the job was correctly done."

"*Muy bien*," concluded Iago. "It was . . . what is the English? It was very nice doing business with you. I could almost regret that we will never meet again."

Though the sea was calm and the winds so light that scarcely a breath ruffled the sails, the *Hive* resembled its namesake more than at any time during the voyage. The waist of the ship was stuffed with prisoners. There was not half enough room for them to sit, and so about two hundred stood, packed upright. Even without space to turn around there were still constant motion and agitation. In the already scorching heat of the forenoon sun, those convicts jammed in the middle of the deck struggled to get nearer to the rail for air, and those lining the port rail fought constantly with a shuffling of their leg chains to embrace the meager shade on the starboard side.

The prisoner population overflowed toward both ends of the ship. Another fifty convicts shared the deck around the foremast with the sailors.

Those remaining, including the women prisoners and infants, were allotted a portion of the quarterdeck, together with the ship's officers and passengers. This arrangement still left twenty-five convicts unaccounted for, and these men were mingled with the group that stood on the high steering platform at the aft end of the ship.

Joseph Burke, Father Talbot, and Pastor Holt were among these, as were O'Halloran, Frayne, and Brophy. The six men stood just aft of the wheel, jammed against the sternrail by the press. It was not a bad spot, Joseph thought. What breeze there was came from dead astern, and the water below was a cobalt blue, rivaling the cloudless heavens.

Despite the overcrowding and the sun, the most uncomfortable people on board the *Hive* were not in the throng of convicts. As six bells of the forenoon watch were struck, Assistant Governor Parker drew out his pocketwatch, cleared his throat, and remarked to his wife, "Eleven o'clock, my dear. This won't take very long."

Unlike the women convicts in their simple prison shifts, Mrs. Parker was swathed from head to toe in yards of cloth and imprisoned by whalebone stays. Rather than abandon a single dictate of fashion, she was faint with the heat and oppressed by being surrounded by criminals.

"Andrew," she hissed to her husband, "how utterly repulsive this is! I cannot turn round without actually touching and being touched by some of these . . . these felons. Do something." Everywhere she turned, Mrs. Parker was being stared at, studied, and all too obviously discussed. It was not proper; it was not dignified. Fanning her fevered cheeks, she said again, "Do something."

Nor was Mrs. Parker the only person suffering uneasiness. The ten guards, normally ample to watch over small groups of prisoners or keep order among larger gatherings of chained men, were woefully inadequate for the present circumstance. The sentries were posted around the outside of the mass of convicts. Six of them were balancing on the railing and clinging precariously to the rigging. Two more hung from the backstays, and the remaining two looked like uncomfortably graceless figureheads as they rode the bowsprit. Despite their uniforms and muskets, all seemed ridiculously impotent. They were fleas riding a bull mastiff, and both sides knew it.

Compensation for this imbalance existed in one form only: Captain

Clarke manned a swivel gun mounted on a platform on the starboard rail. Under the watchful eye of a lone sentry, a similar cannon loaded with powder and a canister of lead balls glowered on the port side, awaiting the return of Jailor Gann.

Gann was at that moment belowdecks in the lowest and foulest area of the bilge, lighting a pan heaped with a mound of sulfur. Rats, some of them grown big as cats, arrogantly studied his actions without even twitching their whiskers.

"Rather run the convicts over the side and keep the honest rats," Gann muttered to himself as he ignited the pile of yellow powder. Waiting only to see that the chemical was well alight, Gann moved quickly along to the next tray and the next, working his way upward through holds and cabins as he went.

Had there been an observer on another ship within a quarter mile of the *Hive*, the preposterous appropriateness of its name would have been so complete as to provoke comment. No more than a quarter hour after Gann ignited the first heap of sulfur, thick, oily smoke poured out of every hatchway and ventilation shaft. The fumes were so dense as to force their way up through gaps in the deck planking and flow out through the scuppers like dirty water. The resemblance to a swarm of bees being smoked out of its habitation was flawless.

The prisoners amidships had new priorities. Instead of hunting shade, the choking convicts wanted to be as far as possible from the rotten-egg aroma of the venting plumes, even if it meant more crush than before.

The quarterdeck, thanks to the direction of the wind, was relatively free from discomfort, but from the mizzenmast forward, all was enveloped in the strangling vapors. Mrs. Parker plunged her nose into a lilac-water-scented kerchief and complained noisily about the smell.

The first rats appeared on deck at about the same time that the smoke first poured out of the stern gallery windows. These less hardy rodents were swatted into the sea by convicts, who made a game of noting how far the animals sailed through the air and wagered on the size of the splashes.

The mood changed abruptly when the rats increased in both size and numbers. Hundreds of the creatures chittered and twitched their frenzied way among the feet of the prisoners, masked by the low-lying smoke. Seeking to climb beyond the fumes, the rats would have been in the rigging if shields had not already been in place to prevent this. The result was that panicked rats climbed convict legs and clawed up convict backsides. It was an experience only funny when happening to someone else, and in no more than three minutes the exposure was universal.

Gann was again at his post at the breech of the swivel cannon when Mrs. Parker shrieked. When a pair of rats dashed into the sheltering folds of her dress, all maintenance of dignity was lost. Yelling "Help, Andrew, help!" Mrs. Parker began shedding clothing as rapidly as possible, aided by genuinely sympathetic women convicts. Parker revolved in place in agitated ineffectiveness, while Joseph and Laurence O'Halloran assisted the female prisoners in protecting the infant children and plucking rats from backs and hair.

That was the moment when Pen Brophy and his conspirators struck. As if Mrs. Parker's scream had been a prearranged signal, Brophy seized Andrew Parker from behind and caught the assistant governor's neck in the crook of his burly right arm.

All over the ship similar tackles were being enacted. In the seemingly random movements of the convicts, Brophy's accomplices had managed to place themselves within striking distance of every guard.

Captain Clarke was dragged from his place without even touching the lanyard of the cannon. One moment he was kicking a rat overboard, and the next he was grabbed about the middle and flung face downward on the deck.

The sentries lining the rails were similarly seized, clubbed, and disarmed, except for one at the stern who grappled with a convict in leg irons and both toppled into the sea, never seen to rise. Of the two guards on the bowsprit, one fired a shot that struck a convict in the face, then missed his footing and plunged into the sea to swim amid the rats. The other guard forward fired a shot that hit nothing, then threw his musket into the waves and set about climbing the rigging to escape. The forecastle was a mass of fighting as unarmed and outnumbered ship's crew were set upon by prisoners.

Jailor Gann was the only officer of the company who remained entirely calm. With a composure born of his total disregard for human life, he jerked the lanyard of the swivel gun and blew a half-dozen convicts into bloody pieces. Those who were nearest the weapon clawed and fought to get away, giving Gann time to ram another charge down the barrel. But before he could add the canister he was swarmed by convicts, pummeled into senselessness, and would have been heaved over the side if the entire battle had not been interrupted by a loud demand from Pen Brophy. "Captain Clarke," Brophy yelled. "Tell your men to stop fightin', or I will kill Parker here."

As he said the words, he tightened his grip on the assistant governor's neck so that Parker's shout of agreement came out a strangled squeak. It was Mrs. Parker, disheveled and weeping, who bellowed, "Do as he says, Captain, please!"

"Stop fighting!" Clarke ordered.

With Patrick Frayne at the helm and Pen Brophy supervising the roundup of the guards who were now prisoners, the takeover of the *Hive* was complete.

Two guards, beaten to death, were dumped over the side, together with the remains of the convicts slaughtered by cannon and musketfire. One guard and two convicts were rescued from the ocean. The rats had been dispatched, and the sulfur fires had burned themselves out.

The members of the conspiracy gathered around Pen Brophy on the quarterdeck. Most of the transportees were pleased with the successful escape attempt and shook their fists at Gann and Parker and jeered, telling them they would soon be food for sharks. Still more of those who had not been in on the secret plan to import rats at

Tenerife and release them on the ship huddled together. They were as frightened of their former comrades as they had been of the former captors.

"This cannot turn out well," whispered Father Talbot to Joseph. "They mean to begin by murderin' their oppressors, and they will end by slaughterin' each other. Look there."

Joseph, Talbot, and Holt formed a tiny semicircle of protection around Captain Clarke, Parker and his wife, and the body of an unconscious guard. The priest gave a slight flutter of one hand toward where Frayne and Brophy argued at the ship's wheel.

"You told me you could con a ship!" Brophy shouted, thumping the binnacle that housed the compass with a belaying pin. "'Many's the voyage I have made,' you said! Now when we *have* the ship, you admit you cannot do it! I should knock you down for lyin'!" He half raised the club to strike.

The northeast breeze, which had been rising steadily, pushed against the *Hive* just as Frayne let go of the spokes. The ship heeled away from the puff of wind and wallowed in the sea, making Brophy stagger. "And how far will you get without me at the helm and to make sail?" Frayne challenged. "I never said I could navigate. That's officers' doin's. I can reef, hand, and steer, and I know how to box the compass, but charts are Greek to me altogether."

"Do any of you coves know how to navigate?" Brophy asked the convicts. There were none who could, or at least none who would admit the ability.

"How hard can it be?" challenged Dawson, a big ruffler from Ulster. "The whole wide Africa coast lies east. Put her nose on the risin' sun, and we'll bump into it."

"And the whole blinkin' Royal Navy, too, you shoneen clot. We need a port for provisions and water and a way to get back to . . ." Brophy's words stopped abruptly as if catching himself from betraying a secret. "All right, then," he resumed. "We'll keep Clarke alive to navigate for us, and we'll kill these and any who oppose us."

"Then you must kill me as well," spoke up Father Talbot. "For I'll not stand by and see cold-blooded murder done."

"Nor me," echoed Joseph and Pastor Holt.

"And I won't help you," Clarke said firmly. "Listen to me," he cried, raising his voice to its usual volume of command. "Many of you have only seven-year sentences and might be paroled in four. Piracy and murder are hanging offenses. Give this up now, and I promise only the leaders will be punished."

"Shut up!" Brophy shouted, striking the captain on the arm with the club. "And any of the rest of you what don't want to follow us can swim for it!"

Brophy might have killed the officer had Frayne not stopped him, saying, "Don't, Pen. We need him!"

Clarke gritted his teeth, cradled his right arm, but spoke again. "Kill anyone, and you must kill me as well. But I will make a deal with you. I will guide you to a French-held port if you will spare everyone else."

"Don't trust him," Dawson argued. "He'll lead us straight to the navy."

"Not if we keep Missus Parker as hostage," Brophy said. Parker, still massaging his throat, protested, but Brophy backhanded him into silence. "If we raise so much as one union jack, she dies. Understand, Captain?"

Clarke agreed to do as the convicts demanded.

"All right then," Brophy concluded. "We won't kill the others, but we can't be bothered with guardin' 'em. We'll set 'em adrift. All except him." Brophy extended the belaying pin toward the trussed-up form of Jailor Gann. "Him we're goin' to flog to death."

Gann was blubbering when they strung him up between a pair of mainmast backstays. "Don't let them kill me! Ah, God, I don't want to die." The jailor was suspended so that the tips of his toes barely brushed the deck. Except for a pair of linen underdrawers, he was naked.

Stripping to the waist, Pen Brophy shook out the cords of a cat and took up position on Gann's left. Brophy's own back was criss-crossed with old scars—the imprint of a life's worth of whippings.

"I need a left-handed man to share in this," he said. "One of the refinements practiced on me in Dublin was two floggers at once, takin' turns. O'Halloran, what about you?" Brophy extended the handle of Gann's own whip toward the boy.

Laurence O'Halloran stretched out his left hand to take the scourge when Father Talbot said quietly, "Don't do it, boy. Do you want to be as bad as he?"

"Go on," Brophy urged. "You would kill a mad dog, wouldn't you? Do the world a service."

Joseph Burke struggled within himself. He wanted to take the whip. He wanted to slash Gann's back. Each blow would have counted for another hardship: there's for my wedding, and there's for the dungeon, there's for my flogging, and most of all, there's for Kate and her needless grief. He moved forward a step, the battle between unsatisfied revenge and his deepest self warring inside him.

O'Halloran touched the knob of the grip, then dropped his eyes to the deck and his hand to his side. He stepped back and hid himself in the crowd.

Brophy's lip curled. "Is there no man among you lot of worms?"

Five other convicts, faces darkening with hatred and narrowed eyes foreshadowing the torture they were ready to inflict, pushed through the crush. Nothing could spare Gann's life, it seemed. Not even Captain Clarke would risk anything further to save the man.

Father Talbot stepped forward. "I have a greater right to this than any of you," he said, grabbing the handle of the whip offered O'Halloran. The convict crowd murmured its concurrence. "I am the one who holds the title to Gann's debt. Give me the place."

Looking doubtful, Brophy reluctantly parted with the cat and stepped away from the whimpering guard. "Know this," Talbot said to the mob. "You are embarked on a course that will end with many of you in much worse condition than you were before. Some of you may die. But if you stand by and watch murder be done, then I will give evidence against you myself."

"What!" Brophy shouted, leaping at the priest. "I gave no leave to be preachin'!" Joseph intercepted the lunge, and the two men struggled for possession of the whip.

When Joseph and Pen Brophy had wrestled to a stalemate, Joseph was eye-to-eye with the man. "He is also mine," Joseph said through clenched teeth. "He marked me back in Spanish Arch prison, took me from my family, beat me for no reason, and now he belongs to me."

"Take him then, and welcome," Brophy sneered. "Get them out of here!" he ordered. "Guards and whipped curs into the boats."

As the boats were lowering, two hurried conferences took place on the quarterdeck of the *Hive*. One concerned Captain Clarke and Joseph. The other was among Talbot, Holt, and Laurence O'Halloran.

"I must keep my crew with me, or the *Hive* would not swim a single day," Clarke apologized to Joseph, "and the women and children would be lost. They will let me give you neither chart nor compass. The best I can do is advise you to keep company with the other boat. Our position is about five hundred miles south of the Cape Verde Islands. If you beat back into the trades you can perhaps reach them or the Guinea coast. The current will be pushing you south. You have water and ship's biscuit enough for ten days. After . . ." Clarke shrugged. "We are not far outside the shipping lanes. You should get picked up soon. God go with you."

"And you," Joseph returned. "You are a good man, Captain, and I hope we meet again under better circumstances."

Across the deck, past where Frayne held the tiller and Brophy kept watch over Gann and the other former guards, the two clergymen argued with the young O'Halloran.

"You must not stay with these pirates, Laurence," Talbot urged the boy. "Brophy is not the only cutthroat aboard. He and his kind will destroy each other till only one remains."

"You must go, boy," Henry Holt said, adding his entreaty to that of his friend.

"But what about you?" O'Halloran asked.

Holt and Talbot exchanged a look of resignation. "I will stay to keep the peace I can and urge restraint," Holt admitted. "Father

Talbot would have stayed aboard, but he is needed to care for the wounded guard."

"I need your help, Laurence," Talbot entreated. "I can trust you." Laurence O'Halloran nodded slowly. "I will go," he said. "No one has ever needed and trusted me before."

The wind was rising as Joseph climbed down a rope ladder hanging from the side of the *Hive*. The small boat into which he stepped was already crowded with men. The wounded and semiconscious guard, Kirkland, lay curled in the bottom at the bow. Father Talbot and Laurence O'Halloran shared a thwart, as did Jailor Gann and the ship's surgeon, White. The stern was occupied by a one-armed convict named John Hoyle, who absolutely refused to stay with the likes of Brophy; he said he'd rather take his chances with the ocean. This was the reduced body of men to whose company Joseph was committed.

The other larger ship's boat lay alongside, rocking in the swells. It was filled with the remaining guards and Assistant Governor Parker. Above them, at the rail, Mrs. Parker screeched for her husband not to abandon her.

After trying to explain that he was being forced to go and that he would return with help, Parker had given up speech. He no longer even looked up at her cries. Eventually Pastor Holt led her away.

Pen Brophy leaned over the port side and spat between the two craft. "Good sailin' to you," he said mockingly. "I wonder how many days it'll be before your tongues blacken and your eyes burn out of your skulls? Then you'll wish I had been merciful and hanged you all. Especially you, Joseph Burke," he remarked. "I thought you were a sensible man and a right'un, but speakin' up for Gann . . ." Brophy shrugged.

"And you," Father Talbot stated, stretching out his finger to point it between Brophy's eyes, "you are responsible for the lives of women and children. God is watchin'."

"Bah!" Brophy spat again. "Cast off!" There were two splashes as the ropes connecting the watercraft hit the waves. At once a gap appeared between the *Hive* and the two frail rowboats as the ship made sail. Within half an hour she had left the castaways far astern and within an hour was hull down over the horizon.

The boat Joseph joined had been the captain's gig. Light of weight, the craft was narrower than the launch to which the rest of the exiles were consigned. He had heard a sailor call the slighter vessel "clinker built," referring to its construction of overlapping planks clenched together with copper nails. Despite its seven occupants it rode very high in the water.

As Joseph sat in the stern next to the tiller, everyone else looked to him for direction. "We must try to keep together with the launch," he said. "We both stand a better chance that way. Let us set about hoistin' the sail."

"And who gave you leave to give orders, croppie?" groused the nearly naked Gann. "Only the doctor outranks me, and drunk as he is, he's in no condition to make decisions. I'm in charge here."

"Man, man," chastised Father Talbot. "Have ye no soul a'tall? Did not Lord Burke save you from bein' killed? And you beggin' to be spared?"

"I am the Queen's officer," said Gann. "And he is still my prisoner. It is my sworn duty to see him delivered to the proper authorities. And you and O'Halloran and Hoyle there, too, come to that. All you've done is keep your necks clear of the noose a bit longer. You are no less guilty of your other crimes, and you are bound to pay in full."

"You are unbelievable," commented Laurence O'Halloran, asserting himself at last. "How can one man have so much blackness in his soul?"

Gann broke into a grin. "Do y'wish you'd let them flay me? I never ask favors of no convicts, and I won't take lip from you either. Now raise that mast, O'Halloran, and get ready to jump when I say."

The sergeant of the guards who was in charge of the other boat directed the launch to row alongside. "What now, Mister Gann?" he asked.

"We head east," Gann replied. "Backs to the sun as it sets. Keep us in sight and show a light at your masthead all night. And hand me that caulkin' mallet." The other guard passed over a wooden hammer used to repair leaky seams. Jailor Gann squinted his remaining eye at the tool and hefted its weight. "Now," he said with satisfaction, "things are gettin' squared away again. Give me your shirt, Hoyle, and your trousers, priest. Better you burn than me."

Adam Kane had recovered part of the appetite he thought he had thrown overboard, but part of him realized that bagpipes would always and forever make him nauseous. Second Mate MacDougall scowled and made noises that sounded like a catarrh of the throat every time the Burke steward came in sight, so apparently the ill feelings ran both ways.

In any case, Kane was able to walk about the deck of the *Blossom* with only minimal discomfort to his stomach, provided he focused on the horizon and not on nearby rolling and pitching.

It was this constant scrutiny of the distant boundary between sky and sea that caused Kane to notice the smoke. Just at twilight one evening he was pacing the leeward side of the quarterdeck and noted a thin trickle of black, like a dark thread only noticeable because it looked out of place against a pale blue fabric. He called it to the attention of Captain Costello. "Do you see that smoke, there, Captain?" he asked.

Costello could not make it out, but he called to the lookout, "Aloft, there! What do you see bearing sou-sou-west?"

There was a pause during which both men on the deck could see the lookout at the crosstrees peering away in the direction specified. A moment later his disembodied voice floated downward, "Below. Smudge of smoke, but it's gone now. No vessel in sight."

The last vestige of turquoise faded into violet, and no trace of the mysterious fumes remained. "Could it be a steamship, Captain," Kane asked, "and no concern of ours a'tall?"

Costello pondered as though mentally reviewing a chart, then shook his head. "Doubtful," he said. "We're out of any likely shipping lanes. No, nor whaler either with his try-pots smokin'—not in these waters. Shall we follow?"

Kane weighed the possibility that the enigmatic smoke was somehow connected to the *Hive* and wondered if his choice would take him in exactly the wrong direction from Joseph Connor Burke. "Could it be a ship in distress?" he inquired.

"That it could," was the response.

"Then follow," Kane stated, his mind made up.

"Helmsman! Sou-sou-west!"

∽ 18 ∽

Colonel Mahon sat atop his second favorite chestnut gelding on the hill overlooking the part of his lands that included the village of Stokestown. Slipe Creek, barely ten feet across at the wettest of wet seasons, was this year completely dry already. It forecast a difficult time sowing the oat crop. The potatoes would undoubtedly be scrawny and unnourishing too. Mahon was pleased.

"Do you see there, O'Shea?" Mahon said to his neighbor landlord, Squireen O'Shea. When O'Shea did not instantly look in the desired direction, Mahon slapped a riding crop against the calf of his hightop leather boot and used the whip as a pointer. "There," he repeated impatiently. "See those women dragging the load of turf? Slatternly creatures. I cannot fathom how their menfolk can stand to touch them."

O'Shea, given to bowing to Mahon's every opinion, bobbed his agreement, even though he still did not grasp the implication. "Aye," he said, "and their passel of children. There must be ten or twelve leapin' around that sledge like . . . like . . ."

"Like fleas!" Mahon concluded savagely. "And like the fleas in the old saw, I shall burn down the house to kill them. See here, O'Shea: there are only three things the Irish peasant succeeds at producing: potatoes, children, and trouble."

O'Shea thought to himself that whiskey and music belonged on the list as well, but he was not about to interrupt the man who was also his own landlord in the matter of some subleased property.

Mahon continued, "I have been patient far too long. You know I have carried a Hanging Gale . . . past-due back rents . . . for three full years and more. Well, no longer! My prize Angus bulls imported from Scotland have been doing their duty; come next fall I will have a tidy herd in need of grazing. Ten acres per animal to do it properly. Stokestown will have to go and soon, so whatever rain we do get will be for grass and not prattie patch and oats!"

Naming the two crops with so much venom made O'Shea regret having eaten oatmeal stirabout for breakfast.

"But what if they scrape together enough to pay the arrears?" O'Shea asked. "You know paddies." Here O'Shea added a conspiratorial wink to prove that he was not a paddy, though Irish-born and Catholic. "They keep back a portion hid in their chimneys or buried in . . ." The angry gleam that sprung into Mahon's eye reminded O'Shea that Joseph Connor Burke had defeated a part of Mahon's grand strategy by exactly such an incident. O'Shea gulped the foggy air and hurried on. "What I mean is, might they not settle up with ye?"

Mahon flourished a folded sheaf of papers from the flapped pocket of his long riding coat. "As a condition of extending the rent three years ago, I had their possessions inventoried. The list is updated annually. Just listen: in all of Stokestown's two hundred families they have, in total . . ." Here Mahon put on his best imitation of forelock-pulling, poteen-drinking, turf-fire-reeking, bog Irish: "One plough, Your Worship, five shovels, Your Excellency, eight rakes, Your Highness, two table forks, twenty-five chairs, sixty-seven stools, one feather bed, two chaff beds, two turkeys, nine geese, one pocketwatch, no looking glass above three pence in value, and four square feet of window glass."

Parenthetically he added, "There was one clock, but it was sold for six pence a year ago to satisfy another loan."

With O'Shea clucking in commiseration at what a hard lot it was for a landlord to have such miserable failures as tenants, Mahon continued, "They don't even possess one wheeled wagon, not so much as a cart. Haul everything on those contemptible sleds. If they had so much as a single spare shilling, do you think they would be living like, no, worse than, barn rats? Not likely! With this year's dim prospects they won't even give me any trouble. Out they go!"

"How soon will you toss 'em?"

"As soon as my gang of dockyard toughs gets here. I have a contact in Galway City to supply me with all the hard cases I need."

The gang of twoscore destructives, including Kirby and Scully, recruited from the dockyards of Galway City to do the evictions for Colonel Mahon, laughed when they saw the village of Stokestown. "What d'we need axes and ropes for?" Kirby inquired. "I could blow 'em down with one breath!"

"Aye," his fellow tough, Scully, agreed. "So you could. But the object is to pull down only the houses and not be killin' all the people at the same time."

Kirby knocked the already dented bowler hat off Scully's head. "And why not?" he challenged. "These miserable sods look like they'd be better off dead. They've been livin' in graves already."

The cottages that made up the majority of homes in Stokestown were built of mud brick to the height of a man, then roofed with grey, tired-looking thatch. The floors were universally dirt—and loose dirt at that. The timbers above the single-roomed structures sagged so badly that many a cabin appeared to have already been demolished, except for the fact that a slender feather of turf smoke still plumed from the chimney.

"This will be an easy way to earn a shillin' or two," Kirby added. "And no regrets neither. Not like pullin' down that whitewashed Mulrooney cottage for Old Marlowe—him that's barkin' mad now. Well, come on. Let's get to it."

The families of Stokestown had been advised to be ready to leave. There was barely enough spark of life force to keep them breathing from one day to the next, certainly not enough for resistance. Besides, they knew their man: since Colonel Mahon had promised they would be tossed on that particular day, most of them had been packed since midnight.

Outside the first cabin, a family of fourteen stood beside a single slipe—a wheel-less contraption constructed of two stick rails and a base bound with rushes. The reed-work sides of this sled contained all that was precious to the household: an elderly grandmother and three infant children.

"Right," Kirby warned. "Off you go then." The family arranged itself into a pathetic procession, marching ahead, dragging the slipe and trailing after. There were no tears, but one dirty-faced young girl pulled away from her mother's hand and ran back inside. She emerged a moment later with a frayed red hair ribbon. "None of that, now, none of that," Kirby challenged. "Don't be takin' nothin' what belongs to the landlord." The girl ducked her head and ran after the retreating forms of her kin. Kirby studied the greasy lace, then tucked it into his shirt pocket.

A crew of fifteen destructives wielding axes and hammers reduced the cabin to a pile of crumbled clay and straw within fifteen minutes. Colonel Mahon, having just arrived on the scene, supervised the proceedings from horseback.

"Shall we save the roof timbers, Your Worship, sir?" Kirby asked.

Mahon sniffed. "Full of a century of peat smoke? Who would want them? Torch the heap, O'Meara. These rabbits will creep back into their warren if any wall is left standing."

"Right you are, Your Worship," Kirby said, knuckling his forehead and laughing. "That's a good one, rabbits is. No creepin' back to be permitted."

The first of the tenants tossed from Mahon's lands passed the iron gates of Burke Park just after sunup. Martin and Mary Elizabeth climbed the oak tree and watched them from the shelter of the gnarled branches. It was a sight unlike anything Martin had ever seen before. He hoped he would never see it again.

There had been other wanderers traipsing along the road through Ballynockanor. Usually they passed as a solitary family: husband, wife, a band of ragged children. In the days of the Donovan dairy, Kate had passed food over the fence. Milk for the children, potatoes, bread, cheese had been offered before it was asked for. She believed that there was no blessing in giving to the needy if the needy put out their hand and begged for it. Every stranger—man, woman, or child—who passed had been blessed with a meal.

But today! How could so many be fed? The people came on up the highway in an endless ragged stream from Mahon's lands. The stronger of the refugees pulled slipes heaped with mounds of household goods, the elderly, and very small children. The people were thin and dirty. Clothes hung in tatters. The faces of children were gaunt and ashen. At first glance it was difficult for Martin to tell who was young and who was old among the company. Starvation had given them all a haunted, ancient appearance.

There was talk that one thousand souls were evicted from Stokestown. It looked to Martin as though there were many more. From the front of the column, the suffering mass stretched over the hill into Castletown and disappeared.

At half past six that morning, Kate commanded that the gates of the park be unlocked and opened. Father O'Bannon appeared on the scene minutes later.

Old Flynn ran shouting from the stables, "Who opened the gates? Strangers! Steward Kane gave orders! No strangers!"

Kate grasped his arm, inclined her head toward a starving child of about four years, and whispered something in his ear that shamed him to silence.

Obediently Flynn helped Fern, Margaret, and Molly prepare porridge in the huge copper laundry kettles. No one in need would be turned away, Kate declared. Everyone was in need.

Mary Elizabeth began counting when the first travelers received their meals at half past seven that morning. She quit counting two hours later when the number was more than eight hundred. Hungry people continued coming through the gates. The high road without was still crowded.

Stokestown was no more. It was, Colonel Mahon explained proudly to Squireen O'Shea as they rode through the ruins, "perfectly untenanted."

Every tree had been hewn down. Only stumps remained, oozing pitch. Tree rings exposed to sun and rain contained the otherwise unwritten record of years and life multiplied to generations when the village had been alive.

"My men will be along to gather the wood. Small trees for the fire. But there's an oak there I fancy will make a fine table. My carpenter says it's seen five centuries. Cromwell used it to string up twenty priests when he conquered Ireland."

At this last item of information Squireen O'Shea looked away as though he had heard enough.

Mahon grunted, "Make you squirm a bit? Ah. You're enough like an Englishman I forget you're a papist. Well, well. What do you say? When I have my table, we'll drink a toast to your dead priests and then to Cromwell. Who says we can't get along?"

There were no branches to stop the wind. Fifty yards up the muddy road stood a door without a house attached. Still in its frame, it was held up by a mound of stones. It banged shut and swung open, forever off the latch, as if angry men passed through and each one slammed it behind himself.

There was no one living in the mounds of rubble. At least no one who dared show himself as Mahon and O'Shea rode by. Emptiness flayed the very earth, and yet there was some presence that made

O'Shea want to whip his horse into a gallop and go home. Mahon was smiling with tight-lipped amusement at the uneasiness of his companion.

"You see, O'Shea, what Ireland can be if we are diligent?"

From the corner of his eye O'Shea caught sight of movement. The flutter of cloth, the flash of something red moving in a ditch.

"Pardon, Colonel." O'Shea's voice trailed away.

"Why, O'Shea, you're sweating. Not superstitious, are you, man?"

"Shall we be ridin' back directly?"

"Why, I thought you'd be pleased to see such a cesspool cleared."

"Aye." O'Shea mopped his brow. "It'll be a fine sight when the cattle are upon it."

"Indeed. The potential for grazing is tremendous. One hundred head on this land alone."

Another burst of mustard color sprang from a mound and slipped into the ditch. O'Shea gasped.

"What's got you, man?" Mahon swung his horse around.

"Somethin' movin' there," he said, panting. "Sure as anythin'. Somethin' . . ."

Mahon spurred his mount to the edge of the ditch. Standing in his stirrups, he peered down to where a makeshift roof had been constructed from one bank to the other. A blanket covered the entrance to this man-made cave. A confusion of bare footprints was in the mud.

"Come out!" Mahon bellowed. "Come out of there!"

From inside came a child's cry and the urgent voice of a woman trying to shush it.

Mahon leaped from his mount and lifted the lip of the shelter with the toe of his boot. "Get out, or I'll use your roof as a bridge. Send my horse across." He stamped his foot on the thin wood as if to make his point.

From inside the woman cried, "Don't do it, sar! I've children within! I beg ye, sar! We'll be crushed! Mercy, Ye Honor!"

Mahon was enjoying himself. He reached into his boot top and flicked out a concealed pistol.

O'Shea muttered, "Don't do it, Colonel, sir. Children. There's children."

Mahon shouted, "Come out, then!" He fired a shot into the mud. There was a terrified shriek within.

The flap opened tentatively. The filthy face of a woman peered out, blinking into the sunlight. "Mercy, Ye Honor! My children!" She raised her hand as if in surrender.

"Get out here! Filthy wretch! And bring your brood with you! Trespassers, all of you!"

Weeping now, she clasped her hands and raised them to Mahon. "Mercy! They're everyone so little!"

Mahon deliberately reloaded the weapon as if he did not hear her entreaties. "Get them out." He aimed the muzzle at the roof of the shelter. "I count to five, and whoever is beneath will get the bullet."

He began to count as the woman cried out and reached in to grasp the youngest and order the rest into the open.

"Five." He fired. The report resounded in the emptiness.

Sobbing before Mahon and O'Shea were seven ragged children from two to ten years in age, clinging to their mother. Clothing hung in ribbons from their gaunt frames. Eyes were large and bellies swollen with hunger.

Mahon looked down his long nose at the family. "Barely human, eh, O'Shea?"

O'Shea did not reply. He swallowed hard and asked the woman, "Where is your husband?"

"Dead, Ye Honor."

Mahon snorted. "Of some plague no doubt. Good reason to burn out these pestilent wallows."

O'Shea questioned further, this time in the Gaelic. "How came you to be here alone, woman?"

She replied in the same tongue. "My husband died last month. We've been living off potatoes dug from our neighbor's fields. Liam, our baby, passed into heaven two days ago. God rest him." She crossed herself, and Mahon flew into a rage at her gesture. He slapped O'Shea's horse with his riding crop and then slashed the woman across the face.

"You'll speak the Queen's English in my presence, O'Shea! Bloody bog Irish! You know the laws against this devil's language!" The whip came down hard on O'Shea's leg. "I'll have your lease for it!"

O'Shea fought with his excited mount. "I was tryin' to get the truth from her, Colonel! No harm! No harm intended, sir!"

Mahon stepped back, mollified by O'Shea's frightened expression.

Only the wailing of the children punctuated the vacuum. The wind came up over the wasteland. The woman struggled to rise from the mud.

Mahon remounted. "What does she say, then?"

"The baby died two days ago."

"They breed like rabbits, these creatures. What's one more or less in the grave to their kind?" Mahon's cheek twitched as he gathered the reins. "Get rid of her, O'Shea." He spurred his horse away, through the ruined town and up the hill.

Martin stumbled upon the camp quite by accident.

He was not supposed to leave the grounds of Burke Park unless accompanied by Nesbitt or one of the Claddagh boys. But since the death of his father, Martin had become accustomed to being the head of the Donovan clan, and it did not set well with him to be idle when he could see chores that needed tending.

So when a cow went missing at the very time Nesbitt and Old Flynn were attending to a collicked mare and the Claddagh folk were busily tending the fields, Martin saw his duty plainly.

He did mention to Kate that he was goin' to see about the moilie, but he did so when she was feeding Tomeen and smiling dreamily about something. Narrowly managing to avoid being caught in a game of sally rods played by Mad Molly and Mary Elizabeth, Martin slipped out the back and over the swale.

Once across the wall, he breathed a sigh of relief. Though perfectly safe, the atmosphere inside Burke Park was stifling to a young man. Too many womenfolk and too many anxious, overprotective servants made for boring restraint. Besides, Martin told himself,

Mahon's watchers had disappeared since the arrival of the Four Horsemen, as Molly called them, and the encounter two of them had experienced with Simeon. Probably scared them off for good.

To a boy reared in the west, a five-mile hike was nothing but a good stretch of the legs, even if Martin's crippled leg ached with the effort. The prospect of scouring the nearby downs, though it took a couple of hours, was of no great concern.

North of Burke Park was an area of uncultivated bogland. The low-lying region was good for pasture and for turf-cutting, but not home to any living creatures save badgers, merlins, and the occasional herd of wild Connemara ponies.

The heifer in question had often shown headstrong tendencies; often grazing aloof from the rest and returning last to the barn as if reluctant to give up her freedom. Despite the extra pains to which Martin was put on her behalf, he was sympathetic.

Since she was a wily one, examining the likely part of the downs for the truant cow took some time. At every suspect clump of gorse Martin noisily rattled oats in a tin bucket and called, "Here, moilie. Come see what I brought you."

A shrill whistle, as if given by a merlin disappointed in its swoop, caught Martin's attention, but only briefly. He thought idly that the falcon's cry was unusually loud for a bird he had not even seen. The boy followed an ancient track down between two low hills. He knew where it led, and the prospect of even harder effort loomed: the path dropped into a bog where unwary creatures often got mired.

"Cush, moilie," he said accusingly. "You haven't gone and got yourself stuck, have you?"

At the point where the ravine widened again, Martin looked across the low-lying swamp just ahead. Instead of a trapped heifer he saw a caravan, a wagon enclosed for traveling, and a makeshift campsite. A pair of draft horses grazed nearby.

That was the view when Martin was grabbed from behind. A skinny arm snaked around his neck and a greasy hand clamped over his mouth. Martin struggled, but the arm squeezed until he saw spots and a foreign accent hissed in his ear, "It is better to not fight, eh, boy? Unless you maybe want me to maybe pluck your head off?"

Hoping he was correctly interpreting which response would give him air, Martin shook his head vigorously. "Good!" the voice pronounced, and the grip relaxed enough for him to draw breath.

A lean, dark-haired form appeared in front of him and in something neither English nor Irish asked his captor a question. The exchange seemed to be in regard to Martin's identity, since he was peered at by both of his swarthy-featured guards.

"What do you do here, boy?" Martin was asked.

"I'm huntin' one of my cows. She's wandered off. What are you doin' here? This is Burke land."

Again there was an exchange of gibberish during which Martin was lifted off the ground and examined like an unusual specimen of bog dweller. "Are you a Burke, boy?"

Not only did Martin answer in the negative, but something in the tone of the query warned him that these were not folks to whom a close connection with Joseph should be admitted. When he was asked his name, he replied, "Martin. Martin McCaslin." This was the truth, since as part of his Christian name the lad had been given that of a great-grandfather's clan. Of the family Donovan he said nothing.

At that Martin was unceremoniously dumped in the mud. The captor who had held him brandished a knife under Martin's chin. "We don't want trouble," the man intoned. "We are just passing, see? No trouble for you or us if you keep your mouth shut. But otherwise . . ." The sentence was concluded with a rapid crisscross stroke of the blade in front of the boy's eyes with the sounds of a throat being cut.

Martin nodded solemnly.

"Good! Now go, and remember what I say."

Martin lost no time in putting distance between himself and the foreigners. When he looked back, he saw only one figure watching him go. This meant the other was following. The boy altered his course so as to go off in the direction of Ballynockanor and not toward Burke Park.

It was not until he reached St. John the Evangelist and was inside Father O'Bannon's cottage that Martin felt safe.

The Tinker is here," Molly said, pointing at Nesbitt, "so it can-not be he."

Father O'Bannon did his best to ignore the fey woman. "From the description of the wagon," the priest said, resuming his discussion with the group gathered in Kate's kitchen, "and from the sound of the two, I say again I believe they are wanderin' folk, Tinkers or what have you." He glared Molly into silence, and she stuck out her tongue at him. "They may be given to thievin' chickens and would not be above helpin' a stray cow through a low spot in a fence, but you say the missin' beast came home of her own accord."

"But wavin' a knife around Martin's throat!" Kate protested. "Is that not somethin' like Colonel Mahon's thugs would do?"

Nesbitt said nothing, but he looked grimly thoughtful.

O'Bannon shrugged. "Mister Nesbitt here and one or two of the Claddagh-folk will go to their camp tomorrow to see what else can be learned. But consider: what use is it to Mahon to have men lurkin' so far back in the downs? Especially men so foreign of speech and tongue that they could not pass any village without remark?"

Kate admitted that this was an unlikely connection. "Tinkers, then, and no threat?"

"The Tinker only threatens those of wicked intent," Molly said indignantly. "And Martin is not wicked are you, Martin?" Screwing up one eye, she hunched over and studied him as intently as the two attackers had done.

Her scrutiny reminded Martin of something. "What about them wantin' to know about the Burkes?" the boy said.

Margaret said, "That foreign gibberish you heard sounds like the heathenish babble the Tinkers speak amongst themselves. And if they was wanderin' tinker-folk, they always want to know who the landlord is. There's some, includin' Old Marlowe, who would have 'em flogged just for trespassin'. No doubt Mahon is the same."

Father O'Bannon continued, "We have enough evil to confront without startin' at shadows. Remain on guard and cautious, yes." Here the priest wagged a cautioning finger at Martin. Molly mimicked the action so completely that the elderly, stubby pastor and the scrawny crone looked like paired images in a badly defective mirror. "Cautious, but not anxious," O'Bannon summarized, self-consciously dropping his hand.

On the following day, Martin led Nesbitt and Simeon back to the bog, but the encampment was gone. They followed the wagon tracks for about a half mile, then the trace veered into shaley ground, and the trail was lost. Martin was satisfied that his chance encounter had only been with potential sheep-stealing vagabonds, but he noted that the troubled expression on Nesbitt's face did not go away.

∽ 19 ∽

As darkness fell again over the Atlantic Ocean, a dimly flickering candle in a brass lantern case was once more hoisted to the top of the thin spar that served as a mast. This fragile reassurance that life continued aboard the gig was answered by a similar spark from the launch. A blanket of high clouds swept over the sea, making the gloomy night still more desolate.

Even before dark on the third day adrift the wind made it difficult to keep the two vessels together. No one aboard either craft had any experience crewing a sailboat. The heavier launch rode deeper in the water and was slower, despite the fact that both were furnished with fore and aft sails. In contrast the gig skimmed over the waves, constantly pulling ahead. When Gann tried to slow their progress by reducing sail, the change in momentum allowed the lighter craft to be slapped about, shipping a great deal of water.

O'Halloran and Talbot constantly bailed while Hoyle gripped the tiller with his one arm. Gann glowered at them from the bow seat where he occasionally nudged Kirkland to see if the other guard still lived. Joseph spelled Hoyle at the rudder, but had been assigned the duty of inventorying their meager supplies.

The provisions allowed them by the mutineers consisted of hard tack and water. These rations, Joseph calculated, amounted to a pound of dry bread and one half pint of water per man each day for a fortnight. When Joseph reported this conclusion, Gann grunted, and no one else said anything. No one wanted to think what would happen if they were not rescued or reached land before the stock ran out.

Father Talbot rested for a time from filling and tossing tin pans of seawater. He leaned toward Joseph and said, "Have y'heard how tortured the poor lad Kirkland is breathin'?"

There was a distinct rasp and a quiver in each respiration. "Can you do anythin' for him?" Joseph asked.

"Not a thing," Talbot replied. "This is no easy matter like a dislocation. There is a hollow behind his right ear. His skull is fractured, sure. I think someone clouted him with a belayin' pin. I tried to get Brophy to let him stay aboard the *Hive* and be taken for help, but I believe now it would make no difference to the outcome. It's a wonder he's lived this long."

Both men were silent for a moment. Joseph employed the bailing cup and allowed Talbot another minute of rest. The priest continued, "The surgeon is useless. If Kirkland dies, Gann will realize that he is one man against all of us . . . and he is more than half-crazy already."

"No talkin' there," the hostile voice of Jailor Gann growled from forward. "Croppies are not to speak after dark."

Joseph was minding the tiller. With neither moon nor stars by which to judge, he could tell only that it was sometime between midnight and dawn. O'Halloran was still busily bailing, but the others all seemed to be asleep. Nothing had been heard from forward for some time from either Gann or the injured Kirkland. Surgeon White was snoring.

There was the smell of rain in the air. The breeze against which the gig fought its way eastward had veered to full northeast, driving the little boat even farther south from its intended course.

The first drop that pattered against Joseph's neck roused him from drowsiness. The alert came only just before the squall struck.

A gust of wind heeled the gig sharply, driving its bow into a wave and shipping enough seawater to threaten the oilskin-wrapped provisions. As Joseph and Hoyle struggled between them to ease the vessel's ride, the others bailed furiously with Gann shouting orders that made no difference.

And then came the rain, "a lashing rain," to quote Joseph's Connaught upbringing. Not yet a teeming rain, but much fiercer than bucketing or pelting.

The wind blew the deluge into the boat faster than it could be bailed out. The level of cold water around the feet of the miserable exiles deepened from ankle to mid-calf, despite the efforts at bailing. Joseph felt something bump against his leg and made a grab for a floating packet of victuals that had come untied from its bindings.

Amid the panic came a cry from O'Halloran. "I can't see the launch's light no more."

The squall passed as abruptly as it had come on. The rain stopped, and the wind abated. Straining his eyes against the darkness, Joseph scanned in all directions, looking for the other boat, but the masthead light never reappeared.

The hired assassin known as Iago whistled softly to his companion. With curt gestures of a knife-wielding hand, he signaled for Sebastian to circle the former Burke stable looking for unbolted doors or unsecured windows.

Iago himself started clockwise around the two-story structure, once the Great Hall of the de Burgos. Across the cobbled yard in the remaining barn, a horse stirred in the night and stamped a hoof. Iago froze in place, melting easily into the shadows between the wall of the building and a stone water trough now planted with prim-roses. When Iago had counted to a hundred and could hear no other noise, he continued circling the building.

Iago and Sebastian had lurked in the hills behind Burke Park for some time. Through a spyglass they had studied the comings and goings of the residents until knowledgeable about the habits of the household. Nesbitt, Old Flynn, and the Claddagh-men were known to sleep in the barn. That left Kate and the three children, the cook, and the housemaid in the hall. The one unknown was a grizzled hag, who appeared to come and go at will. This night she had been seen to leave just at sunset, heading toward a village some miles away. Everyone was accounted for.

Iago and his partner were much more discreet than Mahon's other henchmen. After the accidental discovery of their camp by Martin, they had changed location every other day, avoiding areas of pasture or turf-cutting in favor of the remote and desolate. The two men took turns spying on Burke Park. No one seemed aware of their presence.

Iago was chagrined when he saw Martin living at the big house. Clearly the boy had known more than he let on and could have ruined the plan. Just as clearly his report had not done so.

Softly jiggling the latch on the double doors of the carriage-wide, mounted-man-high main portal, Iago was not surprised to find it securely bolted. His astonishment was that much greater then, when, pushing gently on the sally port in the middle of the expansive gate, the smaller opening fell inward at the barest touch. Iago almost fell over the raised threshold and barely recovered his balance in time to keep the door from banging open.

Someone had secured the huge gates and left the lesser opening unlocked.

Whipping a thin glove from his pocket, Iago pulled the door closed, jamming it on the leather so that the door could easily be opened silently but appear fastened in the meantime.

He went in search of Sebastian.

Martin lay awake in the upstairs bedroom, which was his alone. Next to his chamber and on the same side of the galleried landing slept Mary Elizabeth. Through the open doors Martin could hear her snoring softly, a quiet click followed by a buzz, like a kitten purring.

Across the opening that plunged to the floor of the hall below were the two rooms belonging to Kate and a smaller nursery adjoining in which baby Tomeen rested. The night was waiting without a breath of wind to jostle the leaves of the hawthorn tree outside.

There was no particular thought that kept Martin wakeful long after the rest of the household slumbered. Rather, it was a jumble of images that would not subside: Joseph at his trial, the parade of tossed victims of Mahon's evictions, the flames shooting into the sky from too many burning homes. Martin was doing his best to accept Father O'Bannon's exhortation to only deal with present evil and not borrow or invent trouble. Still, it distressed the boy more than he had ever admitted that life was so fragile. Who could know what tragedy would come next? Would they be turned out at the last? And if they were on the road, where would they go? How would Joseph find them then and the new nephew or niece growing so palpably within Kate?

It did not improve Martin's repose to look up into the rafters and remember the faces of the workmen carved on the beam ends. The images, benign enough by daylight, took on a sinister lurking feel when they were more imagined than seen by the flickering glow of the dying fire. The ominous shadows were further enhanced by the ages-old stag antlers that adorned the railing of the gallery, their spiky outlines reaching into the even darker spaces above.

A door creaked, and there was a momentary clatter, quickly stilled. It could be Kate up tending the baby. Martin listened, but heard nothing from across the way. When all remained quiet and undisturbed, he at last began to doze.

Tomeen stirred and yawned. Although the toddler still had the affectionate title of Little Tom, the truth was that the curly-haired toddler had grown quite independent. At a year and more he was perfectly capable of being by turns demanding, thoughtful, bright, solemn, and curious.

At the moment he was hungry. Tomeen had played so hard that afternoon in the kitchen with Margaret, Fern, and Mad Molly that he had fallen asleep at supper and been whisked off to bed. The sides of his crib were in place, and the oak spindles too narrow to crawl between, but Tomeen had recently discovered the combination of standing on tiptoe and reaching for things. Rather than calling for Mama, he stood upright and grabbed the top rail of his bed.

Bouncing on the fleece-filled mattress made little noise, but it did encourage the child to pull himself onto the railing and hang there. His toes on the turned posts, Tomeen levered himself farther and farther until suddenly he dropped headfirst outward.

The child's plunge was checked by a basket of clean linen waiting to be folded. His squawk at the unexpected dive was muffled just as the landing was cushioned, and he rolled onto the floor excited but not tearful.

The door from the nursery onto the landing was kept closed against drafts, but the one that communicated with Kate's room was open. Tomeen wandered through it dragging a blanket behind him.

The darkness held no fears for the tranquil child, and any anxiety he felt at his adventure was quieted by the sound of Mama's breathing. He approached the coverlet that hung down to the floor and reached for the quilted image of a flower.

A sudden breeze swirled into the room. Kate's door onto the gallery was open to allow air to circulate up from below. The brief gust carried the aroma of extra potatoes still warm by the hearth. The scent called Tomeen away from the bed.

The galleried landing was frightening at first with the big roof overhead and the sense of vastness opening before, but Tomeen had been taught by Kate to climb down the steps backward so that an unwatched excursion would not become an uncontrolled tumble.

One hand on the wall, Tomeen approached the head of the stairs and turned about exactly as instructed. Patiently he dropped to his knees, reached down and back with a questing foot for the next tread, and descended into the blackness of the hall.

Iago deftly withdrew the glove lodged in the doorway and pulled the portal shut behind him. Touching Sebastian, he carefully secured the entry against other intruders.

By the fading gleam of the embers, the two killers studied the layout of the hall: central space surrounded by rooms that appeared to be studies and offices; a hall at one end leading toward a wing that outside observation had already shown to be kitchen and servants' quarters.

Indicating the stairs, Iago signaled that they should ascend. Sebastian nodded.

The two men were dressed in black, their faces hidden by burnt cork. Wraithlike, they flitted across the flagstones toward the steps.

Two steps upward, then three, and so on; Iago tested each tread underfoot for any telltale give in the support that might indicate where a complaining timber would give them away. Above their heads the specters of long-departed artisans and long-dead elk glowered down at the intrusion.

At the top of the flight Sebastian caught his toe on something. He put out his hand to steady himself on Iago's shoulder, and both men halted abruptly. Reaching down, Sebastian freed his foot from its entanglement and lifted a baby blanket. He showed it to his partner, then flung it aside in disgust.

Iago pantomimed that they were to separate, each examining a side of the gallery for their quarry. It was not that they had any moral objection to simply killing all the occupants; they merely were not being paid for more than two murders.

Almost immediately Iago recognized that he had chosen the correct door. Kate's deep, even breathing could only be coming from the one adult living there. And where the woman was, the infant could not be far away.

He would hold a pillow over her face while he slit her throat, he decided. Then he would deal with the child. If Sebastian did not participate in the actual killings, more of the promised gold would belong to Iago alone. He slid the blade out from the sheath at his waist.

The silence of the night was shattered by the sound of crockery splintering on the flagstones. From downstairs came Tomeen's wailing cry.

Kate bolted out of bed at the sound, calling the baby's name. Silhouetted in the doorway, Iago was in the one spot where his disguised form was perfectly visible. Kate added her scream to the child's yowling and then dropped beside the bed, reaching for the blackthorn stick always kept there.

Iago lunged at her, slashing with the knife. In the dark his aim was off, but Kate, striking out blindly with the walking stick, hit the assassin in the shoulder. It was a glancing blow that did no harm, but turned his leap aside.

Shouting for Sebastian, Iago recovered his footing, only to run into a low stool that had been unseen. Kate leaped across the bed, heading for the landing, but Iago was up and confronted her, so she turned into the nursery instead, one hand guarding her rounded belly.

Across the gallery, Sebastian had just examined Mary Elizabeth's room and found that she was not the desired target. He was between the girl's room and Martin's when the commotion erupted. At the crash from below and Iago's call, the second murderer raced forward, only to collide with Martin as the boy responded to Tomeen's cry.

Sebastian had no weapon but his hands. These he tried to wrap around the boy's neck. Martin, yelling for help, kicked and pummeled the intruder. The grappling rolled the pair over against the railing and then back again to thump on the wall. Sebastian's fingers closed around Martin's neck and began to tighten.

In the nursery Kate overturned the crib behind her as she passed, flinging it into Iago's way. As he raged and swore, endeavoring to toss it aside, Kate landed several blows on the attacker's head with the blackthorn stick.

Feet came running from the servants' wing, and Margaret's voice called out, "Missus Kate! What is it?"

Kate shouted back, "Murderers! Get the men!"

At that same moment there came a pounding on the entry to the hall. Nesbitt's voice bellowed, "We heard a crash! Let us in! Lady Burke!"

Iago, snarling with frustration, picked up the crib and threw it at Kate, knocking her back against the wall. Partially pinned underneath it, she was helpless to get clear before Iago slashed down at her. She jerked her arm up to protect her face, and the blade hissed through the fabric toward her throat.

Mary Elizabeth, roused by the clamor, heard her brother's cry for help. Stumbling out of her bedroom, she could dimly make out the pair of figures struggling on the landing. Without panicking, the girl snatched up a water pitcher from the stand outside her room. Seconds later she smashed it down on Sebastian's head.

Martin drew a gasping breath. The boy recovered his wits in time to fling himself onto Sebastian's arm just before the murderer could batter Mary Elizabeth with his fist.

The outside door flung open with a resounding crash. Heavy footsteps and voices roaring in both English and Gaelic echoed throughout the hall. "Lady Burke!" Nesbitt yelled. "Are you all right?"

Iago's stab at Kate turned on a spindle of the crib less than an inch from her neck. He had drawn back the blade to jab at her again when she managed to lever the walking stick up between the bars of the crib. The metal spike on the foot of the staff punctured Iago beside his nose, narrowly missing his right eye.

Enraged, Iago raised his weapon, clasping it in both hands and poising it over his head. He was determined to finish Kate with the next stroke.

But as he lifted his hands to strike, he found both arms grasped from behind and almost wrenched from their sockets. Simeon on one side and Sonny-boy on the other pulled Iago completely off his feet and hurled him back against the wall. Iago's head smacked into a beam, but the hired killer did not drop his knife. He slashed out with it, and the Claddagh folk circled him warily.

Across the gallery, Sebastian had grabbed Martin with one hand and Mary Elizabeth with the other. He shook the children, intending to crack their heads together like walnuts. Lights on the stairs and racing footsteps warned him that his time was up and that escape was now what remained. Jumping to his feet, Sebastian knocked the children aside in his rush. He sprinted away from the approaching steps, only to find his way blocked by Nesbitt. The two men collided. He succeeded in getting his hands around Nesbitt's throat and began to squeeze. To his horror, the assassin discovered that Nesbitt, ignoring the constricting fingers, had locked his own grip on Sebastian's windpipe and was winning the battle of who would black out first.

Lunging forward, Iago cleared enough space for him to dart out Kate's bedroom door. Yelling for Sebastian, he shouted that it was time for escape. With Simeon and Sonny-boy close behind him, and Rusty and Moor outflanking him on either side, Iago jumped on the railing and then downward toward the floor of the hall.

He landed badly on the flagstones, his ankle-bone snapping. Despite the pain, he hobbled toward the exit, which lay on the other side of the room. Just in front of him was Margaret. In her arms was Tomeen. At the cook's feet were the shards of a broken bowl and a trio of splattered potatoes.

Iago snarled as he went for them. He would kill the child at least; he would take his revenge for his injury and still claim the blood money for one killing.

Meanwhile Sebastian, relinquishing his own hold, shot both of his hands between Nesbitt's in a desperate bid to loosen the choking grip. He won his bid, but only gained a foot of room as Nesbitt closed with him again. He heard Iago's roar of pain from below and guessed that his partner had jumped for it. He elected to do the same.

His vision blurred from the suffocation, Sebastian vaulted the rail without looking to see what lay below. His leap took him into a rack of antlers suspended over the void. Man and tines, tangled together, fell toward the stones.

The antlers, knocked over in flight so that their points protruded downward, and propelled by Sebastian's weight, caught Iago on both sides of his backbone. Pierced through both lungs and heart, Iago died instantly, within just paces of Tomeen.

His neck broken by landing headfirst on the flags, Sebastian died less than ten minutes later.

Lights were blazing in Burke Hall. Simeon and Sonny-boy, stout cudgels in hand, had already made a careful inspection of the rooms and outbuildings and declared them free of other intruders.

The bodies of Iago and Sebastian had been removed to the barn and Iago's blood cleaned from the flagstones by Margaret's determined scouring. A damp patch on the flooring was all that remained to show where the two assailants had died.

Kate was weary from replying to Nesbitt, Margaret, Fern, Martin, and Mary Elizabeth that yes, she was indeed all right. Yes, the baby was fine too. She patted her stomach to show that the wee one remained safe.

Nesbitt, bowing and nodding shyly, pointed to the slash in Kate's sleeve. A thin line of blood traced the rent in her nightgown, but only the barest scratch was beneath. Kate shrugged off the concern. "Mahon's men?" she asked.

Nesbitt bobbed his head curtly. "There's no proof on either of them, and I expect none when we find their wagon, but this is Mahon's work right enough."

"They weren't Tinkers, were they?" Mary Elizabeth asked with a shiver.

"No, dear," Kate said. "That they were not."

"From now on," Nesbitt said with authority, "two of us will sleep inside by the foot of the stairs and the rest will patrol outside."

Kate inclined her head in token of agreement. "He will not stop, will he?" she asked.

Nesbitt replied, "Not after this. It is a fight to the death now, and he knows it."

The Claddagh folk, understanding the import if not the meaning of the conversation, nodded solemnly.

Tomeen sat on Kate's lap, wide awake and cheerful. Margaret also cleaned up the broken bowl and the potatoes, but she had retrieved a whole roasted prattie from the kitchen. On this Little Tom was contentedly munching.

Squireen O'Shea anxiously paced the length of scrawny Mahon's library and back again. His neck was thrust forward, and his face displayed fear as he challenged his landlord.

"Colonel Mahon, Squire Mahon, sir, I don't hold to violence against women and children."

"Not violence, O'Shea. A bit of coaxing is what the lady needs. She'll sign. That she will."

"She's hired those Claddagh-men. King's hard bargains they are. And then there's her steward, Nesbitt. There's no gettin' past any of them. Let alone pass through the gates and near the baby or her Ladyship. Those Claddagh-men are closer than nine is to ten around her and the children."

Mahon shrugged. "They'll open the gates wide for us."

"Not until Joseph Burke comes back, they won't."

"I explained to you. Joseph Burke will never come back. Dead already, I'll wager."

"Then she'll not open the gates till you're six feet underground. All your schemes have come to nothin'. You won't get past the portal before one of the Claddagh-boys breaks your neck."

"You're forgetting, O'Shea. Her Ladyship has a fondness for waifs and beggars. The tossing of Stokestown? Kettles of porridge to send them on their way?"

The light in Mahon's eyes passed into O'Shea's expression.

"Over one thousand."

Mahon raised his finger. "That's right. All of them moving freely about the grounds. Resting beneath the oak trees on the lawns. Grateful they were to take her charity. Eating their meals and moving along."

"That was before the Claddagh men came. Before Nesbitt."

"Claddagh be damned. We'll be in before they know."

"But how will we come near the baby? And if we do, how will we get him off the grounds?"

"I've two hundred families farming the strip between my lands and the pastures you sublet from me. Imagine them evicted. Hovels torn down. Where will they go? Ah! Lady Burke is good for a meal. A thousand in the mob. Milling about. One or two to distract her. Another to lift the Burke child and carry him off."

Squireen O'Shea's mouth twitched. "No violence, Mahon. No harm to the child. Upon my soul I'll not have any part in harmin' an innocent child."

Mahon spread his hands, palms up, in assurance. "No harm done."

PART III

*I wish, O Son of the living God, O
ancient, eternal King,
For a hidden little hut in the wilderness
that it may be my dwelling.
An all-grey lithe little lark to be by its
side,
A clear pool to wash away sins
Through the grace of the Holy Spirit.*

—Ancient song of an Irish hermit

∽ 20 ∽

The wind died with the morning and so did the guard named Kirkland. Without ever becoming conscious, the bludgeoned man shook convulsively, gasped for air as if drowning, and expired with an exhausted sigh. All aboard save Gann and the blinking, bleary-eyed surgeon crossed themselves fervently. Gann merely scowled, muttered something about the uselessness of doctors, and helped himself to the contents of Kirkland's pockets: a few shillings, a pocketknife, and a gold locket containing a wisp of honey-blond hair.

Noting the remembrance from a loved one who would never again see her intended and might perhaps never even know his fate sobered Joseph more than the mere fact of death. He grasped the pendant around his own neck and prayed for Kate, and for himself.

"Dump him over the side," Gann ordered Talbot and O'Halloran.

"Not without sayin' a few words," Talbot said firmly. "No man should be sped to his Maker in so careless a fashion."

"I'll allow no papist mumbo-jumbo here," Gann countered. "Kirkland was a good Protestant, and I'll have no witch's spell put on his soul."

"Very well," retorted the priest. "Then *you* must speak."

Gann screwed up his face so that the undamaged side was contorted into creases like the wounded part. "I can't do it," he finally admitted.

"Mister Gann," Talbot said softly, "it is one and the same Lord to whom we pray and one and the same judge of men's souls before whom Kirkland now stands." At the religious talk Gann's visage compressed into an even more tormented grimace, but he said nothing. "If," Talbot continued, "poor Kirkland was, as you say, a good Protestant, then he is under the savin' blood of Jesus. And no one has a higher regard for our Lord's precious blood than me and my brothers and sisters of the Roman persuasion. May I not do him the same service I would wish for myself?"

Still glaring, Gann gestured for the priest to do as he wished. Father Talbot conducted a simple ceremony, commending Kirkland's soul to God, petitioning God's mercy for the departed and for all of them as well.

"Take his clothes," Gann said without emotion when the prayer ended. "He don't need 'em anymore. And tie a weight to his feet. We don't want him bobbin' after us."

Kirkland's body disappeared beneath the waves without a splash and left no trace of his passing.

Joseph reported that the squall had soaked two days' worth of rations. They must eat them immediately, or they would spoil. To this Gann gave a grudging permission. "Good job Kirkland died soon," he remarked bluntly, "'stead of eatin' up vittles and then dyin' anyway."

There was no sign of the launch anywhere about, nor could any other ship's presence be detected on the whole broad breast of the sea. It was as if the six remaining men in the insubstantial boat were alone in the world.

Up at dawn on the *Blossom* for several days after sighting the smoke, Adam Kane was continually disappointed to learn that no sign of any ship had been seen during the night watches, nor was there even a sail in view in the daylight. The vacant expanse of sea mocked his efforts. Adam Kane wondered why more sailors did not go blind or delusional, what with having such featureless surroundings day after day. More than once his strained eyes deceived him, as when he mistook a chip of wood for the distant hull of a ship or when he spotted a petrel skimming the surface and confused the bird's wings with sails.

The steward had never possessed much of a head for heights, but he reckoned it was his duty to employ every means available in the pursuit. Accordingly, he stuffed his pockets with rock-hard ship's bread and climbed the foremast ratlines toward the platform at the head of the lower mast, called the *top*. Over and over he reminded himself to not look down.

But when he arrived at his chosen vantage point, Kane discovered that the set of the foretopsail obscured his view. With a deep groan of resignation, he grasped the shrouds and continued upward until he reached the crosstrees above all but the highest of the sails.

It was then that the steward noticed how much the elongated height of the mast exaggerated the roll of the ship. Side-to-side motions, barely noticeable on the deck some sixty feet below, were distorted into a prodigious swaying. The timber around which Kane wrapped his legs seemed about to part company with the ship and go its separate way.

Getting used to the slingshot sensation took some time. Kane wondered if he would ever have enough nerve to climb down again, then decided he would not give the bagpipe-playing MacDougall the satisfaction of seeing him be afraid. That score settled, Kane returned to observing the horizon. The added height extended his circle of vision so much that he must surely be able to see the Americas from up there.

What he did see was a ship. Could it be the *Hive*? Could the long chase be over and a happy conclusion in sight? Kane grew excited at the thought.

The unknown craft was quite far off, the dark speck that was its hull barely visible. Also it was not where Kane had expected it: this vessel bore southeast from the *Blossom*. Nevertheless he called out proudly, "*Yoo-hoo*, Costello!"

The Scots burr of MacDougall bristled back at him, "That's *Captain* Costello to you. What do y'want?"

"I see a ship!" Kane said, pointing, not trusting his sense of compass directions enough to say. "That way. Tell *Captain* Costello, and be quick about, me *boy-o*." The steward carefully and gratefully returned to the deck.

Costello came from his quarters with spyglass in hand. He congratulated Kane's eyesight, studied the other vessel as its sails lifted higher above the horizon and its hull became visible . . . and proceeded to dash Kane's hopes.

"Well," Costello said, "it cannot be our ship—not *Hive*, I mean."

"How can you be tellin' already?" Kane inquired. "Doesn't one three-masted ship look much like another from this distance?"

Costello shook his head and offered the telescope. "See for yourself. That bluff bow and fat sides—she's a whaler. And from the depth she's ridin' in the water I'd say she's homeward bound and satisfied. Definitely not our quarry." Kane looked crestfallen, and Costello continued. "But her course will carry her near us. We'll speak to her and see if she knows ought of *Hive*. Maybe she has news."

Kane reluctantly accepted this verdict and turned toward the hatch leading to his cabin. Second Mate MacDougall stopped him. "And another thing: *yoo-hoo* is seldom heard aboard ship, me *boy-o*."

It was just past noon when three mates and Peter Chase, captain of the American whaling ship *Eliza*, boarded the *Blossom*. An aura of whale blubber permeated the visiting foursome. Clothes, beards, hair, and skin all carried the unmistakable scent of the hunt—months of smoking try-pots rendering oil from the kill. Kane's nose wrinkled as they took their places in Captain Costello's cramped quarters for the noon meal.

"The *Eliza* is full of oil to the gunnels," remarked Captain Chase as he downed a thick slice of cheddar in one gulp. "A year and a half out of Nantucket, and the harvest has been plentiful."

The officers of the *Blossom* conveyed the latest news from Europe, including the events in Ireland. The monster meetings for Repeal; the arrest, trial, and release of Daniel O'Connell; the transportation of Joseph Burke; all made fine fare to accompany the French wine, Valencia oranges, and Irish cheeses from the captain's store.

With the information that the *Blossom* was attempting to intercept the convict ship and obtain the release of Lord Burke, Captain Chance tugged his beard and raised his eyes in contemplation.

"We likewise spotted smoke from a burnin' ship. Downwind, we were, and heavy in the water due to our cargo. We tried to reach her, but had no luck. All night we lumbered along. Had three men in the crow's nest tryin' to spot the flames, but no luck. Mornin' came, and we had lost her altogether."

"Not the smoke from a whaling vessel like yourself, sir?" Kane asked.

"Lord, no. No whales in these waters. And the stench from the smoke of a whaler is unmistakable. Aye. I can catch the scent of the harvest from miles away." His lower lip protruded. "Here it is. Whatever ship it was burned and went to the bottom. And all hands with her I'm surmisin'. We sailed east to west, north to south for two days lookin' for survivors. Found one body floatin' on a flat calm sea. The fishes had been workin' on him, poor soul, but he was wearin' the striped shirt of a convict."

Adam Kane's thoughts were as darkly morose as the normally cheerful man ever experienced. Things looked bleak indeed for Squire Burke: both *Blossom* and the whaling ship had seen another vessel apparently on fire, and then the body of a dead prisoner, obviously from the *Hive*, had been recovered. What other conclusion was there to draw? The transport ship had burned and sunk, and Lord Burke was lost. Should Kane have the *Blossom* abandon its search? Was there nothing left to do but carry this appalling verdict home to Lady Kate: Joseph is dead, and so are all our hopes?

Costello counseled against despair. "They had boats," he said. "Even a ship afire has time to get her people off. We'll cruise about and seek the survivors."

This was the right course, clearly. But the other conclusion at which both Costello and Kane arrived, neither of them voiced: there was no way that *Hive* carried enough boats to carry all her passengers to safety. What were the odds of one particular convict being spared?

Days of coursing up and down brought no result except to carry the *Blossom* beyond the reach of the steady northeast winds and into the region of the variables. "Any boat that survived to drift so far is as good as lost," Costello admitted. "The winds here are as likely to drive a vessel towards the Rio de Janeiro as toward Africa . . . or leave it adrift in mid-ocean . . ." The unspoken finish to the sentence could only be read as, "until food and water give out."

It was decided that no further good could be obtained in the trackless sea. There was no conclusive proof that the *Hive* had burned. They had no absolute certainty that connected the floating body with a disaster on board the transport; the dead convict could have fallen overboard, died of disease, or even been executed for some offense. "I think it is time to take *Blossom* on toward the Cape," Costello said.

"I cannot disagree," Kane said sadly. Then, on a more energetic note, he added, "And what if *Hive* is already there? She might be readying herself to go on toward Botany Bay, might she not? All said, Captain. Let's not make this pursuit any longer than necessary."

Mahon leaned back in his chair in the library of the manor and put his feet up on the oak table made from the ancient hanging tree of Stokestown. He passed a glass of wine to O'Shea. "I told you we'd drink a toast, eh, O'Shea?"

O'Shea attempted to smile as he remembered the source of the wood from which the enormous table had been made. "That you did, Colonel, sir," he mumbled.

"A lovely thing, is it not? Cross-grain." Mahon thumped his heel down hard on the surface. "Somewhere right in that ring is when Cromwell hanged your priests." He raised the glass. "To Cromwell and your twenty priests." He sipped.

O'Shea considered the liquid in the glass, shrugged diffidently, but did not drink. "No thanks, Your Honor." He raised his eyes in a challenge to his landlord.

"What?" Mahon enjoyed the game. "No salute to brave men?"

"To brave men, then." O'Shea drained the cup.

Mahon's smile faltered. "Do I sense some dissatisfaction, O'Shea?"

"No, sir."

"Disapproval, then?"

"No, sir."

"Well, that's fine. Indeed. Because if I believed for one minute that the man who sublet the largest tract of land from me was somehow in opposition against me or my methods . . . Well, O'Shea?"

"Opposition is a strong word."

"A strong concept. One which would lead me to believe that I must cancel your lease, O'Shea, and find a tenant who will do things my way."

O'Shea's shoulders sagged. "What do you want from me?"

Silence. "That's more to my liking. Docile. Obedient. Like my dog. I've not had a cur I liked so well since I was forced to shoot Flint. Remember Flint?"

"Aye. Flint. The dog you set upon the Donovan cattle just so you would have reason to make Kate Donovan speak to you."

"Lady Kate Donovan Burke. I won her trust by setting right a small disaster that I created. Shoot the dog. Pay for the loss. Replace the heifers. Flint was my only real sacrifice. Loyalty. It is a requirement for anyone in my service."

"You killed the dog."

"I would have killed him had he refused to rip the bellies out of the cows. He died for a good cause."

"He's dead anyway."

"I might have spared him." He poured himself another glass of wine. "And I might spare you as well."

"So you might. But then again, sir, pardon me, Colonel, but I've seen with my own eyes how you reward those who serve you best."

Mahon offered a tight-lipped smile. "There's enough acreage from the Burke estate to give you your own little fiefdom, O'Shea. Twenty-three-years' lease on say, five thousand prime acres? Interested?"

"What choice do I have?"

"None."

"I thought not," O'Shea said dispiritedly.

"If I let the word out that it was you, Squireen O'Shea, who hired the lads who tried to kill Lady Burke and the brat . . . and Lady Burke in the family way. How long do you think you'd last? You, a Catholic too. A traitor to your own kind, they'd say. Betrayer to Kate, the Lady Burke, who'll feed any beggar who comes to her gates! Why the Ribbonmen would be upon you this very night." He took his feet off the table and tapped his finger on the tabletop. "Then we could say Squireen O'Shea was hung along with his priests. And gathered into hell among his kinfolk."

"I've sold my soul in your service."

"And look what you gain."

"Five thousand acres. Not even the whole world," O'Shea replied in a monotone. "What do you want?"

"I need the use of one of your subtenants," Mahon replied brightly. He rubbed the palm of his hand over the polished grain of the hanging tree. "It was in Stokestown the plan first occurred to me, you know. I shall always remember that day pleasantly. The woman living in the ditch with her ragged brood? Remember the look in her eye? That's where the plan was born full-blown. Bring me someone like that woman, O'Shea. A widow. Someone desperate, with more wretched little beggars crying at her skirts than she can feed."

21

The weather that had driven in the storm and riven the *Hive's* boats apart continued to be as fickle as it could be frightening. The days following Kirkland's death continued cloudless, breathless, and featureless. With no wind to stretch the sail, the castaways were reduced to rowing; two pairs of men manned the two banks of oars.

Gann, in his position of command, would not row, and Surgeon White was almost useless, so the effort fell on the four convicts. Hoyle, despite missing his left arm below the elbow, was so strong at one starboard oar that he had to skip every third stroke or drive the gig in circles.

All exhibited blisters on faces, ears, necks, and arms from the sun and the constant exposure to the abrasive seawater. They contrived to shield their heads from the worst of the blazing sun, but the damage was accumulating anyway. Gann's appalling facial wound was made even more hideous by the scorching, but it was the doctor who suffered the most.

Bloated and yellow from his self-inflicted abuse, White panted with the heat like an old dog. "Give me more water," he demanded through cracked lips. "I must have more water."

"Show some backbone in front of these outlaws," Gann ordered. "Besides, you drank your share already. No more till tomorrow."

"The man may die before tomorrow," Talbot observed, the pudginess completely melted from his round features from the exertion and the meager diet. "See how pasty he is? Can we not spare him a drop?"

"Do you want to give him your share?" Gann inquired. "Otherwise, shut yer gob and pull."

Having no instruments or charts aboard, it was impossible for the exiles to know whether they were progressing directly toward rescue or accidentally avoiding it. East was the watchword; it was all there was to do.

Another night passed on the open ocean. It was unremarkable except for the momentary excitement when a school of flying fish, chased by some unseen predator, skipped and glided over the swell. A half dozen of the fish, one for each castaway, fell short on landing, and collided with the gig. Most were devoured raw to supplement the miserable ship's biscuit, but Joseph observed that John Hoyle laid his aside beneath the thwart.

The next mid-afternoon found the four men leaning on their oars. After having rowed for several hours, all except Hoyle were too fatigued to continue, and by common consent they rested.

Hoyle had contrived to bring a fishing line and hook into the gig, and this he baited with the hoarded flying fish. "I was right fair angler when I had both me mashers," he said, shaking his remaining fist. Joseph had discovered that Hoyle, though unobtrusive by nature, had a cheerful disposition in the midst of hardship that made him a valuable companion. Reserved but not taciturn, he would respond to questions. "I was stevedore on Wexford docks," Hoyle explained, "though port is siltin' up terrible. Soon nought but mussel-catchers will harbor there. Anyway, me and mates often fished off docks. I learnt that a wee fish is needed to catch bigger one."

Hoyle carefully prepared the bait and flipped the flying fish far astern again. With simple jerks and twitches he artfully made the creature appear to dance as if alive.

Though Joseph had not asked about the missing arm, Hoyle was without shyness where the subject was concerned. "Load of pig iron dropped from cargo net," he said with a shrug. "Crushed it. Lucky I didn't bleed to death. Surgeon there whipped it off in no time. Ended dock work, course."

O'Halloran, his eyes widening as the story grew, blurted out, "How'd you come to be transported, then?"

Now Hoyle did look chagrined, and O'Halloran mumbled an apology for violating the convicts' code of privacy. "I'll tell you what for," Gann burst out harshly. "He strangled a man . . . a Protestant militiaman who was in lawful search of hidden Catholic weapons!"

"I have a temper when I've pegged a few pints," Hoyle admitted. "And they tell me I throttled some'un. It might be so. 'Course," Hoyle added slowly, "they say he had fingermarks on both sides of his throat."

"You've got one!" O'Halloran exulted suddenly. "Look there!"

A shining silver flash exploded from the crest of a wave just where the bait was trolling. The line uncoiled in Hoyle's hand as the larger fish felt the hook and jetted away. Despite the lack of rod and reel, Hoyle exhibited his talents. He skillfully let the fish run with the line, then took it up again by twirling it about his hand like a spindle when the dash slowed.

"Not too tight," Father Talbot offered.

"He'll throw the hook if you give him too much slack," Surgeon White muttered.

The battle raged for a space of some minutes, and then the exhausted fish was drawn toward the boat. "What is it?" O'Halloran inquired. "Mackerel? Codfish?"

Only a dozen yards of water remained between the captured fish and the boat when the fin appeared. Blunt and stubby, greyish and tipped with black, the dorsal fin of a shark appeared in the wake of the struggling catch. Though the body of the predator could not be seen, its actions could be inferred from the questing motions of the fin as it hunted back and forth like a hound following a scent.

Another fin broke the surface behind the first. "Shark," Hoyle
observed quietly.

"You mean two sharks," O'Halloran corrected.

"No, boy," said Talbot. "That's the tail of the same creature."

It was an unthinkable distance from the dorsal fin to the tail, half
the length of the gig.

Laurence did not yet perceive the danger to the boat from this
new arrival, only the threat to their trophy. "Reel in faster!" O'Halloran
urged needlessly. "You'll lose your catch."

"Worse: we'll lose the hook," Hoyle grunted, sweating and winding the line faster than ever. Joseph, hauling hand over hand, took
up the retrieval when Hoyle showed signs of slowing.

A cavern in the water opened as the shark opened its mouth to
engulf the fish. Close enough to see jagged teeth, Joseph yanked
sharply on the line just as the jaws clamped together.

The severed head of a large mackerel flew aboard the gig, smacking Surgeon White in the face.

O'Halloran exclaimed with disappointment at the loss, not noticing that the triumphant shark, rather than swimming away, was circling the small boat. A baleful, dark eye could be seen regarding the
craft and its occupants.

The first bump appeared accidental. The spiraling shark rubbed
against the rudder with a slow grating noise. The bulk of the beast
pushed the boat sideways, but then he seemed to lose interest. The
enormous predator swam an unhurried figure eight with the gig at
the center of the rear loop.

"Do we row?" O'Halloran asked Joseph. "Or do we pull in oars
so he won't break 'em?"

"He don't want us," Gann said. "He got his supper already." But
for once, there was a lack of conviction in the jailor's tone.

Hoyle shuddered, and the sweat beaded in great drops on his
forehead. "Are you takin' sick?" Joseph asked. "You don't look well."

"Ever since me accident," Hoyle replied, his eyes never leaving the circling shark, "I had dreams that t'other arm was ripped from me by monstrous teeth. Bids fair to come true."

Gann laughed roughly. "Fish that big'll swallow you whole," he said. "You only get one . . ."

What object Gann had in mind with which to conclude his thought was never expressed because that was the moment chosen by the shark to cease investigating the watercraft and taste it instead. Missing a pass as Father Talbot raised his oar out of harm's way, the creature continued straight in. His jaws clamped down on the gunwale, tearing out a chunk of wood just beside the priest's knee. "I think rowin' may be in order," Talbot said.

Four oars hit the water in agreement, but the shark's aim had changed. Charging directly in again, he dived at the last second. The gig unexpectedly shook from side to side like a rat in the grip of a terrier. "He's got keel," Hoyle shouted. "Drive him off!"

Flailing their oars, they did succeed in making the killer fish release his hold. An instant later he was back, this time attacking from the other side. It was impossible to slap the surface anymore, since the castaways had all they could do to hang on and not be tossed into the waves. A jug of water did shoot overboard.

Joseph could see anger and terror mix on Hoyle's face. With a supreme effort, the one-armed man jabbed downward with the oar, thrusting the wooden plank into the shark's mouth. The two forces, man and animal, wrestled for only a few seconds, and then the three-inch-thick pole snapped in two.

Hoyle drew back the remaining piece. The end was shredded, but the desperate measure had worked. With a last flick of its tail, the shark disappeared into the murk.

"Well done," Father Talbot remarked.

Hoyle wiped his face and nodded. "Boat couldn't have stood more of that," he said.

Joseph added his congratulations, then looked down at his feet. Had there been that much water in the bilges before the shark's arrival? As he watched, the level of the liquid rose perceptibly.

Gann saw it at the same moment. "Bail!" he screamed. "He's split a seam. Bail as you love your miserable hides!"

There's a plank sprung, certain," Hoyle announced gravely. Every bucket and cup aboard the gig was employed in bailing but still the water level kept rising.

"Can you make out where the leak is?" Gann demanded.

"No," Joseph replied. "It's beneath the duck boards. I don't think it's all the way to the keel. More like three-quarters of the way down on the starboard side."

"What's to do?" O'Halloran asked nervously. Despite the fact that the shark had been gone for some time, he still looked around carefully before tossing each pan of water over the side.

Joseph, who had been examining the problem, suggested, "Maybe if everyone sits on the portside gunwale, we can tip the boat enough to expose the leak."

Even Gann had no protest at this notion. He even assisted Father Talbot in moving Surgeon White into position. The craft heeled more and more sharply to its left as everyone aboard shifted their weight, raising the right flank clear of the water.

"Now, Laurence," Joseph instructed, "you are the lightest of us. Lean out and tell us what you see."

Stretching his skinny body over the now steeply inclined side, O'Halloran announced, "There's a plank pulled loose, about three strakes from the bottom. It's not bit in two, praise be, just sprung."

"Can you reach it?" Joseph asked.

Try as he might, no amount of crouching on the elevated rail and extending his arms would permit the boy to touch the damaged spot. "No," he said apologetically. "I cannot."

The boat was allowed to slump back into the water, and with it the hopes of its occupants slumped into dejection. "Bail," Gann ordered again, but the fierceness had gone from his voice.

"There's only one thing for it," Joseph said at last. The squire of Ballynockanor looked at his companions: the slack-jawed doctor, the youth, the aging priest, the one-armed man, and Gann. "You must lean the boat over as far as you can without me. Then I slip into the water with the mallet. If we tear up the floorboards, then perhaps Mister Hoyle can press against the spot from inside while I reclench the nails."

The sea into which Joseph slipped was cold and brilliant blue. A few feet below the surface, light refracted and diffused by the water scattered dagger-pointed star patterns. Joseph thought it was like perching on a shattered pane of stained glass above a thousand-foot-deep abyss. He trembled. Best to get done quickly and back inside the imagined safety of the boat. "I'm ready," he announced. "Shift her now."

The overlapping boards of the gig's flank glided upward past Joseph's outstretched arms as the transferring weight inclined the craft away. The one refinement to the plan that Hoyle had insisted on was a length of rope tied around the squire's middle. The other end was firmly grasped in Hoyle's good right hand as if Joseph were a new fish being played on a line. "Can't have you driftin' off," Hoyle remarked cheerfully. Then the big man said more solemnly, "I won't be lettin' anythin' happen to you."

The caulking mallet, secured to Joseph's wrist by another length of cord, bumped down the planks as he pulled it after him into the water. Joseph drifted along the side until he was opposite the damage. "I see the place," he called up to Hoyle. "Put your feet three strakes up from the keel and about two feet behind the second oarlock." These relayed instructions were necessary so that the one-armed convict would know precisely where to back up the hull. Otherwise Joseph's hammer blows would not be effective, and the planks would merely rebound. Since the other castaways were leaning close to the water on the far side of the gig, they could not see what Joseph was doing, nor was it easy for them to hear.

"Ready!" yelled Hoyle.

Swinging the hammer while clinging to the upturned side of the boat was not simple. When Joseph drew his arm back, the motion pushed him out of position. When he swung it forward, his body moved away from the gig, and the blow had no force. Several attempts accomplished nothing except a hollow booming sound like an ancient Celtic war drum.

By wrapping the safety line three times around his wrist and bracing his feet against the narrowly protruding strip of keel, Joseph was at last able to launch a solid strike on the sprung timber. He was pleased to see a length of board tighten up against its fellow below. Since they had no additional nails to use, this had been a crucial moment to see if the gig could survive. "It's working," Joseph called out, getting a mouthful of seawater for his pains. He resolved to keep his mouth shut and celebrate after he was back aboard.

Two more blows followed in quick succession, then Joseph yelled for slack in the line so that he could move over a space. He felt like a workman on the sheer face of a clock tower. Three more strokes impacted against the hull, pulling the slackened strip of wood back into place.

One more shift along the hull. A few more hammer strikes, and the job would be done. The wood, scored by jagged teeth and missing fist-sized splinters, still looked sound enough to serve.

The shark attacked very suddenly, without any warning or preliminary circling. It was only an approach from in front rather than behind that gave Joseph any notice at all. A gaping maw opened in the water, and Joseph shouted and swung the mallet wildly. The blow hit the killer fish on the point of the snout. Not enough to lessen the momentum of the rush, it was just sufficient to turn the shark's head aside.

The weight of the animal's body pressed Joseph's legs against the side of the gig as it brushed past him. It was like being pressed against a wall while your flesh was scored with a rasp. "Pull!" he shouted. "Pull!"

No one in the boat knew what was happening, but the panicked urgency in Joseph's voice made Hoyle react with instantaneous force. Two things happened in rapid succession: the part of Joseph's body that had not been scraped by the shark's hide was abraded on the hull as he was dragged aboard in one brawny tug of the rope; there was also a resounding splash and a strangled cry for help.

The gig rocked and bounced as the occupants were flung about by the commotion. Joseph, streaming blood from a dozen gouges and scratches, lay half across a thwart and half on Father Talbot. Who had screamed?

The noise of floundering and sputtering was cut off by a single horrible cry, and then the body of Surgeon White disappeared beneath the waves. A streak of blood in the water, like a wake left by a wounded ship, jetted off toward the horizon.

Joseph sat huddled in stunned and shivering silence. It was some time before anyone even noticed that the repair had worked; the gig still swam and five still lived.

∽ 22 ∽

On board the *Blossom*, MacDougall was off watch; but that fact did not mean the Scotsman was below—far from it. As his duty ended, he retrieved his bagpipes and began practicing an air of his own composition—a ballad of Bonnie Prince Charlie. The second mate strode up and down the deck, measuring time with his heavy tread on the planks. To Adam Kane, the combination was ghastly. The pace was lugubrious, more like a dirge than a heroic saga. MacDougall's playing was a half step behind his built-in metronome, and if all that were not enough, the high C note screeched like an alley cat being pulled inside out by the tail.

Kane buried himself in his cabin, stuffed balls of candle wax in his ears, and tried to think. He had been struggling for days with what to write to Kate. Should he endeavor to explain what he had seen so far or make no attempt until after reaching Cape Town? It was a dilemma.

So absorbing were his musings and so packed were his ears that

Kane missed hearing MacDougall's plaintive wailing change to an excited chorus of whistles, toots, and squeaks.

Costello inquired if a mouse had got under the mate's kilt, but when MacDougall finally got his lips disentangled from the chanter, he was yelling that he'd seen something in the water.

A whole scurry of pounding feet and an abrupt course change got Kane's attention. An instant later Costello banged on the cabin door.

A small boat tossed in the waves off the port quarter. No movement could be seen, but through the captain's spyglass Kane could make out a number of bodies within the frail hull. The steward shuddered at the double meaning within his thoughts.

Beating up the light winds took an unconscionably long time, but finally the *Blossom* lay alongside an open craft carrying a single sail. The features of those lying scattered about the hull were swollen, reddened, and chafed out of easy recognition. Kane could not distinguish Joseph Burke among them, but then none of the faces were unmarred. There was one figure of the squire's height with bleached blond hair. It might be he.

First Mate Doheny perched on the tumblehome, the inclined upper side of the *Blossom*, and extended a boat hook to snag the rigging of the drifting vessel. As he did so, a feeble hand struggled upward to help. "There's one alive here!" Doheny called out, a statement greeted with cheering by the *Blossom*'s crew.

Three living men were carefully lifted onto the deck. All were dehydrated and suffering from exposure to the sun. Three more lay dead.

None of them was Joseph Connor Burke.

The first among the *Hive* survivors to recover the power of speech was a prison guard named Fleer. Younger and stronger than the others, he was able to talk after downing a gallon of water in enforced sips and having his leathered skin greased with salve.

He told the story of the takeover and how the two boats of exiles had become separated. "There come a great storm," he said, "and not one of us knew sailin'. We got rolled clear over by havin' too much sail. Lost all our provisions . . . all our water. Mister Parker . . . him as was the new governor fella . . . is drownded. Others, too. Shields died two days since, but we hadn't strength to set him over the side."

There was a respectful silence for the lost lives and also for the fact that young Fleer apparently did not know that two more of his companions had also died in the last forty-eight hours.

Gently, Kane asked, "And the other boat? Do y'know who it contained?"

Fleer screwed up his face in thought, wincing as his parched flesh creased. "There was Jailor Gann and another guard—name of Kirkland," he reported, "but he was terrible wounded. Then a priest, Talbot, I think his name was. Two more prisoners; I dunno their names . . . and a political fella."

"Political?"

"You know, connected with the Liberator some way or nuther. Burke, I think his name was."

"And was this Burke . . ." Kane hesitated. "Was he wounded? Was he all right?"

There was a longish pause. "I wouldn't hold out much hope for him," Fleer said. "Gann had it in for that one. I'm surprised he'd lived so long already."

Costello drew the brooding Kane aside. "There is still a chance," he urged. "But our course is decided. Piracy and murder must be reported, and the fates of Missus Parker and the others seen to. We must make speed for the Cape, whether another boat remains adrift or no."

Colonel Mahon held a perfumed kerchief over his nose and mouth as he walked around the woman O'Shea had brought to the stable of the manor house.

She was perhaps thirty years old, but grinding poverty and too many children made her look twenty years older. Her brown hair was streaked with grey. It was uncombed, wild and loose about her shoulders. Dark eyes were dull from hunger and grief.

"A widow, is she, O'Shea?" Mahon spoke over her head as though she could not comprehend what he was saying.

"Her husband passed two months ago of scarlet fever." O'Shea answered in the tone of a man giving the history of a horse or a cow on sale in the market square.

Mahon grunted his approval. "Filthy. Hideously ugly, don't you think?"

The woman winced as though his words were a blow.

O'Shea remarked softly, "Missus Joyce was once a beauty, I imagine."

"It's the way with them, isn't it? Marry at fifteen. A child every year. They're finished by twenty-five." Stooping lower, he looked closely at her and asked, "How many children?"

She glanced furtively at O'Shea.

"Answer Squire Mahon," O'Shea instructed.

"Eight still livin', sir," the woman replied quietly.

Mahon inquired, "How many dead?"

"I've buried four babies, sir."

Mahon clapped his hands once as though to say he had guessed the number. "Twelve! You see, O'Shea? I rest my case."

Mahon paced to the gate of a stall and back, turning on his heel and smiling kindly at her. "Since your husband's death, Widow Joyce, how have things fared for you?"

She kept her gaze fixed on the ground. "Not well, sir. We'd be on the road if it weren't that Squireen O'Shea let our rent hang awhile."

Mahon clucked his tongue in disapproval. "The Squireen let Gale Day come and go and your rent unpaid?"

"Aye. For the sake of the children." She looked suddenly terrified that she had let O'Shea's mercy be known.

Mahon's eyes hardened. "We can't let that stand. O'Shea? What have I expressed to you about unpaid rents of tenants? Everyone will be expecting that, for the most inconsequential matter, they can shirk their responsibility."

O'Shea ducked his head unhappily. What was the point of this? "Colonel, Your Honor, so many mouths to feed and a husband gone."

Mahon shook his head. "There's a hard-luck story on every acre of Ireland. Missus Joyce will have to pay the Hanging Gale or leave."

She dropped to her knees. "Sir! We've no place to go! My children are so small, sir! I've a wee one who's not even six weeks on this earth! She was born after her father passed. Have pity, sir! Please! I'll do whatever I can to set it right!"

Mahon tugged on his lower lip as if in deep thought. "Perhaps there is . . . well, I can't imagine you'd be right for the job."

"Please, sir! Anythin' a'tall! Say the word."

"Are your children hungry, Missus Joyce?"

"I do the best I can. But there's hardly enough for them each to have one spud a day. It tears my heart to hear them cry at night for hunger. Afraid I am that they'll die from starvation or the scurvy."

Mahon raised the kerchief to his nose again. "What would you give to see them fed and clean and with a roof over their head? Secure."

"Anythin'! Oh, Squire Mahon, kind sir! What can I do to see such a day?"

Mahon nodded at O'Shea. "I think the Widow Joyce may serve us well, Squireen O'Shea."

The climbing roses beside the kitchen window of Burke House were in bloom. Kate was out with Tomeen in the warmth of the morning to gather the red ones.

"Daddy loves red roses," she said to the child. No day passed without Kate talking to him about the things Joseph loved most. "You'll know all about him when he comes home, Tom. As if he's never been away. Come, we'll cut a bunch of red roses for Daddy."

Mad Molly wandered out from the stableyard where Sonny-boy was shoveling a heap of manure onto a cart and Simeon was shoeing the grey pony. Molly paused and looked hard at Kate's rounded belly. "Oh, Daughter of Eve," she said with a sigh. "Ye'll have to forgive her when she comes through the gate. Though the pain'll nearly break your heart. Can't be helped. Poor Eve. Still fightin' the curse she brung upon her own kind. Side with the devil, she will, if she thinks it'll save 'em. Poor Eve. Have t' pity her for it. Ah, what a woman'll do to save her wee babes." She reached down and patted Tom on the head. "Hullo."

"Hullo," the child answered.

"Well, ye's brighter than most," Molly said, chuckling. "Steer clear of strange women, Tom. They'll steal your heart." Then to Kate she added, "Tribulation like birth pangs, he said. It'll be somethin' terrible if it's like birth pangs."

"It'll be fine, Molly dear," Kate replied. "I'm not afraid."

The old crone raised her eyes heavenward. "Do ye hear that saints and martyrs? Herself is not afraid!" She grunted and walked slowly toward the gates. "Not afraid, she says. No one ever listens."

Kirby O'Meara and Scully Deane were admiring Colonel Mahon's oak table when the colonel, accompanied by Squireen O'Shea, entered the room. Both thugs bowed and tugged at their forelocks with elaborate deference. "Fine piece you have there, Colonel," Kirby said, fingering the table with hands as coated with dirt as his words were covered with flattery.

"Get your filthy paws off that, you ignorant clot!" Mahon barked. "You'll ruin the finish!" Kirby jerked his hand back.

"You are not here on a social call," Mahon warned. "See that you remember your place."

Mahon sat in an armchair on a raised platform much as an ancient clan chieftain might have occupied a throne. He did not ask any of his visitors to sit, not even O'Shea. The squireen smarted with humiliation; even though it was unspoken, he was being admonished to remember his place as well.

"Tomorrow is the tossing of Ben Beg," Mahon said. "As that is Squireen O'Shea's village, he will be present, but I will not be."

"Yessir, Your Honor, sir," Kirby agreed. "We'll do a right fine job, just like on Stokestown. No trees, no walls . . ."

"You will do nothing of the kind!" Mahon snapped.

"Sir?"

Scully intervened before his mate got them both in trouble. "What Kirby here was tryin' to ask, Your Honor, was what special orders you had for us."

"Keep your mouths shut and listen! Squireen O'Shea will have his own driver supervise the destructives. You two, and twelve more you pick who are especially able hands in a dustup, have a particular chore."

Breaking into a wide grin, Kirby showed by the conspicuous absence of all his front teeth that he was familiar with the notion of a dustup. "Right, sir! Twelve able and brawny it is, sir."

Mahon eyed the thug with distaste as if wishing he could reconsider his choice of agents, then continued. He spoke slowly and distinctly, the same way he would have instructed a particularly ignorant and backward child. "Now pay attention. Just over the hill from Ben Beg is the village of Clonakerry. Do you know it?"

Kirby looked blank, but Scully put in, "Indeed we do, sir, indeed."

"You and your men are to assemble on top of that hill at dawn tomorrow. Make sure everyone is dressed like villagers."

"Sir?"

"In rags, man! In tatters! Do I have to spell it out for you? When half of Ben Beg has been tossed, and not before, you are to descend the hill as if you were coming from Clonakerry and it also lately tossed. Do you follow me?"

"Rags and tatters, hill at dawn, half tossed, right," Kirby and Scully echoed.

"If anyone asks, you will say that your village has been destroyed. You will mingle with the Benbegers . . . that's a good one, eh, O'Shea? Benbeggar, get it?"

O'Shea stared at his boots and said nothing.

Mahon resumed, "You will join the procession of scurvy beggars turned out of Ben Beg and go with the crowd to Burke Park to get fed."

Kirby's eyes lit up with sudden comprehension, and he waved his grimy paw like a schoolboy. "And that is where the shindy, the dustup, will happen?"

"I've already told you what I have planned," Mahon said. "Tomorrow is the time. Do this right, and there will be a reward in it for you. But heaven help you if you muck it up!"

"Heaven help someone," O'Shea muttered.

"Eh? What was that, O'Shea?"

"I said, 'Right you are, Colonel.' Right you are."

∞ 23 ∞

Even though the ration was now split into only five portions, the water situation was crucial as Joseph and the others continued to drift in the small, open boat. There was no longer any attempt at rowing. It was all the castaways could do to conserve their energy, to survive one more day of the relentless heat.

The scarcity of water made the short food allotment seem unimportant. Eating the dry, salty hardtack made the thirst worse. It was barely possible to choke down the minimum required to keep the spark of life glowing and then only if the day's minuscule liquid portion followed immediately.

The dreadful day that Laurence O'Halloran was caught slyly dipping up a handful of seawater and was pummeled by Father Talbot for his simplemindedness was followed by an eventful night.

There had been no relief from blazing light all day long and then, as if mocking the tortured castaways, a cloud no bigger than a man's hand appeared at sunset on the western horizon. The moon chased the sun across the sky before finally dipping behind the small cloud. Joseph, sleeping in the stern with his head lolling on muscles almost too weak to support it, distinctly heard the sound of water gurgling from a jug.

He awoke with a start, convinced that it had been only a tormenting dream when the noise came again from the bow of the gig. At that moment the setting full moon reappeared below the cloud and revealed Jailor Gann drinking his fill from a clay water bottle.

"What are you doin'?" Joseph croaked as the others also roused. "You had your share at sundown, same as all of us."

"Keep back!" Gann threatened needlessly, since no one had moved. "We're done for, or almost. Why should I keep you croppies alive to hang? From now on, the water is mine."

Hoyle staggered upright. "Put the stopper back right now," he said through blackened and cracked lips. "Or I'll throw you to the sharks."

Gann picked up the mallet and waved it about. "Can't scare me, croppie." The two men glared at each other as the light failed again, leaving a tense air of anticipation on the diminutive craft.

There was a rising west wind, but no one noticed it at first. The insignificant cloud swelled and grew to fill a third of the sky, then half, then hung overhead like a curtain being drawn over the stars.

"Hoist the sail!" Gann ordered. "We can use this wind."

No one moved.

"Hoist, blast you!"

"Not while you . . . steal water," Father Talbot countered. There were painful pauses between words while the priest recruited his voice to continue. "If it is . . . the end, it is so for all. You are . . . ten times more the thief . . . than any man who was ever transported."

The full force of the wind struck, and for the first time in days, there was a reason to have Hoyle's hand on the tiller. Lightning flashed around, illuminating the occupants of the gig as if they were outlines with tongues of fire.

"Hoist the sail," Joseph said abruptly.

"Eh?" Talbot questioned.

"Smell the rain? We can use the sail to channel the water into the flasks. Hurry!"

There was barely enough time to form the sail into a makeshift funnel before the downpour was unleashed. The boat was driven eastward at a prodigious pace as the rain bucketed down. Laurence O'Halloran laughed and cried as he slurped the drops from his arms and upraised hands. Clamping the tiller beneath his stump, John Hoyle wiped his face and lapped the moisture from his calloused palm.

Joseph maneuvered a fold of canvas so that it drained into the water jugs held by Father Talbot. The rain continued even after the containers were filled. Drinking and drinking, the bellies of the castaways swelled until each felt as if he would burst.

When the storm at last relented, the sail was set, the tiller was lashed in place, and all fell into a deep sleep.

It's salt!" Laurence O'Halloran's wail floated over the post-storm afternoon like the dying anguish of an entire Irish generation.

The west wind had continued all night and the whole long day that followed. Without a clue as to their location and the distance yet to be traveled, the refilled bottles had still given the exiles a renewed sense of hope. With their bellies full of fresh water and hardtack and the belly of the sail full of a steady breeze, it seemed that things were at last looking up.

That sense of hopefulness existed right up to the moment when O'Halloran uncorked the first of the jugs filled the night before. "It's salt," he screeched again.

"What?" Gann demanded. "Let me see that!"

Taking a long pull at the container, Gann spat, spat again, and rinsed his mouth from the bottle under his feet. "You, Prisoner Burke," he said, waving the brine-permeated flask. "Check the others. Maybe this one fell over in the bilge and got recorked that way."

Joseph did as instructed, although he was careful to dip only a fingertip and taste it cautiously. "This is bad too," he remarked.

"As are these," Hoyle announced quietly, having pulled the remaining corks.

"How can that be?" Father Talbot wondered. "We filled them from the sweet rain that fell from the sky. What evil miracle is this?"

"No miracle," Joseph said bitterly, "though evil for all that. It was the sail. The sail was impregnated with salt water . . . saturated with it . . . and folded up to dry that way. The drops carried the salt." There was no need to continue. The whole grim picture was clear at once. Instead of another two-week supply of drinkable liquid, the gig was no better off than the previous horrible day.

"That means," Talbot said bluntly, "that we are entirely out of fresh water. Except for the bottle Mister Gann has beneath his feet."

"And that stays where it is, croppies," Gann vowed, reaching for the caulking mallet. "It's mine."

"Let's get him," O'Halloran urged sharply. "He can't stop us if we all go after him at once."

"And what will happen to the gig if you do, croppie? Were you forgettin' what's in the water besides salt?"

Nervously scanning the billows for the grey shadow they feared, the boy still entreated the others to back him. "He can't stay awake forever, can he, Hoyle? What about it, Burke? Then the water will be ours."

"I think," Joseph said, standing upright and straining his eyes to see forward, "I think I see breakers ahead."

It was so. Though the view eastward was hidden by a low bank of mist, an unmistakable line of white water appeared directly across the course of the boat. "And breakers mean . . . land."

From high in the branches of the oak tree Mary Elizabeth could see over the stone wall of the Burke estate and all the way up the highway to Castletown.

"Someone's comin', Martin," she said. "Give me the eye-looker."

Martin had already pressed Nesbitt's spyglass to his eye and was focused on the face of the wild-haired woman in the tattered dress. She was holding one baby in her arms and seven other children were clustered around her. Their faces spoke of hunger. The bundles they carried told the story of eviction. As so many other vagrants had done over the last few months, she was headed toward the gates of Burke Park.

"Go get Kate," Martin ordered.

"Get her yourself," Mary Elizabeth spat. "And give me Nesbitt's looker." She grabbed at it, losing her balance and nearly tumbling out of the tree.

From below Nesbitt rebuked them both. "Get down from there and stop quarreling. There's much to do."

Martin swung down from the perch. "Someone's comin'."

"I saw them first!" Mary Elizabeth cried. "A ragged woman and children with her."

"Aye," Nesbitt said softly. "Poor thing. Simeon saw her in Castletown. Joe Watty told her your sister Kate would feed her and the wee ones."

"Go get Kate," Martin instructed Mary Elizabeth.

She opened her mouth to protest, but Nesbitt put his finger to his lips and with a flick of his hand pointed the way to the house. "Tell the Lady Burke you saw them first, Mary Elizabeth." This instruction sent her skipping.

"There've been so many," Martin said.

"Many more to come," Nesbitt added. "They're tossin' the village of Ben Beg tomorrow."

"What? Squireen O'Shea? The priest will excommunicate him for it."

"'Tisn't heaven O'Shea fears half so much as Mahon."

"But it's O'Shea's land."

"Sublet from Mahon. And Mahon's got his purpose. Entirely his own."

"If you ask me," Martin grumbled, "he's out to bankrupt Kate. She feeds every beggar who passes by the gates. Word is out. Every hungry soul in Ireland comes searchin' for Kate, the Lady Burke in Galway."

"And she'll never have to beg because of the mercy she's shown."

"Maybe not, but I heard you talkin' with her. I know how empty the coffers are."

Mad Molly ambled out with Old Flynn trailing behind.

"Another one?" Flynn called, rattling the keys.

Martin answered, "A woman and eight."

Molly sniffed. "Pieces of eight. Their bones are knockin'. The other Eve. Cast out of Paradise. Her own doin', it was. Poor woman. Sold everything, she did, to feed them. Well, she's made a bargain." She scowled into Nesbitt's face. "I suppose you say she's got to eat."

Behind her Kate replied, "I say it. Let them in, Flynn." With Tom on her hip, she shielded her eyes against the glare of the afternoon sun to observe the little band of wanderers. "Margaret heard O'Shea and Mahon are tossin' Ben Beg."

"Aye, ma'am," Nesbitt said. "There'll be five hundred here tomorrow like that one."

Molly leaned her back against the oak. "Don't ye let them in."

Kate looked worried. "At least we've got some warnin' this time. We'll set the soup cauldrons there. And the tables there."

Molly interrupted. "Ye'll not be lettin' them in."

Nesbitt crossed his arms and spoke over Molly. "Tomorrow ye'll be stayin' indoors with Tomeen, ma'am. You're headin' toward full term, and I'll not have you liftin' and fetchin' when there's the rest of us who can do it."

"Pass potatoes through the bars to 'em," Molly sang.

"They'll be needin' a place to rest awhile." Kate glanced up at the spreading branches of the oak. "They cut down every tree in Stokestown, I hear."

"They'll do the same in Ben Beg," Nesbitt agreed.

Molly prattled on. "Don't open the garden to her! Flamin' angels bar the doors! Eve's heard the devil's lie and made her bargain."

The beggar woman and her children stood waiting, silent and downcast, at the gate.

"Let her in, Mister Flynn," Kate remarked.

"No one ever listens." Molly plunked down on the lawn and eyed the arrivals with simmering hostility.

It took four changes of water in the tubs to clean the Joyce family properly. Margaret and Fern tended to the girls and Mrs. Joyce. Old Flynn and Rusty carried water to the boys. Cakes of soap and brushes scraped off a shell of mud to reveal human skin beneath it. Rags that had passed for clothing were not worth the saving and so were burned.

The Joyce children, bathed and dressed in fresh clothes, were still thin, pale, and sickly, with dark circles under their eyes. Mrs. Joyce, washed and curried, was a younger woman than Martin and Mary Elizabeth had guessed. She had an anger in her eye, Martin thought, and stared at the door of the house as though she resented anyone living in such a fine big place when she had nothing. She smiled when Kate was looking, but the pleasantness vanished when Kate turned away. A table was set for them in the shade beside the climbing roses. They did not offer thanks to God for their meal, which Mary Elizabeth remarked upon as strange indeed for people whom an hour before had nothing and now were dressed and clean and being served their food.

After Kate went inside and left them to wolf down soup, potatoes, milk, bread, and butter, Mrs. Joyce said plainly that she did not want to see Father O'Bannon when he came for mass that evening. "No, I'd rather not."

There was a girl, only a bit younger than Martin. She tended the two-year-old boy with a kind of surly resentment. Two brothers, perhaps a year apart in age, took pleasure in tripping the toddler as he attempted to walk to his mother.

"I don't like them," Mary Elizabeth said to Martin from the tree where they watched. "Except the tiny baby and the smallest boy."

Martin nodded. "They're too young to know anythin'," he said. There was a knife-blade edge to their hunger that cut away civility to one another. Though there was plenty before them, they squabbled about a single slice of bread as though there were no other. Like dogs they were, Martin thought, warring over scraps when the dish was overflowing.

"I'll be glad when they go." Mary Elizabeth swung down from their perch and dusted her hands.

"More like them comin' tomorrow from Ben Beg." Martin followed her.

The great shadow of a Claddagh lad fell across their path. He said quietly in the Gaelic, "Not like them. Not coming from Ben Beg."

Martin looked hard at the family group again and asked, "What do you mean?"

The Claddagh-man shrugged and patted him on the shoulder. "Lock the doors tonight, Martin. Keep the windows closed. We'll stand the watch, but you must be vigilant."

It was almost nine o'clock in the evening, and the sky was still light. Father O'Bannon had arrived four hours earlier and now snored happily in the guest room. He would be on hand in the morning when the grieving homeless of Ben Beg arrived. Mary Elizabeth and Little Tom were likewise tucked into bed. Kate, Fern, Margaret, and Martin were peeling spuds for tomorrow's huge cauldrons of stew. Nesbitt and two of the Claddagh boys patroled the grounds with lanterns in hand. This very visible presence was a warning to any who might attempt to force their way onto the estate.

Fern, like Martin and Mary Elizabeth, had noticed the rough manners of their guests. Martin shared that the Claddagh brothers had some misgivings about Mrs. Joyce and her children.

Kate responded to Martin's information with small interest. "And does it make them less hungry?"

"No, but . . ."

"Hundreds are being evicted in the West now. Before men like Mahon came along, they were farmers like us."

"There's somethin' about her, Kate."

"Probably afraid we'd turn her away."

Martin tapped his knife on the rim of the bowl. "I wish you had."

"I wouldn't. Did you see the little ones, Martin? The one is no bigger than Tomeen. A sweet thing he is. A pretty boy once he was dressed in Tom's clothes. And the infant . . ." As if on cue the baby within her thumped a code.

She smiled wistfully and took Martin's hand to let him feel the movement. "If it was myself on the road and you, hungry, and Mary Elizabeth . . . Tomeen and now this little one comin' . . ."

Margaret sucked her teeth and wrinkled her nose. "Ain't the same. Never seen such greasy creatures as them. Water's free, ain't it? Don't matter how poor a person is, water for washin' is as close as the nearest river. And we don't lack for water in Connaught."

Fern bobbed her head in agreement. "It's true. Plenty of water here."

"Nesbitt and the Claddagh boys . . . ," Martin continued.

Kate cut him off, holding up her hand. "That's enough, Martin. Your grumblin' will steal our blessin'. Nesbitt and Simeon will sleep downstairs tonight. We'll lock our doors and bar the windows, although it's a fine clear night, and the air is sweet."

So Kate put an end to the talk. The last tub of spuds was carried out and divided among the stew pots. The household prepared for bed.

Still in the kitchen at half ten, Kate poured herself a glass of milk. There came a soft rapping on the window. Kate lifted the candle to see Mrs. Joyce's face peering in at her through the glass.

Words and warnings rattled through Kate's mind. She hesitated a moment with her hand on the key of the door.

"Your Ladyship." Mrs. Joyce's muffled voice penetrated the pane. "May I have a word?"

Kate could not see past her in the darkness and thought better of opening the door. Instead she raised the window.

"I seen your lamp light burnin'," Mrs. Joyce said almost apologetically. "A friendly sight."

"It's late. Is your room all right?"

"Fine. Aye. Oh, your Ladyship! A lovely place it is for myself and the children." She leaned inward against the sill. "Well, what I mean is . . . You're a generous person, Ladyship. And there I was all clean and abed, and I seen your light and yourself movin' across the window like. So it came to me I've not said thanks to ye." She looked down at her hands. "So, thanks."

Kate smiled in acknowledgment. "You're most welcome, Missus Joyce."

"My given name is Eve," said the woman. "If ye'd care to call me by it, I'd be honored."

"Thank you kindly, Eve. Are your children sleepin' well?"

"They are. Better than they have in months. They're not bad'uns. Just that we've been livin' rough for some time. Ye've saved us. Truly ye have."

"I'm thankful to help."

"The very thing. I've forgot my manners, Ladyship. One day I want to return the favor."

"Then again I thank you, Missus Joyce."

"Eve." The woman sounded relieved. "And here we are, leanin' on a windowsill like two old gossips. A fine way to end the day it is. Lord keep ye." She gave a cheerful wave and stepped back out of the circle of candlelight.

Kate closed the window and set the lock.

The tread of a footstep behind her made her jump.

"Ma'am." It was Nesbitt. "I heard voices."

"Missus Joyce. Just sayin' thanks."

"Aye. And you should get some sleep, ma'am."

"Sleep." Kate said the word as though it were a foreign concept. "I am weary of all of it, Nesbitt. I miss the days when I could walk out my door and tend my own field and my own cows."

"You're the treasure of the Burkes, ma'am. Yourself and Tomeen. Now that baby you're carryin'. There's none but yourself to carry on."

"I long for my husband to be home again."

"So do we all, ma'am. Now go upstairs to bed. Rest easy. I'll stand the first watch."

24

Ben Beg perched on a hillside within the shadows of the Partry Mountains. It was not a prosperous place, but each family tended a prattie patch of its own, and each household among the five hundred inhabitants was able to raise a pig to contribute toward the rent. Had it not been for the failure of the potato crop a year previous, the leases would not be past due. Now the Hanging Gale was being called in.

For a month, ever since Squireen O'Shea had announced the tossing, Ben Beg had scrimped and starved in a last-ditch effort to accumulate the payment. All the pigs had been sold. All the oats had been freighted away. All the hay that could be cut in the meadows within half-a-day's walk was scythed, bundled, and carried to market. Hungry men waited outdoors at noon so as not to have to watch their families consume a paltry few potatoes for their one daily meal. Every economy that could be practiced had been. At the end, they had failed.

Squireen O'Shea stood on a boulder beside the road that wound down into the valley. A stream of people flowed away from the village, the dam that had upheld a generations-old pool of life irreparably cracked. Under the direction of O'Shea's driver, a man named Broghill, the destructives were already hard at work, hammering on walls and cutting down trees. Forty of the village's eighty squalid cottages were no more than dusty mounds.

A barrow, empty except for a single, three-legged stool and a wooden hayrake, passed by O'Shea. No one in the group of six around the conveyance looked up at the landlord. Perhaps they feared that if he took notice of them it would be to demand they give up their last belongings or their meager clothing to pay the debt. Better not to make eye contact at all.

A small child, too young to know the depth of the destruction, was being carried pickaback by his father. Joyfully he smiled at O'Shea and waved. When O'Shea scowled, the toddler's lower lip quivered. The child's mother looked apologetic and hustled her family away.

From over the hill behind the village came a file of ragged men. Dressed in frayed shirts and worn-out trousers, the newcomers nevertheless looked better fed than the others. Also, they stared around defiantly, visually challenging every onlooker. No one from Ben Beg took up the dare.

A slide, pulled by a woman and a young girl and containing a crippled boy, hung its left-side runner up on a rock. As if being stuck would somehow inconvenience the watching landlord, the two redoubled their efforts, yanking frantically at the handles. Resisting all attempts to free the pole, the sled would not budge. The desperate tugging threatened to rip the already scanty wickerwork and spill the lame child onto the muddy path.

O'Shea stepped off his perch and reached toward the pole, but someone cut in front of him. Kirby O'Meara and Scully Deane wrestled the trapped runner loose.

O'Meara turned his head and winked at O'Shea. "Never be soilin' your hands, Squireen," he said. "We'll take it from here." The woman clasped her hands in gratitude at the assistance of the two strong men from Clonakerry who would help her in her trouble.

Squireen O'Shea frowned and bit his lip as he watched the caval-
cade wind down the hill and out of sight.

Though Martin would never have admitted that he was com-
peting against a girl—much less his own sister—he nevertheless was
compelled by her previous victory to climb higher and faster than
Mary Elizabeth. When the oak branch on which he perched was so
thin as to bow and wobble with his weight, Martin judged that he
had ascended far enough. Looking down, Martin was satisfied to
note that his sister was not even trying to follow, having stopped
some four levels lower.

"What do y'see, Martin?" she called up. "Are they comin' yet?"

Looking away to the east Martin scanned the brightening east-
ern rim of sky above the valley of the Cornamona. That was the
direction from which the victims of Squireen O'Shea's tossed village would appear. "No," he shouted back. "Not yet."

The lack of refugees on the road did not mean that Burke Park
was unprepared to receive them when they did arrive. Long before
dawn Kate and Margaret had governed the assembling of the soup.
Cords of split, seasoned oak had been hauled by Nesbitt and Moor
to the front lawn of the Burke estate. Rusty and Sonny-boy dug pits
in the earth between the main gate and the house, and roaring blazes
were therein kindled. Thereafter the four men tended the fires and
assembled mounds of sliced soda bread in heaps like snow-covered
islands floating on the Burke green.

The kettles were giant cauldrons with legs. They stood fat and
round over the flames like the try-pots of a whale ship. Kate supported Tomeen on one hip, and her other arm rested on her stomach as she and Margaret discussed the amount of soup boiling in
the vessels and how many people it would feed. Fern, not trusted
to cook the broth herself, was kept shuttling between kettles and
pantry for salt, barley, and other ingredients. Margaret remarked to
Kate that it made the housemaid feel useful while keeping her out
of trouble.

The sight of Fern bustling importantly back to the house, keeping out of trouble, reminded Martin that there was another person being kept out of trouble this day: Mad Molly. So that Molly would not be scaring children or accosting adults to whom she conceived a dislike, Molly was detained within doors, guarded by the remaining Claddagh man, Simeon.

"They're comin'!" Mary Elizabeth cried triumphantly.

In his interest in the proceedings on the lawn, Martin had neglected to watch the road. Swiveling his head back around, he grudgingly admitted that his sister was correct. A thin black snake, stirring skyward a pitiful trail of dust was advancing into view on the near side of the river.

Martin knew that the folk he beheld had only been walking since the previous day. Yet they looked so bedraggled and bone-weary that their arrival at Burke Park seemed the end of a thousand-mile journey instead of the first steps toward an unknown future. Many of them appeared as walking skeletons; sharp angles where their limbs protruded from their tattered clothing. And the leaders, Martin knew, were the stronger ones, the younger ones, the ones who were better fed.

A family of six, all barefoot, arrived opposite the observation post oak. A mother carried two infants, and two more children walked, bearing small sacks. The father heaved a bundle over his shoulder, passed his family by about ten paces, set the burden down, repassed his brood to a duplicate parcel, hoisted it, and repeated the process. Martin calculated that the man was walking three times farther than the others. No wonder he looked ready to collapse.

Already Old Flynn and Father O'Bannon were together opening the gates. "Come in," Martin heard Old Flynn offer. With his growing deafness, the stablemaster's proposal was made so loudly that it sounded like a command: "Come in and eat!"

No one refused. The first of the dispossessed staggered over the threshold while the file stretched into an apparently limitless distance.

"Climb down, Martin," Mary Elizabeth urged. "Let's go help!"

Kirby and Scully stepped aside from the flow of evicted farmers just at the corner of the wall guarding Burke Park. "We're here," Kirby announced.

"I know that!" Scully said sullenly. "I got eyes, don't I?"

Given the peculiarities of Scully's vision, Kirby would ordinarily have made some scathing rejoinder to such a leading statement, but hearing the hostility in his mate's tone, he elected to skip it. Instead he adopted a note of congratulation. "That's a rum thing you're doin' there, limpin' an' all. Quite a show you put on."

"Show be hanged!" Scully exploded. "I got blisters on both feet!"

"That's good too!" Kirby allowed. "Gettin' ready for the dustup, like. You sound real angry."

"Listen, you clabber-brain," Scully stormed. "I ain't actin' yet!"

"Oh," Kirby responded. "Well, it's most time. Here come the rest of the boys."

So as not to appear too obviously distinct from the stream of refugees, Mahon's men traveled only as loners or in pairs. As each passed Kirby, he flicked the end of his nose with a stubby forefinger. *Get ready*, his signal said. *You know what to do.* Then he and Scully tied kerchiefs across their faces and rejoined the mob of homeless.

The slow, shuffling momentum of the crowd toward the food, the silence of families too broken to speak, and the reek of misery in the yard drove Martin and Mary Elizabeth back into the limbs of the oak.

High above the five hundred exhausted refugees, Martin could see everything clearly. The image of sorrow burned itself irrevocably into his memory.

There was Kate, big with child. She passed out slices of bread with one hand and braced Tomeen on her hip with the other.

"They're too beaten to even say thanks," Martin said.

On the heels of that thought, he remembered Mrs. Joyce and her brood. Neither had they seemed grateful. Martin spotted the woman moving among the crowd. Like Kate, she carried her two-year-old boy in her arms. He was asleep, his golden head against his mother's breast. She kissed his curls and stroked his cheek. It was a tender sight, and Martin regretted the harsh judgment he had passed on the poor woman the day before. Clean and clothed in a calico dress, Mrs. Joyce now seemed out of place among the people of her village. No one spoke to her, and she did not seek out anyone in particular. The other seven Joyce siblings sat huddled together on the lawn beside the lane that led up from the main road. Martin recognized his own outgrown clothes on the brothers. Each child carried a bundle of food tied up in a kerchief. Kate was true to her word that they would not be sent away without something to sustain them on their journey. But how far was their journey to take them? Martin wondered how many of these had traveled the roads of hope with Daniel O'Connell last summer? Where would they be now if Repeal had not failed? If O'Connell had not been arrested and a man like Joseph shipped out of Ireland?

The certainty that every man would be tilling his own land if things had gone differently made Martin seethe inside.

"I won't forget what they've done," Martin said through clenched teeth. "O'Shea and Mahon'll not get away with it, Mary Elizabeth."

Mary Elizabeth replied, "They got away with everythin'. And now how's Kate goin' to feed everyone they toss? There won't be anythin' left a'tall."

Scully and Kirby made their way through the line. Each received a pair of slices of soda bread and a dollop of sweet butter to go between them. Kirby took a bite. "This is real good," he observed to Margaret. Taking in the woman's pleased expression, he added, "Bet you're the one baked it, right?" When the cook nodded, he said, "Best I ever eat."

The line moved along toward the stew. Scully hissed, "What're you flirtin' with the cook for?"

Kirby sounded peeved at having to explain. "Colonel . . . ," he said, then remembered he was not supposed to give himself away.

Lowering his voice, he resumed, "His Honor said we was to mingle so as to get the lay of the land, didn't he? Well, I'm minglin'.'"

Each of the evicted carried a dish or bowl of his own, and it was into this container that the steaming brew was ladled by Fern. "Scully," Kirby said suddenly, "we ain't got no bowls."

"Here you go, then," Old Flynn shouted, tapping Kirby on the shoulder and handing each man a tin cup. "Can't hold stew in your bare hands, can you?"

"Much obliged," Kirby yelled back. "Very kind."

The two men hunted a vacant stretch of lawn on which to recline while eating. Just before they sat, Scully spotted Kate serving the second bread line with the curly-haired Tomeen on her hip. "Lady Burke," he said, nudging his companion. "Right there she is. Keep your kerchief pulled up."

Nesbitt was talking to Rusty as the two men used long-handled iron pokers to evenly distribute the embers under the stew pots. "I have never seen such starvation in my life," he said in the Irish. "I've seen shipboard fever waste a man to nothing. I've seen scurvy-eaten sailors with their teeth falling out. But I've never seen the like of this."

Rusty agreed that the Ben Beg folk were especially tragic. "And to think they were turned out by one of their own," he said.

"I don't think any of these would ever claim O'Shea as one of theirs," Nesbitt observed caustically. "Can't you just see what would happen if he were here right now? Course, he would stand out a mile, so sleek and well fed and all."

Rusty stared toward a pair of men seated on the green. "Like those?" he suggested. "Their clothing is ragged, but they don't look like they have missed as many meals as these others."

"Mister Nesbitt," Old Flynn interrupted before the steward had seen Rusty point out the incongruous duo. "Mister Nesbitt," Flynn persisted, "Lady Burke says you and Rusty here are to bring the reserve loaves from the pantry."

"Tell her we'll see to it right away," Nesbitt replied.

Mrs. Joyce ambled among the outcasts of Ben Beg singing softly to the little boys in her arms.

Where are you goin' to
little one, little one?
Where are you goin' to
after I'm gone?
Whose arms will hold ye
little one, little one?
I'd never leave ye
but my heart it is torn . . .

Tears rolled down her cheeks. But none among the mass noticed. What was one additional tear, more or less, when a sea of tears had been shed for Ireland?

The woman raised her eyes toward two thickset, well-fed men sitting together on the lawn.

With a sly smile and a curt nod, the one called Kirby announced to her that it was time she play her part in the drama.

She looked down at her child and then away, sorrowing for the loss of him. And yet, perhaps Lady Kate would have mercy. Perhaps she would see that he was raised without hunger. Surely Kate Donovan Burke was a woman with a kind heart.

The servant, Fern, was spooning bowls of stew. She was the one Mrs. Joyce had chosen yesterday. The plan was simple.

Mrs. Joyce walked slowly toward Fern, who was no longer smiling and had given up making small talk an hour ago.

"Why, Mrs. Joyce," Fern remarked in surprise, "you're weepin'."

"And is there a sadder day in all the world?" Mrs. Joyce replied. "But look. Your mistress is there toilin' in the hot sun with the baby Tom in her arms. Go help her, and I'll stand in here."

Fern replied, "She'll work till she drops, that one. And herself in the family way as she is." She pressed the ladle into Mrs. Joyce's hand and scurried off to spell Kate.

Mrs. Joyce dished up two bowls of stew then, pleading the need to see to her children, passed the job to another.

Kirby watched the departure of Nesbitt and Rusty with ill-concealed glee. "That's tops," he exulted. "Steward and his watch-dog gone. Must mean it's time."

Ticking off the necessary items, Scully double-checked each require-ment as Kirby muttered them aloud. "All our blokes inside the gates and spread through the crowd."

"Aye."

"Lady Burke and child in sight."

"Aye."

"The woman and her brat."

"Yep."

"At least two of our boys near each of the Claddagh folk?"

This took a little longer to determine, but at last Scully was able to confirm the truth of the statement.

"Then it is time," said Kirby grimly. "Time to earn our pay."

25

The sun climbed higher, beating down on Kate's back. Tomeen drowsed in the crook of her arm as she worked the line beside Father O'Bannon and Old Flynn.

Five hundred and eighteen had passed through the gates, according to Flynn. Father O'Bannon stated that there had never been a wake so solemn as this nor a gathering of Irish who spoke so little.

Fern tapped Kate on the shoulder. "Two hours you've been at it. Will ye sit down and rest then?" she asked Kate.

"No. Not so long as there are mouths to feed." It was not enough for Kate to provide the bread and butter. She wanted to stand before the line and offer sustenance with her own hand.

"Let me take Tomeen." Fern lifted the baby from Kate, who relinquished the child gratefully. "He's growin' so. He can sleep in my arms as well as your own."

The passing of Tomeen Burke into the willing arms of Fern set the plan in motion.

Trembling with the anguish of what she must now perform, the Widow Joyce kissed her own baby boy farewell, embraced him one last time, and beneath the watchful eye of Mahon's thugs, hurried to Fern's side.

"Beg pardon, Miss Fern. Would you mind holdin' my boy for just a moment while I see to my others? The sun is burnin' his fair skin, and you've the only shade left in Galway. Lord! Where are those children? They've wandered off in this mob, and I can't see them."

"Aye! He is turnin' a bit pink, ain't he? What's his name again? You've got so many I've forgot this one already."

"Robert. After his grandfather, Miss." The widow's voice quaked, but Fern seemed to pay this thin veneer of control no mind.

Fern, who was absently rocking the sleeping Tomeen, spread her shawl on the grass, sat down on the cool, shady patch, shifted him on her shoulder, and then accepted the sleeping Joyce child onto her lap without complaint. "Well now, Robert. That's better, ain't it?" Then to the mother she remarked, "He's a handsome boy. Sunburn makes 'em cranky. Can't be too careful on a day like today. I'll stay right here. Won't they have a fine time if they awaken? They're of a size. Two peas in a pod."

"Thanks."

One final touch of Robert's cheek, and the Widow Joyce hurried away to watch and wait.

Smiling with satisfaction, Kirby watched the Widow Joyce deposit Robert on Fern's shawl and move away from the children. He stood and motioned for Scully to do likewise. At the top of his lungs, he bellowed, "You made me spill my stew, you blighted sot!" Kirby hooked his toe underneath Scully's tin cup and flipped the remaining contents into his comrade's face.

Scully launched himself at Kirby's throat, cursing. The two men tangled in each other's grasp, rolled over and over on the lawn, crashing into bystanders who had only just turned toward the noise.

In the scuffle the two thugs knocked over many cups of stew. "Leave off. Get by, there," protested a Benbeger.

"You want some of this?" challenged Kirby, releasing his hold on Scully. "Here it is, then!" and he socked the complainer in the face. When friends of the man tried to intervene, Scully took them both on, grabbing them around the necks and bashing their heads together.

A woman, trying to snatch a child out of harm's way and save a bowl of stew at the same time, was bowled over in the scuffle. Her child wailed, and she yowled, both at the maximum volume.

Rage breached the surface in a dozen places, then splashed down upon the startled citizens of Ben Beg. With astounding violence and rapidity the invented conflict rolled across the gathering, sweeping up men who could not know the true purpose of the battle.

The Widow Joyce, twenty paces away, kept her eyes fixed on Fern. When the servant leaped to her feet to discover the what, the who, and the why of the ruckus, Mrs. Joyce sprang into action.

Gathering her skirts, she ran to Fern's side.

"What is it? What's happened?" she exclaimed.

"There!" Fern pointed over bobbing heads crowding closer to see.

"Lord have mercy!" Mrs. Joyce shouted above the din. "Watch out! They're comin' right at us! They'll be crushin' the children! The babies!" In an instant, she scooped up red-haired Tom and dashed into the wall of onlookers.

At her warning, Fern followed suit, snatching small Robert Joyce out of the path of a half-dozen brawling, swearing, Connaught men. She held the baby close against her, shielding him as she dodged the flailing body of a man who tumbled across the shawl where the two babies had been sleeping just a moment before.

Despite Mary Elizabeth's desire to help with the food distribution, the crush of the crowd was too much and the rush to get everyone fed so intense that she and Martin were shunted aside. In order to at least see the proceedings, the two Donovan children clambered onto the stone wall and balanced there.

It was from this roost that Martin first spotted the disturbance. Looking toward an outbreak of sudden shouting he saw a man with wiry tufts of hair grab two others and smack their heads together.

To the boy's surprise, six other combats broke out across the green in widely separated spots at almost the same instant. Martin was scanning past a burly figure standing peacefully in the bread line when the fellow pivoted abruptly and clobbered the man waiting behind him, for no apparent reason.

"Vermin!" he heard a voice shouting. "No-good scum!"

"What's happenin', Martin?" Mary Elizabeth wondered. The girl extended her foot toward a lower stone as if to climb down.

"No!" Martin exclaimed, grabbing her arm and dragging his sister roughly back up. "Stay here!"

A Claddagh man, Moor, by his complexion, tried to separate a pair of brawlers. Instead of successfully calming the fray, he was grappled by the two and in a trice was underneath them both and being kicked in the side by a third.

"It's a regular donnybrook," Martin muttered. "Who'd think starvin' folks could have so much fight in 'em?"

"Can you see Kate? Is she all right?"

Martin surveyed the mob. "I see her," he said. "She's with Father O'Bannon." Then in a worried afterthought, he added, "But I don't see Tomeen."

The kettle of the fracas boiled over toward Kate.

"Let's get you indoors," said Father O'Bannon. "You are in no condition to be brawlin'."

"But the children!" Kate protested. "Not without them!"

Six men battling eight others stumbled against a stew pot, knocking it over and pouring the broth into the fire. A cloud of steam sizzled upward, and the combatants jumped awkwardly to avoid being scorched.

"Yes, you will!" O'Bannon ordered. He took Kate's arm and dragged her toward the kitchen.

Nesbitt and Rusty came at a run from the house. "I heard the commotion clear inside," Nesbitt said. Taking in the clash at a glance, he said to the Claddagh man, "Help the good father get her inside." To O'Bannon he added, "Keep her there, Father." Then to Kate: "Don't worry, ma'am. We'll get this sorted out soon."

A trio of brawlers surged toward Kate as if to sweep her into the waves of the battle, but Nesbitt leaped between her and the combatants, and Kate was hustled away.

Nesbitt, Father O'Bannon, and Kate were in the kitchen.

"It was nothin' a'tall." Father O'Bannon patted Kate on the back. "Not a thing. Emotions a-boil, that's all. No evil intent. They've calmed down, ye see. Gentle as lambs they are. The trouble-makers gone. Down the road they went and away."

Kate, ashen, had not taken her eyes from the window since it all began. "Where are the children? Where's Tomeen? Martin and Mary Elizabeth?"

Martin called from outside as he pounded his fist against the door. "Kate! Are you in there, sister?"

"There, see? What'd I tell ye?" Father O'Bannon mopped his brow and shuffled to let the children in.

At the turning of the latch, Martin and Mary Elizabeth burst in. Mary Elizabeth charged Kate, wrapping her arms around her neck. "O, sister! I was so afraid! I seen everything! I thought they'd come back to kill you!"

"There, there," Father O'Bannon consoled.

Martin's hands were shaking, his lips pressed tightly together. "Where's the Widow Joyce? Where's Tomeen?"

Kate stood with difficulty. "Fern has him."

Martin looked hard at Nesbitt and said, "Fern's got the other one."

Nesbitt's spine went rigid. He spoke quietly. "What are you tellin' me, boy?"

"Fern's lookin' for the Widow Joyce. Fern's got her baby boy. The one they call Robert. Now she's searchin' everywhere for the Widow Joyce. Thought the widow would be here with Kate. She says the widow took up Tomeen and saved him from harm when the brawl . . ."

Nesbitt opened his mouth as if to speak. Kate read the meaning in his expression.

"Where are they?" Kate cried. "Where's the woman? Where has she taken Tomeen?"

Martin hurried from one cluster of refugees to another. "Have you seen the Widow Joyce?" he implored. The tall crofter to whom the question was addressed shook his head wearily without removing the bloodstained rag he pressed to his lip.

"The Widow Joyce?"

"Not since back in the village, before we was tossed."

"The Joyce family? A woman with a whole brood includin' a wee boy?"

A short fellow with a smashed nose stared dully at his own wife and five children, then answered in the negative.

Escaped from the guardianship of Simeon, Mad Molly paralleled Martin's course. "Have you seen Eve?" she wondered aloud. "The bargain struck will not bless her children."

Gritting his teeth, Martin continued asking, "Seen the Widow Joyce?"

A response in the affirmative from another of the tossed was so unexpected that the boy almost said thanks and passed on. "You did?" he said.

"Aye," repeated the man as he tied a makeshift bandage around the head of a friend despite the sling with which his own arm was encumbered. "Saw her goin' out the gate just before I got meself clobbered."

"Was anyone with her?"

The refugee snorted, then winced with pain. "Only her whole litter," he said. "She must be a prophet to know when to get clear."

"Locked up the wrong madwoman, did ye?" Molly peered into Martin's face. "He'll lock her away till it be safe. Listen to Molly. Lock her away, he will!"

Kate controlled her voice only with difficulty. "We are so few," she said, "and the country so big. How can we find him?"

Fern, holding little Robert Joyce, who was unconcernedly playing with a wooden spoon, snuffled and looked about to wail again. Nesbitt ordered Margaret to take the maid and the changeling out of the room. "This is Justin Davitt from Ben Beg," he said, introducing a stoop-shouldered man with grey hair. "I knew his cousins in Galway City. They are good people."

"I also vouch for him," added Father O'Bannon. Davitt nodded his appreciation.

"The Ben Beg folk know what has happened," Nesbitt continued. "Many of them want to help. Davitt here will pick out the most reliable. Since they all know him, there will be no trouble. Any doubtful ones among them are already gone."

"We'll comb the hills and the downs for the wee one," Davitt said. "We can field such an army that not even a rabbit will go unnoticed."

Nesbitt added, "And we'll start at once. Whatever trail the woman left will still be clear. You mustn't worry, Lady Burke. We'll find him."

❦ 26 ❦

The smell of land—earthy, warm, dry land—reached the exiles through some freak of heated air that flowed over the cooler sea breeze driving Joseph's boat. "We're saved!" Laurence O'Halloran exulted.

"Saved," Father Talbot murmured.

"We haven't landed yet," Joseph observed. "Look at the size of those breakers! We must lie along the shore and hunt for a place to beach safely."

With Hoyle's firm grip on the tiller and Joseph trimming the sail, the gig coasted parallel to the line of white water. Although Joseph felt the land's presence tantalizingly near, it was as yet unseen. Just above the streak of rolling surf, a dense mist, the visible border between the aquatic and terrestrial kingdoms, hovered overhead. "How can we sail into that?" Laurence asked. "Even if we pass the waves, there may be rocks. What's to do?"

What indeed? The gig, one moment responding to rudder and

trim, was in the next being carried headlong through the water in the grip of an unsuspected current. The racing flow defeated every attempt to turn aside. With the wind dead astern, it was impossible to veer back out to sea.

The frail boat rocketed southward, heading directly toward where a mass of the fog bank protruded into the ocean. The roar of the breakers reached the ears of the castaways. Whatever was going to be their fate was about to be decided.

"When we're in the surf, we must set the nose on shore!" Joseph yelled over the reverberation of the waves. "If we broach to, we're done for! Break out the oars!"

The gig was in the rollers. Hoyle put the tiller hard over, committing them to whatever shore lay in front of them. "I can't hold it!" he shouted.

Joseph, on one side, and the one-armed Hoyle, on the other, wrestled against the current for possession of the rudder. Laurence and Father Talbot laid on the oars. In the bow, Jailor Gann huddled beneath the peak of the prow. The waves piled up faster behind them than the ship was traveling, and the boat slewed sideways. "Turn her! Turn her!" was the cry.

The men fought the vessel back to perpendicular, only to be tossed by the following sea and lose all steerageway. The next wave crested almost on top of them, filling the boat with spume and the eyes of the crew with stinging spray. "God have mercy!" Talbot prayed.

"Rocks ahead!" O'Halloran screamed, glancing wildly over his shoulder and pointing to a jagged outcropping that rose like a demonic battlement from the hissing sea. Without any pretense that the pitiful humans controlled the course, the gig shot between a gap in the crags so narrow that both oars splintered with cracks like musketfire.

Then the waves, circling round the rocks, toyed with the gig, striking it first from one side and then from the other. Like a shuttlecock, the tiny craft was batted from crest to crest, no direction or action more likely to lead to safety than to destruction.

Finally, as if tiring of the game, an enormous wave rolled up behind the gig. The stern rose higher and higher in the air, half its length posed on the very peak of the roller. With a last dismissive slap, the breaker flipped the gig forward, stern over bow, tumbling puny men and pathetic belongings into the boiling surf.

Gagging and retching, Joseph coughed up more seawater than he would have believed he could hold and still live. He was in no hurry to move; not just yet. The coarse sand felt warm under his face, and his body wanted only to absorb energy from the sunlight before forcing itself to move. It was good to be alive—and surprising too. Joseph Connor Burke wanted to wallow in the sensation for a time. It was not until a returning tide tickled his feet that Joseph roused himself, suddenly fearful that a seventh wave might drag him backward into the cauldron.

Opening one lid, he saw eye-to-eye with a ghostly pale crab that scuttled away from the movement. Rising up as far as his knees, Joseph scanned the beach for signs of the others. About thirty yards away, John Hoyle was likewise stirring from a prone position. Joseph stood, brushing gravel from what remained of his clothing and from the sun-bleached beard that made him look a hundred years old. Sitting on a mass of seaweed and trailing more of the same from his head and shoulders was Father Talbot. He was cradling Laurence O'Halloran across his lap.

Stumbling across the shingle, Joseph joined the priest. "Is he . . . ?"

"Oh, nay," responded Talbot, smiling. "He's had a knock about the head right enough, but he'll come round soon I'm thinkin'."

Reassured, Joseph studied the shoreline. The line of monstrous breakers through which they had passed stretched in unbroken succession out of sight in both directions. It was miraculous they made it across alive. Of the faithful gig there was no trace, save one forlorn bit of oar rocking in a tidepool.

In the other direction stood rank upon rank of sand dunes. Each hillock loomed larger than the one before. The orderly files of mounds seemed purpose-built to shelter this expanse of strand. *Or imprison it*, Joseph thought.

Rejoining Hoyle, Joseph asked, "Have you seen ought of Gann?"

"No," Hoyle said, pounding the side of his head to drive out the water from an ear. "I saw him once when we were flung from boat. He was clingin' to the bow, like, only the bow weren't still attached." The one-armed convict shrugged and then added, "Should go look I 'spose."

Northward the finer sand was too hot under bare feet, so they directed their steps south along a line of thin vegetation that grew at the juncture of the gravel and the dunes. Lizards scuttled away from their approaching shadows, and once a lizard-sized scorpion ran from one scrawny weed to another. "There is life of a kind here," Joseph observed, "but it does not appear welcomin'."

"And just where is here, figger?"

"I have no way of knowin', really," Joseph admitted. "It looks like what I've read about the southwest coast of Africa, and we were driftin' that way, but God only knows."

"And rescue."

"God only knows."

They climbed one dune, faced another, climbed it and the third, then allowed themselves to be daunted by the yet taller and steeper one beyond and returned to the shore. Hoyle was in the lead when they rounded a crook in the coastline, and he let out an excited yelp. "A ship! I see a mast!"

Moving as rapidly as weary limbs and malnourished bodies would allow, they staggered over a rocky knoll. The two men were already waving and yelling hoarsely to attract attention.

Both halted abruptly as the absurdly high, boxy quarterdeck of the goal came into view. It was indeed a ship, but it lay two hundred yards from the water, and it swam in a pool of drifting sand that buried it up to the level of its gunports. It was a derelict vessel, driven ashore in the unknown past and left behind when even the ocean abandoned it to the desert.

"Should we look for survivors?" Hoyle asked doubtfully. "Or food or water?" The forecastle was missing, and the remaining half vessel was only curved timbers and the stump of a mainmast beneath the top deck.

"Tools, maybe," Joseph said. "Those who sailed her have been dead these three hundred years. She is . . . was . . . a Spanish galleon."

"Keep away," warned a voice more animal than human. "She's a treasure ship, and she's mine, see?" Jailor Gann emerged from the ribs of the hulk and confronted the dumbfounded convicts.

"Are you completely daft?" Hoyle inquired. "We're stranded here now with no food and no water a'tall, and you're thinkin' of gold?"

A roar that exceeded the greatest bellow the waves had produced echoed among the dunes. Into view only two hills away east strode a magnificent lion. His shaggy, golden mane billowed around his massive head, and he disdained to notice the pack of jackals that yipped and barked around him. From his jaws dangled the carcass of a full-grown antelope. The lion toted the deadweight with nonchalant ease.

"You may have found this treasure ship," Joseph said softly to Gann as three men backed away toward the shore. "But I think someone with a stronger claim may be returnin'."

O'Halloran was sitting upright and rubbing the back of his head when Joseph, Hoyle, and Gann returned to the shingle. The priest had formed a shelter of sorts, using seaweed draped over the bleached bones of whales. The sun had passed beyond pleasant to stifling, and the swirls of wind only drove handfuls of stinging sand against already raw flesh.

After listening to Joseph's description of the surroundings and their animal neighbors, the Cashel youth asked, "And what sort of a place is this we have fallen into? Trapped between salt and sand with no water and in the midst of ravenous lions. Are we in hell, Father?"

Talbot shook his head. "No, lad," he said, then added, "But it is a fair enough replica that it should make any sinner flee the real thing." Turning to Joseph, the priest asked, "It is clear we cannot remain here. With no water to hand, we cannot live above two or three more days. Can we cross the dunes, do you think? Or must we chance followin' the coast?"

"I say inland," Gann said, though no one was looking at him. "There must be grass beyond the dunes to feed the grazing creature the lion killed. And where there is grass, there is water."

Joseph and Hoyle compared opinions and concurred before Joseph replied, "Along the shore, I think. That there is water inland may be so since there are animals who must need it as we do. But I fear gettin' lost in a trackless waste to no purpose. And if ships ever venture upon this skeleton-like place, we may yet be rescued."

"Inland, and that's an order!"

It was apparent everyone was ignoring Gann. What threat could he impose on them now? What command could he give or punishment inflict that would make their lot one bit worse? He was welcome to follow their plan or not, as he chose, but that was all.

"There may be seabird eggs in the rocks for food, or fish trapped in shallow pools," Joseph said. "We'll leave tomorrow before sunup. Tonight we'll rest and recruit our strength."

There was no way to build a fire, so the five survivors huddled close together for mutual protection from wandering beasts. Gann sat a little ways apart from the others, but when a hyena cackled from a nearby dune, even he scooted closer to the rest.

There had been scant pickings from the rocks, but it did not seem to matter. Without water it was the same dilemma all over again: no one's hunger competed with their thirst.

Before sleep claimed him, Joseph occupied his time digging a cone-shaped pit in the damp earth just above the high-tide mark. At the bottom of the concavity, he arranged a layer of the cleanest dry grass he could locate. From the circumference of the hole he trailed the long, skinny leaves of a desert plant downward to meet at a point in the plucked stems of grass. A trip to the shoreline provided a double handful of smooth, round pebbles with which to secure the edges and the bottom of the creepers.

As the first light of dawn rose over the dunes, Joseph went to examine his contraption. The night fogs had swept damply over the land and condensed on the tendrils of the plants. The heap of grass in the burrow was moist with water; a modest amount to be sure, but fresh water for all that. By distributing portions of the clippings into eager fists, each castaway was able to squeeze a few drops of the precious fluid into desperately parched mouths.

Of the whole contrivance, only the pebbles might not be easily reproduced, so Joseph pocketed them to carry as they rose for the tramp along the shore.

In the frantic search for small Tom Burke, men were assigned their duties by landmarks: the lone hawthorn above the waterfall, the ancient stone circle across the downs, the fairy rath on the hillside, the stone cross, the ruined village up the river. It was Nesbitt's plan to disperse his army of searchers over the widest possible area. Instead of giving the Joyce woman time to escape the county altogether, they would travel farther and faster than she could. Then, like the cords of a net, the pursuers would draw together toward Burke Park.

Martin and Father O'Bannon visited every home in Ballynockanor. "Had any strangers been seen near the village?" they asked. "Any woman with a red-haired child? Any one at all?"

Together they examined every tumbledown cottage, outbuilding, stable, every hayrick and turf mound. They found nothing.

Nesbitt rode to Allintober, alerting that village about the kidnapping. He extracted from the people there a vow that any unknown would be reported to him. Two dozen more men volunteered to join the hunt.

Simeon and Rusty, Moor and Sonny-boy, went in pairs to the loneliest spots in the bogs. There was no cave big enough to admit a badger that they did not explore, no trickle of smoke they did not investigate, no traveler campsite they did not scrutinize.

All the searching came to nothing. No report of any unknown woman, with or without a red-haired child, produced any useful information. The Joyces and Tomeen had vanished.

By the third day of the quest to find the baby, Nesbitt was reeling in the saddle. He had not slept in seventy-two hours and was so stiff that Simeon had to help him get off the horse. A jug of tea and a biscuit was all he would permit himself before the steward was out again, organizing the next phase of the quest.

A line of men, no farther apart than a stone's throw, extended from the west bank of the Cornamona all the way back to Burke Park.

The column moved north extremely slowly. Every cairn of stones was studied, every freshly turned burrow dug up. Though unspoken, it was understood: they were no longer hunting only a living child.

With her chin in hand, Mad Molly sat on the low step outside the kitchen and stared off toward the river. She had been mute since the first day of Tomeen's disappearance. She would not speak to Nesbitt or so much as look at Kate. Simeon could not make her smile. Old Flynn could not make her rave. Margaret could not make her eat. It was a worry to all. When Fern sniffled past, holding poor little Robert in her arms, fat tears silently coursed down the creases in Molly's face. At this one sign of emotion, Kate observed that Molly had lost her sanity the night small Joseph Connor Burke had vanished nearly twenty years before. Perhaps the old woman remembered and so wept for Fern as well as for Tomeen.

"She's set her heart on dyin'," Father O'Bannon said when she would not speak to him. "She clutches the crucifix her husband held the night he passed. She'll not turn loose of it."

"And die she will," Nesbitt concurred solemnly. "For she has not had any nourishment, but only lapped water from the rain barrel."

Martin and Mary Elizabeth decided she must be saved. All day they sat, one on each side of her. They spoke of Kate and the baby soon to be born. They talked of Joseph's pardon and things hopeful. When Mary Elizabeth said that surely Tomeen would be found sound and healthy, the old woman put her hands over her ears and squeezed her eyes shut.

"Don't talk about Tomeen," Martin whispered. "See what it does to her. If she was a snail, she'd go into her shell and never come out again."

Mary Elizabeth, so sad and frightened herself, put a hand on Molly's grizzled head. "Wouldn't you like to go down to the river, Molly? Come and catch frogs with us, will you?"

Molly lowered her gnarled hands and raised her chin to look away, far off toward the mountains of Ben Beg. She said nothing in reply.

Martin tried. "If you won't catch frogs, then will you come watch the hurlin' match at the cemetery between the dead folk of Ballynockanor and them from Castletown?" This was one of Molly's favorite pastimes: wandering through the gravestones and calling out which friends long gone had scored the goal. She claimed the Ballynockanor team always won. This had always brightened Molly's darkest day.

Molly did not seem to hear Martin. She made the sign of the cross upon her breast and kissed the crucifix. Did she see that she'd soon be playing among her heavenly kinfolk?

Kate, who had her own grief to bear, tried to cheer Molly even as she comforted Fern. Kate came out into the summer afternoon and, curling her legs beneath her rounded self, sat in the cool grass.

She took Molly's hand and placed it on her belly. "The baby's kickin' again, Molly darlin'. 'Tis Joseph's child. You'll not be leavin' us before you hold Joseph Connor's babe in your old arms, will you?"

Even this evoked no response. Frail and brittle as an autumn leaf, Molly swayed a bit when the wind came up. She lifted her finger into the air as though to test it. Or perhaps she was pointing toward heaven.

"What's she doin'?" Martin asked.

Kate replied in a choked voice, "She's searchin' for Tomeen. Like all of us. She's searchin' her mind and wonderin' how it might have come 'round differently." Kate covered her face with her hands and wept. "What could I have done differently?"

Molly did not look at her, but stood and slowly wandered off toward her room at the far end of the stable.

Nesbitt came around the corner and watched Molly go. In a quiet voice he said to Kate, "You've heard?" he asked, seeing her tears.

She gasped. "Oh, no! Is he dead then?"

"Not that, ma'am. I'm sorry to give you a fright. It's just that the searchers have given up. We've combed every inch of ground. He's just not there. And that's a good thing, ma'am. Not finding him means we can still hope, doesn't it?"

Kate, exhausted, could only nod.

27

Joseph wiped sweat from his brow. Each day followed a similar pattern: trek from predawn, when there was enough light to keep from stumbling, until just before midday, when the oppressive heat made any movement draining; doze under whatever shelter could be improvised until late afternoon; hike again until darkness fell. Everyone imitated the success of Joseph's condensation trap. There had been no easily located basin of shiny, round pebbles such as he carried, but they managed. Some mornings it was possible to drink dew drops off the spiny tendrils of desert-loving plants. It was enough, but just barely. For food, the castaways plucked seaweed and mussels from the rocks and gathered a few seabird eggs, which they ate raw.

Each night they saw glowing eyes ringing their encampment; each morning revealed jackal tracks and increasingly frequent glimpses of the tawny-coated, black-backed scavengers. If the exiles did not find rescue soon, it was clear what the fate of their remains would be.

One late twilight, when by Joseph's estimation they had covered no more than ten miles since the previous day, Hoyle, who was leading, motioned for them to stand still. "Listen," he urged.

At first it was difficult to distinguish the sound that had caught his attention from the constant roar of the nearby waves, but there was something additional. It was a not-too-distant rolling growl like the coughing rumble of a lion, only not so deep. "It sounds like hundreds of them," O'Halloran noted nervously. "Maybe we should go back the other way. What if they smell us?"

Gann agreed. "Turn around," he said. "Now."

"Can't go back," Hoyle argued. "We're near done in."

Joseph pointed to the spur of a rocky ridge that ran seaward just ahead of them. "Hoyle and I will climb up and look," he volunteered. "The rest stay here."

As the two men scrambled higher up the craggy slope, the noise grew louder until it overwhelmed the boom of the breakers crashing on the shore. The sound also resolved from a uniform reverberation to something more like grunting or barking. "It's not lions," Joseph said, scaling the last of the grade, "it's . . . seals."

That observation was an enormous understatement. The semicircle of bay that appeared below the two men was home to thousands of seals, perhaps as many as a hundred thousand. The constant roaring was deafening and confusing to the senses. Barking, biting, basking, the seal population claimed the beach from one side of the inlet to the other, and the waters of the gulf teemed with them as well. The only stretch of cove not alive with wriggling, reddish-brown creatures was that occupied by the sailing ship anchored in the center.

Within an hour the castaways were aboard the *Sigurd*, a fur sealer owned by Captain Joachim ten Eyck of Cape Town. All five exiles had to be repeatedly cautioned to drink slowly of the abundant water. The *Sigurd's* crew of black, Dutch, English, and Portuguese sealers marveled at the haggard features on those who had staggered out of the desert.

The Dutch heritage of the captain made his English a trifle thick, but his sincere amazement was evident when he said, "You joost lucky men. No vun comes out of der Namib alive. Unt today iss der last day of sealing. Vee sail for Cape Town today."

That triumphant moment, when John Hoyle had dropped to his knees and Father Talbot was humming a hymn of praise to God, was chosen by Jailor Gann to speak: "I am an officer of the British Crown," he said. "These are prisoners, convicts. I want 'em kept in irons till we see the governor at the Cape."

Colonel Mahon traced the rings on the oak tabletop with his finger. "You're a fool, O'Shea."

"They've given up! He's too small to tell where he comes from or speak of who his parents are. What I'm sayin', Squire, is that this can be done without sheddin' the blood of a child. An orphanage in Belfast. Who's to know?"

Mahon slammed his fist down hard. "It's his blood or ours! The son of Joseph Burke is dead in the imagination of every man from London to Galway City. Why disappoint the world? Kill him!"

O'Shea shuffled uneasily. "I can't do it."

"You *will* do it. Every finger will point to you if he lives and is found!"

"I've left him in a fine safe place. With Widow Joyce, he is!"

"That one! You mean you've left her alive to breath and prattle about all she knows?" Mahon clutched the lapel of O'Shea's jacket. "She dies with him, and the truth dies. She lives, the child lives, and it's your neck in the noose!"

"Not mine alone!"

Mahon flung him away. "Indeed it is yours alone." He gestured at the clock. "I'll give you till tomorrow, O'Shea. Kill the heir of Joseph Burke, or the rumor mill will grind you to dust."

"And you."

"It's all your own doing. I've made certain I'll not be implicated." Calmer now, he unlocked the top drawer of his desk. He pulled out a stack of bound documents and held them before O'Shea's face. "Affidavits from those you hired to stage the fray at Burke Park that day. All properly sworn, and none who say they knew your purpose. Two who saw your carriage take the Widow Joyce away." With a grin, he tucked the evidence away. O'Shea was beaten.

"Kill him, you say. Then damn my soul."

"You're damned already. You sold your soul to me long ago." Mahon inhaled as though breathing fresh, cool air. "I'll want proof."

"Shall I bring his body to your doorstep as proof?" O'Shea asked bitterly.

"His heart will be enough."

Sunlight and shadow played upon the great granite terraces of the mountain that climbed behind the ruined village of Ben Beg. There was a cabin perched upon the crag. The earth dropped away behind it two hundred feet into the river canyon.

O'Shea kept a store of food and blankets at the shelter for his own use when he remembered his roots and longed to escape what he had become.

This was where he stashed the Widow Joyce and her brood of children.

O'Shea's eye picked out the finger of peat smoke from the chimney. It swirled up and was lost in the mists that circled the mountaintop. He was certain no one else would think to look in such a place. No one would suspect. At any rate, talk throughout the county was that they had given up the search—all except the Lady Burke and Nesbitt, her steward, and the Claddagh men.

Reckoning murder, the soldiers stationed in Cong had, in some show of concern for the son of an Irish lord, dragged the pools of the river where the body of an infant might fetch up after a while. In this way they hoped to say to the populace that they had nothing to do with the slaughter of the Burke child. Officials as far away as Dublin put the word out that this vanishing and certain death was the doing of Irish militants who still held a grudge against Joseph Burke and Daniel O'Connell for the failure of politics to free the Irish. It was hoped by Dublin Castle that the child's body would never be recovered and the crime never reconstructed. Atrocities that remained undiscovered left room to accuse whatever political faction was on the rise in popularity among the Irish people. To be blamed for the murder of an innocent child, no matter what the reason, was sure to cast a cloud over the Ribbonmen of Western Ireland.

Except for the smoke, there was no sign of life within. The widow had minded well O'Shea's warning that she could not show herself without risk of being hanged for a child stealer. No doubt the older children had spotted him coming hours ago and scuttled away out of sight as he approached.

He rode up the steep path, leaning into his horse to ease the ascent. At the top of the trail, he paused and looked back. "There ought to be a view around the world from this place if the clouds would ever part," he said, patting his horse.

Dismounting, he waited awhile before he called. "Woman!"

There was a rustle within. The hinges of the aged plank door groaned back. The filthy face of the widow peered out at him suspiciously. The Widow Joyce still had learned nothing about soap and water, it seemed.

"Ah! It's yourself, Squireen O'Shea, sir! We'd nearly given up hopin' ye'd come fetch us. The vittles are near gone."

"Is the child alive?" O'Shea asked, hoping that some disease had carried Tom Burke off naturally, leaving nothing for O'Shea to do.

"That he is, Your Honor! Took fine care of him, we did. He ain't my Robert, but I took a comfort in him all the same." Over her shoulder she called, "Maeve! Bring the Burke boy."

O'Shea did not enter the cabin. The brood tumbled out into the open. A girl of about eleven, carrying Tomeen in her arms, emerged last. The baby's shining red locks were matted with filth. His eyes were dull, and his color sallow.

It came to O'Shea that even the son of a lord could be mistaken for one of the litter when left in the mud of a pigsty.

"Now, Your Honor," the woman said, turning her eyes upward in a disgusting imitation of coyness, "I've kept my bargain. Will ye keep your own? A place for me and my children. I know y'will."

O'Shea observed her bitterly. She was as trapped by Mahon as he was. "The colonel says I should kill you and be done with it."

At his words her demure cheerfulness faded. Fear and doubt chased each other across her face, and then a thin smile bravely reappeared. "A fine jest, Your Honor."

"No jest."

Now terror seized her in earnest. She dropped to her knees and clasped her hands together to beg him. "But I've done all ye asked. Every bit of it! Ye can't mean to do me harm."

Coldly O'Shea replied, "He thinks you'll talk. You and your brood. Those who can talk, he says, will talk."

"I swear! Not a word!" She wept. "Please, Your Honor! Just let us go! I'll keep my oath! Spare my children!"

O'Shea riveted his gaze on Tom Burke. This was where it began and where it ended. Kill this child, and Mahon would never care about the Widow Joyce or her brood of beggars.

"I intend to let you live," he remarked without emotion. He did not add that he had always intended to let them live. He would not have any such shabby, filthy, wretched ghosts appear to haunt him in long nights.

Widow Joyce prostrated herself before him. Sobbing with gratitude, she dug her fingers into the ground. "Lord bless ye, sir! A good man ye are!" She kissed his boots as her children cowered against the wall of the shack.

"Get up." Repulsed, he turned away. "Have done with the keenin', or I'll kill ye to put an end to it."

Abruptly she ceased her wailing and sat up. "Anything a'tall, sir!"

He jerked his head downward once and said to the girl, "Put Tom Burke down. That's right. On the threshold."

The girl obeyed. Tom, deprived of even that meager physical comfort, whimpered weakly.

"He looks half starved," O'Shea noted. "I told you he was not to suffer."

"We've fed him right along, Your Honor. So many mouths to feed . . ."

"Shut up," O'Shea said, snapping his fingers. "Now listen, you filthy, ignorant baggage. Take your litter of shoats down to the river and wash the dirt from yourselves entirely."

Widow Joyce nodded vigorously. "As ye say, sir."

O'Shea continued. "I've brought a valise full of clean clothes. Put them on. There's money for you to make a fresh start and passage purchased for you to sail on board the *Ivory Tess* out of Galway City."

"Leave Ireland?" Her eagerness diminished.

"Or die."

"I've always wanted to see the world." She rose and dusted herself off. "Where are we bound?"

"There's a shortage of women in Australia. Even a widow with seven children will have no trouble finding a man."

She curtsied. "Lord bless ye, Squireen O'Shea. I'll pray for ye every day!"

He stepped forward threateningly. "You'll pray for me never! Speak my name never! Remember my face not at all! For if you . . . or these . . . so much as think of me, the devil will whisper it in my ear, and I'll have you hunted down. Is that clear?"

She gulped and crossed herself. "Sure. I . . . we . . . never a word then. And what of the Burke boy? What's one more . . . more or less."

"Leave him to me. Take the valise. A mile down the path there's a waterfall and a pool. No one will recognize you without the coating of grime. You've a week to get to the ship. Don't miss the sailin'. Now get on with you before I change my mind."

O'Shea watched the retreating backs of the Joyce family till they were out of sight.

Tomeen Burke pulled himself up on the doorframe and toddled toward O'Shea. Unbalanced, the boy clutched at O'Shea's trousers with both hands and looked up into the squireen's face with some expression of relief.

"They haven't used you well, young Burke."

The streaked face of Tomeen lit up pleasantly at O'Shea's voice.

O'Shea frowned, stepped back from the grasp of the tiny hands, causing Tomeen to sit down hard.

Patiently the child picked himself up again and, on uncertain legs, walked to O'Shea and reached up to be held.

"I'm here to kill you." O'Shea pulled his hunting knife from its sheath. Sunlight glinted on the blade. He caught sight of his own pained reflection. He muttered, "Cut out your heart, says Mahon. Lord knows he's seen it done enough in the wars. Women and children too. Means nothin' to him. But I?" He picked up the baby and walked to the edge of the chasm where the river tumbled two hundred feet over the cliff and down into the steaming hot spring below. "I'm no butcher. You'll die of your own account if I leave you here. Or hunger if you last. Or you'll totter over to the brink and fall. But I'll not be here to see it, now will I? Not I. You'll not last long in such a place. Broken to pieces by the rocks. Dead before you ever touch the water. But it won't be my doin'." He placed the baby near the precipice where solid ground plummeted into space. The baby whined softly, not from fear of the danger, but because O'Shea had left him. "You're in God's hands now," O'Shea remarked, not looking back as he mounted his horse and rode down the mountain.

28

Molly was gone.

Simeon and Old Flynn brought the news to Kate before breakfast.

Simeon explained softly in the Gaelic, "She spoke to me last night. In the old, old tongue, it was. She said the brook began on the top of the mountain. The very top. The water is cool in the summer and warm in the winter. It is a curious thing. Her husband told her of it, she said. Steam rises from the water like the breath of an ox. Wee Tomeen is where it begins and where it ends." He tucked his chin. "This is what she said to me. I rejoiced that she had spoken, ma'am. Although I thought she spoke of death."

Though everything within her commanded that she sit down, Kate rose from her chair and went outside. Shading her eyes against the early morning light, she gazed east toward the peaks beyond Ben Beg.

Nesbitt followed her onto the steps. Simeon and Flynn came after.

"What is it, ma'am?" Nesbitt asked.

"Steam like the breath of an ox," Kate repeated. Then she asked Flynn, "My old da, Tom Donovan, used to fish for trout up there. Do you remember, Flynn? Bathe in a stream where there was a hot spring?"

"Aye. So did we all in our youth. With the lumbago, I've wished I could do it again. On O'Shea's property it is now, ma'am. Forbidden to fish or bathe either. Trespass on O'Shea's fishin' and be arrested. Been closed to common folk these many years."

"She's there," Kate remarked with certainty. "Gone there to die, I suppose. Go after her, will you, Nesbitt? Simeon? I can't bear to think of her up there alone. Bring her home to St. John's to be buried if she's dead. Either way, just bring her home."

You're not goin' without me!" Martin blocked the path of Nesbitt's hunter and clung to the bridle of Simeon's grey mount.

"The old woman'll be dead when they find her," Flynn argued gently. "Ye don't want to see her dead."

Martin scowled. "Saddle the pony for me, Flynn. If Mad Molly ain't dead, she's more likely to come home with myself than these two. They're strangers in her addled brain. She's known me always and . . ."

Nesbitt snapped his fingers. "Aye. The lad's right. Saddle his pony. Flynn. Martin'll ride with us."

Mad Molly's trail led the trio of riders through Stokestown, past the stump of the hanging oak, and then on to the ruins of Ben Beg.

It was as though she had to see for herself the desolation of what had always existed in her lifetime. She had often said her husband's family had come from Ben Beg. Often she had threatened to move there when a brooding had come upon her. She never had gone back to visit, however. Until now.

As she had done the night before, the searchers spent the night on the outskirts of what had been the village. It was a haunted, mournful place, it seemed to Martin. The winds swept over it as if it had never been alive at all. Martin was grateful for the company of Nesbitt and the Claddagh man.

Squireen O'Shea took a wandering course from the hillside of Ben Beg toward Colonel Mahon's estate. *The child is certainly dead by now,* he thought, *but the guilt is not on me. I spared him. If God chose otherwise, it is not my doing.*

But what of the proof to satisfy Mahon?

Tucked back into the boglands was a village too small to even have a name. A half-dozen cottages were grouped beside a spring.

The cabins were low huts, windowless and without doors. A few scrawny chickens scratched idly in the dust. From inside one of the hovels came the sound of a grunting pig.

"Hallo the cottage," O'Shea called.

"Who comes here?" demanded a one-legged crofter using a turf spade as a crutch. "What do you want?"

"Sell me that pig."

"Can't," the man said suspiciously. "It's rent pig for Squire Mahon."

"What's the rent amount? What is the pig worth?"

A sly look crept into the farmer's eyes. "Three shillin's," he said.

"You are a bad liar," O'Shea said. "It cannot be more than one. But I am in a hurry. Here's your three." O'Shea tossed the coins on the ground. "Now kill the animal."

"Sir?"

"Do you want the money or not?" O'Shea fairly shouted.

"Yes, Yer Honor, indeed, yes."

"Here," Squireen O'Shea added, flipping his knife so that the point stuck in the ground at the man's feet. "Use that."

A few minutes later, O'Shea was on his way again, a pig's heart folded in a bundle of straw. "I am not guilty of the child's death," he repeated as he hiked. "I am not guilty of the death of the child."

She is not moving feeble," Simeon said with admiration as he examined the barefoot tracks of Mad Molly on the trail. His Gaelic words sounded like a song to Martin's ears. "Straight up she goes with a long stride like a man." Squinting into the dust, he studied other signs for a long moment, then added ominously, "She's not been alone on this path, Nesbitt."

The huge, hairy man led his horse as the incline grew steeper and more treacherous. Cliffs fell away into the depths of a wild canyon carved from the course of the river.

One misstep, and a body would never be found. Martin wondered how Molly would survive such a climb, and if they would ever find her to bring her home for burial in her own familiar churchyard.

Even with Simeon on foot, the progress was swift. On a stretch that would have winded any other man alive, Simeon's gait gobbled up the distance as though he were walking on level ground.

Above them the mountaintop vanished into banners of clouds. Beneath them Connaught spread out in a panorama of emerald greens and the cobalt of a hundred lakes connected by shining ribbons of rivers.

The strip of packed earth that marked the way became almost invisible at times. In the lead, Simeon stopped frequently, examined the ground, and then pressed on without complaint.

Captain ten Eyck refused to put the four transportees in irons for the two-day sail to Cape Town's Table Bay, but he did agree to lock them in below at night. This was acceptable to John Hoyle, who said, "Lock Gann away from us!"

The second morning after leaving the desert coast, the *Sigurd* sailed into the South African port of Cape Town. A thick layer of mist curled over the edges of the plateau looming above the settlement. The rocky massif of Table Mountain was covered with a draped tablecloth of cloud.

Ten Eyck brought the prisoners out for the sunshine and the air and allowed them to eat their boiled lobster and fresh-baked bread on deck. He might not argue with Gann about the prisoners' ultimate fate, but he saw no reason why they should be mistreated.

Gann, on the other hand, exulted in reminding the convicts that this arrival at the Cape restored them to their journey to New South Wales. Waving toward an ugly, stumpy tower on a barren rock in the middle of Table Bay, he remarked, "Prison. 'Spose that'll be your home, croppies, till next transport ship arrives. Better enjoy your last meal what isn't gruel and salt beef!"

As if taunting them about their condition was not enough, he returned to terrorizing O'Halloran. "Take a good look," he said. "Last city you'll ever see, croppie. You won't survive your term at Botany Bay. You haven't seen floggin' like they do there. Drop your spade on work detail, and it's four hundred lashes. Skinny as you are now, just one blow of the cat'll cut you in two."

"Leave him alone," John Hoyle said. Joseph and Father Talbot echoed agreement.

"Oh, ho?" scoffed Gann. "Gonna threaten me, croppies? Like you done on the boat? Think I forgot? Not me. Have ever' one of you strung up before long." He gestured toward an anchored ship flying the flag called the *Blue Peter*, recalling its crew from shore leave for departure. "Dutch captain says ships sail from here back to Ireland in a month or two. Best wave, 'cause none of you are gonna live to see home again."

O'Halloran was trembling all over, and he lunged at Gann, grasping the lapels of the guard's coat. "My sentence is only seven years," he protested. "I'll go home in four . . ."

Gann knocked aside the young man's grasp, then backhanded the boy's ear. "Touch me, eh? There's two hundred lashes right there." He laughed. "Want more? Here's a down payment," and the jailor cuffed Laurence again.

"Stop it!" Joseph said. "That's enough!" Gann turned toward the new protest, but revolving toward his blind side, he never saw the fist that Joseph threw overhanded from the full reach of his arm. It collided precisely with Gann's forehead. The guard's head bounced against the davit of a lifeboat, and the resulting rebound snapped his face forward again just in time to meet another descending punch.

Jailor Gann slumped to the deck. Joseph stood over the recumbent form, clenching and unclenching his fists.

"That's the end," he said.

"Aye, lad," said Father Talbot. "They'll hang you, sure. You must flee like Elijah from Jezebel."

Hoyle was judging the diminishing distance to the moored cargo ship. "Do you have the strength enough to swim?" he asked, pointing toward the three-master. "Anywhere it's goin' be better than here."

"That's it," Talbot agreed. "It's over the side with you, and stowaway as best you can."

Joseph was instantly across the rail and swimming easily through the calm water. A moment later the *Sigurd* made her turn toward the docks of the foreshore, and Joseph was lost to view.

"Wretched sinner as I am, I have no objection to lyin'," observed Hoyle to the priest, "but a man of the cloth . . . ?"

"Have no fear on that score," Talbot said. "I can say truthfully that I don't know his fate nor whereabouts. That should suffice."

The surface of the oak table glowed dully in the lanternlight. The dark wood, bathed in the flickering gleams, reddened in the dim room until it appeared a pool of old blood.

"Well," Colonel Mahon demanded of the haggard and stumbling O'Shea, "have you done as you were told?"

Wordlessly breathing through his gaping mouth as if laboring beneath a great weight, O'Shea nodded and locked the door behind him. From under his arm, he produced a collop of thatch. This he unfolded with care and elaborate patience.

"Hurry up!" Mahon barked.

At last the parcel was unwrapped. Something dangled from O'Shea's hand. He tossed it onto the table to land with a sodden thump.

"Excellent!" Mahon mockingly praised. "That wasn't so hard, now was it? Now there only remains the woman and her unborn brat, and you can rest easy."

O'Shea shrieked, "No more killin'! I'm done with it and with you!"

"Oh, I don't think so," Mahon corrected. "Not after the child. I don't think you will ever refuse me anything . . . not ever."

The bellow of rage that erupted from the little man was heard by Mahon's new steward, who was polishing the silver at the opposite end of the house. So was the clamor when O'Shea heaved the oak table up on edge. The glob of bloody flesh flipped across the room and hit the floor beside the fireplace.

"Ha!" The colonel laughed. "Your anger is so pathetic, O'Shea. What do you hope to accomplish by upsetting my furniture?"

With another roar of wrath, O'Shea shoved the heavy oak piece toward Mahon, backing him toward the mantel.

"This has gone far enough!" Mahon cried. "Stop this!"

Another furious onslaught trapped Mahon in a corner between the mantel and the wall. Shoving against the pressure, the colonel's step was planted on something that squished and slid underfoot. He lost his balance and fell sideways.

Mahon's head landed across the firescreen, his shoulders dangling below. O'Shea dumped the table over on him, pinning the colonel beneath. Mahon's neck was stretched as for a hangman's noose.

Then O'Shea jumped repeatedly on the oak panel. Over and over he recited, "I am not guilty of the child's death. I am not guilty . . ."

The steward pounded on the door. "Sir! Colonel! Is everything all right? What was that noise?"

Above Colonel Mahon's mantel was a brace of crossed dueling pistols. Both were loaded. O'Shea stopped leaping to examine them and selected one that he fancied.

Before the steward, helped by Scully and Kirby, had managed to break down the door of the study, the booming report of a gunshot echoed through the manor.

Inside the room were two dead men: one with a bullet in his brain, the other with a broken neck.

The rumble of the waterfall drowned out all conversation between Martin and the men. It was late afternoon when they arrived at the place where the river roared through the narrow gorge and dropped away into the steaming pool. Hot springs bubbled up to the surface.

In spite of the grimness of the task, Nesbitt smiled at the beauty of the place. He dismounted and motioned for Martin to do the same. Leading their horses to the edge of the water, they let the animals refresh themselves and rest. Human footprints were visible everywhere in the mud. Large and small, they canceled out one another and appeared somewhere else. Among them all was the firm impression of an iron-shod hunter and the boot of a man.

Simeon handed the reins of his horse to Martin and strode deliberately toward the north end of the pool.

He knelt, cupped his hand as if to drink, glanced up, and let the water slip through his fingers. What was it he was studying?

Martin lifted his eyes along the cliff face past clumps of heather and protruding stone. At the very top, there was a flash of color. Red, it was, like the petticoat Joseph had given Molly the day he married Kate.

"She's there!" Martin cried, pointing upward. "It's Molly, sure!" Did she intend to jump? His words were lost beneath the rumble of the waterfall.

Simeon sprang to his horse, spurring it to gallop up the last serpentine mile of trail. Nesbitt raced after him. Martin's pony brought up the rear. In spite of Martin's urging, the creature would not move faster than a ragged trot.

As Martin's pony crept up the last rise, the voice of Molly Fahey rang out.

"She loved hot water, that one did! But she's too lazy to keep the fire beneath the kettle! No place for hot water, but the hermit's pools. 'Tis a place no man will dare to look. O'Shea's own trout swim there. Where better to hide? The monk's shanty. A bath! She needs a bath, says I to myself! Lost things is always in the last place you think to look. I lost my shoe once, and where did you think I found it? I can't remember now. But here he is. I fed him lunch and breakfast. He's had his supper too."

Martin jumped from the back of his mount and half ran, half hopped the rest of the way to the plateau where the shanty leaned toward the cliff.

Three of them sat cross-legged in a triangle on the ground: Molly, Nesbitt, and Simeon. Between them, safe within the circle of their protection, Tomeen swayed happily, uncertain whom to run to first.

"Tomeen!" Martin cried joyfully.

The baby spied him, laughed, and raised his arms to be held.

Molly's face twitched with pleasure. "And look! It's Martin come for supper. You're late, Martin. We've been waitin' here for ye to come."

The South African reception given Captain Costello was that of a hero's welcome for his role in the rescue of the surviving guards. A fast British frigate was dispatched to carry word of the piracy to London and a pair of gunboats were assigned to cruise northward to see if news of the *Hive* had made port on the African coast.

A flurry of action followed Costello's report, and the unassuming officer was himself feted and cheered in the streets.

The greeting accorded Adam Kane was somewhat more ambivalent.

At first he shared in the *Blossom's* glory, but when it was discovered that he was present in the Cape colony on behalf of one of the *Irish convicts* . . .

Even after quoting the guard Fleer that Lord Burke had actively protected sentries and officers and was cast adrift for his pains, it was still socially awkward.

The governor was too busy to see Mr. Kane, the governor's secretary reported, but could he be of assistance? Kane tried to explain about the pardon, but was interrupted by the booming of the noon gun from Signal Hill. "Terribly sorry," the secretary said, bowing away. "Must see to the luncheon for Captain Costello. Certain you understand. Come back tomorrow."

Disgusted, Kane wandered down toward the center of the city bowl. No word had reached Cape Town regarding the fates of either the remaining castaways or the *Hive*. It was time to write to Kate, but what could he say that was truthful without devastating the poor woman? Since there was no more to be done so far from Ireland, Kane made up his mind not to send a letter at all, but to return to Connaught himself on the first available ship. He did not relish the meeting that would follow, but at least he would be in a position to offer concrete assistance instead of just written sympathy.

Eager to let his mind move off sorrow and grief, the steward permitted his attention to focus on the Cape colony. Such fascinating confusion Kane had never witnessed, not in a Galway City fish market nor even in the presence of Mad Molly. Adderley Street, which black workmen were busily widening by cutting down venerable oak trees, was as busy as any thoroughfare in Dublin and the mix of cultures ten times more fascinating. The ruling class of British society rolled by in carriages, attended by black or Malay servants. Loads of furniture, wagons loaded four tiers high with beer barrels and an equally burdened conveyance heaped with elephant ivory, vied for room on the pavement. The scent of the sea spiraled up from the docks to mingle with the aroma of curry from alleyways. A Dutch-heritage farmer, in broad-brimmed slouch hat and tall boots, in from the veldt, stalked angrily down the street.

On the corner opposite him, Kane saw the mirror of himself. A wizened native, wearing a breech clout, strings of beads, and little else, stood wide-eyed on one leg and leaned on his walking staff as he contemplated the hubbub. Kane touched the brim of his hat in salute. "I know exactly what you're thinkin', me *boy-o*," he said. "This is no place for a sane man to be!"

Second Mate MacDougall trotted down the hill to find him and located the steward beside the star-shaped stone fort. Kane stood on the promontory beside the castle and looked out over Table Bay. Far out in the harbor, a ship with sails set was leaning into a beginning voyage. Another ship was unloading bales of seal fur on the quay. "Where have you been, mick?" MacDougall asked. "Don't you know you're wanted at the governor's soiree?"

"Not me," Kane countered. "Irish are not invited."

MacDougall cleared his throat. "Why, you're daft, but then all Irish are. Be that as it may, there's news! More of the *Hive* castaways have come ashore, the ones who were with Lord Burke!"

Despite MacDougall's piping, his wind was not good enough for him to ever catch up with Adam Kane on the entire sprint back to the governor's mansion.

*D*ear *Lady Burke,*

Adam Kane wrote from the desk in his Cape Town hotel.

> *At last I have news worth the telling. Your husband, Squire Burke, though surely you knew that, having no other, is alive and well or was so no more than twelve hours ago. Today reached here, that is, Cape Town, British settlement at the Cape of Good Hope, at the nether reaches of the dark continent, the surviving castaways of a shipboard mutiny.*

Kane went on to recount with vivid description the gruesome details of the *Hive* voyage, as reported by Father Talbot and supplemented by Hoyle and O'Halloran.

> *The noble squire, stout lad that he is, kept the more inflamed among the convicts from doing cold-blooded murder, but got himself set adrift because of it. After surviving hunger and lack of water by sea, he was shipwrecked and suffered the same again, that is the deprivation, not the shipwreck, in*

*the most hellish spot on earth, to hear the good priest tell it.
Oh, and almost eaten by sharks, but that part came before
the desert, to my way of thinking, only the retelling by the
priest was interrupted by them others.*

Here Kane digressed into a discussion of what a jewel of a man
Father Talbot was and the other two convicts as well. Then he wrote,

*But there was a devil in their midst all the time. That
self-same Jailor Gann was personal tormentor to Lord
Burke and, it is said, even attempted to do him injury. But
praise to the Almighty, the squire is out of that madman's
clutches at last. In fact after hearing all their tales, Governor
Napier took it upon himself to pardon the three other convicts and is sending them home on the next ship. (Devil
Gann is being shipped back as well; bad luck for Ireland
in that!)*

Here Kane grew apologetic for arriving tardily at the Cape. He
also defended himself in print since if they had located the lifeboat
at sea it would have

saved Lord Burke from terrible trials.

But in any case, it was not the decree of Providence that Kane
should be his master's rescuer—not just yet. By the space of some
few hours only, Kane had missed letting Lord Burke know that all
was pardoned. Kane was assured, however, that Joseph was on board
another ship, and the steward was still on his trail.

There's just one wee problem . . .

he explained.

*No one is certain what ship the squire took in his escape.
It may have been an Indiaman bound for . . .*

Here Kane made several attempts to insert different succeeding words, then crossed them out, and concluded the letter with,

India, or some other heathen place. But have no fear, Lady Burke, I am in pursuit.

⟨ Epilogue ⟩

Adam Kane's letter from Cape Town was open on Kate's desk. "There is only one problem . . ."

Joseph was somewhere in the vast oceans on a ship with no name. There was no way to tell him to come home. She had read and reread the steward's letter a dozen times since its arrival yesterday. She could not hide her disappointment. Joseph would not know he had a baby due to arrive any day. Kate would face the birth without him.

There was barely room on Kate's bulging lap for Tom to fit comfortably, but he would not be denied. It was naptime. Fern had already taken Robert upstairs to the nursery and to bed. Tom insisted on being rocked. Kate did not have the heart to resist.

"Sing, Mama," he said, his small voice clear and bell-like.

She obliged as he studied his fingers and clasped his hands together.

> *Ag an bposadh . . .*
> *At the wedding that was at Cana,*
> *the King of Grace was there . . .*

The blast of the trumpet from the Galway mailcoach interrupted Kate. Three times it signaled: the indication that a letter had come.

Fern twittered in the corridor. "A letter! Maybe another word from Adam for me! Maybe he's found the squire's ship, and they'll be home together after all!"

Tomeen puckered his face in disappointment at the interruption to his song.

She tapped his nose. "Patience, darlin'. Maybe a letter from Daddy," Kate explained, although she had almost given up hope since Kane's last communication from Cape Town.

Martin and Mary Elizabeth exploded into the room. Martin, waving the envelope, skidded across the floor on the carpet runner.

"Joseph's handwritin'! Kate! Sister! It's his own hand that wrote this!"

Mary Elizabeth took Tomeen, and Martin passed the letter to Kate.

"God be praised!" Kate breathed as the servants crowded into the room. She was trembling, barely able to tear away the wax seal and take out the sheet of paper.

Scanning the cramped handwriting, tears of joy sprang to her eyes. "What's it say then?" Martin snapped.

Kate began to read:

> *My Dearest Wife, my Kate,*
>
> *I write now in freedom from a French ship bound for Morocco. I am no longer in chains, but with God's help have escaped the suffering by which I was so lately bound. I am safe and well, and except for longing for you, I am happy. I have much to tell you of the last months of my journey . . .*

Kate's voice cracked with emotion as she read his story. And she laughed aloud when he ended with, "I trust Adam is managin' everythin' well for you and pray daily that your life is pleasant and dull."

About the Authors

BODIE AND **B**ROCK **T**HOENE's eight ECPA Gold Medallion Awards, including the 1997 award for *Only the River Runs Free,* Book One in the The Galway Chronicles series, affirm what millions of readers have discovered—the Thoenes are master stylists of historical fiction. Their books, which have sold more than seven million copies, include *Shiloh Autumn, The Twilight of Courage,* The Galway Chronicles, The Zion Chronicles, The Zion Covenant series, The Wayward Wind series, and The Zion Legacy series.

The Thoenes may be contacted at www.Thoenebooks.com.

OTHER BOOKS IN THE GALWAY CHRONICLES

Book One
Only the River Runs Free

It was four o'clock on the afternoon of December 24, 1841, in the village of Ballynockanor, county of Galway, province of Connaught, Ireland. There might have been a song of promise on the breeze that Holy Eve, but no one in Ballynockanor could decipher the words.

On the first day of Advent, the old woman Mad Molly Fahey had told Father O'Bannon that a great miracle was coming to visit the poor of Ballynockanor. Indeed, the village is in sore need of a miracle. Struggling under grinding poverty and a greedy landlord, Ballynockanor is the story of a thousand Irish villages where an English usurper is despised by his Irish tenants.

When a stranger crosses the river and enters the village on Christmas Eve, Molly proclaims that he is the herald of freedom and change. Is this quiet man the spark that will stoke the fires of Irish nationalism and bring freedom in a troubled time? Or will he bring the destruction of an entire way of life?

0-7852-7016-7 • Paperback • 300 pages
0-7852-7128-7 • Audiobook

Book Two
Of Men and of Angels

Joseph Connor Burke has reclaimed his ancestral acres and the manor he was born to rule. But in a turbulent time when Ireland is struggling under an English oppressor, Joseph's dreams of a peaceable kingdom are inevitably shattered by violence and betrayal. Soon the village of Ballynockanor will be swept into storms of political strife that will eventually spread to the entire Emerald Isle.

Just when hope for a better life seems brightest, the darkness of evil and tragedy could snuff it out. Will Joseph stand up for what he truly believes, no matter it costs him? And when he makes his stand, will the woman he loves choose to be at his side?

0-7852-6929-0 • Paperback • 320 pages
0-78527477-4 • Audiobook

Book Four
All Rivers to the Sea

It is October 1844. With the death of the evil Colonel Mahon and the greatest harvest of potatoes in memory, it looks like peace and prosperity are finally on the way to the village of Ballynockanor. But this is only the calm before the storm. Politically, British invaders threaten to undermine the movement for Irish independence, but it is the impending potato blight that very well may end all dreams and destroy a centuries-old way of life.

As Kate waits for the birth of their baby, Joseph is in hiding in London, trying to find a way to come to Ireland and assure himself of his wife's safety. But plot and counterplot stand between him and a sweet reunion with those he loves.

Will Kate and Joseph find safety in each other's arms? Can the villagers of Ballynockanor survive the potato famine, a disaster which will forever change the face of Ireland? Who will live to see another spring within the sound of the river in green and lovely Galway?

0-7852-8076-6 • Hardcover • 320 pages
0-7852-6622-4 • Paperback • 320 pages
0-7852-6935-5 • Audiobook

OTHER THOENE NOVELS FROM THOMAS NELSON PUBLISHERS

Shiloh Autumn

This novel is a compelling portrait of an American dust bowl family going through the heartbreak and struggle of the Great Depression. Based on Bodie's grandparents' lives, *Shiloh Autumn* takes readers back to experience Depression-era life, from possum hunts to mass migration, penny auctions to the Veterans' March on Washington.

X80669SAM • Hardcover • 480 pages
0-7852-7134-1 • Paperback • 480 pages

The Twilight of Courage

An award-winning World War II epic, *The Twilight of Courage* is an extensively researched and beautifully crafted glimpse into the most terrifying era of modern history. With drama and detail, the Thoenes have brought to life the men and women living their lives in the face of danger during the early days of the war. Readers are transported into hope, loss, and passion through the Thoenes' visual and engaging writing style.

0-7852-7596-7 • Paperback • 524 pages

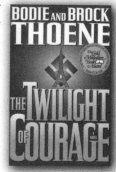